FORTRESS SOL

By Stephen Baxter:

NON-FICTION

Deep Future
The Science of Avatar

FICTION

Mammoth
Longtusk
Icebones
Behemoth
Reality Dust
Evolution
Flood
Ark
Proxima
Ultima
Obelisk
Xeelee: An Omnibus
Xeelee: Endurance
Xeelee: Vengeance
Xeelee: Redemption

NORTHLAND

Stone Spring
Bronze Summer
Iron Winter

THE WEB

Gulliverzone
Webcrash

DESTINY'S CHILDREN

Coalescent
Exultant
Transcendent
Resplendent

A TIME ODYSSEY

(with Arthur C. Clarke)
Time's Eye
Sunstorm
Firstborn

TIME'S TAPESTRY

Emperor
Conqueror
Navigator
Weaver

WORLD ENGINES

Destroyer
Creator

Galaxias
The Medusa Chronicles
(with Alastair Reynolds)
The Massacre of Mankind
The Thousand Earths
Creation Node
Fortress Sol

FORTRESS SOL

STEPHEN
BAXTER

First published in Great Britain in 2024 by Gollancz
an imprint of The Orion Publishing Group Ltd
Carmelite House, 50 Victoria Embankment
London EC4Y 0DZ

An Hachette UK Company

1 3 5 7 9 10 8 6 4 2

A CIP catalogue record for this book is
available from the British Library.

ISBN (Hardback) 978 1 399 61461 0
ISBN (Export Trade Paperback) 978 1 399 61462 7
ISBN (eBook) 978 1 399 61464 1
ISBN (Audio) 978 1 399 61465 8

Typeset by Input Data Services Ltd, Bridgwater, Somerset

Printed in Great Britain by Clays Ltd, Elcograf S.p.A.

www.gollancz.co.uk

To
Molly Alice Baxter, b. 17 July 2021
Micky Ray Moylan, b. 18 September 2023
Elsie Muriel Baxter, b. 20 February 2024

And to the memory of
Mary Shepherd née Ramsey, b. 19 February 1930, d. 18 June 2007
and
David Shepherd, b. 12 March 1928, d. 21 February 2024

And to the memory of
Patricia Leila Nathan, b. 19 August 1949, d. 21 March 2024

Prologue

AD 2198

Edwina Revil, captain of the pioneering deep-space mining ship *James Watt*, was the first human of any authority to see a lume. She and her crew named the lumes, in fact, and were the ones to make the first rough guesses as to their nature and consequences.

The first to make decisions about lumes. Decisions that shaped human history, for good or ill.

At the time, all she was concerned about was the disruption of her own mission. Edwina Revil, leader of the first group of humans to visit the edge of the Solar System.

They had come as miners.

At the crucial encounter, the *Watt* was four years out of Earth.

Or, strictly speaking, four years out of the L5 Lagrange point, a position in Earth's orbit whose gravitational stability had encouraged the development of an elaborate industrial complex. There, at L5, the ship itself had been assembled, and its capacious tanks filled with hydrogen propellant – and its fusion reactor loaded with a trace of precious helium-3, an isotope laboriously mined from vanishingly sparse lodes in the Moon's regolith. Treasure from meteor-churned layers of lifeless grit.

Helium-3 gave you the best possible fusion-energy performance – at least outside of the hydrogen-hydrogen processes that caused the stars, like the Sun, to shine, a process still beyond the wit of humanity to replicate. It was the sheer scarcity of the isotope on Earth – indeed across the universe – that made the use of helium-3 such a challenge. Everybody accepted that scarcity was acting as a brake on humanity's development on Earth, and increasingly off it.

But there was plenty of the stuff if you knew where to find it, and were able to retrieve it.

And *that* was why, as Revil had had to explain many times over to politicians and investors, the *Watt* was sent to Neptune.

Even given its universal scarcity, there was plenty of helium-3 to be had in the Solar System's outer planets, just because the planets were so *big*. A small percentage of a hell of a lot was still a hell of a lot. In Neptune, for example, there was around two hundred *thousand* times as much of the stuff as in the Moon's regolith. And in fact Neptune had the smallest helium-3 lode of all the giant outer planets – Jupiter, Saturn, Uranus . . . But that lode was large enough to mine efficiently, and more than profitably, with the use of bergs suspended in the giant's deep air: floating factories patiently filtering out the precious isotope, and periodically firing the result back to orbit for collection by the *Watt*, and eventual return to Earth.

More than once, when facing policy-makers, or even ordinary citizens of the nations of Earth, Revil had had to explain the what, why and how of all this. Why, for example, were they starting up this outer-planet mining industry with the *furthest* lode, in Neptune?

There was a deeper logic. Jupiter and Saturn, gas giants, were much larger, and indeed closer, but provided more challenging environments than Uranus and Neptune, the ice giants. The gas giants had deeper gravity wells, ferocious radiation belts – and, in the case of Saturn, a suspicion of life in the high clouds.

So, after building up mining facilities at Neptune, thus proving the technology and establishing industrially useful supply flows, a move inwards to Uranus, about two-thirds Neptune's distance from the Sun, would enable a rapid expansion of supply when it was needed. And then on to Saturn, and massive Jupiter itself . . .

Well. All that for the future.

For now, thanks to that laboriously gathered lunar helium, it had taken a mere four years from Earth to Neptune, outermost of the Solar System's recognised planets.

And so here was the *James Watt*, orbiting close to Neptune's innermost moon – called Hippocamp – only three planetary radii above the cold cloud decks of the primary, completing an orbit in a little less than an Earth day. From here Revil and her crew monitored the progress of the robot mining stations they had suspended in that high cold air, saw the intra-orbital ferry craft bringing back helium-3 in increasingly massive and useful loads to the *Watt* . . .

Step by step, building the future. And Revil watched over every one of those steps.

Edwina Revil was very controlling, she knew. Meticulous to a fault. Qualities that didn't always endear her to her crew, but made her an ideal fit for this mission of exploration, and the proving of advanced technology.

But she was a visionary too, so she believed. When she was forced to be, anyhow. Oh, she knew the numbers – she had production targets to meet, demands to fulfil – but she also understood the potential of her project. The implications. The potential of all this was huge, for all mankind.

Consider the twenty-second century, just closing, and the energy usage of a humanity still mostly confined to Earth, in that century. The helium-3 available from Neptune alone was believed to be as much as *twenty thousand times* as much as humanity had used in all that century. And the other giant worlds together would contribute about six times more yet.

That was the dream. Given the short-term costs and challenges, Revil knew she had to capture the true meaning, the significance, of all this in each report she made. Beyond the dry lists of tonnes of helium extracted, of technical triumphs and glitches, of lessons learned for the more expansive mining projects to come in the future, she had to emphasise the existential value.

Enough daydreaming. She tapped a screen to wake it up.

'New file. Notes for speech to be given at – the next appropriate occasion.'

The tenth anniversary of the *Watt*'s launch? Maybe an anniversary of James Watt himself?

'Note to self. Humble. Practical. Not triumphant in tone. As I sit here—'

Marcia Bell's face pushed its way into her display. 'Hold that thought, captain. We've got a problem.'

'Problem?'

'Some kind of . . . incursion. Take a look.'

She did.

And everything changed.

Revil swiped the screen to clear it, and saw something new, subsidiary images around that central focus of her chief engineer's face. Images of – *what*? A blue arc, the pale, dimly lit air of Neptune, the usual dark background beyond – but now, a kind of sparking at the rim.

'That's the problem? Magnify novel imagery. Stay with me, Marcia.'

'Oh, I will . . .'

The blue limb of Neptune was soon so heavily magnified that it presented as almost flat. Stars behind. And – something approaching that blue straight-edge. Something . . . *glowing.* At first she thought it was a single mass, but when she tapped for further magnification it broke up into isolated points, each gleaming, any detail on those points too diminished to make out. Falling on Neptune.

'Like a rain shower,' she murmured. 'Or an insect swarm. Falling on the planet.'

'Or an artillery barrage,' Marcia said.

'Hmm . . .'

Later, Revil would wonder if, had Marcia not made such references early on – if somebody more scientific, and lacking Marcia's own military training and background, had made the first reports – if so, would Revil herself have been so quick to assign labels like 'barrage', 'swarm', 'incursion' to the event? The future might have been different.

Or not.

Because in the next few seconds, the footage reached a point where the enigmatic sparks she was following started to smash into the pale, innocent hulk of Neptune. There was an immediate pinpoint of light at each impact, bruises of blackness spreading over that pale Earth-blue face.

The energy of each impact – and subsequent perturbation of the blue air – was evident.

'Shit. What *is* this? Give me some numbers,' she murmured, not taking her eyes off the screen, tapping by instinct to pull up more data, more angles.

Marcia had numbers ready. 'Well, each of those – bolides – must mass no more than a few tonnes. Those things are small, physically – no more than a metre or so in radius—'

'So is it just ice? Rock, then?' Revil's mind was working faster now. 'A shattered comet? The remnants of some busted-open moon, after a collision with a bigger, badder—'

'No, no. Not as simple as that. When they hit the atmosphere, the bolides don't just – burn up. We are seeing much more massive detonations beneath the upper air layers. A couple of our deep-sampling probes got lucky with the proximity; we were able to estimate the energy release—'

'How much?'

Marcia hesitated. 'Far more than the kinetic energy of a comet fragment. Nothing on the scale you'd expect. In terms of order of magnitude – we're talking multiples of Earth's insolation. I mean, how much energy Earth gets from the Sun per *hour*. That's one comparison. *Per fragment*. It *can't* be kinetic energy. We can see the size of the things, just a metre or so . . . Such objects, with such energy densities, ought to just disintegrate, outside their natural gravity fields.'

'So, what then? Some kind of fusion bomb? Or a cluster of them—'

'Not even that. Given the mass, the physical size, you have to say that this is still more energy-dense than fusion.' She hesitated. 'Some of the guys are saying this must be antimatter. Total annihilation of matter and antimatter, colliding.'

Revil's imagination was running away with her now. 'A few tonnes. *E* equals *m c* squared. That would do it, to deliver that much energy. Matter and antimatter – somehow kept apart until they hit the . . . target.'

'Yes. And it does look like Neptune *was* targeted, by the way. We've seen precise hits along the equator. Well, you have the images. Concentrated bursts. If this was some random cosmic event, that's all highly unlikely. I mean, it's unlikely a planet would be hit at all, let alone with such precision. *Apparent* precision.'

Revil caught that hesitation, the caution.

Marcia, like Revil, was surely already thinking of the implication for the mining operations here. Endless hearings to come if all this turned into some kind of disaster – and there were plenty of vested interests who would enjoy seeing this long-shot Neptune experiment crash and burn. You had to be careful what you said, even here, here now, in anticipation of the hearings to come.

Still, Revil hesitated to say it out loud. 'You're suggesting targeting. Of what – fusion bombs?'

'Not fusion—'

'Marcia, *is this some kind of weapon*? If so, who, or what, might be behind this?'

'Nobody human. I think we can be sure of that. If some aggressor could manufacture an antimatter weapon like this – these luminous menaces – these *lumes*, let's call them, the guys here are calling them—'

'Lumes. I'll buy that,' Revil said.

'If they had *that* they wouldn't need to go dredging helium-3 out of Neptune or anywhere else. Believe me, we'd know about it—'

'No human aggressor. Then what?'

And that stopped the conversation, again.

Still the brilliant specks of light fell upon the face of the planet; still the grey-black bruising spread across that pale blue surface.

Revil tried to process this.

She said at length, 'I think I'd better start making some calls. Wait out the usual lightspeed-limit hours for reply from Earth. Then we'll see what's what. In the meantime, keep watching. Do you have a draft technical report I can attach—'

'Here it comes.'

'Downloaded. Got it.' She looked into the screen displaying

Marcia's face. '*Lume*. Yes. That will do for a label. Let's get to work.'

That was the beginning. The first discovery of lumes in the Solar System.

Their naming.

In the days that followed, humans across the System watched the travails of Neptune, through the eyes on Revil's mining ship, and on other automated watchers.

Spacebound telescopes, meant for deep-field astronomy, looked out further. It was seen that the lumes were coming from deep space, their origin unclear – far beyond the planets of the Solar System, if not beyond the outer System, the realms of the comets and icy dwarf planets.

And still the bombardment of Neptune was unceasing.

A continuing stream of sparks of light fell into the increasingly bruised air of the planet, and, suspended in that air, atmospheric probes, intended to support the mining operation, were hastily adapted to follow the 'lumes' in. The imagery and sensor data they returned showed that some of the sparks were falling down, down into the deep layers of Neptune, towards water-ice strata thousands of kilometres thick, down to the rocky core itself. They looked like torches dropped into a mist.

And then, as hours and days passed, more integrated observations, statistics, suggested that more lumes were being observed reaching those deeper layers *than had come in through the upper atmosphere*.

Somehow the light specks were reproducing, even as they fed on the carcass of the wounded planet.

Breeding.

*

After that – weeks later – huge explosions, deep inside the planet's air, dwarfing anything observed before. Gouts of the substance of the planet were thrown out into space. Ejected debris rapidly formed a ragged ring around the planet's equator.

It could only be the lumes – even before drone imagery confirmed it. The lumes' breeding evidently done, they had, it seemed, begun to give up their mass-energy, each one.

The raddled body of the planet tried to absorb the energy, the inner heat. Neptune itself began to expand. Edwina Revil knew what was to come. If a planet were injected with enough energy – if that injection was greater than what was called the 'binding energy' of the planet – then that planet, any planet, however large, would disintegrate. For Neptune, eighth planet, the end was inevitable.

Humans could only watch.

Revil followed this process, right through to the end of her life. Somehow she would always feel responsible.

But beyond that lifetime, still it continued.

Ultimately Neptune was gone. The process took centuries.

In its place a remnant of the rocky core amid a swarm of rubble, like a cluster of asteroids lodged somehow out of place, far from the Sun's heat. Still the tiny lanterns of the aggressors, the 'lumes', swam through the debris. Some settling in groups, almost as if inhabiting the ruin. Some casually orbiting, all the same dimensions, a couple of metres across, each no more massive than a sack of water the same size – yet replete with energy. *Lumes*. The name hastily assigned by Captain Revil's crew would stick for these unwelcome visitors.

Revil and her crew eventually stood down, retired. Their place in history unwelcome.

Before Revil died, though, more teams of humans, cautiously probing beyond Neptune, venturing into the Kuiper belt beyond the planets, discovered the wreckage of another planet – another ice giant, smaller than Neptune, destroyed hundreds of millennia *before* Neptune.

Another lost world.

And long after Revil's death, significant alarm was raised when lumes were seen drifting in towards the Sun itself.

More alarms when the first lumes reached the clouds of the next ice giant: Uranus.

By now people, considering this apparent pattern, had begun to perceive a threat. A story behind that pattern, that threat.

Perhaps unseen alien warships had come in the dark. Perhaps they had fired out the 'lumes' as if they were semi-sentient cannonballs. Maybe the purpose was to steal the Solar System, in effect, to reduce its worlds to rubble, one by one, moving steadily in towards the centre, mining the treasures of those planets. Why not? Humans had mined their own origin world for millennia.

But this was different. *The Solar System was under siege.* That was the belief complex that emerged, over decades.

And human society, and government, responded.

No defence was known.

No weapons stood against the lumes.

There was no apparent source, no invading armada – nobody with whom to negotiate.

And the fear intensified when it was observed that lumes, just a trickle of them, had already drifted in through the inner Solar System, even fallen into the Sun itself.

What then? The Solar System could not be *moved* . . .

Well, perhaps it should be *hidden*. The whole of the Solar System.

And in this period of chaos and fear, a person known only as the Architect emerged, offering a vision of rebuilding: of order, of stasis, of symmetry, defying the interstellar chaos.

A plan slowly congealed – outrageous – bold, ambitious – fearful. All the worlds of the Solar System – the survivors – would be rebuilt, repurposed. Society itself was reorganised.

The Solar System was to be – hidden.

Even the Sun. Modified.

Some objected. Some said this was a retreat to medieval thinking, to constructing a false, *safe* cosmos.

Others argued this was a psychologically necessary retreat.

Others yet advocated flight. In case the Solar System was ultimately lost, ships were to be built, capable of carrying humans to the stars, the journeys planned to take many generations: a backup strategy, based on ships ironically powered *by captive lumes themselves*, for humans had found no more efficient and effective an energy source.

That was how it started. In the Solar System, guided by ever more powerful leaders, people en masse huddled, or fled. Or waited.

Beyond the System, the tiny ships scattered, all heading away from Sol.

The ships' passengers, looking back as the generations passed, watched the Solar System turn invisible.

A thousand years wore away.

AD 3207

1

We're following the light, that's all. Just following the light . . .

Rab Callis, as he grew, would always believe that he could remember that nightmarish flight with his mother. A flight through the aerial catacombs of Venus. And how that flight ended.

That was even though he could not yet have been two years old – years measured by Earth standard, as counted by the Unity of Mankind, the body which governed the Solar System from Solar Wrap to System Mask, as the proverb had it.

By Earth standard. A measure, more cynical Venusians would say, devised for a planet rotating two hundred times faster than their own, a planet now largely abandoned. So what use was that? . . .

So in a sense there was no surprise for Rab – after he had grown into a position, junior but responsible, aboard the Mask, his permanent station – no surprise when he was finally able to access the files held on him, as on each of the System's teeming billions, living and dead, in finally finding a confirmation of the truth of his mother's flight, and its grisly culmination.

She really had done this thing to him.

His own mother. The flight. The – *act*.

But that wasn't enough. It was easy to confirm the facts, barely remembered – but what about the *motivation*? What desperation could have driven any mother to such an end?

There was little about her to be found in the records. Nothing much beyond the bare details of the fact, the act itself, the consequences – the subsequent banishment of Elinor Callis, for that was her given name, to the pits of Mercury. In fact Rab found little more than the record made by the officer, the Lieutenant, who had tracked her flight, had apprehended her – had resolved the situation as best he could, it seemed. A brief, ghastly epilogue as she was prosecuted for her crimes.

And after that, a slow but pervasive impact on Rab's whole life.

Eventually Rab even found the officer's name: Constable Jeo Planter, a solid Earth-dynasty pedigree. Three years older than Rab's mother, in fact. Later even met the man . . .

Of the incident itself Rab knew nothing more, could remember nothing and knew little for sure. He had been an infant.

And yet he thought he did remember that desperate climb to the light. And his mother's voice, reassuring, deceptive, so soft as she dragged him on, or bundled him in her arms . . .

'Just following the light,' Elinor said, growing breathless as she climbed. 'Just following the light . . . the lovely glow of all those lumes, up in the sky . . .'

But just now they were still deep in the underbelly of the berg, and were climbing a steep, winding stair, the only light coming from her own headtorch, a splash ahead, her own shadow below. This deep in the lowest uninhabited sections of the berg – with only a few levels of workers' dormitories below – there was no handrail of any kind, and the walls and the step surfaces were slick, smooth – thankfully dry. But her boots, flat-soled, were not made for climbing, and were prone to slippages even so.

She just had to climb this sky-berg one step at a time . . .

(Eventually Rab would learn the ident code of the berg itself: UY-HG-TDFC. One of a hundred *billion* that crowded the upper air of Venus, shoulder to shoulder.)

Climbing, climbing.

Little Rab was tucked up in his harness on her chest. He might be safer on her back, she knew, but she liked having him in front of her, so she could wrap her arms around him to protect him – so he could see her, and she him. And she promised herself that she would break her arm rather than fall on top of him.

Climbing, climbing. But this was Venus, with a lesser gravity than Earth – so the climbing was easier. Like Rab himself, Elinor had been born and raised here. Humans had been living on Venus – and rebuilding it – for centuries now, but not long enough, the scientists said, for significant adaptations in the human body stock to have occurred yet – especially since mechanical aids made it unnecessary, in any case, to have the body start evolving away from the Earth-spawned template.

In her own time, Elinor had spent too long in the light gravity of Mercury, a smaller world yet. But years on Venus had made her strong again.

If they fell, she was confident she could protect her son.

Mostly confident. She stepped cautiously as she climbed.

All the surfaces were the same. Slick and slippery. Pretty much everything in this interior space was manufactured from carbon-fibre constructs – as was the whole of the great berg and its fellows, in their immense interlocking clusters that floated on and contained the dense lower atmosphere of Venus. Carbon fibre because all of this had been manufactured from the thick dense air of Venus itself, and *that* was, or had mostly been, carbon dioxide.

She imagined people rarely came this way, save in emergencies:

a route connecting the lower chambers of the berg where workers like Elinor lived and worked, and the upper surface, the playground of the rich and privileged. She sighed, 'Otherwise these damn stairs would be more human friendly. How about a handrail?'

It got slowly harder. Soon her back was playing up, that old deep stiffness in the lower spine. A souvenir of her stay on Mercury, a relic of an ancient injury. She'd rather not be taking these risks, making this ludicrous flight at all, of course. But she couldn't see any alternative right now. No alternative if she was to save little Rab from being taken away from her, and cast down in his turn into the pit that was Mercury, that ball of hot metal circling the wrapped-up Sun.

And so she climbed on.

She glanced down at little Rab's round face, wide-eyed, staring up at her, his mouth open. She had him in a sling on her chest, his legs dangling down. It wasn't as convenient an arrangement as she had hoped it would be when she had improvised it from other gear – in fact the harness was a relic of her own Mercury-surface suit, intended for working in the mines, a souvenir.

At least it was still tough enough to hold baby Rab's weight, she thought. He seemed to be growing fast and strong – not that that was a good thing in the circumstances. It was possible that she couldn't have attempted this ridiculous climb much later in his development.

Now, staring up at her, he was pushing his thumb into his mouth – his right thumb, his *right* hand. She sighed. 'Make the most of it, kid. Because if the worst comes to the worst—' But it hadn't come to that, not yet. That wide stare. She could *see* the intelligence in those deep, hypnotic eyes. 'You're too smart for this world, kid. Too smart for me . . .'

Something in that made him smile, and his whole face lit up.

And she lost it, just for a moment. She crumpled into tears, folded over him – one hand held out flat against the wall to keep stabilised.

She sat on a step, and sat him up on her lap.

'Plenty of time for breaks, kid,' she mumbled. 'Seven kilometres from bottom to top. Either they're on to us or they're not. And if they are they'll no doubt be tracking us with exquisite precision.' She faked a big beaming grin. 'My only hope is that they'll fuck up more than I have, and we'll get away with it, without my playing my wild card . . .'

The cuss word seemed to make him smile.

And with her heart melting like a snowflake on Mercury, she fumbled in a pocket, pulled out a bulb of water. He took the nipple hungrily, reaching for the bottle with his hands, those precious, intricate little hands . . .

'I'm teaching you bad habits, little boy. Or the wrong habits.'

Hold it together, Elinor.

He was so young. She'd waited until he was weaned, at least, before embarking on this desperate escape attempt. Still, he was barely two. But already the various ability-potential tests he'd had to take – so soon after his birth – had mapped out his career, and his fate.

A fate she was determined to defy. She shouldn't wait any longer.

He wasn't done with the water, and was playing with the bottle with those tiny, precious hands. She couldn't take her eyes off his hands, such was her mood.

He had always been a curious little boy, it seemed to her, from the moment he opened his eyes, in her arms. The preliminary psych-potential had confirmed as much. It was ironic that, she suspected, much of that potential had come from the father, now a senior manager at Caloris on Mercury, who himself had been the subject of what had seemed a harsh allocation decision, a double-length assignment. After her own assignment to Mercury, Elinor had returned to Venus, pregnant. Her lover had never complained about his fate, her reassignment, his being kept apart from his son after she'd gone – not to Elinor. All the way up to his own premature death.

And now, her son.

They won't take him too. Mercury can't have him.

Rested, her determination reinforced, she tucked away the bottle, got Rab settled in his harness, and stood up cautiously. After a grizzled protest, he nestled against her chest once more.

And she continued her plod upwards along this steep, apparently interminable stair.

As she settled back into her rhythm, Rab quickly drifted off into a kind of half-doze, as he glared around at the mostly nondescript surfaces around them.

Nondescript, maybe, but not unchanging, and before setting out on this desperate flight Elinor had worked out a route that ought, she thought, to keep her away from the more populated volumes in this particular berg.

Berg: a simple word, a word little Rab might learn soon. He was a bright little boy.

Berg: in the context of Venus that word summed up something magnificent – or hubristic, she sometimes thought. A *berg*: a segment of the artificial world humans had built around this planet.

The bergs were a planet-wide clustering of balloon-like vessels, like upended airships, that literally floated on the crushingly dense, warm air below, far above the lethally hot ground of the planet itself. All seven kilometres long, crammed together, side by side, built to support a habitable surface above, they were a geometric layer of huge interlocking segments.

That was where the privileged lived. On that comfortable upper tier. Even the gravity was about right, kinder, in fact, than Earth's.

It was a world of engineering. At the vessels' base, the air was thirty-six times as dense as Earth normal; at the top, the density was just about Earth-normal – and Earthlike, with nitrogen, oxygen imported by humans or processed from Venus's primordial atmosphere . . .

It was all a legacy of ancient engineering, it was said, put together *before* the Solar Wrap had been assembled within the orbit of Mercury to harvest all of the Sun's energy, *before* the Mask had been spun around the Solar System, just inside the orbit of ruined Neptune – *before* the invasion from deep space. No, the remaking of Venus had been earlier than that, an epic venture that must have caught the imagination of generations – only to be dwarfed by the tremendous feats that followed, when humans had even blocked out the light of the Sun, and had hidden from the stars themselves.

When people had first ventured away from Earth, their attention had naturally been drawn to the inner planets, and their moons, if any. And for the inhabitants of the third planet, Venus, second planet from the Sun, must have seemed a prime target for exploitation, for colonisation. Venus was a world of iron and rock, similar in size to Earth. But, being so close to the Sun, Venus had had a surface temperature some four hundred degrees higher than Earth – any water had long been boiled off – and an atmosphere, mostly of carbon dioxide, *ninety times* as massive as Earth's. Oh, and its 'day' was over a hundred Earth days long.

The first generations of pioneers and their robot predecessors had battled these conditions with little success – until they observed that while Venus might be an inferno on the ground, it was Earthlike *in the clouds* – some fifty kilometres high – where the air pressure was about that at Earth's sea level, the cloud temperature no worse than at Earth's surface. The upper air itself was usable – so long as you filtered out the acid clouds.

So while mining machines toiled on the surface far below, people started to live in airships, floating in the sky. Such ships grouped together, soon linked to make floating islands, the bergs, which huddled together in great herds . . .

Why not go further? If you had the resources, why not cover up the whole ground? Why not make a new surface up in the sky, where it was moist and temperate, enveloping the *whole world*, leaving the useless rocky ground far below, and the remnant bulk of the lethal atmosphere, all that carbon dioxide, useful only to be mined for its carbon . . .

So, for centuries, generations had lived in these crowding cloud cities, high above the planet's glowing-hot surface, fed by sunlight and water from the sky, and by metals and minerals extracted by robots from the ferocious Venusian landscape below – a landscape studiously ignored save when ancient volcanoes erupted, and the jostling bergs moved or rose to escape damage.

Farms and cities, floating in the sky.

So successful were these enterprises that Venus had soon started to *export* food to Earth. The mother world was under its own agricultural pressures, as ecologies were reconstructed – as farmland was replanted with forest and savannah, some of it for the first time in millennia . . .

That was before Neptune.

The attack on the ice giant and all that followed – the dousing of the Sun, the expulsion of the stars – meant little immediately to Venus, or the inhabitants of its island-crust world. The engineers simply spun a new transport web around the planet, indeed the *planets*, that allowed lumes, carefully controlled, to shed their mysterious light on the roof-world of Venus, emulating that of the shrouded Sun. And eventually a new transport net, the Frame, brought water across the Solar System from ice moons, water that rained down on Venus – and turned it into the breadbasket of the Solar System. That, and a workshop. As for the bergs, aside from their basic function of supporting the habitable surface, the bergs contained a host of necessary infrastructure – storage, sewage processing, waste disposal, air and water processing.

Population boomed. But even as the bergs grew downward in sophistication, so there was a population crisis on the upper sunlit roof-worlds above.

Soon, the workers who maintained this strange planet had to live *inside* one of the great bergs. Lived and worked there. Elinor and her son among them, like generations before them.

And now the Unity police were coming to take her son away, to cast him down into Mercury, Elinor could think of only one means of escape from this aerial maze. If she was to find sanctuary, there was nowhere inside the berg, her home, to hide. She needed to reach the top deck, the roof, the lifted landscape of a transformed Venus. There, in an environment not so heavily patrolled and controlled as her own level – one where no one knew her – she might find refuge, for herself and Rab.

All this was a horribly vague plan. To hide among the rich and powerful and privileged?

And to get to that refuge above, she had to climb.

It was all she had. Save one fallback, she reminded herself. One fallback if the worst came to the worst . . . She struggled to her feet, secured Rab, and resumed her climb.

That was when she became aware that she was being tracked.

*

She froze.

It had been an echo that wasn't quite an echo.

Coming from below.

Not an echo of her own clattering at steps. Not the metallic chime as her harnesses hit the ladder. Not even an echo of Rab's occasional gurgles.

It was all unravelling. So quickly. She knew that she was already in trouble. Even by making this unauthorised climb so far, especially with a baby in hand, she was breaking several ordinances. Most probably she could be arrested, apprehended.

Her baby taken away, even earlier than otherwise.

She stared into Rab's intelligent, inquisitive eyes. He gurgled, burped and smiled at her. She'd had to try, she told herself, had to save him if she could, given the slimmest hope of evading Mercury.

And on the other hand she wasn't actually apprehended yet.

There was still a chance. There was no reason not to go on as long as she could, until there wasn't the slightest chance of winning through. As long as Rab came to no harm.

So she took a deep breath, and climbed up further, through the next hatch.

And emerged into another vast, enclosed space.

She saw shadowy forms high above her. There was plenty of plumbing up there, she noticed. It was like looking up into the stomach cavity of some giant anatomical model: memories stirred, of ancient emergency-medicine training on Mercury.

'This isn't a lived-in place,' she murmured to a wide-eyed Rab – she would swear he was curious, staring around. 'This bit, all this complicated stuff, supports places you *would* live in. Up there, beyond the ceiling. All those pipes taking power in and waste heat out, and water and food in and sewage out, and air to be breathed in and out and then cleansed of all the carbon dioxide—'

'Those who work here call such places catacombs,' came a male voice.

It sounded as if it came from the bottom of the latest ladder she had used. Close, then.

Elinor grabbed her baby and flinched back.

The voice called again. 'You are Elinor Callis?'

She closed her eyes. Was the game up already? 'You know who I am?'

'May I come up? I mean you no harm.'

'I – do I have a choice?'

'Good question. All the choices you do have, apart from surrendering, will probably have worse outcomes for you, if not for your baby.'

'I don't know who you are.'

She saw him now. He was a dim, blocky form climbing slowly out of the darkness beneath.

'My name is Planter. Jeo Planter. My rank—'

'Constable.'

'Good guess. Can you see my insignia?'

'No. Do I know you?'

'Not personally. Rab's nursery alerted my commanders when you . . .' His voice tailed off.

'You can say it. When I abducted my baby.'

'Baby Rab. He's safe? Well? Uninjured?'

She flared at that. 'He's safe. He's with me.'

'I had no doubt. It was a formality for me to ask. But I have to ask even so. The only harm done in the eyes of the state, so far, is that he has been taken away from his nursery school before role allocation. But I'm guessing that's the problem here. The allocation itself. I've seen the records. You protested against what seemed to you to be a likely unjust life-vocation assignment, based on his age-group tests. And I see you were given the same assignment, at a similar age. To Mercury. You came back after—'

'Have *you* been to Mercury?'

'Not to work—'

'Then you don't know what you are talking about.'

'I *have* been to Mercury. An orientation trip; we get a lot of refugees from down there . . . It is a mine. Would you say that? A planetary mine. Closest of all planets to the Sun, it is a world of nearly molten lava. Of course now that the Mask has blocked the solar insolation—'

She said, 'A world of cooling lava. Five billion years of heating cannot be shed in a few centuries. A human can't venture out on the surface save in the heaviest of protective gear . . .' She was speaking rapidly, she knew. Letting it spill out. 'You may say the mining of metals is largely automated there. Of course it is. But in such conditions, even after centuries of development, still a human presence is necessary. And the toll of accidents and deaths, even today—'

'I'm aware of the statistics,' he said softly.

'Statistics are one thing. The misery inflicted on the humans sentenced to serve there, as I once did—'

'Such an assignment is not a sentence but a duty to be fulfilled—'

'You parrot jargon. *I served there.* You know this. I survived. Others of my cadre, of my friendship groups, did not. The death toll is shockingly high. And now my son—' Her voice caught; she clenched, refusing to break down. Strength was the only option. Especially if her plan, such as it was, had to be followed to its bitter end. 'And I'd still be there, labouring in those damn mines, if not for my own injury.'

'Yes, I read the file. A minor back injury. And so you were reallocated to the sky farms here . . . For all our engineering prowess, all our experience, we still need people to work down here, and frail human bodies still come to harm. And yet Mercury with its metal-mining is a linchpin of the whole Solar System economy. And it's a source of other materials, such as silicates in the crust – did you know that? That is why we must go there.'

'*We*.' She made the word sound as bitter as she could. '*You* need not go. I have been. My son will *not* go.'

'But if he is needed there – and we all must serve the Unity where we are needed, and where we are fit to serve—'

'He can serve the Unity here. I know what Venus is. And I know that this world of floating farms was built, or modified, before the Solar Wrap was completed. When the sunlight was lost, a network of lumes was installed to match the lost solar insolation . . . I *know* this. So let my son be a farmer, here, on the planet where he was born. Let him feed all those other hordes as they pursue their own noble goals.'

That sour remark made the constable laugh. But he pressed the point. 'And if we have enough farmers?'

'Then let him learn other skills. You've seen his preliminary assays – you must have. He is intelligent, or will be. He will have a technical intelligence I do not share – or you, I dare say, constable – and he would prove to be a great asset. More so than in what amounts to manual labour in the lava fields of Mercury. Send him to the Wrap!'

'They have no need of him at the Solar Wrap. Not when he matures—'

'The Mask, then.' She thought she heard her voice catch at that.

And it seemed as if the constable reacted to that. 'The edge of the Solar System. Where he will be as far from you as it is possible to be?'

'I will have to accept that.' She stared at him frankly. 'I think you are not without – empathy, Constable Planter. Or we wouldn't be having this conversation at all. But I would sooner he be far from me and safe, than close to me and in danger: in the dull, stupid, inevitable danger of the Mercury mines.'

He seemed to muse over all this. 'This cannot end well, you know,' he murmured. 'I mean, without your giving up the boy one way or another.' He waved a hand. 'It wasn't the most foolish idea to hide out on the top deck. Criminals from up *there* generally flee down *here* . . . You have gone the other way.' He studied her. 'But you failed. I am trying to disabuse you of the notion that there is anywhere you can run or hide. Why, I have caught you already. Even if you were to evade me, the automatics will never forget you. You have to end this attempt to flee now.'

He sounded genuinely sympathetic.

She nodded. She thought through her response, one more time, and she knew she was certain.

She grabbed little Rab to her chest, and with the other hand she rummaged in a pocket, produced and held up a tool.

'This is a metal-cutter,' she said.

The constable seemed shocked. He held up empty hands. 'Elinor . . .'

'A metal-cutter,' she repeated. 'It's capable of slicing through hardened steel the thickness of my own finger.'

Planter hesitated. 'What do you intend to do with that?'

'Not use it as a weapon. Do you have an emergency medicine kit?'

'I—'

'Do you have the kit?'

He seemed to suppress a sigh. 'I have the kit. Tell me what you intend to do.'

She sat little Rab up against the wall, making sure he couldn't fall or come to any harm. He looked up at her, wide-eyed. Expecting a game, probably.

Smiling at him, she wielded the metal-cutter. He grabbed for it as if it was a toy, but she kept it out of his reach.

The constable asked again, ominously, 'What do you intend to do?'

'You have seen Rab's test results. You know that intellectually he would make a suitable recruit for service at a high-intellect posting such as the Mask. But physically, too, he is fit and strong; so he would also make a suitable recruit for labour on Mercury . . .'

The very brightest and best, everybody knew, were generally meant for the complex engineering of the Mask, out beyond Uranus, or possibly the equally complex management of the Solar Wrap, at the very heart of the Solar System – or even the Frame, the great integrated transport network that connected the worlds. But where you ended up, as you matured to allocation age, depended as much on need in different locations as on availability of human potential.

'It's not *fair* so much as *rational*. But when it's my own child . . .'

The constable nodded, as if confirming her own thoughts. 'But there will probably be no postings at the Mask, or the Wrap come to that – at least there will not be in a couple of decades' time when he is ready to serve. Whereas on Mercury, we know—'

'I will not let him be sent to Mercury. Not – *him*. Not my boy.' She held up the cutter again.

'Ah.' The constable, evidently, now saw her plan. 'He is

physically able to work on Mercury. You intend to disqualify him from that work through – disability.'

She hesitated.

He spoke no further.

Deadlock. The moment stretched. He was forcing her to respond, she realised. All he had to do was to wait until she lost her nerve. This cop was too smart to be bluffed.

She was going to have to go through with it.

'Sooner longevity with a disability than a short life on Mercury,' she said.

She opened the cutter and, gently, laid her son's tiny arm over it, so that the blades would close over his wrist. He looked at her, and at the tool, and giggled.

'He thinks you're playing a game,' the constable said softly.

'No game.' Still she hesitated.

'You'll kill him.'

'No.' She tapped a pocket of her suit. 'I have a smart med pack. The wound will be cauterised – I have already administered an anaesthetic—'

'But even if he survives, he may be crippled. After such a clumsy procedure it might not be possible to fit a prosthetic.'

'That's a chance I'll have to take.'

'*What mother would do this?*'

She looked at him. 'A desperate one.' She swallowed. She braced herself, prepared to close the cutter—

'*No.* Wait.'

She hesitated.

'Don't make me wait long, Constable.'

He touched his ear, looked distracted. 'Let me . . . my superiors are debating this, umm, fiercely.'

'They've been listening in?'

'Of course they have.'

She shook her head. 'You, and they, can't stop me—'

'Wait, I said! There is an option.'

'I won't move from this spot until the thing is done, one way or another.'

'I believe you,' he said, still listening to unheard voices. 'Let us – let *me* help you. I can call in a med drone. Capable of making this – amputation – surgically, if it must happen at all. With no pain, minimal damage to the wider body. There are proper ways to do this. Under general anaesthetic for one thing. The operation isn't simple, not if complications are to be reduced and the maximal use of the limb maintained, with prosthetics. But we could do it right here, right now . . . I've just had that confirmed for me. He would have a much better chance of survival than – *this*. And – yes, look, later in life, such a, a disability—'

'Anywhere but Mercury.'

'Yes. Anywhere but Mercury.'

She hesitated. Tried to hold her nerve. Still Rab stared at her, a kind of puzzled smile on his face.

Planter was distracted; she heard the faintest of transmitted voices. He looked away, touched his ear.

She snapped, 'How do I know you won't trick me?'

Planter shrugged. 'You have my word. You must trust me.'

Still she hesitated.

'Then do it.' She dropped her head, and held out the metal cutters to him.

Planter let her hold little Rab until the med robot drone arrived, sleek and efficient.

Planter, consulting his comms kit, listened to multiple channels. Whispered headlines, strange images. 'Have you heard the news? They say they've detected a signal from a starship. A human starship, on its way towards us. A *long* way, still twenty years out, but on the way. Must be some of the diaspora from the Neptune attack. Or their distant descendants . . .'

Elinor cradled Rab. His eyes were wide.

'What use is a starship to me?'

AD 3230

2

When Captain Tavar issued the long-awaited call for the crew of the starship *Lightbird* to assemble at the Carousel podium, Muree was working at the lume tank. As usual. And as usual she didn't want to leave.

Ship-wide summonses like this were infrequent: Tavar called her two-hundred-strong crew together in this way, in person, maybe once every few weeks – almost always for some fairly trivial purpose. Or sometimes a death or birth. If nothing else it was a good drill to keep the crew alert to their captain's authority.

But this time Muree knew what such a call, made just now, must signify. That the ship's century-long flight from Ross 128, her home star, was finally, formally, over. That it was time to look outside this ship, this cosy interstellar shelter, and to think about what was to come when the journey was completed – when the *Lightbird* finally sailed out of interstellar space and, perhaps, entered the edge of the Solar System itself.

And she felt complicated about that. As if her own life were ending, only to be continued – differently. Unknowably.

Still, when the captain spoke, you jumped. That was the one golden rule drummed into every crew member from birth.

And now, peering up and around through the windows of her

station on the ship's axis, close by the lume tank, Muree could see people already responding. Making for the down shafts that took you to the Carousel.

Reluctantly, she closed down her work, and followed.

The main body of the *Lightbird* was essentially a fat, hollowed-out disc – or you could think of it as a flattened cylinder, two kilometres in diameter, with just twenty metres between the upper and lower plates. The whole arrangement spun on its axis once every minute, to give a 'standard gravity' at the spinning rim – the 'Carousel' – although Muree wasn't sure whether that 'standard' referred to the gravity of the *Lightbird*'s home world, Rossbee – formally the planet Ross 128b – or the gravity of Earth, a similar-sized world where, she had been taught, humans had evolved . . . It didn't really matter, she supposed.

The result was a strip of habitation, a hoop just over six kilometres long. People ran races, regularly, around and around that perimeter. And people lived in compartments built into the side walls, 'above' the Carousel, with decreasing spin gravity as you climbed towards the axis.

The axis itself was the spine on which the great habitable structure spun, and served as mount for external components. The ship's massive engine block. The huge radiation screens, the even huger heat-dump radiators. The vast propellant tanks – now, with the journey to the Solar System nearly done, all but depleted of their hydrogen contents, though with sufficient residue left to explore what might be found at journey's end.

And the breeder farm, where a hundred lumes, give or take, swarmed and tumbled – and delivered one new lume every day, give or take, to the ship's internal store, its tank. Just as they had done over the last century, all the way from the orbit of Rossbee – and as a similar community of lumes, she supposed, had brought similar ships to the star Ross 128 a thousand years before.

That begged the question, of course, of how the crew were to get back home – if they needed to, if they weren't made sufficiently welcome – if they *attempted* to do so in this ship. Sure, they would have the lumes, self-reproducing power packs, but acquiring enough propellant in the form of liquid hydrogen – or perhaps water or oxygen – might not be an easy task. When the ship had left the orbit of Rossbee the tanks – now nearly drained – had contained around two million tonnes of liquid-hydrogen propellant: as much as *four times* the dry mass of the ship's structure.

Would the inhabitants of the Solar System be generous with such materials? Muree had literally no idea. She could barely imagine what such people might *look* like, after a thousand years apart . . .

She longed to return to the lume tank, the farm, where she belonged, which was home enough for her, away from all this unwelcome clutter beyond the walls of the ship.

And she knew why she felt that way. Because, since the loss of her parents in a major air breach, the jostling lumes were the nearest to a family she had.

But orders were orders.

Obediently, she made for the lines for the elevators down to Carousel level.

Captain Tavar and her staff, and their predecessors across a century, had done their best to instruct generations of youngsters in the facts of the geometry of the ship that sustained them.

Such as, facts about the monstrous engine which had hurled this huge spinning top from one star to another, from Ross 128 to Sol, in just under a hundred years. Through those years, the propulsion system had unceasingly pushed the ship with an acceleration of half of one per cent of the Carousel's spin-gravity – a field itself about the same, Muree had learned, as the natural gravity of both Rossbee and Earth.

At its peak, halfway through the interstellar journey, the *Lightbird* had reached a quarter the speed of light, which had resulted in a slight relativistic bending of time for the crew as compared to the outside universe. Thus the work of a star-straddling engine.

And at the heart of *that* was the lume farm. Every day or so, on average, a new lume was born – a mysterious process which seemed to break the walls of the universe itself, as the lume infants came sparking out of nowhere.

And every day, on average, one more lume, mature, was extracted and sacrificed to the ship's energy store, yielding up its mass-energy for the sake of the ship, the journey, and the humans whose mission this was.

Not that Muree, born on the ship nineteen years earlier, had any but the dimmest understanding of that mission. *We're going home* – that was all her mother had had time to teach her, before her untimely death.

Untimely – and the cause of a deeper loss. *She had never told Muree who her father was* – evidently a choice of the genetic diversity panel, a donor who had opted not to have anything to do with his daughter. Who might not even know she was his daughter. Which wasn't unusual . . .

She was dreading the end of this mission, this strange backward-looking voyage of exploration. She didn't belong on Earth, even if it still existed, or ever had, that strange, lost world, a world from which her ancestors had fled a thousand years ago, in the face of some bewildering invasion.

On the other hand Muree wasn't *from* Rossbee either. That

was just the alien place, the strange gravity pit, into which her ancestors happened to have been born. She was an orphan several times over.

As far as she was concerned, where she was *from*, where she belonged, was on this ship where she had been born, and the end of its flight was a source of fear. For whatever lay beyond that ending would not, could not, could never be as familiar and *hers* as the ship was.

And, in particular, once the journey was over there would presumably be little need for her to spend her days with the lumes.

Thinking that over now, she longed to go back to her station, return to her duties. And the lumes.

But captain's addresses were compulsory.

So she followed her workmates to the elevators.

She found an empty compartment.

Entered it, tapped a panel to close the door, murmured 'Carousel'.

And immediately felt the familiar jolt that told her the boxy compartment was moving down, down along a radius towards the Carousel, the rim of this flat, spinning, circular tank. Then a steady build-up of spin gravity. Another jolt to stop.

As the elevator car settled, curiosity pricked. What *was* the captain going to say? Maybe the crew would at last get some kind of briefing on what they might find at the Solar System, the origin of humanity, which, as Muree knew, as everybody knew, had remained resolutely silent despite signals from the approaching *Lightbird* – signals sent for decades – and despite an energy flare from their decelerating engines that must have been visible across light-years.

No signals from Earth. No signals from anywhere. What could that possibly mean? According to the rumours Muree had heard, there might be stranger news than that in the offing, held close for now by Captain Tavar and her senior crew.

Well, maybe today would be the day they all found out more. For better or worse.

With a sense of anticipation, or maybe dread, she reached the Carousel level. But before the door would slide open for her, various warning systems whispered in her ear: how to raise the alarm in case of some disaster, how to access emergency supplies – and, crucially, how to access air. In this long-duration starship – as in the fully enclosed habitats people lived in back on Rossbee with its thin carbon dioxide atmosphere, or so she'd been told – whatever the emergency, human beings were never more than a few seconds from a supply of oxygen, by design. The mantra had been drummed into Muree and other youngsters from infancy: *If I take your food away from you, you might last weeks. If I take your water, you're dead in maybe days. If I take away your air, you are dead in minutes* . . . An uninterrupted air supply was an existential right. So you were reminded every time you moved through the ship's levels. People were encouraged to carry their own masks and emergency packs at all times.

Toddlers learned all this before they learned to walk . . .

At last the door slid open.

And Muree emerged onto the Carousel, into quite a bustle.

She knew she wasn't far from the podium, a modest construction but a magnet at significant events. Now a respectable crowd had already gathered ahead, including a few officers. She was close to the action, then.

She made her way forward – and her interest perked up when she overheard gossip among her crewmates that Captain Tavar did indeed want to brief her crew on what had been discovered so far about the star system they were fast approaching. But it seemed the milling crowd was of the opinion that Tavar's news was going to be – unexpected.

Muree got her bearings, and edged through the crush towards the podium.

But she staggered a little. That was the Coriolis force, the sideways push you always got when trying to walk across a spinning floor. She stayed close to one wall where there were handrails, purposefully placed there for the benefit of axis-dwelling zero-gravity refugees like herself.

She had no shame in taking hold of the rails, letting her hand slide along as she walked on. She did get a couple of looks, not from anybody she knew. *You stay up there too long, you don't follow the exercise protocol* . . . She weathered that. Too right. She hadn't exercised her time away. Not when she had the existential wonder of the lumes to tend . . .

But as she got used to walking again she took in the architecture of the ship with new eyes.

Here in the Carousel, she was at the rim of a flat, circular can that was spinning on its axis – an axis visible overhead, a thousand metres up, where a knot of cloud had gathered around the hub. The Carousel's main drag, just twenty paces wide, lined in places by lesser buildings, was mostly kept clear for foot passage and transport, and it was bounded on either side by the main outer walls of the Carousel's structure.

Aside from that touch of Coriolis she had no sensation of being on a spinning artefact at all.

This was a linear town, if not a city, fenced in by towering walls to either side – walls just twenty paces apart – and the thing was, you could *see* the curvature of the roadway, as it lifted up ahead of you and behind. And if you leaned back, looking beyond the side walls, dense with their own structures and detail, and up above, beyond the hub structures at the centre of it all, you could see a mirror-image of the thin landscape strip you stood on now. Well, not quite a reflection; up there was parkland, a narrow strip of it, vivid green and photosynthesising busily under the rays of the sunlight lamps – lamps mostly powered by the brief lives of her lumes.

And all these *people*. So many of them when they were all out of their cabins.

OK, there were only a couple of hundred people on board at any one time; births and deaths over the century's flight had continually churned the identities of the living population. She'd once been told that the population density – numbers of people per square kilometre – was actually a little lower than in the cramped habitats on Rossbee, but was apparently typical, she'd learned, of cities and towns on old Earth, before – well, before starships like the *Lightbird* had gone scattering mankind across the cosmos. How odd it must seem to anybody who had spent at least part of her growing-up on a proper planet, like mythical Earth. Or so she imagined. Maybe, if they had visitors from the Solar System, that would be obvious. Curious.

'Watch where you're going.'

The voice, the sudden presence before her, startled her.

'Or rather, look *down* where you're going. You spend too much time up there in the axis hub.'

She forced a grin. This was Brad Tenant, a little younger than she was, heavy-set, short, in a coverall uniform identical to Muree's. Not a surprise since he worked with her, in the lume bays. He habitually joshed her. She habitually joshed him back. 'Shouldn't you be at work?'

That was her standard line for him. But this time he shrugged. 'The captain has something so grave to tell us that she's allowing all non-essential stations to stay uncrewed.'

'What is it?'

Tenant shrugged. 'Kind of a dumb question. We'll know when everybody does, I guess.'

'Your mother and sister?'

'Back home. Everybody's supposed to listen, but parents have been told to filter the news for the kids. Meaning under-tens, I think . . . Oh, here comes the captain.'

Following his lead, Muree turned to the podium, where Captain Tavar approached – but the crowding was such that Muree got a better view from the nearest viewscreen, high on a wall.

And when the captain started speaking, the audio output filled the air, as if she whispered in Muree's ear.

'. . . should say sorry for cutting into your day like this. You know me; I don't like to grandstand.'

A pause. Then some nervous laughter. Muree wondered if that actually was a joke, or just a lame introduction.

She looked around, at the screens that hovered around Tavar as she spoke. Screens full of faces, save the central panel above her head, showing the captain herself.

Tavar was a short, squat woman, about forty-five, her prematurely greying hair drawn back from the dark skin of her forehead. She always looked at her best when she was being deadly serious, Muree thought. Not a bad attribute for a commander. Even if her jokes lacked something.

Now Tavar waved away the laughter. 'OK, that one didn't deserve a laugh. But maybe that best sets the mood.

'Look, people – you all know that we've been surveying Sol system since we arrived here, and even from further out, as we approached. I haven't wanted to disseminate any news, or non-news, until we had some kind of confirmation about what we've found. I mean, specifically, that if we had received some kind of signal, we would have reported it to you immediately. Either a response to our own hails – or some kind of recognisable leakage, even if not intended for us, perhaps . . .

'I have to tell you now that no such signal has been received, or detected.

'In the absence of such a signal, however, I decided to wait to speak to you until I had *something* to say, however partial, however – alarming, perhaps. Disturbing . . .'

She spread her hands, turned around, surveyed the ship, her crew.

Tenant snickered. 'She looks almost – magnificent.'

'Give her a break,' Muree said. 'I think she's finding whatever she's got to say difficult. Which kind of implies—'

'It's going to be difficult to hear.'

'. . . *Disturbing*,' Tavar repeated. 'Look – you all know the deep background of all this. Every schoolkid learns it.' She waved a hand. 'Once, humans lived *here*. And nowhere else. In this solar system. We evolved on the third planet, Earth. There were eight major planets in all, from Mercury, closest to the Sun, to Neptune, the eighth, an ice giant out at the inner boundary of what was known as the Kuiper belt – the domain of ice moons and comets . . . A family of planets much as we found, or our ancestors did, at Ross 128, *our* star.

'And – Neptune. I'm sure you know why that's significant, why I mention it. Because it was the disruption of Neptune that sparked the human exodus from the Solar System, a thousand years ago. An exodus, a swarm of ships like our own ancestors' . . . Even though most of Earth's population, of course, was left behind.

'Now, if you were standing out here, oh, before the age of spaceflight – if some power had transported you here – you'd have been able to *see* all those planets, maybe with the help of a telescope. Including Earth, first home of mankind. All illuminated by the light of the Sun, Earth's star. In fact that's what our own ancestors would have seen, looking back aboard an earlier version of our own beautiful *Lightbird*, as it sailed, regretfully, away from the light of the Sun – from Earth.

'And you know why they had to leave. Our ancestors, and crews on those other ships – it was no *mass* migration. That was impossible, given the billions of humans spread across the inner Solar System at that time. After the destruction of Neptune, *they* were prepared to stand and fight for their home. But, as an insurance policy, they sent out – *us*. Our ancestors. In ships like this, small ships, small bands of pilgrims heading for nearby stars, where we thought there were planets we might colonise, where the story of humanity might continue – if the worst came to the worst.

'Because that worst was already breaking over us – so our ancestors thought. Because the Solar System had come under attack.

'It began at Neptune, as you will know. That outermost planet was bombarded – *broken up*. That's not a trivial task; you have to lift much of a planet's substance out of its gravity well. It was a technology beyond us, then. But people went exploring, probing into what was left of Neptune. Most of the planet's atmosphere of ices and gases had been stripped away, though much of the core still survived . . . *and there we first encountered the lumes*, busily using their matter-antimatter annihilation energy to, well, annihilate the eighth planet.

'You can see the logic – the fear. If Neptune were lost, what next? Uranus, Saturn? Jupiter, which massed more than all the other planets combined? . . . *Earth?*'

'So we ran,' Brad muttered to Muree.

'So we – our ancestors – fled,' Tavar echoed him, unconsciously.

'And we don't fully know what followed. The full details of what was planned, what was hoped for the billions who remained in Sol system, are not clear, in the scraps of history we have – like scraps saved from a burning building, fragments of broken treasures a thousand years old . . . We know, of course, that very quickly we humans took some of the invaders' lumes from the wreckage of Neptune, learned how to cultivate them – it is the lumes' energy that enabled ships like ours to escape. A swarm of ships carrying just a handful of humankind, including our forebears, to ensure the survival of humanity, even if the Solar System were lost . . . Even then there would be hope of survival. That was the logic.

'And in fact that has turned out to be a wise strategy. For here, in the Solar System itself, the process of destruction did not cease with Neptune. Evidently. And now we can see it for ourselves.

'Or rather, *we can see the ruin that was left*.

'Neptune remains, a drifting wreck. We have imaged it, kept our distance. Neptune is – was – a battlefield. There the lumes still swarm. We presume. But we're going deeper in. Given the ancient records, we *should* be approaching planet Uranus soon – but we haven't detected it, believe it or not.

'And of the other planets, I have to tell you – from Uranus to Mercury, including their moons – *including the Earth* – there is no trace.'

That brought a murmured reaction.

'And,' Tavar pushed on, 'and the Sun itself is – changed.'

There was a grave silence. Unconsciously, it seemed, Tenant held Muree's arm.

Captain Tavar gazed around, at those before her, around her, above, peering from balconies on the side walls – even those two kilometres above her head, at the opposite point of the Carousel, like flies on a ceiling.

'All of this we anticipated, to a degree,' Tavar said now. 'Sol was visible from our home planet, Ross 128b. *Or should have been.*

'Centuries ago that vision, that remote star, was – lost. And as there was no word from the humans of the home system, it was assumed that some natural obscuration was, well, in the way. A dense interstellar cloud. Such features are not unknown and would have cleared eventually. We thought.

'We – this crew, our forefathers who first boarded the *Lightbird* – were not briefed about this by previous captains and their crew. And in my present role, on reflection, I have taken the decision to continue that policy – until now. We were committed to the journey; there was no point in causing alarm about what we might find at journey's end. I inherited the policy; I continued it – but now I believe it was flawed. That you should have known the truth. Even as we have it, partial only.

'Over the last decades of the mission, as we have approached Sol system, it's become apparent that the standard explanation for the silence – a gas cloud – *can't hold.*

'Think about it. An intervening cloud should have expanded in our vision as we approached. Even if it were somehow small and compact – if it were directly in our line of sight – we ought to have seen neighbouring background stars eclipsed by the dark, across a wider and wider field of view. We saw none of that; only the Sun was – obscured. *There is no cloud.*

'Further. The cloud should have been absorbing the Sun's heat, all these years. Re-radiating it. There should have been a strong infra-red signature.

'We found no such signature . . . *There is no cloud.*

'So, given all that, there's only one conclusion.

'The Sun no longer shines.'

She let that hang.

Muree was aware of the silence of the crowd around her.

'What we *do* see,' Tavar said now, 'is something that may be the Sun – but only a plundered relic.

'For we have other, technological senses. *We can sense the Sun's gravity*. It's there, that huge mass is *there*. If not, the outer debris belts might have dispersed even more by now. So we know the Sun itself is there, its brute mass. But not the Sun we knew. No sunlight. Not any more. What we *do* see . . .

'We think the Sun may have been collapsed into a black hole.'

Muree was starting to feel lost. Revelation upon revelation.

Tavar said, 'What we *can* see looks like leakage radiation from a black hole – that is, gravity waves. Faint: the Sun's mass would make for a tiny black hole – but detectable, and unmistakable.

'Perhaps this is the doing of the marauders who wrecked Neptune. Perhaps *they* are building something new. Or have built it. The . . . solar object . . . is spinning, you see. And you can tap such an object, a spinning black hole, for industry – or even, maybe, for exotic biological purposes – as long as the spin lasts. All you are taking is the spin energy, not the mass-energy of the hole itself. And as far as we can see the spin energy of what was Earth's Sun is all but depleted, compared to what we *know*, from our own records, we should be seeing.

'So, those who came here – following the destroyers of Neptune – perhaps they dismantled other planets, and even collapsed our Sun into a black hole, and have mined its gravity field, its spin, ever since. Mined it to exhaustion. Perhaps they used that energy to go on to other stars, other worlds, consuming as they go . . .

'As for us – there is nothing for us here. In this solar system. Evidently.

'So what do we do, in this – unanticipated scenario?

'Well, for now, we intend to approach Neptune, or the wreck of it – if it is Neptune at all – and do our best to – well, to replenish our supplies, particularly of hydrogen propellant. Lumes, perhaps. And then we go on – we go home. All I can offer you is another star flight, with all its privations. But a century from now, at least your descendants will see the light of our own beloved Rossbee again. And they will be able to tell those we left behind of what became of the home worlds . . .'

Tenant shook his head. 'I guess I'd better go help my family get their heads around this.'

But Muree hesitated. 'Something's not right here.'

He looked puzzled.

Puzzled herself, deeply disturbed, she walked away.

3

As soon as she could, she got away from the people, the crowds.

As much as you could call any gathering of no more than a couple of hundred a crowd at all.

In the last few years – the final years of the interstellar flight – Muree had become more curious about the world, or worlds, to which she was returning. Once, she knew, Earth itself had been crowded with people: on land, ultimately even on the rising oceans, on vast raft-like floating cities. More nascent crowds in space, in huge orbiting habitats, on the surfaces of other planets, other moons. And she had swiped through images of those crowds, hundreds of thousands of people crammed into vast bowls for political rallies, or mere cultural or sporting events. Some sinister assemblages, military, more thousands marching behind displays of lethal weapons. Crowds in which all the people she had ever met, or heard of, in her life, would be lost, invisible.

That was the Earth she had expected to find – despite the lack of messages to welcome the approaching craft, or even to warn it off. Despite the lack even of leakage signals, overheard conversations between noisy, crowded worlds.

She had expected to be wary. To be overwhelmed by unimaginable throngs. Perhaps she would have dived back into the security and confines of the cosy *Lightbird*.

But, all this strangeness, the silence . . .

The captain had been making reassuring noises. The lack of signals up to now had been understandable. Maybe humans didn't broadcast noisily and indiscriminately any more. Maybe they had developed planetary, even interplanetary messaging signals based on cables or tightly focused, energy-efficient beams.

But even so, why not make an exception for a returning human starship?

Surely none of the *Lightbird* crew had expected this utter silence. This apparent desertion. At least, this *shunning*.

What did it truly mean? What *could* it mean? She needed time to think it through. Calmly. And she could find that time and calm with the lumes. Even while working.

She retreated to the elevator she had taken down to the Carousel, rode it back up to the axis, and worked her way along the zero-gravity axis to her compartment.

It was not that her duties were onerous, in a sense. All she had to do was watch the lumes – and raise the alarm if anything went wrong with the mysterious processes of lume self-generation, of their yielding their energy stores for human use. The lumes: their births, their lives, their deaths. And even that 'watch' was a falsehood, for she could only glimpse the lumes, through robust monitoring devices, as each was born, grew, and finally dissipated.

And one lume sacrificed daily yielded the energy needed to drive a starship across eleven light-years in a century.

Their utility was one thing. For Muree, that wasn't even the start of the miracle that was the lumes. What fascinated her still more was the nature of the lumes, and how humans had acquired lumes to harness for their use in the first place.

The first lumes exploited by humans, so the thousand-year-old tradition had it, had actually been retrieved from planet Neptune – or rather from its lume-induced ruin. And since then the lumes had been – bred. As they were aboard this ship. Indeed the first starships had been built around the lumes' remarkable and very useful properties. And, later, more lume exploitation developed in orbital stations around humanity's other worlds, her own ancestral home included – Rossbee, Ross 128b, first discovered planet of the star catalogued as Ross 128.

But what *were* lumes?

Scientists and engineers who studied these things had come to believe that lumes, when gathered together, were able to access some other realm from which such materials could *leak* into our own universe, something like matter and antimatter, but neutralising each other without immediate detonation. The best theoretical guess, it seemed, was that lumes were the product of a flaw in spacetime, a flaw that dated back to the creation of the universe itself. Maybe, in that initial chaotic, destructive overlap, wild ecologies had flourished and died – ecologies out of which, so the best theories went, the lumes themselves hastily evolved. Creatures that lived, somehow, on this overlap of antimatter and matter.

Materials, energies, *living things*, brought across universes, to be used for the petty purpose of driving a shipload of messy human beings from one chilly planet to another – or even for warming shelters for humans in their colonies . . .

Muree had always wondered what the lumes' own purpose was. Nobody seemed to ask that. Did they have a role in some pan-universal ecology? And that question seemed to nag more often as she grew older – and closer to the lumes.

Oh, she had watched lumes, even as she had grown up, as closely as anybody alive – so Captain Tavar had once told her. And she thought she had seen signs of sentience in them – not intelligence, perhaps, but at least the raw instinct to swarm, to create anew.

And to know when to die, it seemed, for the lumes appeared to *choose* to isolate some individual when the time was ready. There would be a kind of withdrawing encouragement from the rest, before the release of the dying one's energy cache.

It was a behaviour that humans had observed, and learned to exploit. On a regular, even industrial basis.

Lumes were invaluable tools. Captain Tavar, giving pep talks, had told the lume-handling team more than once that humanity would have had no realistic technological way of crossing the vast gulfs to the nearest stars without them. Certainly not so early as the era of the post-Neptune exodus. *Even though* the lumes seemed to have arrived at the Solar System as part of the invasion that had smashed Neptune. Brad Tenant had overheard cynical senior officers saying it was as if humans had picked up exotic weapons from the field of a lost battle, and adapted them for their own purposes.

But to Muree and others who worked with the lumes, who cared for them, the lumes were more than energy caches. They were clearly animate, even sentient (Muree believed) creatures rather than artefacts of technology.

She knew that most of the crew didn't believe the lumes were even alive. Still more didn't care one way or another, so long as they continued to spill their energy into the ship.

She knew too that there were plenty of people – cynics, friends and superior officers alike – who thought she was treating the lumes as surrogate family to compensate for her lack of human relatives. Muree didn't wish to probe into such matters too deeply. Most of those who lectured her on her emotional damage, she comforted herself, hadn't even *seen* the lumes. Or at least, hadn't seen them properly. Especially when they bred, when three or four or five lumes would huddle around a new-arrived infant, nudging it gently until it grew, learning to swim confidently through the net of electromagnetic fields generated by and supporting the lume clusters themselves . . .

The biggest questions of all about the lumes were still unanswered, as far as Muree knew. Most thoughtful people would surely wonder how humanity had encountered the lumes in the first place. Why had lumes come to the Solar System? Could it really be true that they were no more than planet-buster weapons, wielded by some unknown foe? They seemed too sophisticated, complex, for that. Too *alive*. But – *remember Neptune* . . .

All fair questions, but Muree was interested still more in the origin of the lumes, their destiny, their own ultimate purpose – if such creatures could be described as having a purpose, and if so surely nothing to do with humanity at all . . .

Once, she had read an old speculation, penned by a crew member fifty years dead, that perhaps the lume had evolved to serve a purpose in the *future*: to fit an ecological niche that the wider ecology of the universe didn't 'know' it needed yet.

That seemed fishy to Muree. How could evolution anticipate anything? But Captain Tavar, encouraging her curiosity, had pointed her to sources describing evolution in the Solar System, the intricate webs of ecological links that had bound up the planet. Evolution had no kind of foresight, but was more an emergence of a complex net of causes and effects. Feedback. Grasses, for instance, didn't *know* to evolve, but once they *had* evolved – and had developed the neat trick of being able to withstand being browsed down to ground level without being destroyed – they were able to cover much of Earth's temperate continents, even supporting unprecedentedly large herds of heavy herbivores. A new, rich phase in Earth's ecological adventure had begun – but it had taken the grasses *and* the later evolution of the browsing animals to fulfil that adventure.

Muree got the idea, she thought – vaguely. There was even grass growing in some stretches of the Carousel. But if she didn't understand grass, how the hell was she supposed to understand lumes?

And why had they come to the Solar System?

She had toyed with these questions for years. Arriving at an enigmatic Solar System didn't seem likely to provide answers. Not quickly, anyhow.

That night, keeping herself to herself, she watched her lumes for long hours, through her monitors. Followed the steady cycle of their brief, hugely energetic lives. She didn't sleep for a long while.

But she did sleep.

And when she woke, she found herself listening to a recording of Captain Tavar announcing that they had already passed the evident wreck of the planet once called Neptune. Now Tavar intended to take the ship further into the Solar System. Further in, to see if the other apparently broken-up planets had left any traces – even, perhaps, in towards the deeply mined black hole, or whatever it was, that seemed to be all that was left of Sol.

Muree called Brad Tenant, asked what he thought about that.

Brad was cynical. 'Great. Let's go down into the pit and get eaten by the wild lumes like the rest of mankind before us. What was the point of all that running away to the stars after all?'

But the conversation was interrupted by a complex alarm signal.

'Hold that thought,' Tenant said, evidently accessing data feeds.

Muree downloaded data for herself. '*Radar anomalies ahead*? Oh – that's why there's a call for you?'

'My second job,' he confirmed.

Tenant, like most of the crew, had more than one role, depending on circumstances. So, for Tenant, lume farming *and* radar monitoring in a crisis – usually concerning the close approach of some piece of interstellar debris.

'We thought there was nothing there. Now we're seeing something huge. Huge and all but invisible, even close to.'

'A huge and invisible *what*?'

'Don't know yet. We've got to keep those lumes fired up to get us out of here fast, if we need to.'

Muree checked a monitor. 'I've picked up my rads for the day.' Humans could still be harmed by over-exposure to the complex electromagnetic and other fields associated with lumes, despite centuries' worth of technological development. It was precautionary, but—

'Rules are rules,' they said together.

Brad said, 'OK. And orders are orders. Now I'm to spell you here, and you're wanted on the bridge, on comms.'

Her secondary job. 'I know.' She felt vaguely thrilled. Working comms, of course, usually meant issues intra ship, on this lonely vessel, and was a dull chore. But today, everything was different.

Tenant looked – conflicted. 'It's all going crazy out there.'

Muree grabbed her stuff, comms, personal monitors. 'Most of me wishes I was staying down here.'

'I wish you were too . . .'

She grinned. 'I'll tell you all about it. And I'll tell our lumes . . .'

4

'It's all going crazy out there . . .'

So muttered Rab Callis. His station was a wall of blaring screens. It was as if the whole of the Mask's monitoring systems were malfunctioning, all of a sudden, right in front of him: a plethora of different alarm types, manifesting across most of the subsystems he was supervising. Absently he scratched the back of his scalp with his prosthetic hand.

Why me? Why my shift?

Rab was, officially, about to go off duty. He was one of three in his rota group, supervised by Lieutenant Planter. And each group took a four-hour shift, spread around the clock. So the chance of this anomaly, whatever it was, showing up right at the end of his watch in this small, cramped monitoring hub was . . .

He deliberately set aside the petty calculation. He tried to focus on the alarms. He had to respond.

Where to start? . . .

Rab Callis knew the inside of his own head.

He knew he was always too eager to over-analyse the most superficial aspects of any given situation. A habit he had developed in the course of his life, he knew, ever since Commander Revil herself, senior officer of this stretch of the Mask, had come to the Mask's cadet academy to interview Rab. Then he was just a promising student, aged twelve, recently selected. In the interview, Rab had to be taken once more through the long chain of circumstantial improbabilities that had separated him from his mother in the bowels of some ancient Venusian floating sky-berg, and brought him *here,* to a vast artefact at the very edge of the human Solar System. So close to that edge, Rab had liked to think, that he could almost reach to *touch* the Mask, the very boundary of human reality. He wouldn't even get vacuum burns if he used his latest prosthetic hand to do that for real . . .

But now, thirteen years later, at twenty-five, if he didn't focus on this latest alarm, if he didn't handle it competently – or so his immediate superior, former cop Jeo Planter, had frequently promised him – he would be shoved out of an airlock. Good hand first.

Focus aside, his main problem here was that he was getting a mush of unfamiliar signals in unfamiliar patterns, and he was taking too many seconds to analyse the likely source, or even *type* of source . . .

Oh. Now he saw it. Something he had only seen in simulations, training exercises. He knew what this must be.

Without taking his eyes from the screens, he activated an alarm. Hopefully the right one.

A starship.

One minute later Lieutenant Planter came bursting into the monitor hub.

'What in the Architect's name is going on? Tell me why those boards are all lit up, Callis? . . .'

Rab was aware of snapping to attention, straightening out of the slumping posture he usually adopted, even as he kept working at his boards.

He needn't look round to see who it was. Nobody on this station – none of the thousand crew cowering behind the huge sweep of the Mask in this sector – *nobody* moved like Lieutenant Jeo Planter. He was just as when Rab and his mother had first encountered him – short, heavy-set, badly shaven – maybe a little greyer, but still strong, adaptable, ingenious.

It wasn't luck that had brought them together here at this posting. The constable, having 'rescued' a little boy from mutilation (or at least from an amateurish amputation) by a supposedly clinically insane mother, had lapped up the commendations for his empathetic handling of the incident. But Rab knew that the extraordinary episode had stayed with Planter too.

And so, just as Rab had been saved from Mercury, so Planter had leveraged *that* to get a transfer for himself out from the dingy underworld of Venus to *this*. This, one of the twelve control hubs of what had to be mankind's single most ambitious piece of engineering: the Mask, a smart shell thrown all around the Solar System itself . . .

Rab had thought it was just his bad luck that, twenty-three years on, the constable, now in his fifties, now a lieutenant, had been put in charge of him. But it wasn't luck, good or bad, Rab now realised, nor a coincidence. It was a display of a kind of institutional conscience that had brought the two of them together, so long after such a traumatic, unusual event—

'Midshipman Callis!'

'I'm on it, Lieutenant.' Actually, he wasn't. Daydreaming hadn't helped. He scrambled to report. 'Umm, you can see the proximity alarm pattern, sir. There's a large mass approaching the Mask. From outside—'

'How large, damn it?'

'Mass order of half a million tonnes. Length scale in the kilometres.'

'So what? Ice moon? Comet nucleus? This is the inner circle of the Kuiper belt—'

'Not that, sir.'

'What else? Why raise this level of alarm?'

'It's not the right radio reflection. Too many sharp edges.'

'Then what—'

Let him speak, Lieutenant Planter.

That disembodied voice belonged to Commander Revil, controller of this one-twelfth sector of the Mask.

Rab, already sitting straight, snapped to attention.

The boy was right to raise the alarm. He was the first to do so. And I can tell you why the alarm systems have gone crazy.

The Lieutenant, too, turned rigid in mid-air. 'Hearing you, Commander.'

Midshipman. In your own words. Tell me what you see.

'Sir, yes, sir. It's obvious when you look at it. This – object – approaching the Mask. It's no inert mass. No comet. It's too complex in the imaging. There are structured signals we can detect in its leakage radiation. Though not a hail I can recognise.

'And – *it's changing course.*'

Now Lieutenant Planter gasped. 'Oh. Wow. I hadn't seen *that*—'

I myself have never seen this before, Revil said. *Not outside simulations and such . . .*

That astonished Rab. *So what does this mean for the Mask?*

As the commander kept talking, he tried to think. Ran through briefings, some by Revil herself, that he'd endured on such unlikely scenarios:

. . . Look, people, let me remind you that the Mask is a fragile construct. A sphere of smart, whisper-thin graphene, smart carbon, entirely surrounding the Solar System, at the orbit of Uranus. Graphene manufactured from methane that was itself mined out

of the upper air of planet Uranus. Only a few per cent of that air, though . . . an economical design.

And let me remind you what the Mask is meant to do. It's smart. Its surface is holographic. It's supposed to make itself *look invisible. And it's supposed to* show *any incomers what we want them to see – a broken-up set of planets, a sun itself reduced to a remnant black hole sitting there, not even spinning . . .*

'Nothing to see here,' Rab said aloud, parroting his training. 'That's our mission. Nothing to mine, nothing to plunder. No planets to shatter. Take a piece of Neptune if you like, as a souvenir – that's already lost . . .'

As you say, midshipman, the commander put in. *Remember the big picture. After the loss of Neptune, humanity tried to hedge against further attacks, against extinction. We sent a handful of fragile colony ships out to the nearest stars. And we tried to – camouflage – our solar system. The Mask is a key measure in that. Obviously.*

But it has to work, continually, perfectly. We can withstand random punctures by interstellar comets and such – even impacts by objects out in our own Kuiper belt, Oort cloud. The Mask is big. *We can fix it. But if an intelligent agent comes snooping—*

'Camouflage,' Planter said gravely. 'That's what the Mask is. The best we can do. If you can't defend yourself – or at least if you're not *sure* you can do that – you hide. But now, that strategy has broken down. There's evidently some kind of craft incoming. It looks as if we have been detected after all. Still, we may be able to . . . hit back.'

That shook Rab. From the earliest days of his training here he'd always understood the purpose of the Mask as being, yes, to *hide* a rich, intricately developed Solar System, hide it from would-be predators or destroyers – foes who might come to demolish others of the System's worlds as, so it seemed, they had long ago demolished Neptune.

Hiding was one thing. Fighting back was another. What if they just provoked a worse response?

'Or we could try to talk,' he said on impulse. 'Try to communicate. Find out what they *want* here—'

That would be a fine sentiment if not for precursor events, said Commander Revil. *You know the outcome of the previous incursion. The outermost planet, Neptune, destroyed. My own ancestor was a witness to that terrible event . . .*

Lieutenant Planter grunted. 'No reason to believe they won't come back for more. And then . . .'

Rab knew the nursery-rhyme warnings, drummed into the children of Sol, even in this remote place. He intoned, 'First they came for Neptune, and it's gone. Next they'll come for Uranus, and when it's gone . . .'

Planter snapped, 'So what *do* you want us to do, sir?'

Well, the Mask hasn't yet been breached. It may be that the camouflage strategy will still work. If not, we may have to withdraw some portion of the Mask's structure—

Rab had been coached in how to open apertures in the Mask surface, carefully timed and planned, in the case of a dumb threat approaching – a rogue comet, or a fragment of shattered Neptune. But this . . .

'If this is a crewed ship, a human ship, we'd let them in, commander?'

That is how it's been war-gamed. If there's no immediate threat we take in the intruder – human or otherwise – and we analyse, we act accordingly. At least we'd discover what larger threat we face. Planter, when this is all over we probably ought to coach this stuff more intensively into the junior staff here.

'Noted, Commander.'

For now, Midshipman Callis, you're on the spot. The idea is, yes, we do just that: we let them inside, thus saving the Mask from a collision, perhaps deliberate damage, perhaps an uncontrolled breach – and deal with them inside. But it's all going to have to work to maximum efficiency and efficacy – and timing. Beginning with the opening up of the Mask in this sector.

Lieutenant Planter nodded. 'Formal permission to proceed with said Mask manipulation, please, Commander Revil. For the record.'

For the record – do it, Lieutenant. But may I suggest . . .

'Yes?'

Fast reactions may be crucial. Use the boy. His unique attributes.

Planter looked surprised. Maybe even disappointed, Rab thought.

But the Lieutenant nodded, and rested his own flesh-and-blood hand on a startled Rab's shoulder. 'Establish the linkage, lad. You know what to do. Through your prosthetic to the Mask itself. You've done it a hundred times.'

'Only in rehearsal,' Rab said – shocked, if not terrified at the responsibility.

'A hundred breaches at *least* in training, simulated and physical. You're a long way from that cadet you once were, green from the Uranus training camps. You'd barely arrived before the senior officers spotted the potential of that smart prosthetic of yours, and not just as a weapon.' He grinned. 'You can thank me later . . .'

Do it, said the commander. *Brief him, Lieutenant Planter. Inform me when he's ready.*

You'd barely arrived . . .

From the beginning, at the Mask, Rab had had to learn to fight.

He'd come to this place on his eighth birthday. A long way

from Venus, from his home world. Already, he'd travelled to the limits of the Solar System. Green and innocent – with a prosthetic hand on the stump of an arm that sometimes ached, from that mutilation he still remembered from age two. To his fellow trainees he was nothing but the Venusian, from a scorned place, a world of scrubby farms and scrubby people, and a source of recruits for the Mercury mines. *And* disabled.

Very quickly, though, his aptitude with the left-hand prosthetic, along with an obvious general intelligence, suggested special uses to some of his mentors and tutors.

On his eleventh birthday he had been put through a further course of aptitude tests, away from the Mask itself. This had been his first flight into space since his arrival from Venus, which by then he barely remembered.

He was taken to another enormous structure – dwarfed by the Mask, but impressive enough if you were eleven. The System authorities had built a regional command post into what had once been, long ago, pre-Neptune, a tremendous solar energy farm, in the orbit of Uranus, constructed to capture the energy flow of sunlight – a farm necessarily enormous to be able to capture a worthwhile amount of light, so far from the Sun. The energy would have been used to mine the volatile-rich clouds of Uranus.

Of course once the Solar Wrap had been closed, the sunlight excluded, the farm had become redundant for that purpose. But in the hands of the post-Wrap, post-Mask Unity of Mankind, such antique sites had their uses – in this case for training purposes, readying recruits to serve on the still more enormous structure of the Mask.

And there Rab had undergone a formal assessment of his talents and limitations, his potential usefulness – as all Unity citizens had to endure. In his case such talents and limitations were obvious. Just as his mother had intuited, he was – potentially – smart enough to serve in very complex technological environments. Of which the Solar System was replete, given that every environment was based on a life-support technology that had to be flawless. That was true even in the case of Earth itself, since, once the Wrap was in place, natural, undirected sunlight no longer fell on the origin world.

And, as his mother could never have guessed, the mutilation by which she had sought to make her son unfit for Mercury turned out actually to be a boon, not a handicap. His fake hand, with a little modification, was proved to work as an interface between Rab's own nervous system and the intricate systems of modern technological environments – such as in his training on the abandoned sunlight farm, and later on the Mask itself. All spotted by a wise enough mentor in Lieutenant Planter – probably guilt-ridden on some level, Rab thought – who had always kept a kindly, if remote, eye on Rab. It was all about looking at things the right way – and seizing opportunities to exploit unanticipated capabilities.

And as Rab had grown further, he had begun to learn all about the Mask.

The Mask: nothing less than a smart hide that contained and concealed a whole solar system. So smart, in fact, that it ought to hide the system from the view of any predators of the kind which appeared to have left planet Neptune in ruins.

The logic behind the Mask was simple. If any predatory visitors 'saw' only an exhausted star-mass black hole, surrounded by the drifting debris of Neptune, a single planet – why, perhaps the remnant of Sol system, and of mankind, would be left alone. But it all depended on one monstrous lie.

Rab had no real idea how long the Mask had been here, hanging in this place, a tremendous spherical curtain around the Solar System – and a smart curtain at that. Centuries at least. But no human construct was perfect or eternal.

Rab himself had worked on minor repairs required to the Mask. These were generally occasioned by clumsy deflections of Kuiper belt debris that still drifted in from beyond the planetary system: fragments of smashed planets and moons, or of worlds that had never coalesced at all, fragments following their own long, slow, often highly elliptical orbits. Mostly such debris would be deflected or destroyed long before any damage could be done to the Mask, or indeed the worlds of mankind. But if feasible, sometimes the Mask would be *opened up*, to allow the rogue object to cross through the space enclosed by the Mask without damage, to be dealt with by heavy-duty equipment within the Mask itself.

Rab hadn't had to do this yet himself, except during practice.

But now, it seemed, he was being ordered to make the most significant opening yet, if not the most significant in scale . . . This time, sailing in towards the Mask's invisible, deceptive surface was no comet head or fragment of a shattered moon . . .

This time it was a craft. A human craft.

He had no idea who these humans were, or where they had come from, or why they had shown up here and now. Not even if they *were* humans, in fact. Aliens in hijacked human technology? Why not . . .

He tried to focus. He had his job to do, that was all.

And so he laid his false hand on an adapted sensor plate.

And –

He could *feel* it, feel the Mask itself.

As if it were some tremendous set of wings fixed to his own shoulder blades. He *felt* those imaginary wings tremble, even as the ungainly form of the unknown ship came closer.

Eventually he could *see* it, not directly but through multiple technological eyes: he saw a central, heavily spinning disc-shaped main hull, mounted on an axial spine that supported a technological clutter of engine and propellant tanks, radiators and comms gear and instruments. In fact the view he had was more like an engineering diagram, crusted with floating labels, some with question marks if components were not recognised.

Lieutenant Planter reported in. 'Only an hour left, commander. An hour before it reaches the proximity of the Mask. Weapons systems online . . . We're continuing to pick up signals but it's what appears to be leakage radiation. We haven't yet been hailed by them. And we haven't hailed *them*. If there is a meaningful "them" . . .'

They know we're here, Revil said. *And we know they're out there. Hold the weaponry. Let's gamble.*

Midshipman Callis of Venus. Allow them in.

Rab lifted his left hand, flexed and spread his metallic, shining fingers – and laid them on the nearest screen.

It always . . . prickled . . . as the nanotubes spread upwards from the screen and into the smart metal of his prosthetic hand. Prickled as they began the intricate linkage of his hand, his body – his sensorium – to the structure of the Mask itself, or at least that portion of it that could be reached by lightspeed signals in times that matched the reflexes of his own nervous system.

Rab lifted his arms – he had a heavy sensation as if he were hauling at vast curtains, literally – and he *felt* a great rent in the Mask open up.

Directly before the incoming ship.

And immediately he *saw* it, not some engineering analysis, but a vision as if seen through human eyes, channelled through the linked systems. A ship, yes, a ship like a huge drum spinning on a long axle . . .

His eyes stung. He was weeping.

The ship wasn't exactly beautiful.

But in a solar system that been in stasis for centuries, this was something *new.*

5

On board the *Lightbird*, the lumes in their tank were going crazy.

And Muree was handling them alone.

She tried yelling for Brad again. 'Tenant! Wherever you are on this damn ship, get down here right now and do your job!'

This was the third time she'd called, if you didn't count the automated summoning call made by the smart systems when it became evident even to *them* that Muree alone wasn't able to handle the job.

Crazy. She had no other label for it. She'd never seen the lumes like this, their big massive forms, replete with potential energy, rolling, pushing against each other, as if jostling to escape. The only way to handle this, she knew, was to let them loose to join their hundred or so companions in the big external farm. Out there, they could usually release all the pent-up energy they wanted, a trickle of matter-antimatter annihilation turning into a stream of energy – energy usefully siphoned off, even now, to run the ship's various systems.

But that would leave the ship without its primary energy sources, at a critical moment.

She yelled again. 'Tenant! Get down here—'

'I'm here, I'm here.' He pushed his way through the door, grabbed a radiation-proof coverall and pulled it on before joining her in her compartment – then halted, mouth agape, at sight of the monitors. The roiling of the lumes in their chamber. 'Wow. I've never seen them like this.' He paged through records on a screen on his sleeve. 'There *must* be precedents . . . It's all going crazy out there.'

She risked a glance at him. 'Captain Tavar is still determined to take us further in?'

'Yeah. She says what we're encountering makes no sense, in terms of the Solar System as we thought we knew about it . . . Makes no sense? I'll say. The planets are *gone*, Muree. Even their moons. Even the asteroids! The best theory is that they were dismantled to build some kind of engine around the Sun itself—'

'To collapse it into a black hole?'

'That's the guess. That's what we *see*, in the gravity-wave radiation at least. But . . . it sounds crazy. Implausible? We know it's a thousand years since the exodus from the Solar System, our ancestors' flight to Rossbee and other maybe-habitable worlds. Only a thousand years, that's all. Maybe forty human generations, to do all *this*? To – what, move, demolish the planets? Even to collapse the Sun?'

'Implausible, you think? . . . Even with lumes?' Muree asked.

'Even with lumes—'

An alarm flashed on one panel.

'Now what?' She bent down to see the panel. 'Look at this. The environment scanner. It's picking up a change in the local gravity-wave structures.' She looked at him. 'How can *that* be?'

But he was distracted by outputs from other monitors. He virtual-grabbed the output from one screen and threw it over to another near Muree. 'Look at *that*.'

A scratch across space, vertical. Pale light against the black.

She looked at the new image, trying to unscramble it in a head that was already too full of novelty. *Think, Muree. You see darkness, star-littered, with – what, a vertical slit? Superimposed? More like some kind of wound, opening, widening . . . A wound in what?*

'And this.' He pointed.

That was easier to read. 'Anomalous gravity waves. Coming out of that – breach. A breach in *what*? In spacetime?'

He shook his head. 'The Captain is having all this probed . . . Muree, listen. This is all crazy, but – standing here, we thought we were looking at space – the distant stars – and the Sol black hole. The planets and moons, gone. But now, this – *gap* . . .' He touched a plug in one ear. 'The observations are coming in from across the ship. Captain Tavar is trying to make sense of it, even while she's snapping out orders to keep calm . . .'

'Just tell me, damn it.'

He half-laughed. 'Muree, *we've been looking at a blank wall.* A wall that was hiding the Sun – save for its gravity waves. Making it look like this is an empty system – empty apart from what was left of the Sun.'

She shook her head, trying to shake the pieces of all this into some kind of sense. 'A wall?'

'You can see for yourself. Look! It's as if a vast curtain has been thrown around the whole system. Around it at this radius from the Sun. The *whole* of it. And now it's being drawn back. Purposefully – it has to be.'

She held her breath.

'Revealing what?'

He peered into the screens, tapped for more information.

'Planets.'

'Planets?'

'Planets! And what looks like some kind of interplanetary – structure. A network? This is crazy. But that black-hole Sun is right where it should be.'

'All of it hidden until—'

'Until we got too close,' he said. 'I guess they had a choice, to let us in – or what? Blow us out of the sky? It has to be some kind of response to the Neptune incident.'

She frowned. 'This is moving so quickly. After a thousand years . . . So, what now?'

He touched his ear. 'There's a regular brainstorming session going on down there in Captain Tavar's briefing room. But I think she's deciding to take us in further and see for herself.' He glanced at her. 'I'm serious. We're going in, *the ship*. Into the Solar System – or whatever *this* is. Through the hole in the wall. We've got work to do.' He glanced around. 'We're going to need more lumes ready to energy-spill. I . . . Shit,' he said. 'I can feel the acceleration already. We really are going in, aren't we?'

She had to smile. 'For better or worse. Then let's do this. You start lining up the lumes. I'll brief the captain on our capability and time frame—'

Not so fast.

That was the Captain's voice, her face on a couple of screens.

I see you smiling, Muree. Well, you were.

'Sorry, Captain. I didn't mean—'

Never mind. Listen Muree, we need to speak to our – hosts? And I need a friendly, competent face to point at them when we achieve a link. That's going to be you. And not scared.

'But, Captain—'

No argument. You're on.

6

Shit, said Commander Revil. *They really are coming in, aren't they?*

Revil's face filled several screens set in the walls of this local-control hub.

To say the situation was tense was a wild understatement. There had never been a comparable crisis in Rab's memory, even given his own youth. And Rab didn't think he had ever heard the commander swear before, however mildly.

Rab risked a glance at Planter. 'Shit,' he said softly.

Planter snorted. 'That's shit, *sir,* to you.'

Revil, if she heard, ignored the banter. *All right,* she said. *Planter, Callis, you're on the spot. I've given the order to open the Mask. The reconfiguration is already underway. We've rehearsed this procedure often enough—'*

'True enough, Commander,' Planter said, 'but never using scenarios with assumed agency.'

Can you give me that without the jargon, Lieutenant?

'Sorry, commander. Cop language. That is, previously when we rehearsed opening a Mask panel, we imagined it in the course of an encounter with an inert mass – some rogue object from the Kuiper belt or beyond. Generally we could destroy or deflect such threats long before they came near the Mask itself. If not, since we can't move the Mask out of the way, yes, we would open a rent in the surface, plot a course for the intruder through the interior – hopefully avoiding the more densely built-up volumes within. The main challenge there might be dismantling some of the Mask's structures, get them out of the way to allow the mass to pass through without damage – not so difficult generally as the incomer's hyperbolic course could be assumed to be pretty much a straight line. Not so difficult to plan, at least.'

Rab nodded. 'Like a bullet passing through a body. Tunnelling through.'

Thank you for that, Midshipman, Revil said dryly. *But that's not a bad analogy. If that 'bullet' were to hit an organ, by analogy – a planet, a moon, even a significant Frame node – a great deal of harm could be done. And so we worked on deflection and destruction scenarios, did we not?*

'Along with some war-gaming, commander,' Planter reminded her. 'When we got the chance. We found we could break up even a fair-sized asteroid without much harm. But how would we cope with some agent that might be tougher than mere rock and ice – let alone some kind of smart or guided craft that changed course, or even actively tried to evade us?'

Yes, Revil said, sounding doubtful. Rab heard fingers tapping on a desk top. *Well, that's what we face. And your suggested solution?*

'Probably our only recourse would be to use missiles – small, light craft powered by a single lume, perhaps two. Probably have to be crewed if it's needed fast.'

A missile. Even inside the Mask?

'Even inside. An inert missile of that kind can move pretty quickly, and we have the smarts to steer it without difficulty. Even its kinetic energy alone will make it a pretty devastating warhead . . .'

Revil hesitated. *Given we don't know what we're dealing with, that sounds – unethical. Not to mention highly dangerous. Depending on whether we're firing at enemies or friends.*

Planter said nothing.

Revil sighed. *But we need a defence. So tell me how many we manufactured? Is there a stockpile?*

Planter nodded. He was evidently distracted by the data flows from the oncoming craft, responses to queries into his own screens. 'I wouldn't call it a stockpile. We manufactured a couple of dozen, partly to iron out the design flaws. Just in case.'

Revil said, *Just in case. How many remain? And where are they?*

Rab was doing his own checking. 'Found them, Commander. A dozen remain, operationally speaking. The others were broken up for spare parts as their maintenance period extended—'

Get to the point. Where are this dozen?

Rab glanced over at Planter, who checked his own sources.

Planter reported, 'In clusters. Spread around the Mask, Commander, near the equatorial control stations, a couple at the poles.'

Hmm. Shit. I wish it had come anywhere but here, on top of us. I'd rather not have to make this decision.

Rab was startled at that admission.

Planter caught his eye, tilted his head. Rab could see what he was thinking. *This is what command really entails, kid.*

OK, said Revil. *And so, do we any have such missiles nearby? Near this station?*

'Two,' Planter said. 'Two close enough to – well, to reach the target before it goes too deep into the interior of the Solar System.' He glanced around at his other displays. 'But as the distance closes, that opportunity's going to shut fast. The missiles simply wouldn't be able to reach the target before rendezvous.'

How long?

Planter checked. 'We have three minutes left for a launch decision.'

Shit. The commander hesitated for a heartbeat.

Rab held his breath.

Then, evidently, Revil came to a decision.

Launch them. Launch them both. But put them in some kind of – holding pattern. Don't put them on any course that would intercept the intruder – not until I say so specifically. Just be ready—

'Sir,' Rab said. 'I know I dug this up. This possibility. But do we want to threaten it at all? The incoming ship. We've been studying it. We can make some assumptions about *them*, the people on the ship. And we infer people *are* in there, given the geometry – like the spin for Earth-standard gravity at the equator of that big carousel – we can infer that even if it is a weapon, there are people inside. People more or less like us. And they use lumes. As we do. We can *detect* the lumes they have, directly, from gravity-wave signatures.'

Revil frowned. *I'm not intending to attack, damn it. Just taking precautions. Precautions that, I hope, will prove unnecessary.*

Planter glanced over at Rab. 'Callis – captains, leaders, commanders have to make these kind of choices all the time. Pray you are never in such a situation.'

Says the man, Rab thought, who once had to decide whether to cut my hand off.

'OK, Commander, we're running out of time,' Planter said. 'First deadline coming. That big heavy ship, full of momentum, will be committed to coming through the aperture unless their captain gives the order to turn aside very soon. And we don't have much more time if you do intend to use the weapons—'

Launch the damn things, said Commander Revil.

*

Rab had been setting it all up as they had spoken. Now he swiped one screen over to the Planter's console. 'Launched, commander. Holding pattern as you say—'

OK. Now collapse the Mask, Revil snapped. *Locally, in front of that ship, as ordered. Midshipman, you set it up. You have the control. Do it.*

Rab's heart hammered. This did mean violating the Mask's prime purpose, its ability to hide. Worse yet, if this was a screw-up it would be entirely his fault. Reflexively he glanced over at the Lieutenant, his immediate superior.

Planter nodded his head once, sharply. 'Open it. Open the Mask.

Just locally, mind, the Commander said. *Just here. Just enough to let the damn thing through.*

'As ordered, Commander.'

Rab had worked this all out in advance. Now he set his controls, checked and double-checked, moving rapidly with his prosthetic-hand link. Planter hovered at his shoulder. Revil murmured further detailed instructions through her own systems.

But even as he worked, as fingers prosthetic and flesh manipulated the screens, Rab thought about the wider picture. He couldn't conceive what might come next. But he suspected his life was about to change, for ever.

Oddly, he thought of his mother. He wondered how she would feel to see him like this, at this seat of power. He couldn't even visualise her face.

He glanced around, at Planter, at Revil. 'Ready, sirs. Final confirmation, please.'

Do it, Revil snapped.

And Rab pressed his synthetic hand against a screen, once more.

*

The screen seemed to expand, virtually, to show a wider section of the Mask. A blank, black surface. A staggering feat of engineering, whichever way you looked at it.

A feat of engineering under attack. A superfine surface which now crumbled, cracking, revealing a lesser dark beyond, paler than the pitch black of the nearly lightless interior of the Mask.

And there was the ship – he saw it at last, against *a background of stars.*

Rab had seen images of the ship before – even interior visions of it, painfully reconstructed from stray radiation picked up by spy probes, even from deflected gravity waves originating in the ship's lume tank at the hub of that great turning wheel. Now, framed in the rent in the Mask, it seemed enormous, complex, ungainly – magnificent.

And it sailed calmly through the rent.

Planter blew out his cheeks.

'We have a visual link from the intruder,' Rab said softly.

About time, Commander Revil murmured. *Take it, Midshipman.*

. . . On Rab's screen, a woman's face.

Her hair a kind of silver-grey, her skin dark, her eyes an empty blue.

In his screen, Rab's own face was superimposed on hers. Where she was dark, he was pale – her hair sculpted, his head shaven. She looked surprisingly young, given the hair colour – about twenty, perhaps.

Rab felt his mouth drop open.

And she hadn't yet so much as blinked.

Nor had he. Planter muttered, 'Pull yourself together, Rab.'

Purposefully he nodded. 'I am Rab Callis. Midshipman Callis.'

She smiled back, if stiffly, formally. 'My name is Muree. Chief lume-wrangler.'

'Greetings, Mu . . . ree?'

'Greetings to you, Midshipman. My commander wishes to speak to yours.'

'And mine yours.'

She was now grinning widely.

'Quite a responsibility we share, Muree.'

'Yes. But I think they only put me up *because* I'm one of the youngest on board with any responsibility. And I have a nice smile.'

Rab nodded. 'What responsibility is that?'

'Handling lumes, usually.'

'Wow. That is a responsibility.'

'What about you?'

'I happened to be on duty when we made our first encounter. I report to *him*.' He jerked his prosthetic thumb at Planter.

Muree shrugged.

Lieutenant Planter laughed. 'Two worlds reunited, through their children.'

But Revil sounded more serious. *Don't mock, Lieutenant. These are the products of two branches of mankind, reunited after a thousand years. And close enough for the translation circuits to make a linguistic bridge immediately. Remarkable.*

Rab hadn't thought of that. He'd just *assumed* this woman would share the common argot of the Solar System. Why not? She and her people must ultimately have come from the Solar System, indeed from Earth itself. But – a thousand years of separation? And yet, evidently, the groups hadn't diverged so much that their machines could not translate for them. Or maybe efforts had been made to sustain that ancient, common tongue . . .

As he was thinking this through, Lieutenant Planter leaned over, tapped his shoulder, and pointed at another screen. 'There's another view vouched only to a handful for centuries. Don't miss it, Venus boy.'

And Rab found he was looking out through the rent in the Mask. A scattering of bright dots against the black, some brighter, some not, making teasing patterns.

'*Stars*,' he said.

'Stars, child,' Planter said. He grinned. 'You've come a long way from the sewers of Venus . . .'

Still most of Rab's attention was taken up by the woman in the screen. Muree. Despite the stars.

(*The stars!*)

Now she glanced away, at somebody out of the screen's image.

Another voice broke in, from the visiting ship, a stern female, with no accompanying image. 'I am Captain Tavar. In command of the *Lightbird*. You see us, now that you have opened your hide – the Mask, did you call it? – and now we see more of your world – or rather, worlds. Muree's assistant believes that our lumes are disturbed because, with your Mask dropped, they sense another nest of lumes, much larger, not far away.'

Revil said, *Greetings, Captain Tavar. That's possible. The Mask is designed to scramble gravity waves as well as other spectra of—*

'You have many planets here,' Tavar said. 'At the centre of it all, a mass the size of a star, though we detect no stellar radiation. Everything inside has been hidden by this – Mask.

'But we found a planet outside your Mask. Wrecked. Infested by lumes. Our tradition says that such a planet, called *Neptune*, was destroyed in the war, the invaders . . . Can you confirm that such is the name you give that planet?'

Revil broke in again. *I . . . can confirm that. Yes, that was Neptune. My name is Revil, rank Commander. I am in charge of this installation, but have no authority to speak to you further of these things. If you would care to send ambassadors from your ship, we will take you—*

Tavar snorted. 'Are you wary of us? Even though you allow us and our ship into your Solar-System-sized cage? Ah. This is why you hide. In case the Destroyers come again.' She thought that over. 'You thought *we* might be the Destroyers?'

Revil said sternly, *That word will serve. It might seem outlandish. Our caution extreme. Yes, your ship resembled a human craft. But we need make only one bad guess, and we might face the extermination of the species, here at least. Remember Neptune.*

'And that is why you hide.'

And that is why your ancestors fled.

Captain Tavar stiffened. 'Well. Perhaps we two branches of mankind should reunite, or try to. Talk at least before we indulge in mutual annihilation. You must come to our ship. And we must visit your worlds.'

Rab smiled, and reached out, to his screen, to Muree. 'You should come here first. You will be amazed . . .'

But Muree was staring. 'What happened to your hand?'

7

It took days before the crews of Mask and *Lightbird* were allowed to meet each other, to mix.

The delay was going to drive Muree crazy, she thought, after the first couple of those days. Even though she understood the reasons – the time needed for a certain amount of integration of the crews.

There was obvious care taken against mutual infection – though no harmful vector had been found in either population. Once you had gone through the inoculation process, whether you were crew of ship or Mask, you had to display a sigil painlessly tattooed onto the back of your hand, to be shown at all times when you weren't wearing a pressure suit or similar – and even then there were badges to be worn.

Beyond that the problems were technical more than political. There was a need for a basic understanding regarding limits on the exchanges of people, and for communication networks to be established between the command hierarchies – and even that had taken some doing, given the drift of their respective vocabularies from what had evidently been a common root stock a thousand years ago. Translation software helped, but confusion was rife and had to be resolved.

And then there was a similar challenge of interfacing two divergent technologies.

Here was an interstellar worldship, with its own technical demands and design aspects, the product of one of those technological branches. And on the other hand the Mask, as Muree was learning to think of it, like a ship going nowhere, dedicated to the monstrous task of *hiding* an entire planetary system.

The crews of two such diverse vessels could hardly have had more different environments to work in. Even the most basic social aspects that you might expect to be held in common were different, Muree saw. And the most technical too.

Take subsidiary transport. If crew had to leave the *Lightbird* – if they needed to access the craft's exterior and couldn't manage their task by following the system of rails and cables and simple transporters fixed to the outer hull – they had small runaround crewed craft, powered by chemical propulsion: hydrogen burning in oxygen, the ingredients of water. Whereas on the Mask, this tremendous spherical hide, if major work had to be done it seemed it was almost always quicker, easier and safer to move people, machines and materiel through the *interior* of the Mask itself, and emerge from the hull at the point where they were needed.

An interior Muree and the rest of the *Lightbird* crew had yet to see, just as nobody from the Mask had come across to the *Lightbird*.

Mauree told Rab Callis, in one of their (hopefully) private conversations – still sitting in their separate domains, still peering into screens like everybody else – that, from the hints she'd been given, she imagined the interior of the Mask as being like one of the big holds inside the structure of the *Lightbird*. 'Big empty spaces strung with ropes and cables, and people and machines pulling themselves around . . .'

Rab laughed at her guesswork. 'Which isn't so far wrong, I suppose. If you break it down to its simplest terms. But there's much more to it than *that*. And you probably can't imagine the wider picture. The Frame. You need to visualise worlds . . . tangled up in spiderweb. Whole worlds. Umm, do you have spiders on the *Lightbird*?'

'Of course we do . . .' She thought about that. 'I say "of course" . . . Spiders are too useful not to have around, aren't they? But that means somebody must have released whole species of spiders over the ship once it was commissioned and launched. I never thought of that before.' She laughed. 'What a job. Having to *think* of that.'

He nodded, and scratched his chin with that odd artificial hand. 'But come to think of it, somebody must also have carried spiders around from Earth to the other planets and moons, the habitats we established all over . . .'

Other planets.

Earth. Neptune.

They were the only two Solar planetary names she had learned so far, and even what she knew of them was from her own past, her people's treasured fragments of history. *Earth*: the legendary origin world of mankind. *Neptune*: where humans had met the invader, and lost, and as a consequence some of its children had fled to the stars in a scattering of tiny ships . . .

And here at home, so to speak, there had been a different, much stranger response than mere flight, it seemed.

Rab, empathetic, intelligent, tried to tell her something of it, despite the security restrictions that still frustrated communications between the crews.

'You'll see it all,' Rab said. 'Soon, I'll bet. You've heard about the Architect. Whose vision led the rebuilding of the Solar System – the connection of the surviving planets after the invasion . . .'

Except, she was learning now, the legend of that invasion

was surely incomplete. The sudden opening of the Mask, the revelations within, had made anybody on the ship who saw it all question their basic assumptions about what was going on here, she suspected. From outside, it was all an immense lie. She faced the basic proviso. *If there had been a battle at all.* If these people hid and lied about the past, maybe they lied about the present too.

. . . *All* of them, countless billions of them. Or perhaps the mass of people were lied to also.

She didn't know how to frame such questions, even with Rab.

Still, they had some common ground. Traces of old Earth lingered in both their overlapping cultures, she and Rab slowly learned.

Time was measured in hours and days and years, on the Mask as back on Rossbee. And, she discovered now, even on Rossbee, everybody grew up using a dating system designed to measure time on distant, legendary Earth, and most of them probably didn't know it.

In fact the continued use of Earth's calendar at Rossbee was practical, Muree came to understand – not that she'd thought much about it before. Rossbee – named formally by astronomers on Earth, long before the attack on Neptune, as Ross 128b – was a small planet that orbited a small star, a red dwarf. And it sailed so close to that star that its rotation was locked – it kept one side facing its sun all the time. So a 'day' on Rossbee was the same as its 'year', and each was almost exactly the same as ten days on Earth – but neither of those yardsticks was any use for measuring time on a detailed human scale. So, Earth dating had been preserved, a race memory made solid in a calendar – with adjustments for the slippery time dilation incurred by relativistic space travel.

Away from their daily sessions, as she pondered what she was learning so quickly, Muree thought she and Rab were developing a genuine friendship here, as they talked about such matters – despite the barriers of translation filters and physical distance, and an awareness of the strange politics of this unique situation, this coming together of two branches of mankind. But it was no ordinary friendship, if only because she *believed,* but couldn't be sure, that their conversations were being monitored, that their relationship was being *allowed* to develop as it would. Because it was useful. Politic, even.

She imagined a discussion between the commanders. A dialogue between the two communities had to start somewhere, so why not with these two youngsters?

But, as those first days of contact wore on, she sensed that there was a continuing wariness about the encounter at the top levels of command on both sides.

'What strikes me,' she said on the fourth day, 'is that nobody on my ship is even being *told* about this. Aside from the upper officers, I suppose, and the likes of me, who happened to be involved in the first contact. I mean, from the *Lightbird* anybody can look out and *see* your Mask.'

Which, so close, showed no signs of curvature. Aside from the recent opening, it was like a flat, black, nearly featureless wall, stretching off to infinity in every direction. Existentially strange, she thought. Like a monument to death itself . . .

She'd hesitated, she realised. Staring out of the monitor, Rab was watching her as she gathered her thoughts. 'And I suspect the images we *are* seeing, aboard the *Lightbird,* are heavily censored.'

Rab leaned forward, closer to his screen. Not that that helped in terms of the privacy of this conversation, Muree knew.

He said, 'I've been thinking the same thing. About the secrecy. I don't know for sure – to be honest, inside the Mask, even in normal times you tend not to hear a lot of news away from your usual locations – where you live, work.' He glanced at a second screen. 'But at least you can *see* it all, the Frame, the struts, the worlds, the traffic . . . Everybody inside the Mask can see it, I guess, on a good day, from the Mask on the outside to the Solar Wrap on the inside and the worlds and Frame struts between . . .'

Frame. Mask. Wrap. Struts. There was so much she still didn't understand. It seemed this 'Wrap' was literally a wrap around what was left of the Sun, now a mined-out black hole. Even if that was correct – why? Why build such a thing? For the natives, she suspected – even for inquisitive Rab – all this was taken for granted, without need for explanation. But then—

'But then,' she said, 'I don't suppose you can imagine how *my* life is – shut up inside a worldship that used to seem roomy until we came upon *you*. Oh – here come the bosses. In person this time.'

She could see, over Rab's shoulder, Mask Commander Revil walking into the Mask cabin – and another man, Lieutenant Planter, who Muree knew was Rab's immediate superior in the apparently vast human hierarchy of command and control that maintained the Mask, and indeed spanned the Solar System.

And she knew, too, now, about Rab's strange relationship with this man, from Rab's tales of his childhood. Another enormous divergence of experience . . .

Rab seemed startled to see them both. Hastily he turned and made to rise.

But Planter squeezed his shoulder. 'It's all right, Rab. Stay there.'

'More than all right, Callis,' Revil said. She leaned down and glared into the screen, at Muree. 'We've a job for you two.'

Rab frowned. 'A job, Commander?'

'A job. Look – you know you've been monitored, from the moment the pair of you were thrown together in the earliest stages of the encounter – somebody had to make first contact, after all. Correct? And it was you two, by chance. But you did a good job, both of you, through the language filters and so on, but informed by a facility, a, a *willingness* to communicate with the stranger, which, I suspect, is a faculty many of us lack, for better or worse. I can tell you that both sets of command officers, on the Mask and the ship, have been impressed with your contributions. Both of you. Your *ongoing* contributions. I can say that on behalf of your Captain Tavar also, Muree, with whom I'm in regular contact.

'But now we're going to ask more of you. You know that contact between the two, umm, populations has been limited so far. And for good reasons which I'm sure you'll understand.'

Rab said, 'Yes, Commander—'

Revil ignored him. 'Cultural for a start,' she went on. 'Consider the divergence. We have been able to establish, or confirm, from the very genetics, that our two populations have indeed been separated for a *thousand years*. Just as we were told by the records we keep here on the Mask, and the historical accounts brought back aboard the *Lightbird*. A thousand Earth years. You know, we might have expected a greater divergence of languages. We're sure of that possibility given Earth's historical records – I mean from the epochs before Neptune. From right back in the age humans were confined to Earth and still lacked fast transport, when cultures could develop out of contact with each other—'

'But we can speak to each other,' Muree said. 'Mostly. With the computers' help for now. Even though we've been out of contact so long.'

Planter bent to see her. 'That's it. We are two highly

technological cultures – or rather, we are descended from what must once have been a single global culture. And we've both evidently maintained records, since the divergence. That, we think, has had the effect of freezing both our languages close to an ancient, common form. There's some novelty, some linguistic drift – and some new words, or new *usages*, as time has gone on, as our technologies and other cultural aspects have diverged . . .'

Muree grinned. 'Tell us about it. Before coming here I would have used the word "wrap" to mean a bit of smart paper I would keep my lunch in.'

Rab frowned. 'I didn't really think about it. From the beginning we, Muree and I, have just got on with it and – talked. Worked it out as we went along.'

Revil said, 'Well, you followed your instincts, and that's been a good thing. The first contact, as mediated by you two – and a few others, I may say, in similar positions – has gone well. Which is why we want you to take a step further. *Together*. Captain Tavar and I and our staffs have worked it out between us.'

Muree felt excited at this slowly emerging situation. Or perhaps wary. She thought of the *Lightbird*'s lume tank, without her. How long was this going to take?

'What do you mean, Commander?'

Revil held her hands up. 'Look. Talking heads in screens, that's all very well. It hasn't been difficult to make contact that way – well, as you can see, you two have been using this for days already. But—'

'Physical contact,' Muree blurted. 'You want me to go over to the Mask – or Rab to come here?'

The commander gave her a wry smile.

'Easy, now. You won't be alone. We'll exchange parties, not just individuals. But – well, you two have established a certain – profile. And that's symbolic, you see. If you two can get along, why not the rest of us? So you need to be the first, or among the first.'

Muree exchanged a glance with Rab, who raised his eyebrows. She thought she knew what he was thinking.

Are we symbols?

It's all a little – manipulative, isn't it?

She responded with a slight shrug. *So what? It'll be fun.*

She said aloud, 'Of course we'll be – honoured – to do this.'

Rab nodded. 'Of course. I guess there will be more quarantine protocols?'

Planter now chipped in. 'That's one side of this. After a thousand years of separation, even mild mutations of common diseases could cause havoc in isolated populations.'

'But it's more complicated than that,' Revil said. There's also a technological interface to be built. Look – after a thousand years apart, the *Lightbird* and the Mask come from two pretty divergent technological traditions, which were *not* designed for physical contact.'

Muree thought that through. 'I guess that's obvious. The *Lightbird* tech is basically designed to land on planetary bodies – or maybe for docking with space facilities, like we have orbiting Rossbee, the supply facilities, the jig factories—'

'Correct,' Revil said. 'Whereas the Mask was not designed for any such interfacing. Remember too that the purpose of the Mask is concealment – which has meant that it is pretty complex, and pretty fragile, for all its size.'

Rab nodded. 'I get it. The *Lightbird*'s runabouts would be too massive, too energetic to bring close to a structure like the Mask.'

'Also our defensive structures would react to any such – um, intrusion. *But* a craft from the Mask—'

'Could come to the *Lightbird*,' Muree said eagerly.

'That's the idea,' Commander Revil said. 'And what we do have is a number of small, independent, private ferries to hand, which we use for small excursions outside the Mask, usually for maintenance purposes, and also for travel inside the Mask – usually ferrying to the Frame, and access to the rest of the Solar System.'

Muree nodded. 'And one of these ferries could come to the *Lightbird*.'

'Anyhow that's the proposal, for the first contact event at least. I've talked this through with Captain Tavar. We need to manage a first meeting between our populations. That will be spearheaded by you two. But the way it's going to work, Muree, at least in the beginning, is for Rab, with others, to go to you. To the *Lightbird*.'

Muree and Rab looked at each other through their screens. Muree saw that Rab was grinning as widely as was her own reflection.

Revil said, 'I hope that sounds acceptable. It's a fair responsibility, there will be some attention on you both . . . However. That's the scenario. All good, Rab, Muree? Fine. Well, all we need to do now is to set up a secure quarantine regime, to be absolutely sure that the two branches of mankind don't kill each other on first contact . . .'

On impulse Muree held out her hand and laid it flat on the screen. 'Welcome aboard.'

And the hand Rab held up to match hers was that spidery robotic construct. She thought she could hear a scraping of metal on the surface of his screen.

8

First contact was set up for the next day.

Right on time, the ship from the Mask slid briskly through the space between that great semi-infinite surface and the waiting starship.

Muree, sitting in her own small cabin on the Carousel deck, watched the approach on various monitors – as did, probably, much of the ship's population. The ferry, it turned out, was called the *Styx* – small, its hull, rounded, shell-like – and it was dwarfed by the structure behind it, the Mask, which filled the screen.

Sitting there, she quickly learned from the senior crew that this craft's owner was actually independent of the Mask and its command structure. The *Styx* was a ferry owned and run by a solo trader of some kind – a woman called Angela Plokhy – and it somehow startled Muree to be learning about this person. An independent trader in the environs of a system as large, and as controlled, as the Mask. But it seemed to make sense, as the crews communicated back and forth, as she learned more. An installation like the Mask, even one of its local stations, generated a lot of traffic, and private enterprise of some kind could help in carrying that traffic in a flexible way.

And also an independent ship, used to making a wide range of contacts, would be useful, indeed practiced, in maintaining quarantine as the first passengers crossed between Mask and starship; apparently the *Styx* was equipped with such suitable facilities.

Brad went for dark humour. 'And if you do bring out a plague bug we can just shoot that little ship out of the sky.'

Muree snorted. 'Stay away from my funeral . . .'

But as she watched the craft approach, the next day, the bulbous little ship only served to emphasise the vast scale of the Mask itself, from which it came. Every so often Muree had to remind herself that *humans made this*.

In its final manoeuvre, the ferry headed for the axis of the great wheel that was the main body of the ship – where the *Lightbird*'s own small ferries docked.

Muree knew there was a thick layer of shielding around the axis, as around the rest of the craft, to guard against radiation and meteorite impacts – as well as a rack of laser cannon to back up the passive shields in case of an unlikely contact with massive fragments during interplanetary, indeed interstellar flight. Even between the stars space was not empty but littered, sparsely, with comet cores, meteorites, asteroids, objects lost from Oort clouds or Kuiper belts on the fringe of planetary systems.

The ship's defences were controlled by smart tech that, today, all needed to be carefully persuaded by its human masters that the incoming object, though strange, though not in the ship's archive of friendly craft, was not some rogue interstellar mass, and therefore was not to be harmed.

The final approach, therefore, was understandably slow, ultra-cautious, as the ferry approached a dock at one end of the starship's spin axis, where a counter-spinning mechanism made it easy for the newcomer to dock with a stationary port.

Physical contact was to be made by the mating of two halves of a transit sleeve, hastily assembled by engineers from ship and

Mask working together. But Muree learned that the little ship's ports were designed to accommodate a wide variety of interfaces anyhow.

And, at last, more monitors told Muree that the docking was in progress.

Muree longed to *feel* the contact. In the end she told herself she had, that the craft from the Mask had caused a gentle shudder as it mated with the much more hefty hull of the *Lightbird*.

Finally a single green light told her that the ferry and starship had securely docked.

'Show time,' Muree muttered to herself.

Before she left her cabin she checked over her gear once more. Today, like everybody else who might come close to the visitors, she was wearing her personal survival cum quarantine suit – basically a lightweight, unobtrusive, airtight coverall with gloves and helmet, as issued to every crew member on the ship. Such suits were standard pieces of ship kit, were reissued as you grew, and practice in using them every few days was mandatory. The suit protected her against decompression, toxicity in the atmosphere, radiation leakages, and other calamities.

Before the arrival of the ship at the mysterious Mask, Muree had never really imagined she would need to use the suit in anger. Even the notion of a return to the Solar System, to fabled Earth itself – the nominal purpose of the mission, a return had been expected in her lifetime – had never seemed real.

But here she was.

Check complete, she pushed out of the door of her cabin, and made her way to the hub elevator cluster. Here, six shafts, set out radially, could be accessed. Each one would take you down from this central hub to the Carousel, reaching out to descent points spread around the circumference.

Muree knew which of the six shafts to pick – in fact she would ride the elevator to which Rab and his disembarked handlers from the Mask ferry would soon be guided. For now she had it to herself.

She closed her faceplate, a standard bit of protocol. The descent took less than a minute; as always she braced against the ever increasing gravity load as she travelled outwards from the hub.

At the bottom, she stood straight for a few seconds in the heavy gravity, letting supports in her suit take some of the load, making sure she felt comfortable, her legs, her spine, her neck.

And she took one deep breath before opening the door.

She emerged into the bright 'daylight' of the Carousel.

She was immediately aware of people everywhere, waiting, hanging back around the elevator shaft – a diffuse crowd gathered, not for her, but because this was where the visitors from the Mask should soon arrive. All of them in quarantine kit of their own, it had been agreed.

Muree pushed her way out through the crowd, heading for where she knew Captain Tavar would be waiting. She tried to be brisk, tried not to show her nervousness – tried not to make eye contact too often.

Muree knew these people, of course, some of them well. There were after all only two hundred or so people living in the worldship – like a 'reasonably sized farming community on Venus', Rab had told her, using vocabulary she barely followed. And everybody knew she had a role to play today. So now people didn't quite crowd around her, but were drawn to her through curiosity – maybe – especially those who knew her best.

But for now she had to keep quiet. She was labouring under a command for secrecy. Tavar and Revil had ordered that this first encounter at least should be controlled, monitored – aborted if anything went wrong. Muree saw the logic. Both ship and Mask were fragile in their different ways, that much was evident. And given the centuries of separation of these two branches of humanity, despite all their precautions the possibility of various kinds of harmful cross-contamination loomed large.

But still she didn't like the idea of secrecy, of dividing such a small, fragile community. Although, she thought guiltily, if secrets had to be kept she would sooner be on the inside, *knowing*, rather than wondering from the outside.

She felt a complicated relief that her mother wasn't here. It had been five years since her death. It would have been hard to keep secrets from her . . .

Now she was emerging from the loose crowd of onlookers around the shaft. Here was Captain Tavar, waiting. She beckoned to Muree. In person Tavar was a stocky, impressive woman, with an air of effortless command, Muree had always thought.

Alongside Tavar were a couple of crew wearing quarantine suits, as was Tavar herself. The crew were armed, Muree could see; they each had stun prods tucked into their suit belts. All contingencies covered, she thought.

Tavar nodded to Muree. 'Right on time – noted.' She glanced at the elevator shaft, rising up to the central hub above their heads. Muree saw the pale green indicators on the shaft's smooth wall, indicators that tracked the cabin's kilometre-long descent from the ship's axis to this circular floor.

Captain Tavar murmured, 'Our visitors are on the way down. Between us, by the way, one of the Mask people reported nausea as they started that elevator ride.'

'Coriolis forces? Vertigo?' Muree tried not to laugh. 'These people have put the Solar System in a box, and they get *vertigo*?'

Tavar was grinning behind her faceplate. 'Goes to show.

People are people and no more than that, no matter what they achieve. Not a bad thing for us to have a sense of superiority over these solars in one small aspect at least, don't you think?'

Muree allowed herself to grin back. She did get Tavar's point. And at that moment Muree was glad she wasn't a nauseous stay-at-home herself. But on the other hand she'd liked what she'd seen of her main contact, Rab; she didn't particularly want him to be discomfited.

The hub elevator doors now slid open.

'And two worlds meet, after tens of generations,' murmured Captain Tavar. 'Come on, Muree; let's put on a good show.'

The captain led the way forward with brisk steps.

Muree followed more cautiously, alongside the two other crew with her.

Staring at the two figures in the elevator cabin.

Both in all-over environment suits in pale grey, the newcomers halted for a moment, looking around. The ship's internal light seemed bright for them; they both shielded their eyes with gloved hands over face visors. But they seemed to be aware of the sparse crowd of onlookers in front of them.

Then they took a single step forward, together.

As they stepped through the elevator door frame, there was a brief, bright purple flash. Muree knew this was a deliberately visible manifestation of the elaborate quarantine regime that had already been established between spacecraft and Mask – a reminder that these were populations separated for a thousand years. She knew that Rab and his companion would have gone through several such processing stages, starting with their naked bodies being screened even before leaving the Mask itself. And if, when, Muree was ever allowed to make the reverse journey, she would go through similar procedures.

Muree risked a look around. Her crewmates looked on in apparent awe.

As well they might, Muree thought: this was the first time any of them had *ever* met a person who had not been born and raised on the ship itself. At least she had been inoculated from wonder by her talks to Rab Callis, to a degree.

And now he was here . . . but which was which?

She guessed he was the one with the lesser signs of vertigo – the apparently younger, fitter one. She walked forward.

And as she approached, that person – *he* – opened his suited arms, his hands, in a gesture that clearly meant friendship. Still she could not make out a face. But one of those hands, gloveless, was a metallic simulacrum.

She walked up to him and gave him a suited hug.

Captain Tavar followed her, and shook gloved hands with the second Mask ambassador.

The people behind them started to applaud.

There followed a few minutes of basic introductions.

'I am Captain Tavar. This is Muree, who works with our lumes – when not communicating with exotic visitors from the stars. Come. Walk with us, as we talk. The people of my ship are – intrigued – to see you.' Tavar smiled through her faceplate. 'You don't get many visitors on a generation starship.'

Rab introduced himself and his companion in a comprehensible but heavily accented version of the ship's own language. He must have memorised it phrase by phrase, Muree realised. Once they started to speak informally, Muree knew, smart systems would allow for mutual translations, either in the ship or on the Mask.

She dared wink at Rab through her faceplate when she caught his eye. *Good job.*

The other visitor was identified as Lieutenant Jeo Planter.

Tavar began to lead the group in a slow walk along the concourse. People tracked their steps, politely, curiously. There was a background of subdued chatter.

Captain Tavar looked back at them, beaming. 'Welcome to our vessel, our home – Rab Callis, isn't it? Midshipman? Are you comfortable walking with us? If the gravity is difficult—'

'We have centrifuges and such at the Mask,' Planter said, walking alongside Rab, if cautiously. 'Also many of us were born on high-gravity worlds, and have lived there for long periods. Adaptations are various. I served on planet Venus myself—'

'And I was born there,' said Rab.

If he had more to say about that in this slightly awkward exchange, he didn't deliver.

Muree saw he was distracted as they passed a nursery school. A milestone on the itinerary, so the party slowed.

The school's children – a dozen of them – and their teacher had clearly known the party was coming. As they passed, the kids came crowding out of the building into a small garden, green grass with swings, slides, other toys. All this behind a floor-to-ceiling transparent sheets: more quarantine precautions.

The visitors waved back.

It was surreal, Muree thought, the pressure-suited spacefarers walking past the gaudy colours and rounded contours of the school, the happy, wide-eyed kids. But she felt oddly proud of the moment. Proud for them all, residents and visitors.

They walked on, still waving to the kids, and then past a work party. These workers had taken panelling off an inner hull wall, and, with autonomous robot workers, were pushing their way into the deep tangle of machinery that evidently filled the space between the Carousel's inner and outer hulls. Maintenance. Rab slowed to see. In turn the workers paused in their work to stare back at him.

Muree wondered what to say. 'Your – structure, the Mask – it is surely far more advanced than our poor ship.'

Planter shrugged. 'I wouldn't care to hazard a guess. My local command station alone would dwarf your ship. But we go nowhere, whereas you travel to the stars. And the ships have much in common, I'm sure. On one level both are simply machines designed to support human lives, and must both derive from a common technological tradition a thousand years old.' He glanced up, leaning back so he could see beyond his visor. And he stared up at the hub above their heads, at the axis of the great spinning wheel in whose curvature they were standing. 'And we have nothing like *this*. I'm figuring out the engineering. We've been told little, as you know. This – carousel? – spins to provide a simulacrum of gravity. There is warmth, there is air – air that must be recirculated to remove excess water, to be recharged with oxygen . . .'

'We have plants for that,' Captain Tavar said. 'Green growing plants, that are backed up by machinery. In fact the workers over there,' she pointed at the stretch of opened-up wall, 'are servicing some of the air conditioning suite. It is all over the ship, behind the walls, under the floors.'

Rab continued to stare up, beyond the hub, at the inverted corridor of landscape two kilometres over their heads, far enough off for there to be a perceptible mistiness, from moisture in the air.

Muree looked up herself, trying to imagine how it must be for *him* seeing this. Was he impressed? But then she knew virtually nothing of the world, or worlds, he came from – nothing beyond enigmatic talk of vast frameworks, struts and planets hiding behind the Mask: a parcel containing, evidently, a whole planetary system . . .

'It really is a miniature world,' Rab said now. 'This ship.' He looked at her, and down at a walled flower bed, an ornament in the middle of the upcurved way. 'Children, schools. Growing plants? Green plants, with chlorophyll? . . . But without sunlight, between the stars.'

'True. But we have a substitute. Lamps. Powered by lumes, or by the ship's backup fusion pile. That's where I work, in the lume bank. Making sunlight, in a way. Or a substitute for it. Among other things. You are stationed here far from your own Sun – and besides, of course, your "Sun" is a black hole.'

He smiled, behind his visor. 'Sorry. I'm full of questions. As you must be. Are your parents here? Do you have siblings? I never did. I would have pestered mine, I think . . .'

That was a difficult track for her to go down. He wasn't to know *why*. Not yet.

'No parents. No siblings.'

That curtness seemed to surprise him. But he nodded. 'I know your population has to be controlled. Neither too high nor too low . . .'

She turned away without a further answer – but that felt awkward, now.

It struck her that most of the ship's crew, all save the smallest children, would probably know something of why she was sensitive on that subject. It was a small community, she was coming to realise, and her family background was – unusual. Most people would know. Even so she felt an odd, illogical resentment that Rab's questioning had managed to go so deep so quickly.

He said nothing, walking on, evidently aware he had walked into a problem.

Get it over with.

'Rab—'

He turned to her.

Just tell him.

'I had no siblings,' she said. 'None that survived.'

He seemed puzzled at her tone.

She was being unfair to him. He could not *know*. Conversely, there was much she didn't know about him. This encounter was becoming much more awkward than she had imagined.

Embarrassed, she turned away. She *would* tell him. But not yet, not here – not in the middle of this performance.

'Yes, we do have green plants,' she said. Back to safe territory.

Through his visor, he looked at her more cautiously, but picked up the cue. 'Growing in the light of your lumes. With lumes, you have crossed the stars. Whereas for us . . .'

'Go on,' she said cautiously.

'For us, the lumes are everything too.' He waved a hand. 'The Mask. The whole Solar System itself is like a single engine on a mighty scale, all reliant on the lumes . . .' He seemed to crumble a little. 'Sometimes I think this has been too much for me. These revelations, your ship's arrival, the last few days – I'm a pretty junior officer in the Mask, you know, even if it is a shell that holds in the whole Solar System. I just do my job. And now all this. Your ship. *You*.' He grinned, awkwardly. 'Sometimes I feel as if an overfed lume is burrowing into my head, and is about to explode.'

Muree had to smile at that. 'Hiding a whole solar system, though.'

He shrugged. 'You get used to it.'

In this quiet moment, Muree looked more closely at Rab himself. She was a little taller than he was, and she looked down on him now, through his slightly dusty faceplate. That pale skin, so unlike her own. Maybe humans back in the Solar System had kept the same diversity of appearances as had been preserved on Rossbee.

She didn't know what to say. *Try, Muree.*

'This all feels like a mess, doesn't it? Awkard. But we are all just – humans – together. No matter how long we've been apart. You and I got off to a good start anyhow. Maybe we can keep that up, and help – sort things out.'

He nodded behind the faceplate. 'Agreed. But right now I think we'll have to catch up with the rest of the party.'

'Yes. I think they're heading for the Memorial.'

'What memorial?'

She looked at him, surprised. 'The Neptune Memorial. There's one back on Rossbee. One on the ship – as you'll see. Don't you have them? That's a history we share – probably the last bit of history we *do* share, in fact . . .'

He seemed to think that over. 'We've lots to learn.'

'I can agree with that. And maybe we can learn together.' On impulse she held out her gloved hand.

And he took it with his own artificial hand. Its touch was soft, firm, even *warm*, even through their quarantine gloves. She didn't remark on that, as they went to rejoin the main party.

9

The first encounter between the folk of the Solar System and the returning *Lightbird* had been successful from the start, it seemed to Rab when he thought about it later: the reasonably calmly handled mutual discovery, and then an agreed post-contact quarantine period, just in case some nasty slipped through the interfaces between the crews.

Planter was given wide responsibility for the contact management. Back on Venus, he had essentially been a police officer – but he had had some medical training in his background. Mostly emergency stuff: trauma treatments, basic life-saving treatments, and some more sophisticated field medicine. That was one reason why he had been assigned to the pursuit of Rab's mother, in the face of her determination not to let her child be cast down into the mines of Mercury. That had been halfway to a medical crisis, a psychodrama that might have turned yet more bloody.

And now, as well as being hastily assigned as a companion to Rab on the *Lightbird* – Rab, the symbolic, youthful face of Earth as first presented to the incomers – Planter was unofficially lending medical support and advice to Mask Commander Revil and her team, as they cautiously developed their contact with the crew of the newly arrived ship. It was Planter who had most persistently argued for an extended quarantine period to follow the two crews' first mixing, just in case – advice the commanders, Revil of the Mask and Tavar of the *Lightbird*, seemed to have heeded.

Of course, quite apart from medical concerns, they would have recognised that the integration of the two crews – given so long a divergence, such different social backgrounds and goals – needed to be carefully handled in every aspect. A cultural quarantine.

A compromise was struck.

A sixty-four-day medical quarantine would be imposed. In that period only a handful of carefully monitored crew from the starship would be granted access to the Mask, outside the docking area to which the *Lightbird* had been guided. Similarly, only a few Mask crew would be allowed, cautiously, aboard the spacecraft.

And out of those Mask pioneers, polls showed, Rab Callis was the most popular with the *Lightbird* crew.

When Rab first heard the news from Muree he felt overwhelmed. Embarrassed.

'And scared,' he admitted.

'Don't be,' Muree said, over their comms link. 'Just give people what they want.'

'You're enjoying this, aren't you?'

She grinned. 'How can you tell?'

So, after a couple of initial forays to check out the evolving quarantine procedures, Rab, accompanied by Muree, prepared for another tour of the *Lightbird*.

The first stop this time, Rab heard nervously, would be another nursery school – situated right next to a funeral home. It seemed to be a symbolic destination; in his briefing he was told only that it was a location of significance to the starship's inner culture. *Schools and funeral homes* – he thought that an odd juxtaposition, even for a ship no doubt full of anomalies and surprises, and he hoped he wouldn't say the wrong thing.

Muree had assured him he would be fine, but even so, as the two of them rode the elevator down from hub to rim he had the feeling she was laughing at him behind a mask of politeness. But she linked her arm in his – his left arm, the arm with the prosthetic, as if to confirm its irrelevance.

At Carousel level, the door slid open to reveal Jeo Planter waiting, in a bio isolation suit.

The Lieutenant grinned. 'Surprise! Don't worry, I've had all my jabs. You didn't think the commanders would let you wander around down here unaccompanied, did you? Not yet. Anyhow, I can't wait to see you with your public, Callis. Or some of them. I read that poll . . .'

'Yeah, yeah,' Rab said, making no attempt not to sound surly.

Muree squeezed Rab's arm, evidently suppressing a laugh. Planter winked at her.

Muree led the way out into the concourse, the complex, busy heart of the *Lightbird*. Just as before, for Rab it was like walking into a vast corridor, a corridor that sloped disconcertingly upwards, ahead and behind.

They were soon approaching the school that was their first scheduled-but-informal stop of the day. It was a blocky building with big picture windows – and heavy-duty doors, doors that were functional airlocks, he'd been told. As with every building on this ship, in case of a pressure-hull breach this school could be turned airtight in seconds, with its own air supply, indeed its own independent power source.

Now, he saw, protected from air loss and these strange aliens' infections alike, the school's children were lined up behind the plate-glass windows. It was just like his first jaunt through the ship, though this was a different school: more, older kids crowding the windows, teachers hovering in the background. Some kids waved when they saw Rab's party. Others held up pictures, even models – one mess of folded paper might have been the *Lightbird*, another, a big ball crudely painted black, must stand for the Mask itself.

All this was unfamiliar to Rab. There were no children on the Mask, anywhere across its enormous expanse, in the many habitats scattered around the smart-graphene shell of the main structure . . . But here there were children, infants, even a few babies. And the adults who cared for them must have designed as much safety and redundancy into their systems as they could, must constantly maintain those systems and watch over the children who depended on them, Rab supposed. Children, an essential burden – a burden to be protected no matter what the sacrifice. Just as his own mother had once demonstrated.

Muree nodded her head at the window. 'Look. That little boy has made himself an artificial hand. See?'

A thing of plastic straws, knotted together.

Planter laughed. 'Quite the celebrity,' he said dryly.

'Oh, shut up,' Rab snapped back.

And now a couple of the children held up plastic boards with questions written on them.

Rab squinted. 'I can't read those—'

Planter nodded. 'I've been trying to learn this script. It's not as divergent from ours as you might expect over a thousand years of separation, but still difficult.'

Muree shrugged. 'Let me. Look, that placard the little girl is holding up – can't you read *that*? She's asking what Earth is like.'

Rab tapped a microphone stud in his collar. 'Can you hear me?'

In response, lots of beaming, smiling faces, nodding like flowers in an aircon breeze. More placards were waved with scribbled-on questions, and messages. Rab couldn't make out the script, and Muree had to translate again.

'That one asks the same thing. Have you ever been on a . . . planet? Because these children haven't, remember. Nor have I . . .'

He nodded. 'I've never been to Earth. The only planet I've lived on has been Venus. Oh, that and the Mask, which is just a big building. Venus? . . . I scarcely remember it. I was very small when I was brought away from there.'

Planter said, 'Not so small. You were kept on Venus with your mother after the – incident. For a few years, for your own health.'

Muree asked, 'So can you tell them what Venus was like? Do you remember anything at all?'

'Not really. The light, the green . . .'

Muree translated for him, as he spoke about the rooftop farms and the kilometres-deep infrastructure of the sky-bergs.

'That's where my mother worked. People lived in the bergs, and on top of them. And on the top, where the sunlight fell, there were farms. Growing food for everyone. They still do.' An aside to Muree, 'I hope that made sense.'

Muree nodded, murmured, 'Well done.' She waved her hands, and spoke into a wrist communicator, to the children behind the glass.

The children were clapping. More placards: HELLO SPACE MAN, in wobbly lettering, or so Muree said.

'Looks like you got that right,' Planter said. 'Another question?'

'Maybe one more,' Muree said. 'They'll need to save their questions for other Mask folk . . . Oh.'

Rab glanced at her; she seemed confused. 'What's wrong?'

'Well—' She pointed. 'The little boy who held up the latest placard. Asking a question that's very rude here, I'm afraid. I'm surprised the teacher's let him do it . . . Oh, she's taken it away.'

Rab frowned. '"Rude"? How can a kid that young be rude about anything?'

'Call it a taboo.' She sighed. 'He asked how many brothers or sisters you have.'

That simply baffled Rab. 'Why is that taboo?' He glanced over at the boy once more, who seemed to be quailing under the gaze of his teacher. Then the teacher shrugged at the visitors, half-smiled, and turned away, gathering the children back from the windows.

'Well, that's that,' Planter said. 'Come on. Next stop, the mortuary.' He pointed.

Only a hundred paces away, Rab guessed. They walked slowly.

'So,' Rab asked, 'unless it's too delicate, what's the issue with brothers and sisters?'

'Starship rules,' Planter said. 'So I'm guessing? I did hear about that.' He hesitated. 'And I was briefed on your own case, Muree.'

And Muree frowned.

'My "case". That's personal. Or should be. Such things are supposed to be private.'

Rab was evidently confused. 'What *case*?'

Planter eyed her. 'It might be best if he knows.'

And now she was growing angry. Nobody aside from the medics was supposed to know about her family background, this particular detail anyhow, not unless she chose to divulge it. And now, this.

She tried to focus. Rab looked bewildered. *You're not being fair, Muree. He needs to understand everything.* He *can't hide his hand . . .*

'All right – well, we all study this at school, as those little kids are already learning . . . Look, Rab, the *Lightbird* is a generation starship. Our journey from Rossbee has taken a hundred years. And the key to surviving a hundred-year space mission is controlling your population. A community of people, of just two hundred or so, has to survive entirely enclosed in this space, this – building. Generation after generation.' She waved a hand. 'The main danger is you could have too many children, an overcrowding that might stretch the ship's systems too far. Or of course there can be population *crashes*, through disastrous equipment failures, maybe some kind of mutated disease – or even conflict, war.

'But on the whole, crashes and explosions alike come from a failure of strict population control. Our history tells us that. The numbers are scary, when you first hear them at school. The numbers of that control.

'If you have a population of two hundred, say, as we do, then a deficit of births over deaths of just two per year, on average, every year, would cause your population to be reduced by *two thirds* in the hundred years of your mission.

'Conversely an excess of two births per year will cause your population to be *tripled* in that century.

'This isn't just some mathematical theory. Our ancestors kept in touch with the rest of the fleet from Earth, as long as they could. They heard such disasters play out, over and over.

'And we learned that on a starship, a catastrophic *drop* in population is much more difficult to handle than a rise. Because if you have too many folk, you see, you can just limit births, for maybe a decade or two? That will give you a lumpy demographic, but will keep you functioning, for a while anyhow. Or, if things get bad enough, there's always euthanasia . . .'

Rab just stared at her as she said this.

Planter, on the other hand, shrugged. 'I studied such scenarios once, in training for the police. In fact we've shared notes with your captain, Muree. After all, most of humanity lives in artificial environments now – all save a handful, a few million, on Earth itself. Emulating prehistoric numbers.

'You won't be surprised to learn, Muree, that some divisions of our police in the Solar System have supervisory powers over population density management, if not quite population control. We move people from places that are overcrowded, to places where they are less so. The Frame helps a lot with that – its high capacity.'

Muree still wasn't clear what the Frame was.

'Sometimes whole communities are moved, depending on resources or need for labour. The government decides, and we, the police, implement.' He glanced at Rab. 'Which boils down to the level of an individual being transferred from place to place. Compulsorily if necessary. To where they are more useful, or where there's just more room.'

Rab raised his artificial hand, flexed and opened it.

Planter made no comment, turned away.

Muree had heard Rab's story, realised they were thinking of the boy seemingly doomed to mines on Mercury – but she *knew* there were outcomes of population control far worse.

They were touching her own deepest, darkest secret.

Happily, they seemed to have dropped the subject.

They had reached the mortuary now. Their second stop.

This was a clean, white structure, elegant in its way, if plain, Rab thought. There was nobody around outside – certainly no children waving placards at him.

'I guess nobody died today,' he said softly.

Muree said, 'More likely they postponed any ceremony for

the day, while you of the Mask are introduced to us all—'

He glanced at her. 'What ceremony?'

'We waste nothing here. Our closed-loop recycling systems are too small for us to be able to afford the luxury of discarding seventy kilograms of organic material every time somebody dies. A person is reduced to their organic essentials, a legacy to be returned to the life-support system. We have ceremonies, built around that . . . sacrifice. Captain Tavar always speaks very well. But—'

Planter grunted. 'The colony worlds have similar ceremonies, mostly. Away from the Earth – Mars, Venus, Mercury, elsewhere – many of those started out with very small, very isolated populations. There was a similar need to commemorate the dead, but not to lose their substance from the life-support loops.' He looked at Muree. 'Such colonies long pre-dated the Neptune attack, the flight of the first interstellar ships. These are very old customs.'

'It's so here.' She waved her hand at the school, the mortuary. 'This is the way we mark such things.

'And why you have the school and the mortuary close together. The beginning and the end.

'It's to show even small children how the loop is closed, for all of us aboard, from birth through growth to death, and how, when we die, we must give back all that we are to the ship, the community. Births must balance deaths. So that others may live on, and the mission as a whole continues.'

Planter murmured, 'And sometimes you have to make other sacrifices for the sake of the community. That was what Rab's mother couldn't accept, of course. She did what she felt had to be done – the, the mutilation – to save him from the perils of the Mercury mines, as she saw it. Was she right? Was she wrong? At least Rab's mother's actions had a clear outcome. An origin story. And he's found the potential to follow the career path she shoved him onto.

'But in your case, Muree – I've been talking to your co-workers, your captain – the paths weren't so clear-cut, were they? If the surgeons had chosen the *other* foetus to survive, then who can say what difference that might have made? . . . A replacement compared to an omission . . .'

Muree froze.

Rab was at a loss to follow this new thread.

Muree said deliberately, 'What are you talking about, Lieutenant?'

Planter was hesitating, as if he'd suddenly realised he'd said the wrong thing.

Muree seemed *pale*. In shock? Rab wondered if she might faint, fall. He reached out with his artificial hand. Withdrew it.

She was still glaring at Planter.

'She told you. The Captain. She *told* you.'

Planter said, 'I'm sorry. I was only – look, our briefing was thorough. On every aspect of the ship, your society, as it's had to adapt. On your own background. Yours too, Rab. The ship commanders have had to learn who you are, where you come from, to trust you. You must see that.'

Rab spoke cautiously, picking out the key words: 'The foetus. The *other* foetus, you said—'

Muree snapped, 'What are you saying about me, stranger?'

Planter seemed rendered speechless by her anger.

But Rab was getting it. Slowly, maybe. He reached out to touch her, but she recoiled.

'I think I understand,' Rab said carefully. *'He's saying you were one of twins*. Right? That Captain Tavar told him so. That you were one of twins. Did your twin – die? Your mother never told you?'

Muree took a breath. 'My mother died many years ago, in an air breach. No. She never told me. My father was a donor, by the way, selected following genetic diversity rules. I never knew him even to speak to.' She eyed Rab again. 'Another restriction in such a small population. Have to keep those genes stirred up nicely. As to my birth – on my eighteenth birthday, the teachers at school told me what had happened.'

Now Rab saw why, maybe, she was drawn to the abstract 'family' of the lumes in their tank. And again he hesitated asking the next logical, inevitable question. 'So, evidently, the other twin didn't survive?'

'No, it's not that simple . . .' Still she glared at Planter.

Planter was obviously troubled with guilt. 'Oh, shit. I'm so sorry. I didn't mean to bring this up. The officers were discussing generation ship rules. In the abstract.' He looked at Rab. 'Rules about how, on a worldship this small, you have to budget for *one birth per conception*. Births have to balance deaths. But if the overall numbers are tight enough for that generation, and if it turns out to be a *multiple* conception – you could bust the budget. And, so – well, you have to choose.'

Muree said, 'Are those the words the captain used? *Choose. Budget*. While you analysed my life? About how you choose between two – two foetuses? Two siblings?'

Now Planter reached out to her.

She waved him away. 'How *could* you choose? Identical human beings, not yet born, not even yet formed . . . How could they choose? Could it have been me? I never knew . . . *How could they choose?* I lost a sister. I might have lost my life. And they told *you* about it? About me?'

Planter said carefully, 'Once again, I'm sorry. I'm a stranger here; you know that. But – you know, we have a regime of restrictions too.' He glanced at Rab. 'Our worlds are full too, more or less. And Rab, *you* know that I too have sometimes had to *choose* what to do, in matters of death and life. Muree, our regime is like yours in that. We have to make the best use of our people—'

'The best use. For what purpose?'

Her bitterness was tangible now. Cold, Rab thought.

'What purpose?' she repeated.

Planter, evidently horribly uncomfortable, at least tried to answer. 'Isn't it obvious? The Solar System *was* invaded – was it not? Who is to say that the invaders will not come again? If they do, we will be prepared, at least. We have built our worlds into a fortress, worlds sustained by flows of mass and energy on the scale of the whole System. But it's just the same as for a starship, surely, if on a larger scale. Commanders must manage their finite resources, their crews, as best they can to reach their destination. According to their rules, their pragmatic . . . judgement.'

'Judgement. And for these goals, Rab here was mutilated as a child. By *you*. For these goals, my twin sister had to die without taking a single breath. My mother must have had to choose which of us – no wonder she couldn't bear to *tell* me—' Her voice broke.

Planter reached out again. 'Muree, please—'

She backed away from him. 'Your war is worth none of this. Not a single life.' And she turned and walked away, stiff and angry, marching back towards the school where children were still gathered behind their window.

Rab saw shocked faces at that window. They must have seen them argue, if not hear them.

Small mouths, gaping open.

*

Planter would have followed Muree, but Rab reached out and took his arm. He used his prosthetic hand, and squeezed, hard enough to hurt. Deliberately.

'Let her go.'

Planter didn't protest. Or react to the lock on his arm.

Rab didn't let go until Muree was out of sight, lost in the sparse crowd on the up-curving of the Carousel.

Meanwhile, when he got the chance, Planter's suit downloaded a new set of orders, of priorities from the commanders.

He touched Rab on the shoulder. 'Things are moving quickly. These visits of Mask personnel to the starship have gone well. Now they want to move forward. Now they want to bring ship crew to the Mask, as soon as possible. In particular –' He grinned.

Rab smiled too. 'Muree?'

'Muree. With you. Our new partnership in clean young flesh. And they want it now, today. Think you can manage that?'

A bit bewildered, both nodded.

'And just you two,' Planter said. 'The meetings of the high-ups here are going well, and the Mask officers want to stay. So they'll send you back, just the two of you, on that ferry. The *Styx*. The quarantine regime evidently worked; you can go through it before debarking at the Mask. We already alerted Plokhy – the pilot. Think you can manage that?'

Rab nodded. 'When do we leave, Lieutenant?'

'I guess – when we have apologised to Muree.'

10

The pilot of the ferry *Styx*, Angela Plokhy, was a short, stocky woman who looked about forty.

Once she and Rab had boarded, alone, with no officers cluttering up the space, Muree found her fascinating. As far as Muree could tell, she had no place in the hierarchy of the Mask. She was actually the first Solar System resident not to show up in a uniform.

She owned her craft, the *Styx*, outright, and missions like this in the vicinity of the Mask were only temporary assignments. This was the first human Muree had found, here in the Solar System – including Rab – who wasn't locked into some quasi-military authority.

Plokhy welcomed them aboard with a wide grin. 'Glad to meet you two again, and without any stuffy officers. This is a lot more fun. Even if it is a short trip.'

That sealed it. Muree *liked* this person. She had to smile.

Rab, she knew, was still tearing himself up over the clumsiness about her lost sister. Plokhy knew nothing about the incident, but somehow Muree's hurt seemed to recede in her presence. *He hadn't known.*

She looked over at Rab, who seemed cautious. But she smiled, nodded.

He didn't smile, but dropped his head, and nodded back.

Plokhy just looked on, but Muree sensed she had perceived the tension, had somehow resolved it, saw it was done.

Now Rab thanked Plokhy. 'But you know we have to go through quarantine procedures before we dock.'

'Sure, sure, you didn't want the Mask crew to infect your starship travellers, and conversely we don't want our pet traveller,' nodding at Muree, 'infecting the whole of the Mask. Don't worry, I'm on top of it. In fact that's one reason our commanders used me; I come and go all over the place so I'm up on such procedures.' She glared at Muree. 'In other words, one cough, young lady, and you're in the garbage chute.'

Muree just raised her eyebrows.

The glare melted to a winning smile. 'I think I'm going to enjoy your company. So, we'll decouple and fly out of here in a couple of hours. You need anything in the meantime?'

Rab let out a breath, and loosened the collar of his pressure suit. 'It's been a tough day, and I'm not used to the gravity. Maybe a nap . . .'

Plokhy winked at Muree. 'Diddums. OK, that can be arranged . . .'

The habitable interior of the ferry had seemed to be a unit, a roughly circular space with a bridge control position at one side. Now Plokhy snapped out a few orders, and partitions folded out of slits in the walls; one of these surrounded the bridge position, and another folded around a couch for Rab.

When he was settled, Plokhy beckoned, and led Muree to the bridge position, tapped to make a chair fold up out of the floor. She whispered, 'I need to do some piloting. You want to sit with me, or wander? Not that there's much to see . . .'

*

That turned out to be true.

So Muree spent some time alone.

She wandered around Plokhy's eccentric little ferry. She explored the propulsion system, the hydrogen-propellant tanks – the small lume tank. She found she liked the craft, with its compact efficiency, and evidence of repairs, multiple patches in the fabric of the ship – a patchwork that reminded her of her home craft, which had carried its own century's worth of supplies for repair work. Child-like, she liked the gadgety aspect of the craft, with utilities folding out or away as required.

But she did find herself missing the big inner volume of her worldship.

Maybe that was why she was soon drawn to the windows that gave her a view of the *Lightbird*. Now receding in her view, as the *Styx* made for the Mask. It was strange to think that complex, ungainly structure had been all her universe, effectively, all her life – and, stranger yet, for generations of ancestors spanning a century. A miniature universe in which her baby twin sister had lived out her miniature fragment of a life. The ship seen from without was huge – and yet it was utterly dwarfed by the complex, engineered outer surface of the Mask beyond, a spherical shell so huge that, even from far out, it looked more like a flat wall, flat save for engineering details, ports and access hatches and windows – an infinite, textured wall that shut out half the universe, all of the Solar System within the orbit of ruined Neptune . . .

'You'll lose yourself in it. You OK?'

Plokhy was smiling, as usual. But the smile crumbled into what might have been a mocking frown. 'What, are you going to kiss me or punch me?'

'Not that . . . I'm sorry, Plokhy. It's just that you seem *different* from everybody else I've met here.' She thought it over. 'Just the way you look at people.'

'You learned one thing. Everybody calls me Plokhy. Never Angela.'

'I don't mean to pry—'

'You're not prying,' Plokhy said. 'Curiosity is healthy. It's good to know about other people. I *need* to know about people.'

'Because of us? The *Lightbird* crew?'

'Not particularly. I'm an independent trader, a pilot. In my job I meet a lot of people anyhow, coming in from around the Frame, gliding in along the struts, hitching a lift. The run out to the Mask is just a part of it all, and a pretty dull part given how big it is.'

Muree still didn't know what she meant by any of that. *The Frame. Struts.*

'When people arrive here, you see, at any of the portals to the interior of the Mask, they might have come crowding in from anywhere between Mercury and Saturn, some even from Uranus—'

Antique, legendary, exotic names to ship-born outsider Muree. But she got the idea.

'But the *Styx* is a small boat. I need to know if any individual is going to turn out to be a particular problem before I let them ride in the modest confines of my ship, with *me*.' She looked at Muree. 'Better safe than sorry, always been my fallback. But on the other hand if I don't like you I can always lock a partition between my bridge and the lounge.'

Muree was transfixed. This odd person seemed about the sanest she had met since she had come to this place. She felt a curious relief that such a person as this existed here at all.

Plokhy was looking back, and grinned. 'Just think of me as a useful ally,' she murmured.

But before Muree could follow that up, there was a soft chime.

Plokhy glanced at a chronometer set in the skin of her right arm. 'Have to start my prep for the docking. Twelve hundred already . . .'

The timing mattered to Muree too; she checked her own chronometer, on her wrist. She was expected to attend some kind of high-ups' meeting within the hour. Yet another meeting, before, it seemed, the news of the arrival of the *'Bird* was finally to be widely announced to the hapless hordes of the Solar System . . .

Although that announcement had seen so much prevarication already that Rab had suggested, half-joking, that maybe the arrival of the *Lightbird* never *would* be announced to his fellow citizens. 'Docked for ever to the Mask where no one will see it,' he'd suggested, only half-jokingly. 'A huge great lie at the edge of the Solar System . . . *Another* great lie . . .'

Plokhy saw the gesture, the watch. 'Another meeting with the high-ups? Don't let the assholes who run this place get you down.'

Muree thought she saw a kind of stern compassion in her face. She had to smile. 'What place? What assholes? The assholes who run the Solar System?'

'Powerful assholes are still assholes. Remember, they've done nothing but squat in the System for generations, most of their ancestors right here on this big dumb old Mask and similar palaces, giving each other fancy titles and promotions, while the likes of Rab and his mother toil on Mercury or Venus, and *you* and your ancestors have been exploring the Galaxy.'

Again Muree had to smile. 'Exploring one world at a time.'

'One is a better number than zero.' Plokhy looked at Muree more thoughtfully. 'You are having a hard time with these people, aren't you? Your own high-ups as well as the Mask authorities. Listen. I'm not going anywhere just now . . . You want somebody to yell at, you come yell at me. Better yet, we can share what we know about the lumes.'

Muree's smile widened. 'The lumes?'

'I know you work with them; you've made that very clear. Why not? I work with them too, through necessity. That's how the *Styx* gets pushed along, after all. I've listened to your conversations about them – pardon me. I never heard of anybody who really knows what the lumes are, how they *work*. All that energy. Still less what they are *for*.'

That puzzled Muree. 'What they're for?'

'Well, why *not* ask what they're for? Not for shipping humans around the place, which is what they're mostly doomed to here – and aboard your toy starship. You ever seen a horse?'

Muree shook her head. 'Is that a rhetorical question?'

'Well, if you've never heard of a horse, I've never heard of a rhetorical question, so we're even. Look, once – so it's said – when humans were still stuck on Earth, and they hadn't yet got too smart with engines and such – the horse, this animal, was the main transport engine for humanity. You could ride a horse, you could have it drag your carriages and carts and whatnot . . . But that wasn't what horses were *for*, though. What *were* they for? For making baby horses, and running, running free as the wind. And eating the grass, which was what *that* was for.'

All this was an abstraction to Muree – no horses on Rossbee, or the *Lightbird*, not even any grass save scraps of lawn in the Carousel – but she got the point. 'And you're saying that, even though we use them all the time, we don't know what lumes are *for*.'

'And that they're almost certainly nothing to do with humans. You got it.' That smile widened further.

Muree checked her chronometer again. 'My meeting—'

'You need somebody to talk to, you come talk to me. Don't wake me from my naps, though. There's a schedule on the partition.'

'It's a deal.'

11

A few days later, Mask Commander Revil called a major meeting on the way forward – for the crews of the *Lightbird* and the Mask, and for all mankind in the Solar System.

For days already Muree had been escorted around this vast mass of technology and protocol – through a quarantine procedure, then a series of interviews with or without Rab – who had his own regular duties – and finally some time unescorted. 'A chance for my crew to get to know you,' Commander Revil had told her, smiling falsely.

Now, to get to the relevant conference room, Muree had to find her way through yet more labyrinthine corridors, dug through the fabric of this tremendous Mask.

What a waste in resources, both human and material, this huge boondoggle was, she thought, with a savagery that surprised her. How many ships like the *Lightbird*, or even the *Styx*, might have been built to *go* somewhere, if not for the resource sink that was this immense hide? . . .

Or maybe she was just annoyed that her own personal life story was already current across this monster construction. Full of strangers.

At last she found the right room.

Calm down, she told herself, as she walked in.

*

Once through the door she took a breath to survey the scene. The room was a cylindrical space, wider than it was tall. Like the *Lightbird* Carousel shrunk and set on its side. The central space was dominated by a single circular table, its pale brown surface polished smooth. Chairs set around the table looked deep, lush, with zero-gravity silver belts to be pulled around their occupants.

Rab Callis, already seated, near Lieutenant Planter, waved discreetly. With his real hand. And she spotted what was evidently her seat – an empty space next to Rab. She felt thankful Rab was there already; she would have had no idea where to go, and no doubt would have smashed more protocol in guessing.

She drifted around the curved wall – gracefully, she hoped, pulling herself from one handhold to the next. She was used to zero gravity but not in any chamber of this size.

She and Rab, she realised, were the youngest here. In fact the *only* young people here . . .

And the exotic uniforms on display distracted her. She'd never before seen the ornate costume the *Lightbird*'s Captain Tavar was wearing today: sky blue with golden braids at shoulder, collar and cuffs. It – *dazzled*, almost comically.

But even so Tavar was outdone by the heavy robes worn by Commander Revil of the Mask, sitting beside Tavar, in a fabric that glittered with what looked like golden thread. And Muree could make out images sewn into the material on the left breast: two faces, one smiling, one grimacing – no, they were *masks*, she saw. Maybe some kind of archaic symbol of Revil's duty as the commander of this part of surely the greatest 'mask' humanity had ever constructed.

In their competing finery, the two commanders were leaning towards each other, speaking softly, occasionally glancing around at the rest of the assembled group. With a start Muree realised that they had the same body language, the same quasi-relaxed closeness, the whispered conversation – the same apparent disdain for the rest, for members of the crew of the *Lightbird*, for the elders of the Mask, alike.

She was staring so hard she nearly collided with the back of a Mask officer a couple of seats away from Rab.

Rab himself moved quickly, pushing out of his own chair, in the lack of gravity helping her reach her seat with a confident grip on her shoulder – she felt the slightly harsh pinch of his prosthetic. Rab himself was in some kind of coverall uniform, heavy material, a deep green. Clean enough and intact, but not remotely ornate. He at least was no officer, you could tell at a glance.

As she settled into her seat, she felt unreasonably pleased to have his company.

Still Tavar and Revil muttered to each other, paging through images on the smart surface of the table before them. Still the rest of the seniors in the room spoke quietly amongst themselves, or simply watched the commanders.

Trying not to emulate the leaders' postures in a way that might look like mockery, Muree leaned over to Rab. 'Nice outfit,' she murmured. 'But you could do with a bit more gaudy colour to compete with the bosses. How about bright yellow?'

He snorted, choking a laugh. 'This is my official uniform, if you like. What the high-ups wear on Mercury – which, according to some of the regulations, is where I should be right now.'

'Officially?'

'Officially. Despite the business with my hand. Didn't you know? All this is a – a *temporary* assignment, you see, to the Mask. Even if it takes up the rest of my life.' He nodded at Planter, who was chatting with Brad Tenant. 'And in theory Planter could throw me down there at any moment.'

Muree was still getting used to all this, the huge, wide, hierarchical regime that seemed to embrace the whole of this Solar System, and yet could focus its terrible energy on a single individual – even a child. 'Don't you resent it all?'

He thought that over. 'It's a complicated question. From *their* point of view, to manage the System as a whole, to make it all work, all the jobs that *make* it work have to be filled, and people have to *stick* to the jobs to which they're assigned . . . Isn't it the same aboard your starship? People have to do the jobs that need doing, for the health of the ship as a whole, as opposed to what they *want* to do.'

'Of course. But – it's different. On the *Lightbird* you grow up within the hull – you can *see* the walls. Every time you look out of a window, you see only lethal vacuum. You can *hear* the hum of the air conditioner outlets. You *know* the ship has to be kept functioning, all the time. The work you have to do is obvious, so you do it, or – well, everybody would die. *Here* you have a whole planetary system, worlds and moons. Isn't there room enough for—'

'For irresponsibility?'

That was Lieutenant Planter, leaning over towards them.

He went on, 'Sorry to eavesdrop. No room for that, Muree. Not here in our engineered solar system, any more than in the confines of your ship. It's only a question of scale. Yes, if just *one* person abandons their duty here, whatever it is, the chance of serious harm is smaller than on your ship, I grant you – but in the end *all* must serve the common cause, scrupulously, diligently, and without fail. After all, we are essentially on a war footing . . .'

And he ran down, realising that the commanders were staring around, waiting for quiet, and he'd spoken loudly enough to be heard generally.

Revil, commander of the Mask, said evenly, 'None too edifying a phrase, Lieutenant. *War footing.* But appropriate for the matters we need to discuss – the reasoning we have to work through today. For today we have to decide on our recommendations as regards managing this situation, here at the Mask, with our very welcome guests. Recommendations to the regional authorities – *and ultimately to the Unity itself.*

'Let's be frank. Thanks to the arrival of our guests – our very welcome guests, the captain and crew of the *Lightbird* – we have come to realise that our entire system of governance, our entire human society – and by that I mean the fortified Solar System *and* the colonies like the one that *Lightbird* has come from – is based on *fear.*

'But now, perhaps, given the pooling of our knowledge, we may have to concede that that fear is not – justified. Not entirely, at least. And perhaps we can consider a scenario in which a new driver emerges – a new *hope,* even if the fear can never be set aside entirely.'

Silence.

Revil sipped water from a flask. Theatrically, Muree thought. To give her words a chance to sink in.

Muree glanced around at the other delegates to this odd conference. Some seemed surprised by the commander's words: all the present crew members of the *Lightbird,* save maybe Captain Tavar herself. But of the solars, only the most junior officers seemed taken aback at that mild, yet shocking statement. Evidently there had been prior briefings to prepare the ground.

Where is Revil going with this?

At a glance from Revil, Captain Tavar smoothly took over the narrative – and Muree immediately sensed a kind of collaboration between them.

Tavar said now, 'Much of the understanding of our situation

– and by "our" I mean all of mankind's – was shaped, of course, by the destruction of Neptune. And the later discovery of evidence of a *previous* planetary assault, on a lost, never named world whose ruins have been located in the Oort cloud.

'The logic seemed obvious. That there was a, a *systematic assault* on the Solar System underway, an assault mounted over millennia, or much longer – millions of years, maybe. A creeping demolition. First our unnamed Planet Nine. Next, Neptune, the eighth planet. Nine, eight – the logic was obvious, and the consequential fear. After eight, seven – Uranus – six, Saturn, five, Jupiter . . . Perhaps even the inner rocky worlds, Mars, *even the third planet*, Earth itself. Where then for mankind?

'And so my own ancestors and their ship became part of a grand exodus from Sol system. They went out to nearby stars which seemed stable enough to serve as surrogate suns, and which had planets, habitable if possible, or at least useful in providing resources to build new colonies . . . Something would survive, if Earth and the Solar System were lost . . .'

Muree thought bleakly, *We were saving humanity. But my twin wasn't saved.* She *was snuffed out before she could learn anything of surrogate suns and colony worlds . . . Was it worth it?*

Revil took over. 'And as for the System you left behind, captain – you know the rest now. The energy of the human race, the whole accessible resource of the System, has been dedicated to the endurance of this – siege. For that is how it has been characterised. We, here – our ancestors before us – have striven to fortify our home, to *hide* it from the aggressor. A grand strategy for the defence of our worlds.' She waved a hand. 'Our guests from the *Lightbird* have seen some of the results in this Mask.

'The Solar System has become a fortress.

'Fortress Sol, they call it. In the months and years ahead you star travellers will no doubt see more of it, and I envy you seeing it for the first time . . .

'Whole planets have been rebuilt – if you like – repurposed as fortresses in themselves. Or factories. Or cities, or gardens.

'We, or rather our forebears, have linked the worlds with fast-transit highways. This is the Frame. Much of this follows the unifying vision of a genius we remember as the Architect . . . With such tools, humanity itself has been repurposed, its use optimised.'

At that, Muree saw, Rab glanced down at his own metallic hand. His own repurposed limb. *Optimised*. She wondered if Rab would use that word.

Captain Tavar took up the thread again. 'We've talked this over, from our different perspectives. There is much common ground. I think we of the *Lightbird* might say you have repurposed the whole of the Solar System, as if it were a giant generation starship. The military, defensive aspect is one thing. In a closed environment, we can understand the need for tight control of resources, processes, energy – even people – just as on our own generation ship.'

Revil nodded. 'Yes, you too have survived and prospered – and you will be able to support our own future developments given such experience, I am sure . . . And meanwhile *we have the lumes*. Especially the lumes that have been found in Uranus – we will speak of that. We have been able to – access them. A legacy of the apparent assault on the solar system, and a remarkably useful one. You of the *Lightbird* seem expert in this.'

Tavar nodded at Muree. *Tell them*.

Muree hadn't expected to speak.

Feeling bewildered, utterly out of her depth in this strange, loaded conversation, she stood, slowly. 'It's true,' she said. 'I understand that the lumes were already being – exploited – used for human purposes, at Ross 128b, our star, one of the planets there – an ice giant – even before the *Lightbird* was built.

'And, yes, our ship was designed around the lumes. The energy density they give us is comparable to that of matter-antimatter annihilation.' She glanced around. 'You know all this . . . We have a birthing tank on the ship. Much smaller than the great planetary swarms here, but sufficient . . .'

'Indeed,' Revil said. 'Your technology in that regard is in advance of ours. Here it's still easier to just scoop the lumes up out of Uranus.' Her tone was grim. 'The histories tell of the shock of discovering lumes in the seventh planet in the first place – not long, actually, after the original assault on Neptune. And it took some time – centuries – before it was seen that the assault on Uranus *was actually an opportunity*. That, with care, we could exploit the proliferation of the lumes for our own purposes. If the lues destroy some of our planets – well, then, we will use the lumes themselves to gird ourselves against any attacks on our home worlds. Turn the invaders' weapons back on them.'

Muree was still standing. 'We have a world like Uranus, at Ross 128b. Which our first crew plundered for the ship's initial lume stock. I read about that. I believe that was in place when the first human explorers showed up, after the exodus from Earth.'

Revil nodded. 'It's evident that of necessity you've gone further in studying the lumes than we have, despite our extensive use of them – across the Frame . . . Yes, you cultivate them, even. It's evident that we must pool our talents, our knowledge – as in other areas, other experiences.'

Rab touched Muree's arm. *Sit down now.*

Muree, distinctly uncomfortable, took her seat again.

Revil went on, 'Well, we must speak of common interests. I am the commander of this section of the Mask, remember. This is a military posting. My own ancestor saw the initial assault, the lume storm that hit Neptune, that dismantled that world. And even while we exploit the weapons left behind by our unknown assailant, the official position remains that we have to *anticipate another assault*, an attack using lumes or otherwise. And so we have kept the Solar System masked. Controlled. For a thousand years . . .'

She said it not without pride in her voice, Muree thought.

Captain Tavar asked calmly, 'And what of the Sun, commander?'

And Muree sensed tension in the room. She knew that the *Lightbird*'s officers were still confused about the condition of the Sun itself.

Now Revil nodded. Perhaps she was ready to share more.

'As some of you from the *Lightbird* now know – there is another "mask" around the Sun. We call it the Wrap. Another huge project, the greatest of all. But a project that was essential for the building of the Mask, and the rebuilding of worlds within, the huge Frame which unites them . . .

'And vital, we believe, for the survival of the Sun itself. Even as Neptune was being consumed, we saw parties of lumes – small, to begin with – pushing inwards, through the plane of the planets' orbits – *and we saw lumes falling into the Sun.*

'We, my forebears a thousand years ago, immediately recognised the possible consequences of this. We could afford to lose planets. Even the Earth! We could move out, colonise . . . But if we lost the Sun, all life in the Solar System would eventually be extinguished. Leaving nothing but – lumes – and whatever might follow them.

'So we, our ancestors, tried to make the Sun – unpalatable. We mined it ourselves, partly for that purpose.'

Tavar grunted. 'A monumental project, dismissed in a sentence. To drain the Sun! . . .'

'We constructed the Wrap around the Sun, trapping its heat, its light, its energy. A project itself spanning centuries. And we used that energy to initiate a collapse to a black hole, and then mined that black hole for energy in part to transform, rebuild, the planetary system . . .

'You can only extract useful energy from a black hole by tapping its spin. So the solar hole is now inert, useless, spun down – and with no attraction for any subsequent predator. But where we used to have sunlight, *now we have the light of the lumes*. All of it in our control.

'All this took centuries. We needed the time to implement the grand design . . .'

Muree hadn't known this, not fully, and found it hard to understand. And she – recoiled.

Speak up.

'So,' she said, 'we, my ancestors, travelled light-years to find a new world, under a new star. *While you put out your own Sun . . .*'

Heads turned to her.

She thought it through further. 'But that's made your worlds completely dependent on whoever controls the remnant Sun. Or rather, who controls the lumes, which were sent by your aggressor, your enemy.'

Captain Tavar glared at her. *Be silent.*

But Revil picked up the exchange. 'No, no. These are valid points,' she sighed. 'In a way, child, you've put your finger on it. Our ancestors believed they were in a fight for survival, for humankind, for the Solar System itself. What were they *meant* to think? How else were they *meant* to ensure mankind's survival into the indefinite future? They used the tools, the resources they had to hand.

'And their response, as rational as it could be, was to *use the lumes* as best they could – supremely powerful energy sources

– first to power the scattering of ships like the *Lightbird*, sent to the nearby stars, and then to use the lumes in the rebuilding of the Solar System. Everything designed to maintain the illusions cast by the Mask and the Wrap around the Sun. *Fortress Sol*. We have sustained all this so long—'

'But the invaders never returned,' Muree said.

Planter shot a warning look in her direction. Captain Tavar too. But Muree spoke on. *I might never get a chance to say this again.*

'Commander Revil – your invaders. The invisible raiders. They've not returned in a thousand years. How long should we wait? And while you are waiting, you can't allow – disbelief.'

She earned more glares from Captain Tavar. The youngest here weren't supposed to be monopolising the conversation. But, after a thousand years of stasis, maybe they should listen to the young, Muree thought recklessly.

'Disbelief,' she said again. 'Doubt, in the existence of the invaders, doubt that they'll come again. Because if there was doubt, your whole system of government would fall apart. It all depends on belief. Just as on my ship, generation after generation of us maintaining the ship and its crew – we eked out our own lives in a box, generations of us, *all because we believed in the mission.*'

Revil and Tavar exchanged glances. Even Lieutenant Planter was glaring at her.

Captain Tavar hissed, 'Is all this something to do with your damn sister?'

Her heart was racing, she found, as if she might faint. The urge to withdraw was strong. But she might never get another chance like this.

'Go for it,' Rab murmured.

Yes. The Captain's right. This is for you, my sister.

'Well,' she said, 'Rab said it. *They have not returned.* The predators, the destroyers. What if they *never* return? Why – I'm not sure how our own crew would react. How *I* would react. After a thousand wasted years—'

Revil said, speaking over her, almost shouting, '*My own ancestor was present at the initial assault on Neptune*, a thousand years ago. I have said this before. I was brought up to understand *her*, her actions, to be proud of her. We fought well. *She* fought well.

'As for us, our duty has to be to learn, to comprehend the significance of that battle – what followed. Centuries have gone by, and we have no idea of the likely timeline of a subsequent attack . . . Is it time to forget? Is it time to drop our guard?' She glared around. 'And what would be the consequences for a society that has been entirely *constructed* around maintaining that guard?'

Muree, listening hard, thought that final qualification was a crucial admission. 'You can't afford to drop the guard. That's what you are saying. *Because you couldn't control your people any more.*'

There were murmurs, mutterings around the table.

She forced herself to speak on. 'Even if there is no new attack – *even if you had proof* that no more attack will come – you couldn't release your grip. Because you are frightened of the consequences. The social consequences of liberation—'

Commander Revil held up a hand. 'I think we've gone far enough with this. Clearly the ideas expressed here could be grossly destabilising. And if they represent the thinking of the rising generation – following on from the destabilisation that will inevitably be caused by news of the arrival of the *Lightbird* . . .

'My decision, for now, is that none of this discussion should leave this room. Not until I've had a chance to talk to my superiors on Mars – which will take hours, as you know. Days, for a full conversation . . .'

Rab whispered to Muree, 'Lightspeed delays.'

Revil snapped, 'Thank you all. Discussion concluded for now.' She sat down, leaned over, and began to talk privately to Tavar.

'Come on,' Rab said. 'Let's get out of here while we have the chance.'

They both released their seat straps, and Rab led the way to the nearest door.

The other officers – who had kept silence during the meeting – were now milling around, talking urgently. They uniformly ignored Muree and Rab as they passed.

All save Lieutenant Planter, who was glaring at Rab, an obvious threat, it seemed to Muree. And, similarly, she noticed now, Captain Tavar kept a less than friendly eye on Muree, of her own crew.

Muree turned away, irritated – self-conscious. But what did the commanders expect? That they would just nod along with everybody else? Maybe that was what they *wanted* – as if two such prominent figures as Rab and Muree were meant to be tokens of some kind of acquiescence to the regime's new direction, whatever it was . . .

Somewhat to her surprise, she realised that, led by Rab, the two of them had got across the room and to the door before Planter or anyone else had reacted quickly enough to stop them.

The door. Where they found Angela Plokhy waiting outside.

Muree was surprised to see her. 'What are you doing here?

Plokhy grinned. 'Listening in. Waiting for you two. What a shit show that was.'

Rab grunted. 'I'm just glad it was so short. I just want to get out of this place and go somewhere else—'

'Somewhere else where you won't have to be telling lies the whole time?'

That startled Muree. She stared at Plokhy. 'What do you mean? Why were you waiting for us? Where else can we go?' She thought that over, her mind exploding. 'And how could we get there?'

'Well, I'm about to get out of here myself. My assignment here is done. Next, a regular run to Uranus, to pick up more lumes from the breeding grounds there. Fuel for the *Styx*.' She grinned. 'Yes, you heard me. The seventh planet itself. The departure, the flight's approved. You want to give it a try?'

Rab and Muree exchanged glances. And grinned.

Muree said, 'Sooner that than stay here and get arrested.'

Rab said, 'We'd have to get out of here before anybody notices we're gone.'

Plokhy nodded. 'You only have to get to the *Styx*; I have government-approved identity shielding. Once in there you'd be invisible. And besides, the higher-ups will be talking for hours rather than worrying about two raggedy kids. They might be glad to see you go, rather than kick up a storm here.'

Rab shook his head. 'They won't react like that. They won't want to lose control, even over two insects like us. We should go, now.'

'You've got time to go get anything you have to take.'

Rab grinned and held up his arm. Spare hand. 'I'm packed.'

Muree dared a glance back into the conference room. Lieutenant Planter was glaring at them, but he was evidently ensnared in conversations with other attendees.

They could do this.

Rab was waiting for her response.

'Let's do it.'

Plokhy tipped her head. 'Well, come on, then. Get your stuff and meet me at the lock. Go!'

Muree and Rab got.

12

Rab fetched a bag of essential stuff, just a holdall, and made his way from his cabin to Muree's. When she emerged, he grinned at her in the low light of the corridor, and led her away.

'You OK?' he asked.

She shrugged. 'As OK as I can be in a universe I hate. Well, I've been sleeping badly. Even before all this. This was a big day. Also I've got docking lag, as I've heard you and your buddies call it. Timings out of synch on different habitats and ships . . .'

'It happens,' he said. 'Did you know there's an *official* timescale? Based on Earth. We work and sleep when we need to, depending on the task at hand, the local clock. But when I grew up on Venus we were taught to handle two timescales, one based on Venus's own rotation, such as it was, and the other based on Earth. I was just about old enough to find that irritating by the time I was sent away from Venus for good . . .'

They drifted, weightless, down the long, curving corridors of the Mask, past closed doors, in the subdued sleep-period lighting.

They carried on their conversation, softly. About *calendars*. The use of days and months and years – *Earth* years. Muree thought it all made sense, in an abstract way. A slow, archaic cycle, like the breathing of a very old person. Archaic, and yet imposed on peoples and colonies who had otherwise lost touch with the home world – who, perhaps, had otherwise forgotten about their origins altogether. A kind of institutional memory.

'Of course,' Muree said now, 'all that breaks down beyond the Sol system. Where I come from. And how I got here. Over stellar distances, and velocities approaching lightspeed, simultaneity itself breaks down.'

Rab nodded. 'I learned about all that. A guy called Einstein figured it all out before anybody had put a foot on Venus, let alone started rebuilding it. Basically, if everybody is moving around at any respectable fraction of lightspeed, you have to keep synching your clocks the whole time. And there's no one master clock – not even Earth.'

'But your officers try anyhow.'

'Yes, they try. The senior commanders, from Revil on down, take all this very seriously. As you'd expect. I wonder if Einstein ever knew the Architect. Or if Kepler did. Or if Kepler knew Einstein . . .'

Rab said all this with his characteristic mix of intelligence, wry wit, keen observation – and, Muree suspected, a deep buried anger.

'I saw Earth once, you know,' he said now. 'Only from the Frame. Earth looks pretty these days, but useless in industrial terms. Mined out long ago, basically – long before Neptune. Apparently only a few million people live there now – and lots more genetically-restored animals in a wilderness of forest and ocean and grassland and desert . . . We did pretty much wreck it. And then we saved it, kind of. And still we set our watches by its turning.'

'You never landed there?'

'Earth?' He shrugged. He closed his eyes, briefly, calmly drifting. 'Only time I saw it was when I was brought out of Venus that first time – I was separated from my mother already, put in with a bunch of other misfit kids being shipped to who knows where – we knew we would pass Earth itself, as we worked our way around the Frame on the way further out. It's more that I didn't want to see it. I remember the other kids crowding the ports as we passed.'

'I don't understand,' she said, as gently as she could. 'You didn't want—'

'Well, I was one mixed-up kid. The fake hand was a good fighting weapon. I thought I didn't need people, a home, by that time. I didn't *care* that it was all hidden away.'

'And you're finding you don't feel like that any more.' She looked at him more closely. 'Right?'

He nodded. 'This conference confirmed that, I think. Where the seniors, Commander Revil, Captain Tavar, so casually decided to keep lying, despite the arrival of the *Lightbird*—'

'Lies upon lies upon lies.'

The new voice made them jump. Muree turned, clumsily.

It was Angela Plokhy, pilot of the ferry craft.

'And the commanders will cling to those lies as long as they're useful. Maybe *that's* why you've come here? Both of you? Do you think?'

Abruptly Muree realised that, wandering apparently at random – evidently not thinking about where they were going – they had come to the access port that led out of the Mask interior and through a connector to Plokhy's ferry. One of the few destinations Muree knew, in fact, since she had used this port to get to the *Styx* herself. But even so – maybe some instinct had drawn them here . . .

And here was Plokhy herself, a half-smile on her face. 'I knew you'd come back, once I dropped the hint.'

Muree and Rab exchanged a glance – a rueful smile from Rab

– and Rab shrugged. He said, 'Well, there's nowhere else on this Mask where we aren't being watched quite so tightly, I guess.'

'Maybe you'd better come aboard,' Plokhy said.

Muree nodded. 'Maybe we should.'

So they followed.

They passed through a small airlock and drifted into the bridge cum crew lounge of the *Styx*.

'It looks bigger than before,' Rab said.

Muree glanced at him. Maybe he was feeling the same kind of dislocation as she was.

Plokhy snorted. 'No high-ups been in here recently. *They* take up a lot of room. No crowd. No need for *equipment* for a crowd. All folded back into the walls. An ingenious design,' she said. 'Better yet when it's just me and her, frankly. *Her* – the *Styx*. But you two don't take up too much room. You want something to drink – tea, maybe?'

Muree felt nonplussed. All this was completely unexpected.

Plokhy bustled to a corner kitchen facility. Water was heated quickly, sachets of green leaves were emptied into a pot, then the dark liquid forced through a short dispenser into sealed zero-gravity mugs.

Rab took his mug gratefully. 'During the officer tour I didn't get any of your tea.'

'I ran out.' Plokhy shrugged. 'This ain't no interstellar ship, let alone the Mask, a structure with a crew of, what – millions?'

Rab shrugged. 'Dunno. It *is* a structure that encloses the whole solar system. Maybe orders of magnitude more than millions . . .'

'Well, most of the time *I'm* the only inhabitant of this little ship, and the recycling system is essentially based on me and my intake and personal waste products. So I hope you aren't squeamish.'

Muree thought that over. 'You should make a donation to the Mask. I kind of like the idea of Captain Tavar and Commander Revil sampling your, umm, waste products.'

'That's the spirit. Probably a lot of other things about this little ship you missed first time, too.'

'Such as?' Muree asked.

Rab was looking out of a small port. 'Such as the *wings*.'

That surprised Muree. But he was right, she saw, leaning down to peer out of a port on the other side of the cabin. 'Wow. Big, sweeping wings – on a spacecraft?'

'I think it's a delta-wing design,' Rab said. 'Flaring wings set under this basically cylindrical hull.'

'Quite right,' Plokhy said. 'And you never did notice that before, did you? You don't think about landing a spacecraft – not when you live in a spacecraft the whole time. As both of you do, more or less, if you count the Mask as a big dumb going-nowhere spacecraft. Generally my ship stays in a high orbit, whatever planet we stop at, dock at some orbital station. But sometimes I'll land, and I'll use the atmosphere of the destination world to brake, to lose a little kinetic energy. If there is air. If not I've got plenty of energy on board for the deceleration—'

Muree nodded. 'Lumes?'

'Of course. Says the resident lume-keeper on your own world-ship, right?'

'One of them. Pretty senior, I suppose. Not in rank, but we don't really have ranks below the command crew . . .'

Plokhy didn't seem interested.

'As to the wings,' she went on heavily, 'aerobraking saves a little reaction mass, at least. Although aerobraking is strictly forbidden at the inner worlds, of course – especially at Earth, but also Venus, Mars. The high re-entry temperatures create a trail of toxins – you burn nitrogen, basically.' She smiled. 'But anyhow I also like the wings for aesthetic reasons. Historic. Either of you ever heard of the *space shuttle*?'

'Not me,' said Rab.

'And certainly not me,' Muree said.

Plokhy studied her with a smile. 'Born under the light of another star? You have an excuse. Not you, Rab. The shuttle was one of the first spacecraft, launched from Earth itself – and it was built to glide down from orbit on a big delta-wing. Only partially successful, the history books will tell you, but a heroic design anyhow. So my *Styx* has similar parameters – the orbiter's all-up mass was about a hundred tonnes. A similar *look* . . . But powered by lume energy and hydrogen propellant rather than chemical propulsion. In fact the original shuttle needed boosters to get out of the atmosphere.'

Muree frowned. 'That name of yours. *Sticks*?'

'*Styx*.' She spelled it out, and smiled. 'Black humour . . . A very old myth, more pre-spaceflight stuff, about a ferry crossing a river to the land of the dead. In some versions of the story, the river itself was called Styx, in others the ferry . . .'

Rab and Muree exchanged glances.

'I don't get it,' Muree said.

Plokhy shrugged. 'Well, I've travelled as widely around our precious Solar System as anybody alive, I'd think. And often it's struck me as being like nothing so much as a huge tomb. Their Unity of Mankind is more like a monumental graveyard, waiting to be filled. Not all of it, of course . . . Children play, still. And I suppose some would argue there are surely more children playing today than there ever were back on Earth, where it all started.

'But in the end it's all about lies, isn't it?' She paused, studied them, waved a hand. 'I know it's different for you, Muree. The kid from the stars. Your ancestors' mission was sincere and brave – and successful. And behind you, you have a whole culture, a whole world, a history I know nothing about. It's possible your people were sent out on a false premise, but that doesn't detract from their achievements.

'But then even *you*'ve been lied to since you got here – I've seen it for myself. Why, your – *our* – whole history is based on misunderstandings, and lies by omission, at least. I mean, as the centuries passed, why couldn't Earth have sent out messages, or even messenger drone craft, to all the colony worlds to tell them the truth? That there had been no more invasions?'

Muree had the impression that Plokhy had wanted to get this stuff off her chest for a long time.

'As for the future of the *Lightbird*, you can bet its existence won't be revealed to you if you live on Venus or Mercury or Earth – not even to most on Mars, probably, though that's the capital of the Unity . . . Hellas City . . . Not for a very, very long time . . .'

Muree was feeling distracted, overwhelmed.

Rab touched her hand with his own – the authentic one. *A lot to take in.*

She gave him a weak smile back and tried to concentrate on the conversation.

Plokhy was saying, 'So you see our glorious rulers have but one superpower between them, and that's the ability to lie: to hide, to deflect, to dissemble. And so they have lied, presumably, for countless generations. All of it to maintain a System-wide power structure.

'Look – you might think I'm shooting you a line. But I see it for myself, every time I venture into the interior of the System. Which isn't often nowadays. In fact I think they keep me and my freelance colleagues out here, further out than Uranus anyway, where we're useful but can't pick up or spread too much destabilising information. Tooling back and forth to the Uranus mines, picking up personnel and goods and cargo – mostly hydrogen. And lumes. Due for a trip back there soon, in fact. To Uranus. Quite a ride.'

Muree thought she was hinting at something. She forced a smile. 'There's more than one of you? Independent pilots?'

Plokhy winked at her. 'There's a whole swarm of us, kid. This is a big Solar System; the structures that unite it are big too – the Mask is astounding for its scale, and the Frame is even more so, for its complexity. But its junctions are few and far between . . .'

Muree still didn't know what this 'Frame' was.

'Beyond that, you need me and my trusty *Styx*, and others, to take venturers like you around the place, to exactly where you want to go, and even into the darkness beyond. All at a reasonable price – *and* with a little more personal freedom than most enjoy on the way.'

'Well, maybe you're lucky,' Rab said now. 'If you really have got freedom of movement—'

'We all do to an extent, if we're smart enough,' Plokhy said. 'Being an independent pilot helps. Look – I generally get told to start at A, and finish at B, but A and B can be interesting places in themselves, and you might get a chance to visit C or D or even E on the way, if you can push it. *And* get paid for it. Less so within the orbit of Saturn.' She glanced at Muree. 'Where the outer rails of the Frame run. You're new to all this. You know about the Frame?'

'I—'

Rab said, 'The Frame. Believe me, Muree. That's a whole different thing.'

Muree blurted to Plokhy, 'Have you been to Earth? Yourself?'

'Only a couple of times. Visits are not encouraged.'

'That's true,' Rab said to Muree. 'Supposedly that's because it's been restored, after most of the humans—'

'But also,' Plokhy said, 'because a lot of ancient crimes are buried deep in those recovered landscapes, under the new jungles and deserts, the old ruined cities . . . So they say.'

'There's so much, isn't there?' Muree said. 'In the Solar System. *The original worlds of humankind* . . . And I'm never going to see any of it.'

'Maybe not,' Rab said. 'Not after we shot our mouths off at that officers' meeting.' He grinned. 'But it was worth it, wasn't it?'

'Oh, will you two stop with the negativity?'

Plokhy had spoken sharply, startling Muree.

They both shut up, looked at each other.

Faced her.

Plokhy let herself drift up into the air, where she glared down at them. 'So,' she said. 'What now? You two are in a bad spot, I see that. Not life-threatening, but lousy, for people your age. Because you've both been born into a kind of prison, haven't you? A prison of lies. Lies about the future, lies about the past. And, while you might have thought it was a lucky break to be involved in all the recent excitement, it's not so much fun if you can never tell about it, is it? As if your whole future lives are mapped out, constrained. Well, that's what the authorities here, from Revil and Tavar on down, are going to want. And now that you *have* shot your mouths off, as you said, you're probably going to be even more constrained.'

Rab shrugged. 'I guess that's true. I mean, the smartest move for the authorities would be to keep me here for the *rest of my life* – and to shovel Muree back into her starship and send her home.'

Muree nodded, thinking hard. 'I'm not used to – talking like this. Thinking this way. Breaking the rules. Escaping. *Planning* to escape, to break the rules. You *can't* escape from a generation starship. And the rules are important. Life-critical. But *here*—' She looked at Rab. 'I don't want to lose this,' she blurted. 'Whatever it is. This *chance*. What we have here, right now, sitting here. It does feel like freedom.'

Rab said, 'Or the nearest we're ever going to get. But I don't see how this can last. As you said, pilot, soon she'll be off to the stars, and I—'

'It doesn't have to be that way,' Plokhy said bluntly. 'Because you met me. And I like you.'

Muree and Rab exchanged wary glances.

Rab shrugged. 'What option is there?'

'I'm leaving in a couple of days,' Plokhy said. 'My next assignment – Uranus. Into the spaces inside the Mask. Just a surveying expedition. Routine stuff. Counting lumes, basically.' She looked at each of them in turn. *'And I could smuggle you out of here*. Both of you. Away from the Mask, and all the way to Uranus. Maybe a stop at Saturn later. And then—'

'Wow,' Rab said. '*Saturn*. If we got that far – well, if we could get onto the Frame we really could make a run for it.' He faced Muree now. 'You'd have to trust me—'

'And me,' Plokhy said.

'I . . .' Muree hesitated, surprising herself. *Where had this come from?* 'It means throwing over our current lives. That's what we're talking about, isn't it?'

'Not necessarily, to be frank,' Plokhy said. 'Even if you're caught, you might talk your way out of any sanction. Blame me, if you like. You're a couple of kids having an adventure and you have high profiles, on both Mask and ship, right? I find that exhilarating. Everybody within this damn Mask is old before their time. Give yourselves a break. *Let me help you*.'

Again Rab and Muree shared a look. Muree found she longed to do this. To explore the Solar System . . .

But she still had doubts.

She turned to Plokhy. 'Why would *you* do this? I mean, take the risk of some sort of sanction, I guess, if you were found out—'

'I did something like this at your age, or thereabouts.' She grinned. 'How do you think I ended up like this? Somebody helped me then. Now I'm helping you. Somebody has to.'

'We'd never get away with it,' Rab said.

'It would be tricky,' Plokhy admitted. 'As you know, nothing gets past me. Apparently the commander and captain between them have already detailed Lieutenant Planter and some kid called Brad Tenant to keep an eye on both of you. I don't know those two clowns.'

Muree hadn't known that. 'Well, so Rab is going to find himself under the supervision of Lieutenant Planter once more, just like on Venus. And Brad Tenant's from the *Lightbird*. He's a friend. Some friend!'

Plokhy shook her head. 'Don't blame him. A friend under orders. You'll forgive him, some day. Both these bozos are presumably answerable to Revil, as Mask commander.'

Muree shrugged. 'And to Captain Tavar as long as the *Lightbird* is docked here, I guess.'

'Well, it's obvious what you have to do . . .'

Muree felt helpless. 'What?'

'Before these two clowns get their act together.' She grinned. 'Take it from a master.'

'What?'

'Run.'

To get off the Mask, the two of them tried to cover their tracks, with the help of a few friendly accomplices rounded up by

Plokhy, who seemed to know everybody.

And that worked well enough that they had been gone for three days before their absence was noticed, and Commander Revil, with Captain Tavar from the starship, called in Brad Tenant and Jeo Planter.

13

Jeo Planter, facing the commanders, felt thoroughly out of his depth.

And angry. Standing here before them, Revil behind the big desk in her office, Tavar by her side, Planter felt betrayed by Rab Callis, the prosthetic kid, and now Muree's close friend, apparently.

Revil turned on Planter first. 'You were supposed to be watching them.'

'Sir—'

'And now I'm told that the *Styx*, that crummy freighter, has left the Mask. On the way to Uranus, correct? With these two kids aboard? You should know about ship movements. Part of your job, as I recall, Planter?'

'Commander, I—'

'And you, Tenant, you were told to keep an eye on Muree until things died down, until we found some kind of stable situation here. Or even until the *Lightbird* sets off home. You know the kid; she's obsessed about her lumes for one thing; all you had to do – bah. So how did she talk herself out of your sight for *three days*? I mean—'

'Sorry, sir,' Brad broke in. 'But she told me she had been put on assignment, she and Rab.' He glanced over at Planter. 'And she told me that, for those three days, she had been put under the supervision of the Lieutenant here. Both of them, Muree and Rab—'

And Lieutenant Planter slapped his forehead. 'And at the same time Rab came to me and told me they were both under the sole supervision of Brad here—'

Revil slammed a fist down on her desk. 'You assholes. Both of you.' She glanced at Tavar. 'I'm sorry for insulting your crewman, Captain.'

'Be my guest, Commander.'

Revil glared again. 'All you had to do was to *speak* to each other. What's done can't be undone. But you two are going to have a damn good try, gentlemen. You are relieved of other duties. I've approval for that from your captain, Tenant.'

Tavar nodded curtly at Brad.

'Go find those kids, and get out of my sight until you do.'

She paused.

Tenant and Planter stood rigidly.

'What are you waiting for? Get *out*.'

Once outside the office, with the door slammed shut, Tenant and Planter faced each other.

Brad shrugged. 'So where do we start?'

Planter said, 'Well, she's your friend.'

'And this is your Solar System.'

Planter glared. 'Then let's go.' He turned, and pushed himself off down the corridor.

'Shit,' muttered Tenant as he rushed to follow. 'Shit, shit, shit.'

14

It was going to take seventy days to get to Uranus aboard the *Styx*, Plokhy had said, given how far away the planet was in its current orbital position. Acceleration all the way, a few per cent of Earth gravity. They wouldn't feel a thing, Plokhy assured them.

A journey of around thirty astronomical units from the location where they had undocked from the Mask. Thirty times the distance between a shadowed Earth and a wrapped Sun.

'Which is a well-worn run, since they mostly built the Mask itself out of the substance of Uranus, one of only two ice giants we had in the Solar System,' Plokhy said. 'After Neptune was assaulted by the lumes, only one ice giant was left intact. Now – well, you'll see . . .'

By the second day of the seventy, they had got leaks from allies on the Mask – via Plokhy's contacts – that Jeo Planter and Brad Tenant had been assigned to pursue them.

Muree had spent much of those two days talking to the Mask and the *Lightbird*, apologising for her escape. Her crewmates were predictably mortified – though, she suspected, some were secretly proud of her continuing high profile. In fact, they said, to some she was a hero – and so was Rab, come to that, since his visits to the Carousel.

When he heard about Planter and Brad, Rab seemed dismissive. 'So *they're* chasing us?'

'Sounds like it. What do we do?'

'Well, we'll just have to keep one step ahead, is all . . .'

'After I've told whatever idiot they've put in charge of my lume tank how to do their job, if it's not to be Brad . . .'

With their escape from the Mask completed, and the *Styx* settled into its journey and on course to Uranus, they had a chance to talk – not so much over what they had done, as what to do next.

To start with, once they left the *Styx*, what they were to *wear*? Rab's Mask uniform, a Unity standard issue, was drab and obviously distinctive – but not so much as Muree's gaudy ship-printed jacket and trousers.

Plokhy gave them survival suits from her voluminous store. These items seemed eminently practical to Muree, even if over-elaborate. 'One-piece, self-adjusting, I get that,' she said. 'Integral boots. A hood, even gloves. Intelligent environment control. But – a built-in orthopaedic frame?'

Rab said, 'I've worn such things. It only kicks in if you stumble or fall. Useful in unfamiliar or varying gravity. Specified up to one and a half Earth normal, it says here. Suitable for all the planets up to Earth, and for descent accelerations in tubs like this.'

'But it's so complicated. There's so much to go wrong with it.'

Plokhy smiled. 'You have a point. *Keep it simple* – not a bad mantra. But this is a very mature technology, for us. I mean, for the antique civilisation you've returned to. It won't go wrong. Everybody wears these things outside habitats, or even inside at times. Your only problem is that your designs are seriously unfashionable. Blame me; I stock *Styx* with essentials, not the latest fad.'

Muree persisted. 'But something so complex. Smart. Surely they could be tracked?'

'They'll track us anyhow,' Rab said. 'On the Mask, we were given markers we swallowed with the food we ate.' When Muree recoiled, he said, 'Yes, you too. Didn't they tell you?'

Plokhy snorted. '*That* stuff will wash through your systems before we get to Uranus. I guarantee it, given the smart diet I'll be feeding you. Until then we'll just have to live with it.' She smiled. 'You're probably wondering if this very conversation might be tapped by the authorities. If Commander Revil is listening to every word we say.'

Rab smiled back ruefully. 'You get used to *that* on the Mask.'

Muree shrugged. 'As for me, we were always monitored aboard the *Lightbird*. We accepted it. You grew up knowing that you were in a small and fragile ship. And there was always the chance of an accident, lethal or otherwise. Always. At any time. It might just take one small flaw – or even one person, if they were smart enough and informed enough, and bearing enough of a grudge – to finish us all off in minutes maybe. I know it must be the same on any space habitat, to some degree. So I never thought of the captain listening as – sinister. More like a protective parent, maybe.'

Rab drifted beside her, dangling from one handhold. 'Whereas, on the Mask . . .'

'That *does* feel sinister, if I'm honest.' She thought it over. 'I guess the difference with the ship is that the captain's authority was obviously necessary. We really were suspended in space, between the stars, no help for light-years around. Whereas on the Mask it's different. It's all lies, all of it. The Mask *itself* is a huge lie, a hide to conceal a whole solar system. And if you want to maintain a lie, you need heavy control.' She hesitated, looking to Plokhy. 'I suppose, in here, we can talk more freely than we were ever able to on the Mask?'

'True,' Plokhy said, adding sternly, 'with caveats. Nothing is ever totally secure. I have some pretty useful counter-measures. You'll be as safe from tracking as is possible.'

'Near enough,' Rab said.

'OK,' Muree regathered her train of thought, 'I've been wondering about all this – all that I've learned since we got here – I mean, is it really *all* a lie? About the Neptune invasion and its aftermath . . . People across the System think they are under imminent threat. But they aren't? . . .'

Plokhy just shrugged. 'I've seen no evidence of it, frankly. I mean, no hint of a return of any invaders, either in official or unofficial records. Records that go back centuries. Don't ask how come I know about such records. I tend to keep that to myself. Believe me, all the evidence I've ever seen, in terms of residue from the first attack, across a thousand years, is – the lumes.'

Muree smiled at that, and Plokhy smiled back.

Rab looked from one to the other. 'You know, at heart you two are so similar. It just boils down to the lumes, right? I've seen thousands of them, from a distance. Millions – hell, I don't know – in the guts of Uranus. Strung out on the Frame struts like lanterns, millions upon millions . . .'

That capsule description startled Muree. She still didn't know what this 'Frame' was. Maybe her surprise showed in her face.

Plokhy's grin widened. 'Millions of captive lumes? That shocks you?'

Muree said, 'On the *Lightbird* we have a hundred. That produces one new birth per day. And we, umm, use up about one a day, so the population stays constant—'

'Whereas I only have two lumes at a time,' said Plokhy. 'And even they are barely tapped during my little missions. The estimate is it would take a *thousand* trips like this ride to Uranus before I'd exhaust a single lume. Gives you a feel for the relative challenge of interstellar versus planetary trajectories, right? One would be enough, frankly. I take two just so they have company.'

'I've never actually seen a lume,' Rab said. 'Not up close, save for the suspensions on the struts, of course . . . You have two lumes on this ship? Can we go see them? . . .'

Plokhy grinned. 'Took you your own sweet time to ask. Actually most groundhogs aren't interested at all. They treat them as if they're just another bit of technology, or as good as – even if they know, intellectually, that a lume is actually some kind of life form. Who cares?'

Rab looked confused.

Muree said, 'Plokhy's right. People who have never worked with lumes think they are just – energy lodes. If you do work with them, you soon know different.' She reached out and took his hand – his flesh hand, as usual. 'Let's go see. I'll show you. Plokhy—'

Plokhy's grin widened. 'Follow me to the lume tank.'

So they made their short journey through the heart of the compact little vessel.

And when they got to the tank – well, Muree had to admit there wasn't much to see. Not compared to the crowded birthing chamber on the *Lightbird*, with its hundred lumes – and certainly not compared to the swarms in the carcass of Neptune, and presumably as many or more in tanks aboard the great Mask.

Here, just the two. Big, silvery balloons in a tank.

They rested side by side, on a bare surface at right angles to the direction of thrust. The engines of this little ship didn't offer much acceleration, and so little effective gravity, but enough to hold the lumes in their place.

Of course this lume tank wasn't as well equipped, or nearly

as large, as the facility on the *Lightbird*, but it was good enough, Muree thought.

Plokhy was watching her, smiling. Muree allowed herself to smile back.

Rab, meanwhile, was staring. 'Kind of smaller than I expected. Just big silvery bags of – what? Why, they look almost as if I could pick one of them up. In a gravity field, I mean.'

Plokhy smiled. 'Not quite, not even with that cyborg hand. They've got the density of water, more or less. In zero gravity they settle into distorted spheroids, with a typical radius of a metre, or a little more. So at Earth gravity they'd weigh—'

'Let me figure it. Around five tonnes?'

'Thereabouts,' Muree said. 'They do vary. And diminish as their energy content is harvested, of course. Truth is, even a thousand years on from the first discovery of the lumes – or rather, their discovery of *us* – we still know very little about them. Or so it seems, going by what we of the ship knew, and from what I've learned from the scholars on the Mask since we got here. We don't even know *how* they grow. What they feed on.' She glanced over at Plokhy. 'At least *we* didn't, back on Rossbee.'

'Umm,' Plokhy said. 'You've been too busy being scholars of survival on a marginally habitable world to have time for such issues. But I do know the two crews, Mask and *Lightbird*, have swapped notes. And there are some interesting new ideas floating around about the more complex aspects of the lumes' lifestyle.'

Muree nodded. 'I was involved in some of that, with Brad. My colleague in the lume tanks—'

Rab laughed. 'And now interplanetary cop, in embryo.'

Muree didn't like that. 'He's a decent person. He's following orders. I'm not going to blame him for that.' She took a steadying breath. 'OK, OK. Lumes feed. They reproduce. They feed. They give up their energy, quickly or slowly – mostly, if they're left alone, to make more lumes. They die. Repeat. They can create new birthing colonies, clusters, in the hearts of planets – preferably ice giants. We don't know how or why. They have all the attributes of life as we know it, define it, even if on a completely different basis from ours. And we think they can be very long-lived. A lume won't let itself drain, by choice. It can lose energy, but always tries to acquire more. Drain them too fast, though—'

'Like when they are put on the Frame struts,' Plokhy put in. 'Systematically. Or an overpowered spacecraft. Or even a small craft like this.'

Muree stared at her. *This woman really does care.*

Plokhy said now, 'Nobody knows what their lifespan might be, in the wild. Maybe not much more than we observe of them in captivity.'

Rab hesitated, evidently thinking that over.

Muree smiled at him. '*Lifespan*. Now you're wondering where little lumes come from. That's what everybody asks.'

Rab nodded. 'But not only that, *where do they get the energy that can drive an interplanetary ferry* – let alone an interstellar ship?'

'Actually – we think – from the same place.' She had to laugh at the expression on his face.

Plokhy said, 'Oh, give him a break. Rab – so where do you *think* little lumes come from?'

Rab looked across, clearly fearful of making a fool of himself. 'Well, from Neptune. They landed there, didn't they? Somehow? And took the planet apart . . .'

'Not really,' Plokhy said. 'That's the common belief, yes. Yes, they landed on Neptune, having crossed between the stars in some inert state, we think. At first, in the immediate shadow of the planet's destruction, we, our ancestors, thought a lume was some kind of weapon, a planet-buster – a destroyer spreading from star to star – or rather from the planets of one star to the next. *We* – I mean Commander Revil's distant ancestor and the ignoramuses she commanded.

'Yes, they soaked up a lot of mass-energy from Neptune. Made a mess of that world, for sure. That was what we thought was a conscious invasion. And as you know there is evidence of an earlier incursion out in the Oort cloud, another giant planet chewed up before we humans even knew it was there.

'Yes, everybody thought it was an invasion, and that was understandable. Everybody thought lumes were weapons – mobile, even self-directed weapons. Everybody thought we were under attack, an assault on an interstellar scale, with the lumes controlled by some invisible aggressor. You could say that people panicked, en masse. The governments, the military . . .

'But no fresh attacks came.

'Now there are people who think – *think* – that what the lumes were trying to do was just to get a foothold, feed off the planet's resources, its deep gravity well, all as a means of . . . accessing . . . a deeper energy, something to do with exotic physics. The energy of cosmic inflation, maybe . . . Approaching the theoretical limit of energy density.'

Muree saw that Rab was puzzled. Unsurprisingly. So was she. She hadn't heard any of this speculation.

Rab was frowning. 'I've certainly always been told the lumes were weapons wielded by – something else. Some*body* else. An invading force.'

'That's what everybody thought,' Plokhy said. 'I think because that was how humans had always waged war, every place we went to. But it turned out that there *was* no wider force. No interstellar battleships or missiles . . . just the lumes. Like living, reproducing, bombs.

'But you can see the logic of the authorities at the time. They, or their experts and advisers, were worried that they faced some kind of plague of destruction passing through the Solar System. *Conscious or not.* Maybe there would be more assaults on the planets. Maybe the lumes were nothing but mines to clear a path; maybe an armada of some kind of super-warships would follow. And when that didn't happen quickly, they started to worry about panics and refugee flights and other calamities, caused simply by irresponsible speculation about such *possibilities* as a wider invasion.'

'Hence a lockdown,' Rab said.

'A lockdown. Across all the worlds of humankind, and the traffic between them. It was effective,' Plokhy said. 'And *essentially it's still in place.* And all because we thought that the lumes and their deployment are *like* our own behaviours, strategies, technologies. Destructive technologies.

'But time passed. The world didn't end, the Sun didn't blow up – although we reduced it to a black hole – and Earth wasn't attacked, although there had to be a substitute found for the lost sunlight. And as for the controllers at the time – I guess the kindest thing you can say about them is that they didn't want to make things worse.

'So they just kept everybody's heads down. They maintained the narrative of conscious invaders. They'd sent out the colony worldships, like the *Lightbird,* to scatter humanity so far out it could survive any single blow. They'd built the Wrap around the exhausted Sun. And they'd used lume energy, mostly, to build the Mask. And the Frame, to unite – and control – the worlds.

'And over the centuries they have kept the same paralysis – social and military – in place.

'But, after all this, we still don't know what the lumes *are*. Despite a thousand years of scientific study of these things. Even though we depend on them, here, and on the colony worlds, presumably.'

'And aboard the *Lightbird*,' Muree said. 'And any other colony ships. All we have is—'

'Abstruse theories—' Plokhy said.

Muree snorted. 'Hand-waving, you mean, like you're doing now. But even if this is all so, *why*? What's the purpose of these lumes, save for making more little lumes? We have no idea.'

Plokhy frowned. 'But you might as well say, what's the point of a human being?'

Muree said, 'It doesn't matter. I'm pretty sure that whatever lumes are *for* – if there is a *for* at all – it's got nothing to do with the way *we* use them. Useful as they are. And as much as some of us are – fond of them.'

Plokhy smiled now. 'I'm with you there, Muree.'

Rab sighed. 'How many more days to Uranus?'

'Fifty-nine and a bit.' Plokhy grinned wider. 'So we've got plenty of time to talk about it. Especially since your pursuers have absolutely no idea where I'm taking you, aside from guesswork. Anybody can wear a mask.'

So they talked, and ate, and slept, and exercised.

They never did get around to discussing Plokhy's theories on the cosmic role of the lumes.

Until they arrived at Uranus, as promised.

15

Muree had thought she knew about Uranus.

There had been historical images of the seventh planet in the extensive library of the *Lightbird* – as there had been of all the Solar System's bodies, from the Sun itself through Earth to the Oort cloud on the fringe of interstellar space. Data on Uranus, specifically, gathered from centuries of study through telescopes, then robot spacecraft, and at last human exploration of the moons and the planet itself.

As seen from afar, in human eyes, Uranus had resembled a big fat copy of Earth: a world of greenish-blue air, dimly lit by the distant Sun, streaked with ice-crystal clouds. That was how it *had* looked, anyhow, in those antique images, before the catastrophe of the 'invasion'. And, as she now knew, before the loss of sunlight.

In the subsequent dark, human lume-based resource harvesting had begun on a massive scale.

Early images surviving from that period showed straight-line streaks across that blue-green sky – straight lines, the signature of industrial mankind – where scoop ships had dug into the atmosphere to extract volatiles for fuel and human comestibles. Mostly water was taken, which you could drink, or split into hydrogen and oxygen for rocket fuel, or propellant for use in more advanced drives. Then more ambitious schemes sought other exotic treasures to be had, such as helium-3, premium fuel for the nuclear fusion reactors that powered deep-space ships and colonies, eventually imported back to Earth itself in large quantities.

Muree knew that some on board the *Lightbird*, knowing something about these industries, had been cynical about what they would actually find once they finally got back to the Solar System, after centuries away. If that level of industrialisation of the Solar System had continued, would they return to find nothing but drained worlds?

Muree herself had been hopeful, as she flicked through these antique images, that such spoliation and destruction had been limited. There was no reason why people *had* to drive every extraction opportunity to its limit.

But now, as she learned more about the fate of Uranus after the invasion, she had become apprehensive.

For here, another form of mass-energy extraction had begun.

At last the planet itself loomed. During the final approach Plokhy shut down the external viewers, even masked the dumb ports, wanting her passengers' first impression of Uranus to be made in close-up. And on the night before the big reveal, as the ship swept inwards, she advised them not to judge what they were soon to see.

In the morning of that closest approach, Muree washed, dressed, ate, and joined the others in the lounge cum bridge of the cramped little craft.

And there, beyond the big open ports, she saw Uranus at last.

Or what was left of it.

'It looks like Earth,' Muree blurted. 'I mean, a ruined Earth. A huge Earth, a devastated Earth . . .'

She was looking down on a monstrously thick atmosphere – but an atmosphere that was a relic, Plokhy said, of a much greater reservoir of air. And a rocky inner core that itself looked old, worn down. It featured what might have been mountain ranges, visible under all that dense air, even massive uplifted terrains that might have been continental plates rising above a deeper, more dense mantle.

But what she could see for certain, here and there, were signs of humanity: lights like fallen stars, some of them clustered in what were evidently colonies of some kind. Other lights, chains of them, lining what must be roads or some kind of rail tracks.

And, here and there, much brighter assemblages, glowing scars in the planet's side.

Lume-light. Unmistakable.

'That's not Uranus,' Muree said at last.

Plokhy raised an eyebrow.

'I've seen images. In our ship's library. There was a massive atmosphere of thick greenish air, high clouds—'

'*That* was how Uranus used to be,' Rab said gently.

Muree said, 'So what's happened? It looks like another lume attack. Like Neptune—'

'What's happened,' Plokhy said, 'was humanity. *We needed to build the Mask*, remember. And the Frame, the Solar Wrap. Engineering on the scale of the Solar System. After the destruction of Neptune, our rulers locked themselves into a cycle of fear, of hiding. Even as time passed, as it seemed increasingly unlikely that any more invasions were to come – even as some started to mutter that the first "invasion" might have been no such thing – they felt they couldn't abandon it all, their wary posture, for fear of creating a panic that might have inflicted more damage than that done to the Solar System so far . . . They had to do *something*.'

Muree shook her head. 'But according to your theory Neptune hadn't been – *attacked*. Not by some invading force. Just a wave of lumes, coming from further out in the Solar System . . . But I suppose if you don't understand what you're seeing, it *looks* like an attack. But – at the same time, they learned how to *use* the lumes. Humans did. At some command echelon.'

'Yes,' Rab said. 'They saw what the lumes had done to Neptune; now they saw the *possibilities* that offered if they could use the lumes as, as a *technology* to take Uranus apart.'

Muree nodded. 'And that's how they developed their plans, for the great rebuilding.'

Plokhy nodded. 'All of this was based on the visions of the Architect, as everybody learned to call her, or him . . . Visions of the remaking of the Solar System from Saturn inwards . . .'

She tapped screens to show them the Architect's plans.

'Some of this will seem strange to you. The Architect drew on ancient visions, derived from the dreams of astronomers before Galileo – days when people still believed that the Earth was the jewel at the centre of the cosmos, with the Sun, Moon and planets caught in a divine web of orderly geometric forms – perfect solids, nested, one inside the next, tetrahedra, cubes, octahedra . . . The Architect sought to revive that spirit of orderliness, of safety, and people flocked to those dreams. *Even though it depended on using the lumes, which we had thought a weapon.*'

Muree did her best to follow this. *All in good time,* she thought. *Be patient . . . Although a diagram would help.*

'But,' Plokhy said, 'these immense construction projects needed immense resources. The resources of an ice giant. And since Neptune had already been plundered by the lumes—'

'They came to Uranus.'

*

Rab looked out of the windows, as they sank deeper into the thick air. 'The surface is exposed. Rocky. The core of the planet . . . I see straight edges. *On* that core. Immense quarries? I can see convoys on those roads, I think, moving lights . . . People! They're going so slowly that it has to be . . .' He looked up. 'What happened to the atmosphere? I never dreamed . . .'

Muree glared at Plokhy. 'So what did they do to Uranus?'

Plokhy held up her hands. 'Hey, don't blame me. And I only know a little more than you already, I'm pretty sure.

'Look. Here's the headline. *They dismantled it.*

'Once Uranus was a giant, a world of layers. At its heart, a rocky core, about the size and mass of Earth – the core you see down there now. And above the rocky core you have – had – a liquid water ocean, ten thousand kilometres deep. That alone had the mass of about twelve Earths – so deep you could have dropped Mars into it, whole. Above *that*, another ocean, this of liquid hydrogen, another eight thousand kilometres deep – only a little more than Earth's radius. Oh, and a gaseous hydrogen atmosphere above *that* – hydrogen with a trace of methane, a carbon compound.

'And so the atmosphere was mined for its methane, some of it taken out and used to build the Mask. Which is mostly a graphene shell encompassing the orbit of Uranus itself . . . The carbon from the methane in the air was used to create the graphene, you see: graphene, a very light, very strong carbon-based solid . . . Look, there's centuries of smart engineering in all of that. *And they used lumes to power it all.*'

Muree had been expecting that. 'Yes. Yes, you'd need a lot of energy to lift off that ocean, that atmosphere. A lot of lumes—'

'I worked it all out once – I mean, it's all highly secret, but you can't hide the reality of *this*. To dismantle the planet completely would have taken the equivalent of thirty *trillion* lumes.

You know that lumes double their numbers in seventy years, if left alone? It might surprise you, if you don't know your maths, that, even starting from just two, you only need about forty-five doublings to achieve that number, the thirty trillion.'

Muree frowned. 'And if a doubling takes seventy years –'

'In less than a thousand years, so far, this is as far as we've got. Can you see the logic? From the beginning, the mass-energy of each successive layer of the mantle was used to grow more lumes. Some lumes were siphoned off to power projects elsewhere – including the Mask, the Frame, even ships like mine – while others were used to lift the substance of the planet itself—'

'All those lumes. They lived and died for – this? To build the Mask? A cowardly lie?'

Plokhy frowned. 'To be fair, the original designers, in the aftermath of the loss of Neptune, *did* think they might face another "invasion". They were earnest, hard-working, true believers. But as the decades, the centuries passed, the likelihood of another invasion seemed to decrease. *Belief* waned, at the centre at least. New theories emerged—'

Muree was getting the idea. She said, 'Theories such as it wasn't an invasion at all. Just a swarm of lumes, living beings, animals, just going through their life-cycles. At Neptune.'

'Right. But by then – well, they were committed. I think they feared unrest, chaos, if they abandoned their huge projects – their vast, quasi-divine, centuries-old transport structures. And, worse, always at the back of the mind – what if the "invaders" returned after all? How could we respond?'

Rab looked down at the surface of the 'planet' below. 'And all the people who lived and died down there? And who *still* live and die down there. Were they told it might all be unnecessary?'

Plokhy's expression hardened. 'Of course not. And nobody else outside the command strata can know either. Even now, I mean if it all turns out to have been a terrible mistake, if that were admitted now—'

'The builders will be reviled by history,' Muree said.

'More than that,' Rab said. 'They'll be torn apart.'

Plokhy nodded. 'You see what this means for you? I hope you feel I did you a favour by getting you out of the clutches of those guys, the authorities. But in another way you're now a target. For the rest of your lives. Because you've seen the truth, or some of it – and, what's worse, you have the perspective to grasp it.'

Rab said, 'I *already* feel like a target . . . Plokhy, how come *you* aren't a target?'

She smiled. 'I'm too useful, for now. Rogues like me lubricate the system, you see. I'll be disposed of some day.' Her smile widened. 'But they'll have to catch me first.'

'But us—'

Rab said, 'We won't be killed outright. These are bureaucrats; they don't think that way. There are other ways to silence us – such as by dropping us down there, into. Uranus.'

Muree looked down again at the prison-world. The crawling lights.

'They do some research down there,' Plokhy murmured. 'To be fair. As well as development. Resource extraction. But it's a tough regime. Punishment is brutal. And it's been working for centuries. There are no heaps of corpses – no cemeteries in this *gulag*.'

Muree had to whisper for a translation of that word.

Rab asked, 'Worse than Mercury, you think?'

'Worse than Mercury. I'm told that the bodies are flash-destroyed so their carbon can be extracted, used to process into graphene. Smart carbon, to be used in the next big construction project.' Plokhy looked down at Uranus. 'Some legacy, for a human life.' Then she looked up, grinning. 'So we'd better take you somewhere else.'

Muree was bewildered – dismayed. 'Where?'

Plokhy beckoned her to another screen, another view. 'OK. More conceptual breakthroughs for the interstellar wanderer. 'What do you see now?'

Muree peered into the new screen. Pale dots of light against the dark.

'A star field?'

'Look closer. Not stars—'

'Planets. Oh, I get it. We're seeing the planets of the Solar System.'

Plokhy pointed. 'The position of the Sun – or the Wrap around the Sun – is just about – there.' She tapped the screen with one finger. 'In fact, from the position of Uranus, you're looking at the rest of the inwards Solar System – Saturn, Jupiter, all the way to Mercury, innermost planet.' She moved the finger up slightly, over the screen, above Saturn. 'And what do you see there?'

Muree looked closely. 'A straight line. Extending up from the image of Saturn. Which is a bright dot.'

'What does it *look* like?'

'I don't know. A ring system, maybe? Saturn has rings, right? Particles of ice. I've seen images of that. Rings like a huge dinner plate—'

'Huh,' Plokhy said. 'And humans have been dining off that plate for centuries. All that free-floating ice, laced with organic chemistry – just too much to resist for resource-hungry colonists. Yes, edge-on the rings could look like that. Or they used to.'

'So I'm guessing it's not that,' Muree said.

'What else, then?'

Muree shrugged. 'Some kind of – track. A road across the sky.' She looked at the image again. 'A glowing road.'

'Good enough.'

'So what *is* it? – Oh.'

Plokhy smiled. 'A glowing road across the sky. You're seeing a network of roads that spans the inner Solar System. This is the Frame, travellers.'

Rab, grinning himself, rested his good hand on Muree's shoulder. 'She's teasing you. Yes, it's just a road network. A lot more – utilitarian – than you might think. And it spans the Solar System – inwards from Saturn, anyhow.

And Plokhy said, 'Whatever you think of it, you need it right now, and that's where we're going. Hold on tight.'

16

On the very day it was discovered that Angela Plokhy had taken Rab and Muree away in her private ferry, the pursuit of the three fugitives officially began. A pursuit put in the hands of Lieutenant Jeo Planter – and Brad Tenant, Muree's colleague from the *Lightbird*.

Brad was no cop, but he knew Muree. That was the rationale worked out by his boss, Captain Tavar, and Commander Revil.

And for Brad it started the next morning, when he was woken by an enthusiastic knock on the door of the small cabin he'd been loaned, deep within the Mask.

'Tenant. It's Planter. You moving in there?'

That was an officer's door-knock, for sure. 'Give me five minutes, Jeo,' he called back.

He clambered out of his bunk. Moved slowly to the small bathroom attached to his cabin. A hasty dump. Even a cop from Venus could wait for that.

Five seconds in the exfoliator that shaved and cleansed his skin.

And then a one-piece body suit, that was not so much worn as more or less sprayed over him – and given the ferocious reclamation and recycling regimes on board the Mask station, a spray whose substance had no doubt been scrubbed from the air and reconstituted from detritus, many times over. The boots he had been given, at least, lasted from day to day, even if they too were self-cleaning, self-repairing. But, he thought, as he struggled to pull them on, with all the advanced technology suffusing this place, you'd think they'd give you magic boots that *fit*—

More bangs. 'That's five minutes, Tenant.'

'Yeah, yeah.'

In fact, rather than seeking adventure, Brad found himself pining for his ship, the *Lightbird*, the safe routine of the endless shipboard days – his assigned duties, working the lumes with Muree. Especially with Muree. Every day the same, and once he had sometimes chafed at that. But compared to the chaos that his life had become now, those lost days seemed like a chain of peaceful islands, each governed by routine, by little tragedies, little triumphs.

Especially with Muree.

If only the interstellar journey had never ended, he thought, childish though the idea was. But – why not? If he'd born earlier during the century-long mission, he might well have lived out his whole life between origin and destination without even the *possibility* of his having to be dragged out of that cocoon of familiarity.

And he and Muree might have had time to – well, to figure out their own relationship.

Muree.

It had always been Muree. They hadn't quite grown up together, but near enough. Then they'd worked together, which was no coincidence as he'd applied to work alongside her in the lume bank, as soon as he was given the opportunity.

It wasn't any kind of sexual attraction, he didn't believe. Though that might have come. Maybe it was love, but even that was only secondary. It was more like admiration on his part.

It was just that she was so – gifted – in that environment. You needed empathy to handle such a job well. Empathy with the alien, an understanding of its own strange needs and wants, pleasure and pain . . . She had all that. As well as an instinct for leadership, even if she didn't yet recognise that herself.

And all that was what had kept Brad at her side.

Well, their relationship had never had the chance to reach its climax, its completion, because the damn interstellar journey had finished too early. And conversely, now, it was that past relationship with Muree that had doomed him to this ghastly, scary environment. And an even scarier assignment beyond, it seemed.

An assignment to chase Muree across a bewildering, engineered Solar System, where he was a complete stranger.

Thump, thump. 'Tenant, you ass—'

Brad grabbed a breakfast bar and ordered the door to open.

There was Lieutenant Planter – a local authority figure, he wasn't always 'Jeo' yet to Brad, or to anybody else from off the ship. Not yet, maybe not ever. But today the big man looked as happy as Brad had ever seen him. No, not happy. *Anticipatory.* A job to do.

Planter spoke first. 'You ready? *They've been spotted*. Don't bother to answer. Don't bother to *pack*. Everything you'll need is on the ship they're preparing for us . . .'

'What ship?'

The Lieutenant merely turned away and lunged down the corridor, grabbing handholds one after the other, skilfully hurling his bulk from one to the next in the zero gravity.

Brad followed as best he could, munching on his breakfast bar.

But he was aware that Planter was leading him to the inner

surface of the Mask. The surface where the spacecraft docked.

He really was about to leave here, then. Leave the Mask. Leave to dive further into the Solar System – or what was left of the System. All of which was a thrill, of an abstract kind, for Brad. But it put paid to any chance he had of getting back to the *Lightbird*, where he truly belonged, any time soon, and the lumes . . .

But he would have a chance of finding Muree, he supposed. And he found that felt like a strong motivation.

He tried to focus on his surroundings.

He was hurrying through a corridor fitted out with structures that he recognised from roughly similar fittings around the *Lightbird* – airlock hatches, decon chambers. Ways in from space, ways out into space – interfaces probably standardised long before the interstellar *Lightbird* itself had been commissioned, a thousand years before.

As they hurried past all this, Planter turned to study him, vaguely curious. 'All this strange to you? I guess where you come from, there wasn't much need to go extravehicular. You were a solitary ship, nobody around for – well, light-years. Right? Until you got here.'

That was true enough. 'We did train up for extravehicular. Very occasionally – once a year, I guess – you might get some kind of incident, say a bit of interstellar grit that might do some harm, which needed a repair. There was a rota for such assignments, so everyone got some experience.'

'Sounds professional enough . . .'

Brad hesitated. He didn't enjoy admitting to what might seem less than 'professional' to these strange people with their vast Mask and their apparently unbending rules. Their web of laws, their rigid systems – their untruths, as embodied by the Mask itself. The ship had been different. It was more like a community, and less like a military encampment, like this Mask. Or had been, and he wondered now if he would ever find his way back to it . . .

He felt a little out of breath already. Planter was still rushing him through what was basically a long corridor. But then this Mask might have a corridor an astronomical unit long and you'd never know about it until you found yourself at one end of it . . .

'You were saying,' Planter said. 'Training up for extravehicular excursions?'

'Yeah. On the *Lightbird*. Everybody went through it, from an early age. Babies and infants would be held in pouches in their parents' suits. From age about seven years you'd start going out in your own miniature suit. Always tethered; your parents didn't take chances. So you'd play a bit and get used to it, then try out simple tasks. There'd generally be struts and harnesses to help move us around. You learned about that. And there were small independent craft, but they were used mostly as work shacks on particularly long and difficult jobs, or for retrieving casualties. Craft so small they were almost more like heavy pressure suits, legless, with external manipulators. As you grew up you'd be assigned to exercises in more significant engineering jobs. Relining engine exhaust nozzles was a tough one. All under supervision. You'd get badges for achieving one grade or another.'

Planter snorted. 'Badges? Well, Muree can show me her medals when we retrieve her and that clown Rab . . . OK. Here we are.'

They had come to a port, a doorway almost seamlessly fitting its frame in the smooth inner hull.

Planter grinned. 'On the other side of this wall, hard vacuum – and the Solar System.' He tapped at a small panel set in the wall. Then he laid the palm of his gloved hand over the panel. Security measures, Brad presumed.

And the doorway detached from its setting with a soft snap,

then a hiss as it withdrew and slid sideways, revealing what lay beyond.

Which was dark, for a moment – until bright light flooded the space, and there was a soft hiss of equalising air pressure.

And Brad realised he was looking into the interior of another craft entirely. Small cabin, monitors, a wide window, couches. Smooth, curving walls.

Planter looked back at him. 'This is what we call a runabout. One of the smallest ships we have out here. Most are heavy transport, as you'll understand, given the challenge of provisioning such a big facility. Take care when you follow.' He pushed his way through the hatch, into the light within.

Brad took his advice and followed cautiously. Soon he was inside, floating alongside Planter.

The fundamental designs and purposes of the Mask and the *Lightbird* were very different, after centuries of divergent cultural and technical development. But a spacecraft was a spacecraft. Brad almost felt comfortable here.

Planter was glaring at him. 'You know what I'm going to say.'

'Don't touch anything until you tell me to?'

'And I won't be telling you at all, unless I can help it. Or I get bored. And I might, we've a long trip ahead of us. Even best case.'

There was a soft hiss behind Brad's back. Holding on to the back of a seat with one hand, he turned around.

The hatch was settling back into its frame. When it was done, its oval edge was imperceptible.

Brad said, 'It's like being inside a huge – egg.'

Planter raised his eyebrows. 'You had eggs on a starship?'

Brad had got used to such questions. 'Why not? Hens, other birds – parrots are popular, colourful and smart, and do well in low effective gravity. Also—'

'Never mind. I don't want to know. Seriously, I don't. More to the point, we have the clearance to cast off from the Mask. In a moment—'

Brad started to feel the push of acceleration. He reflexively grabbed on harder to the back of the seat, to orient himself, keep himself steady. Quite quickly, the push built up. The thrust, however it was created, was smooth, soundless, and steadily increasing.

Planter was studying instrument displays. 'All well. We detached from the Mask successfully.'

'I guessed. So we're flying free. *Inside* the big enclosure of the Mask . . .'

'That couch you're holding on to. Sit down and strap yourself in.'

Brad did so, but he was starting to feel resentful at Planter's attitude.

'Look, Lieutenant – I was born and grew up *in* a space vessel. I know what I'm doing, I have reflexes developed over a lifetime—'

'Shut up. Sit down.' Planter just glared. 'Strap in. Oh, and by the way. Shut up. Did I say that already? *Shut up*.'

Brad held his gaze, not feeling like backing down, not so early in this damn trip.

But he could feel the acceleration building, and gave in.

Settling into his chair, he reached for clasps at waist and shoulder – but the seat was as smart as the rest of this vessel, it seemed, and even as he sat, clasps emerged autonomously from the body of the couch, dragging straps in a cross over his torso.

Planter was still glaring. 'Good enough, but slow. If I tell you to get into your couch, or do *anything*, you do it, and fast. Clear?' And he made his way to a couch of his own, flopped into it, and let the straps crawl over his torso and waist.

'Clear enough.'

And now, soundlessly, the acceleration built up further. Brad could feel the couch under him adjusting to the thrust. Moulding itself to support his back, his neck, head. He felt he was sinking, sinking into the intelligent, contoured form, as if into a huge cushion.

He dared lift his head a little, looked around. Planter was sitting securely in his own couch – but working at screens, instrument panels, tapping, swiping, murmuring into a headset that had unfolded out of his seat.

After a few minutes of this, with the thrust still building steadily, Planter looked over at Brad. 'You still with me, kid?'

'Bearing up.' *And I'm no kid.* 'How high is this thrust going to be?'

'Eight times standard gravity. By which I mean, Earth gravity. Not that anybody who matters lives on Earth any more.'

'*You* can tolerate that, right?'

'I'm not about to do handstands. Mind you, I never could anyhow.'

'But you're not from Earth . . .' He remembered what he had been told of Rab's life story. All second-hand from Muree. 'You're from Venus.'

'Correct. And Venus is a rocky world, like Earth, with about ninety per cent of Earth's gravity.'

'Close enough, I guess.'

Planter hesitated. 'You might think so. But I did go up to Earth a couple of times, as a junior cop. They train you up for operations on other worlds. Just in case. So, yes, I got accustomed to heavy gravity. That resilience comes in handy when you travel. But the accelerations you'll encounter around the Frame are only a fraction of Earth standard . . .'

Again, the Frame.

'You said they trained you to operate on Earth.'

'What about it?'

'I thought Earth had no people.'

'Ah. Yeah. Well, not quite. Earth *is* sparsely populated these days. Full of life, but not much of it human. There's similar numbers, I think, to the human population at the time of the stone age. Before farming, before our numbers started ballooning. More like when humans were just another animal on the grasslands – a smart one, granted. A few million maybe.'

These casual remarks thrilled Brad.

'Anyhow, you might stop marvelling at my glittering career and start paying attention to *your* immediate surroundings. What can you tell me right now?'

Brad thought about it. He was gradually sinking into his couch, which was in turn silently adjusting itself further to the contours of his body. 'I can tell you that the acceleration is increasing.'

'Good spot,' Planter said. 'You want to guess how much?'

And Brad thought about that. 'You said you work on Earth. You'll ramp it up to an Earth gravity. Right? Fine by me,' he said defiantly. 'There's a standard one-G in the *Lightbird*'s Carousel.'

Brad thought he could *hear* the grin in the man's voice as he replied. 'Well, that's comfortable enough for an old Venusian like me. And the faster we go the better chance we'll have of catching our fugitives before they get to the Frame. Much harder to catch them then.'

The Frame again.

'Where do you think they are now? Muree and Rab.'

Planter replied without hesitation. 'They've been to Uranus.'

Of course Brad hadn't been briefed about that. From his point of view, Muree, and Rab, had just disappeared. 'Uranus? Really?'

'Really. They were tracked by internal sensors to that damn Plokhy's ship, and *that* was tracked en route to Uranus. Seventh major planet of the Solar System—'

'I know about Uranus. I've heard enough about it here. And I learned about it before, on the *Lightbird*. There was a very old teaching machine that had come from home – from Rossbee – that taught the little kids about the Solar System, the planets, all the way to the Sun itself. A relic hauled out from Earth in the first place, probably. Still worked.'

Planter frowned at that. 'Kids on Rossbee were taught about the Solar System? Earth? A planet light-years away, with no hope of ever seeing it – why?'

To Brad, that seemed a ridiculous question. 'Why not? Wouldn't you want to know where you came from? Your roots, at least?'

'No,' Planter said, without hesitation. 'Maybe basic factual. Who needs detail? Born on Venus. Grew up on Venus. So what? So what if deeper my ancestors came from North America, Earth. Who cares? They're long dead, and North America is all but depopulated. What more do you need to know?'

'You grew up on Venus, like Rab?'

'Rab Callis would have grown up on Mercury, if not for his mother forcing the situation . . . I'm sick of going over that incident, all those years ago. Where were we?'

'Talking about where Rab and Muree were. And where they are going, I guess. If our mission is to catch them—'

'Right. Well, so far as we know, they are still in the care of Angela Plokhy, and riding in her dumb little ferry-boat ship. You heard about any of this?'

Brad hesitated. 'Only that Muree was gone, with Rab. I didn't know for sure it was with Plokhy. But thinking about it there was no other plausible way they could have got out of the Mask, save in the *Styx*.'

'That's true enough.'

'But why would Plokhy *do* that – why give them some kind of dumb free ride?'

Planter shrugged, a relaxed gesture, despite the still mounting acceleration. 'I know that some people think our Solar System, organised and efficient as it is, can be too – rigid. Actually you need a few free agents to shake stuff up. Such as Plokhy. Makes people think, at least. In a way she has a licence to – disrupt a little. There are potential counter-measures if she goes too far. It all tests the resilience of the systems, harmlessly. That's the theory. Her own motives? Who knows? She's a useful pilot. Well, evidently so; Commander Revil uses her.'

Brad had to grin. '*That's the theory*. I take it you don't agree.'

'*I* wouldn't use *her*, not by choice. Too damn clever. The further down the hierarchy you are, the less you need to think. That's what I believe, and it's a shame *that* isn't drummed into little kids' heads at school. I mean, who knows? If Rab's mother hadn't *thought* too hard about the fate of her kid, that damn mutilation, if he hadn't been here to fall in with another "free mind"—' He said that with obvious disgust. 'Well, then we wouldn't have this minor crisis on our hands, and you and I wouldn't have to go chasing across the System.'

Despite his general anxiety and physical discomfort – growing discomfort, as the acceleration built – something in Brad thrilled at that. He'd grown up travelling between the stars, and now here he really was chasing fugitives across the outer reaches of mankind's old home. *Chasing!*

And still the acceleration mounted. Even now, he couldn't get a glimpse of a screen showing an external view, showing anything at all, either through Planter's spite or carelessness or sheer excessive control.

'So we're chasing them. They went to Uranus. Why go there?'

'Well, it is a planet. So far as I can make out none of you have seen a planet before, save through a telescope pointing back at your own Rossbee, right? And also – and here I'm guessing, but given their backgrounds, Muree and Rab might have wanted to go see the lumes.'

'There are lumes at – or in – Uranus? Like in what's left of Neptune?' Brad thought that over. 'OK, I can see that Muree, at least, would want that.'

'And that little bastard Rab probably has a crush on her, as well as an unstable temperament of his own. He'll follow her lead.'

'But why would Plokhy take them anywhere?'

Planter sighed. 'Because she's a born troublemaker herself. A disruptor, just like we talked about. She did it because she could, instinctively.'

'So, Uranus. Have they left there? Do we know where they're going now?'

'To the nearest Frame portal. Obviously. And our best bet is to chase them to that point, hopefully, and cut them off before they even penetrate the Frame itself. After that the chase will be a lot harder.'

'OK. So what is this . . . Frame?'

'Of course, you don't know much about that either . . . You want me to show you?'

Brad shrugged, increasingly bewildered. And even more so by the images Planter showed him now.

At first he saw only darkness in the screens.

But on second glance he saw a rough row of what looked like

bright stars, scattered across a straight line that cut horizontally across the image . . . *Were* they stars?

He glanced at Planter, confused.

Planter said, 'So this is a view from cameras mounted on the inner wall of the Mask. Pointing at the equator, looking into the plane of the Solar System. Pretty much as you'd see if you'd climbed out of this ship, right now. You're looking into the darkness within, right?'

'OK. No distant stars. I've spent my whole life in starlight. Here, it's shut out. And no sunlight. It seems so – strange.'

'So no background starlight. What *do* you see?'

'Those starlike patches, in a row, across the sky?'

'Not stars. Those are the planets. The surviving planets, from Mercury through Earth to Saturn, the sixth planet – the seventh planet, Uranus, is outside the scheme. They orbit the Sun in near-circles, and more or less in the same plane; if you looked down from above, and if the Sun were still luminous, that would be obvious.'

Brad squinted to see. 'And how come the planets are so bright, then? If there's no Sun.'

Planter smiled. 'Because of us. Humans. We light the planets now.'

'Oh. With lumes?'

'With lumes, that are bred out of Uranus and other locations – and here. Some of the planets are industrial worlds, some aren't – Earth is a park, as I told you. You know that word? *Park*. Given over to nature. Or a recovering nature. So the lumes replicate sunlight – the light Earth used to receive from the Sun.

'Aside from Earth itself, Venus is the most Earthlike – sort of. Partially terraformed. Mercury is a mine. Mars is . . . a city. The remaining giants, Jupiter, Saturn, are industrially mined, though on nothing like the scale of Uranus.' He pointed. 'Look

– *there's* Saturn, the outermost in the Frame. Go ahead, look, ask. What else do you want to know about this image?'

Brad imagined that round about now Muree was asking pretty much the same questions of Angela Plokhy. He leaned forward, saw that horizontal line, apparently brilliantly lit. He traced it with a finger, over the screen. 'And so what's this? It runs through the positions of the planets.'

Planter sighed. 'What does it *look* like?'

'A road across the sky.'

'And that's about right. *That* is the Frame. A road across the sky. I'll try to show you . . .'

'Let me tinker with the virtual perspective. There are eyes in the sky everywhere, even if the whole structure is so huge that it suffers lightspeed time-delays, from one side to the other. Delays of two or three hours . . .'

The image on the screen tilted. The single line seemed to split, into two arcs that separated, parted –

'It's not a line at all,' Brad said, feeling oddly excited. 'Rather it's the edge of – something. A *circle*? That we've been seeing edge on?'

'Keep watching.'

Now it felt as if Brad were rising, rising above a great circular arena. That brilliant line was separating into an ellipse, which did indeed grow slowly to a circle . . . And now he saw more circles within the big frame, all apparently concentric. All shining. The planets, seeming to glow by their own light, were set out around this layout . . . The outermost world, a misty globe, sat more or less on that outer circle. Saturn?

'It's as if the planets are caught in some vast – spiderweb.'

'Not a bad model. Keep watching.'

The great frame tilted further. Brad interrogated the smart

scene for detail. More lines became visible, these ones radial – no, they spanned the outer circle from one side to the other, two of them at right angles to each other. And other planets, he counted, six in all, were scattered across this frame, one to each circle.

Brad was simply astonished. 'It's like a – road network. A system of roads, spanning the whole of the Solar System. Roads between the planets? Is that what this *is*?'

Planter nodded. 'That is what it is. That, my friend, is what we call the Frame.' He pointed. 'You can see how you travel around, from world to world. From your starting point, you hop onto the circular track that follows your origin planet's orbit. When you get to a radial track you follow *that*, in or out, to get to the orbit of your target planet. And then you work around the orbital ring to make for *that* planet.'

'At Ross 128 the planets' orbits are ellipses, not perfect circles—'

'Same here. But not very elliptical. The circles of the Frame are pretty close, and the whole thing is smart. You generally get from the Frame to the target world, and back, in short-range ferries.'

'Like Angela Plokhy's.'

'Right.'

'An interplanetary railroad. I know there were railroads on Rossbee, on the planet . . . I've seen images of them.'

'And on old Earth, centuries ago. So the terminology has survived even on other worlds, light-years away?'

Brad was surprised to hear Planter express any interest at all in Rossbee. But overall he just felt overwhelmed by the vision before him.

'It's – magnificent. It's crazy! Why do it that way?'

'Because it works. And it has . . . higher meanings. Cultural meanings. You'll figure *that* out when you get to know the place a little better. Meanwhile we have a job to do, remember? All you need to know for now is that, if our refugees Muree and Rab are anywhere, and still free, they're going to be heading to the Frame by now.'

'How do you know?'

'Because that's where I would go. Because the Frame is a road twenty-four billion kilometres long, that's how I know. They have a head start. But to get *anywhere* they do need to work their way around to the position of Saturn and that inward strut. And so you and I, my friend, have a journey ourselves, from here a journey of about fifteen astronomical units, fifteen times Earth's distance from the Sun, from where we left the Mask, to that location of Saturn on the outer ring. Which is where we can get into the Frame ourselves, and track down our fugitives.'

'Fifteen times Earth's distance . . . How long?'

'I hope you're comfortable in that couch. Four days at eight gravities.'

'Eight gravities . . .'

'I need a nap. Make yourself comfortable.' He turned away.

Meanwhile, elsewhere, the *Styx* was already approaching the Frame.

17

As seen from the *Styx*, the underside of the Frame was a line across the sky. Or one 'strut' of it was.

'Struts.' Muree rehearsed the word.

'Struts,' Plokhy said. 'That's what the engineers call them, the basic construction units of the Frame.' She was looking out absently as she guided the *Styx* gently, gently upwards, towards –

Towards what? Muree wondered.

'The navigation's a little tricky,' Plokhy said. 'I have to match my speed with that thing. Which is far from static. Rotates in seventy days or so – at this radius that means about seventeen hundred kilometres per second, or one astronomical unit per *day*. But luckily the whole thing is smart, and so's my ship, so collisions and such are unlikely.

'Think of it. The whole of the Frame rotates as one. You have to match your speed and land on, or dock with, the Frame, the outer circular rails. Then you catch a fast train, you ride to a junction with an inward spoke, divert down that to the circle you want, then you ride *that* circular rail, heading for your destination – generally a planet. And when you get close to that planet, you land in a spacecraft . . .'

Muree didn't want to admit it but she didn't know what a 'train' was. But –

'That's impossible,' she said. 'Surely. A structure the size of astronomical units, of planetary orbits – no. And there must be safeguards, failsafes—'

'No such thing as a safe failsafe. Most people get by. Have done for centuries . . .'

And Plokhy fell silent, focused, as she edged the *Styx* in towards the roof over the sky.

Slowly that dead straight line became less abstract, thickening from a pure geometric line into a band, still cutting across their line of sight, side to side of the viewing port. Dead black. That Muree could see it at all was because of light shed by the *Styx* itself, splashes of it from lamps evidently installed on her spine to aid docking.

And in that light Muree began to pick out details on the underside of the nearest strut – straight-line ridges, what looked like panels, rectangular, square. All very mechanical, industrial. There was evidence of logistics deliveries too, she thought. Docking ports, transfer for passengers maybe, as well as for fuels and other necessities: air, water, even food . . .

Plokhy evidently registered their silent gawping, their peering to catch the moments of illumination. 'We're rising into the shadow. It's not dark up *there*.' She grinned. 'Topside, on the deck. It's quite the spectacle, isn't it? Even if it is just a fast-transit system.'

'As well as very useful for policing and control, on a System-wide scale,' Rab said.

Muree was awed, if sceptical. Nervous. 'And we're going to dock this little ship with *that*.'

'You bet,' Plokhy said. 'That's one of the things this *little ship* is designed for. That and running away, very fast. Although it's more like we'll *land* on it. On the Frame. Docking sounds a bit – *equal*.' She looked up at Muree. 'You understand all this?

Are you sure you're getting the scale of this thing right in your head? Well, you were able to comprehend the Mask. This is on a similar scale, but is far more – elegant. Your *Lightbird* is, what, three kilometres long?'

'Measured along the spine, about that.'

'So, if you were to land the ship on that surface up there – *sideways* on— Actually, I can show you.'

Plokhy tapped skilfully at her screens – and up came a cartoon version of the *Lightbird*, the big torus, the long spine to the nuclear engines and thrusters at the rear. Then with a flick she cast the cartoon against an image of the Frame. With a mildly sadistic grin, Muree thought, she let the *Lightbird* image dwindle in perspective, ever more dwarfed by the great, complex wall of the Frame.

When the images finally coalesced, Muree tried to do a fast estimate in her head. 'So that wall in space – it's what, six, seven times wider than the *Bird*, which is itself three kilometres long . . . *Twenty kilometres wide*?'

'Near enough,' Plokhy said.

'And how *long*?'

Rab grinned. 'I admit I'm enjoying seeing the interstellar traveller in awe. I guess it's a matter of career path. *Your* ancestors went to another star; mine stayed home and built *this*.'

Plokhy nodded. 'Mine too, probably. Not that many of them had much choice in the matter—'

Muree demanded, '*How long*?'

Plokhy and Rab exchanged a glance.

Plokhy said, 'Do you want the answer in metres? Or *Lightbird*-lengths? Or—'

'Or astronomical units,' Rab said, more gently. 'Come on, Plokhy. Let's quit teasing the tourist. Muree, the Frame, in all, is over a hundred and twenty astronomical units in length.

Including the radial struts. If it was stretched out, it would reach from the Sun to *twelve times* the distance of Saturn's orbit. More.'

Muree tapped a screen. 'A floor area, then, of a hundred and twenty astronomical units times twenty kilometres,' Muree said, knowing her voice was quiet, sounding small. 'If it was all stretched out . . . Wow.'

'But it's *not* stretched out,' Rab said. 'It's a lot more intricate than that. It's basically a kind of travel system. You'll see . . .'

'Not just travel,' Plokhy said, more darkly. 'It's all about control, ultimately. The Frame takes you where it will let you go, not necessarily where you want to go. Why do you think they built it that way? Why do you think I've done my best all these years to keep a hold of my own ship? I relish my independence – even if I have to make a living scooting around the ruins of Uranus and other places . . . Sooner than be trapped in *that* spiderweb. Travel? I go where I like, in the *Styx*. You'll see.'

Muree followed this exchange, but she could see Rab had a more pragmatic attitude to this – Frame – than Plokhy, who seemed to see it all as something sinister.

Well, she thought, maybe they were both right – or both wrong. She'd have to figure it out for herself.

The final docking seemed straightforward to Muree, once the ship had got close enough to the underside of this monstrous piece of engineering.

A massive enough object in itself, the *Styx* edged ever closer to one of a cluster of what were evidently docking ports set into that roof across the sky. The final approach came with both roof and spacecraft travelling at over sixteen hundred kilometres a second, matching relative speeds, and tentatively docking.

Muree vaguely wondered what would have happened if one of the runabouts from the *Lightbird*, small craft designed to allow access to space from within the main ship, had attempted to make this trip, this docking. A craft unknown to the Frame, to its autonomous intelligence, to whatever human controllers assisted it . . .

Plokhy shrugged her shoulders when Muree asked about this. She had her eyes glued to her screens as the docking proceeded, and she didn't turn around as she murmured her answer.

'There is a lot of smartness in the design, all the way through. It's a very old system, centuries old, but it's been continually upgraded through its working life – and it upgrades itself, too. Self-repairing technology can – *improvise* – it can handle pretty much whatever's thrown at it. If it suspected an attack, or even an unauthorised approach, the Frame's systems would report up to human authority. Restrain you if necessary. But then *Styx* is just as smart.' She waved a hand, still staring at her screens. 'So, rather than fight it out, we have two smart systems working to shake hands. What can possibly go wrong? Well, a lot, actually, which is why humans are still involved. Speaking of which—'

She sat back.

'Docking achieved.'

Muree and Rab exchanged a glance. There had been no sense of impact.

Rab smiled. 'Take her word for it.'

'I don't need to,' Muree said. 'I can feel – gravity.' She lifted an empty cup by her chair, dropped it. It fell to the floor – but slowly. 'Spin gravity?'

'Right,' Rab said. 'It's around lunar gravity, one-sixth of Earth, at this radius . . . I guess you'll know all about spin gravity from the Carousel on the *Lightbird*. Same principle. Given a fixed rotation speed, the spin gravity is proportional to the radius. So effective gravity is less, further in. Even out here, it's only enough gravity to be useful, not so much as to strain the whole structure.'

'I think I'm starting to get overwhelmed,' Muree said. She had come to comprehend the Mask, a still vaster structure. But that was just a big dumb bubble – well, not so dumb, if it worked as a hologram to hide the presence of a whole solar system – but *this* was engineering of a scale and complexity and intent that she could barely relate to, barely understand. If you took one enormous generation-starship carousel and wrapped it around a star – granted a dead used-up star – this was what you might get . . .

Plokhy had turned back to her screens. 'Hmm. So we docked minutes ago, and here's a human official already on the way to screen the two of you for your inoculation status. Humans checking humans, still the way, and for once I agree with the protocol. Oh, I nearly forgot. You've got your inoculation sigils?'

Muree showed her right hand, Rab his flesh hand.

'Well, with those things they'll be able to track you from Mask to Wrap. But inoculation and screening goes on all the time, not just because you showed up. Chances are you'll get away with it. Comms can be flaky across the System, given the factors involved over such distance – lightspeed limits, for one thing. But just to be sure . . .'

She produced a pin-like gadget, and pressed it against their sigils in turn. She murmured, 'So your sigils are silent now. If you do need to repeat any of the information you carried, just touch the sigil and say *play*. Glad we remembered to do this before the barrier . . . Getting old, Plokhy . . . In a way it's all because of the Frame. A tremendous technical achievement, but the downside is it's connected the whole of humanity together.'

Muree was starting to see it. 'Oh, OK. So all that interconnectivity is good for doing business and policing and moving people around, but not so good when it comes to containing communicable diseases.'

Plokhy pulled a face. 'That's the reasoning. However, official inoculations are often used to smuggle in other tech – especially trackers. If any of your shipmates from the *Lightbird* are being treated right now, you can bet they'll walk out of there bugged. Whereas I can promise you two a clean bill of health, *and* invisibility.' Plokhy clapped her hands together. 'Anyhow, we're done for now, my work is finished – and you can go face the Frame, and your destiny. I won't tell your bosses where you've gone. Although I might try to invoice them for the ride.' She pointed. 'The way out's over there.'

18

So they stood, the two of them, side by side, cautious in the low apparent gravity, each clasping a small holdall, in front of the exit hatch of the *Styx*.

Now the hatch dilated away, and they passed through a small, cramped airlock. The door closed behind them, and another folded back before them.

Folded back to reveal a vast hall. Or so it seemed to Muree: not so vast as the two-kilometres-wide Carousel of the *Lightbird*, but larger surely than any of the compartments she'd seen within the Mask. And everywhere people were on the move, some masked, some not, some on small vehicles, others on foot, isolated or in groups. Everybody *going* somewhere. A babble of echoing voices.

She looked around, bewildered, as they stepped forward together, and the view opened out. The roof looked pretty high, hundreds of metres up. A high wall behind them, itself hundreds of metres long, if not kilometres, apparently straight, punctuated by doorways – maybe one every hundred metres – doors just like the one she had emerged from.

The light came from cloudy panels set in the roof, and high on the walls. She recognised that light, at least. Lume-light.

At Rab's prompting, she walked away from the entry doors, into the wider spaces.

So much for the ceiling, the architecture. People everywhere, all around them.

And, before her, stretching to right and left, she saw a long cylinder – no, a series of linked cylinders, big ones, a chain, with doors in each section. People milling around, she perceived now, heading into those doors, or emerging. To right and left as far as she could see, the same diorama.

None of this made any sense to her.

Rab was watching her. He held out his hand – the prosthetic, and she took it gratefully, feeling the hardness of the mechanics under the human-soft skin.

He said, 'You OK? You'll get used to it. I don't know how you'd describe it; it's surely like nothing on the starship. This is a – transfer exchange. A travel hub. A station. Where you move from one mode of transport to another. I've checked some of the history – this must be strange to you. But I suspect this basic layout was familiar to millions of people on old Earth, even before the first human reached the Moon, let alone Rossbee.'

She smiled. 'I've spent my whole life in just one form of transport. I'm beginning to see how limited that was.'

'Like I said, you'll get used to it.'

'A *transfer exchange*. So we got out of a spacecraft, and we transfer to—'

He pointed at the linked tubes. 'Into that. A form of train. Come and see. And it's all integrated. From here on we can get *anywhere* in the Solar System. Well, except the Mask and the Wrap around the Sun, I guess. And that's just where we're going. *Anywhere*. Until we drop dead of some exotic plague, or get arrested—'

'Or go crazy.'

Rab snorted. 'Or save mankind. You ask me, and now that I'm looking at it all from outside – from your perspective maybe – I think humanity went monumentally crazy when they built all this, from the Solar Wrap to the Frame, the Mask. The products of centuries of obsessive fear – of inwardness. I was born on Venus, remember, which is a bona fide planet, even if not the one humans evolved on. *That's* where we should all be, on the planets, even if there had to be less of us. Less room, you see. Not all riding around in this huge . . . *cage.*

'On the upside, however, riding the Frame is fun.

'Come on. Let's go find a place.'

They walked together, cautiously.

She pointed at the roof. 'At least I can recognise the lighting. Lumes, right?'

'Of course, lumes. You'd know about that. If the whole Solar System is connected up by trains, so it is all powered by the lumes. They say about ten million of them in the whole Frame network, strung out a couple of thousand kilometres apart, giving enough light, with reflection and refraction, that the whole of the Frame is illuminated as brightly as Earth once was by the Sun. There are light pipes, reflectors—'

'Wow . . . But that's going to drain the lumes quickly.'

'So it is. I believe they all need to be replaced in the course of each year . . .'

This was horrific to Muree. She found it hard to concentrate on her surroundings, even as Rab gently led her forward. *Ten million lumes a year? Used up and discarded? If so there had to be a trapped population of breeders, hundreds and thousands of them perhaps* . . . She recoiled from the raw numbers.

They were approaching the 'train' now. Units that Rab called 'coaches'.

Focus, Muree.

A flight of steps led down from the main concourse level to a door on the side of one of those big cylinders. The door slid open and shut as people approached it, waving their hands at it before climbing inside.

Muree stumbled a little descending those steps in the low gravity.

When they got to the bottom, the big door panel wouldn't open to them. Rab touched his hand – his good hand – to a small side-panel, and encouraged Muree to do the same. Rab muttered, 'This is low-grade security. It's not raising the alarm, but it hasn't seen "us" before, and it does need to tell whether we carry infectious diseases it knows about, or other horrors it can detect – even a bomb in your stomach cavity, say . . . Give it a minute.'

She was tiring in the gravity, low as it was; she shifted from one leg to the other to rest her muscles. 'Is there much of that kind of threat?'

'I don't know. The rail system is high energy; only one bad guy needs to get through to make a huge mess . . . Say, are you OK? I should have thought – there are booths with seats where we could have waited.'

'I'm fine,' she lied.

He shrugged. 'It's meant to be around lunar gravity – one-sixth of Earth's. Spin gravity—'

'I know. We use it on the *Lightbird*, remember. That's a full Earth gravity. But on nothing like this scale.'

'I guess not . . .'

And the door of the carriage finally slid open.

Rab led the way inside, confidently. 'Phew,' he said. 'he tapped his hand. At least my sigil's let me pay for the journey. Open-ended tickets for now. We'll be charged for as long as we ride. Good old Plokhy. '

Once within, as Rab led her through into 'their' coach, Muree was surprised how much room there was.

It was less like a spacecraft than a long, tubular building, with three or four storeys, connected by staircases and elevators. Rab chose a stair that took them through the upper levels. On each floor, aside from open areas set with couches and what looked like restaurant facilities, there were sealed-off rooms, even whole clusters of rooms, which Rab called 'villas'.

'These places can take whole families,' he said. 'Or other groups. Work teams. Military detachments . . . Here we go. An empty villa. If a small one.' He made to touch a panel, set in the door frame. 'If I swipe we'll be registering our presence yet again. Our false identities—'

Muree shrugged. She felt she ought to be more positive about this, confused as she felt. 'Let them chase us. Go for it.'

'Done.' He touched the panel.

The door slid back to reveal a kind of lounge. Seating, cupboards that looked like they held food, drink. More doors led off to other rooms.

Rab led the way in. 'There'll be a bathroom, a kitchen, stored food. A bedroom or two. All small but usable . . .' He was studying her. 'Let's just rest for now, do you think? You OK?'

She sat, cautiously, at a table. 'All this is very strange. A structure that spans the Solar System. With bathrooms. And *sofas*. Cosmic mundanity.'

He grinned. 'Well, you'd get complaints without the sofas and stuff. And the facilities do self-clean between passengers, if you're worried about that. You'll get used to it. If you need anything just say so. Or just ask. Like this.' He tapped the top of the low table between them. The top slid back, revealing trays of drinks, food in anonymous wraps.

She took a bottle of water, which opened itself when she raised it to her mouth. 'So here we are on a vast – wheel.'

'Or centrifuge, if you like.'

'How vast?'

He smiled. 'With a pivot on the location of the Sun, and a rim out here, at the orbit of Saturn . . .'

'Like our Carousel. On the scale of planets?'

'More like the scale of planetary orbits . . .'

'But, huge as it is, it's all – closed in. Uniform.'

He nodded. 'Safe, though?'

'. . . I guess.'

'You have to understand the – psychology – of people here. As it was after the Neptune attack anyhow. Misunderstood as that attack was, maybe. In response, your ancestors fled to other stars.

'But here, people fled into the past, if you like. Into a cosier time, when we thought we lived in a cosier, safer universe.

'And we *fell back*, psychologically – at least this is what I think, and I've seen a lot of the Solar System, and the people who live in it – we *fell back*, kind of, to the inner System. But not the system as it exists. A kind of primordial mental model of it. The Solar System the ancients knew. Before the telescope was invented, they had counted six planets, including their own: Mercury, Venus, Earth, Mars, Jupiter, Saturn. Planets you could *see* with the naked eye. After the attack, people fell back in their thinking on those six – as if that was all there was around us. It was a strange – regression. Just go back to what you can see, a nice orderly array of planets . . .'

Muree did get some of that, she thought. 'OK. So the further planet, Uranus, didn't – *count*. Because you can't see it with the naked eye from Earth.'

'Right. We just used that as a resource lode to build all this. You saw that. As for the rest, there was that genius called the Architect, who had this grand vision . . . Well. Maybe we'll get to see more of it.'

'You said something about finding out more about this Architect.'

'Yeah. Before we left the Mask, I asked around. It's said that there is some kind of memorial to it all on Mars, or maybe Earth. Or maybe both. Maybe designed by the Architect themselves. There's a side-legend that it's in a place of stability – of *extreme* stability. So it will endure, I guess . . . . But Earth is mostly off limits now. I kept my ears open. Tried not to give away why I'm asking about this stuff.'

All this felt abstract to Muree, in the circumstances. She picked up her water bottle, closed it, let it drop slowly to the table between them.

Spin gravity.

She really was in a structure the size of the Solar System. And it was spinning.

What was she doing here? Sinking through a fantasy dream of some long-gone visionary, evidently driven to the point of insanity by the battering of the Solar System . . .

No, she told herself. They were challenging that madness, that deep psychological flaw.

There was a soft jolt. When she glanced around, Muree saw that this 'train' was in motion. Sitting here, still and peaceful, with barely any sense of motion after that initial push, it was as if the great hall of the 'station' was sliding back around her.

Rab seemed distracted by the view outside the windows, by the people gathering in little knots, various bots rolling across the concourse floor.

He said, 'You know, when I first got to ride the Frame, I was – astonished. I was already working – still on Venus, studying engineering – and Venus itself had been extensively engineered, long ago. But a mere planetary rebuild was nothing compared to *this*. The Frame. All built by humans . . . Think of it. An integrated piece of machinery the size of the Solar System. All carefully stabilised and balanced. And the dimensions – here it's set just outside Saturn's orbit, to allow for the orbit's ellipticity.

'It's basically a track, about twenty kilometres wide – wide enough that people can *live* on it. And there are six more tracks, one for each planet. The foundation is the equivalent of rock ten metres thick. Creating *that* pretty much used up about half the mass of Earth's Moon. I said that the spin gravity out here is set at one-sixth standard Earth, about lunar gravity . . . I think that was meant as a kind of tribute to the wrecked Moon. And it's all powered and lit up by lumes.'

The mention of the use of lumes made Muree uneasy again.

'OK. And the spin gravity—'

'Where we are sitting we're tracking a tremendous circle, and the faster you go the greater the centrifugal force. We face a few days of acceleration – a fraction of Earth standard, and you'll barely notice it, because the furnishing in the carriages moulds itself subtly around you – and eventually, in this train, we'll hit sixteen hundred kilometres per second. That is, relative to the track, which is itself moving at a similar speed – these are *fast* transports. At full speed the centrifugal forces hit two thirds of Earth's gravity . . . and we'll be travelling, every day, one astronomical unit – that's the distance between Sun and Earth, per day.

'It can get a little giddying. With the lumes spaced one every two thousand kilometres along the course of the whole Frame, it gets bewildering to the naked eye – two a second. In fact we'll have to filter that out, smooth it out, if we want to get any sleep—'

She held up a hand. 'Sleep, you say. Enough with the stats. I have a feeling my best option is to sleep through it.'

He grinned, self-deprecating. 'Am I showing off? Sorry. And you're no bewildered tourist—'

'"The whole Frame," though. You say that. It really is a single object that spans the Solar System, or what's left of it. Uniting the surviving worlds.'

'Yeah. As well as being useful, I think it was meant to *symbolise* the unity, the recovery of mankind. A very obvious symbol, spanning the sky. But it's a practical system in terms of travel. I'll show you.'

He poured a little water out of his flask, spilled it on the tabletop, and used a forefinger to sketch concentric circles, with lines arrowing into the centre of the display.

'You get the idea, don't you? So to get from Saturn to Mercury, say, first you follow the Saturn-orbit track, until you reach one of the radial tracks, and you change trains to drop down towards the centre. At the junction of the radius with the Mercury track, you transfer again and go as near as the Frame will take you to where the planet is in its orbit. And then a short hop in an interplanetary craft to your destination.'

Muree was struggling to process what she had learned. 'I travelled between the stars. I thought that was the limit of human ambition. But this . . .' She was lost for words.

He grinned. 'It's either crazy, or brilliant, right? I've had this reaction from some of your crewmates, who have seen some of this. The numbers *are* incredible. Twenty-four *billion* kilometres of track. On average twenty kilometres wide, ten metres thick – that doesn't seem very much but it's very smart material.'

'But the Sun is exhausted. Yes? So all the radiant energy you need for life, for civilisation, has to come from lumes? And this has gone on for centuries.'

He angled his head, studied her. 'I think, before I met you, I never thought much about the plight of the lumes.'

'What did you think about?'

He shrugged. 'My work, mostly.'

'And now?'

He raised his arm, and landed his artificial hand on a table surface with a thump.

'People, I guess. The people riding around inside this huge – clockwork. I mean, not just myself. My mother's – agony. And doubt.

'But the doubt was always there. Maybe. You know, there's a lot of double-thinking. The Mask is the outer defence perimeter of the Solar System. That's what it's *for*. But if you live there, if you just look around, you can *see* the – the doubt. There's been no more aggression, if that was what it was, for a thousand years. And in that time we humans have actually begun to repeat the planetary crime that befell Neptune in the first place, according to the official story.'

'By taking Uranus apart?'

'Yeah. And all for – what?' He angled his head. 'Was it a misapprehension. A monumental mistake? And another mistake, when they built the starships like *Lightbird*, and people went off to live and die in space, or on the lethal surface of planets like Rossbee.'

'Requiring sacrifices like my twin sister.' She forced a smile. 'So we both hold grudges. And all of it untruths – maybe. Misunderstandings first maybe, deliberate lies that followed. Lies that are still being told to us.'

'Maybe.' He blew out his cheeks. 'Half an hour in the Frame and we're crashing through taboos already. 'So what are we going to do about it?'

'Find the truth, I guess – whatever the truth is. And then . . .'

The carriage swept under a brilliant light: a lume, Muree saw, caged, high above the track, glowing like a piece of the Sun itself.

Clumsy in the low gravity, she ran to a window, watched it pass.

From here she could see the line of the track, lume-shining in the masked dark of the Solar System. Dead straight, in either direction.

As far as she could see.

19

By the tenth day of the chase, his own interminable ride through this monstrous Frame, Brad Tenant was getting sick of it. With only Lieutenant Planter for company. Waiting for this great wheel to *deliver* him somewhere.

You'd think a generation-starship passenger would be used to monotonous travel. But the *Lightbird* had been a world in itself, if small, mobile. A place where you had a *job*. This was like a mobile prison, not a world. Despite the obvious distraction facilities, the virtual theatres, the gymnasiums – when you could access them.

They weren't alone, of course. He and Lieutenant Planter. There were other passengers around, and at first Brad was intrigued by glimpses he got of bona fide civilian citizens of this strange solar system, as opposed to the command elite of the Mask.

But he soon learned that a healthy proportion of the passengers on this transport weren't passengers at all, but *residents*.

Brad knew that people still lived on the planets – even a few on Earth – under the light and warmth of the lumes. But there was plenty of room to live aboard the Frame, and he started to wonder how many people did just that – spend their whole lives *on the Frame*, in the dull comfort of the carriages, a journey that never *ended* anywhere.

But then this Frame was a *big* construction, bigger than his imagination seemed able to cope with. It had the surface area of a *thousand* Earths, and now united and hosted a population that was perhaps a thousand times a once-crowded Earth's maximum numbers. When he thought about that, about the sheer scale of the operation needed to keep all those people alive – let alone the mundane mission of taking bona fide network travellers to the right destinations – Brad's head spun.

It was a marvel. And he was already sick of it all.

Sick of the very obvious dimming of the interior cabin lights, the so-carefully adjusted opacity of the windows over a twenty-four-hour cycle – clearly based on the turning of old Earth itself, a day-night cycle humans had evidently stuck to wherever they had gone.

Sick of having to absorb the fact that he and Lieutenant Jeo Planter had no control over their mandated pursuit. They were not going to have the slightest chance of getting hold of their prey, not until Rab and Muree alighted somewhere – because *they* were, evidently, in a train somewhere ahead of their pursuers, in this great Frame.

Some chase this was.

Even when they got a report that the fugitives had been spotted changing trains at a radial junction – they seemed to be heading for Mars – all Brad and Planter could do was to patiently wait until the Frame delivered them through the same journey of curves and lines in space. Trains on single lines didn't overtake. In this chase, the pursuers had no control over the pursued.

And that was despite the monumental effort it had seemed to take to get this extraordinary mode of transport in operation in the first place. Planter, in one call back to the Mask, demanded to know why an independent craft, like Plokhy's *Styx*, couldn't have been used in a far more flexible pursuit. But discretion, it seemed, was all: secrecy was dominant over speed.

But what distracted Brad the most, what disturbed his sleep even, was the, to him, very perceptible flickering of the lume-light that illuminated the Frame itself, the whole of its monstrous, Solar-System-spanning length. At full speed they passed one lume every *second* or so, every heartbeat, through the train's arbitrarily defined cycle of day and night.

He thought back to the lumes aboard the *Lightbird*, tended so skilfully and kindly by Muree, assisted by Brad and others when she let them. Every one of those, Muree would swear, was an individual in its own right, each sentient, each different yet allied to its peers – every one of them a live, thinking, feeling *being*. By comparison, he had been told that over ten *million* such beings at any moment were labouring in this vast Frame, every one as unique and individual as those Muree and her colleagues had cared for – had sometimes even given *names* to – but every one of them here isolated through its whole life.

Still, he did his best to put such thoughts out of his mind. Because he knew his reactions were being watched, by Planter. He didn't wish to show any weakness, of any kind.

Similarly he did his best not to ask Planter too many questions about the casual technological miracles all around him, in this unexpected world.

Unexpected it was, though. In his heart he supposed he had imagined, before arriving here aboard the *Lightbird*, that Sol system would be more or less similar to his own home system, with its one not-quite-uninhabitable rocky world where human settlements had been established, a couple of gas giants, a super Earth into whose deep gravity well – twice as deep as Earth's – a handful of helium miners had cautiously ventured. Well, maybe home would look like *this* sometime in the future, after a few thousand years of space-bound civilisation. If you could call this concatenation of monstrous artefacts and penned-in humans a civilisation at all.

It was all a constant conceptual bombardment, for him. But would he have refused making the trip, this Frame journey, if he'd known it was like this? If he'd had the choice to refuse . . .

And, not to have *seen* this – he probably would have spent the rest of his life regretting it if he had missed this chance. Despite the security restrictions. Despite the fact that he hadn't exactly volunteered for this mission. Despite the fact that he understood little of what he was seeing and hated most of it. Despite the taciturn company of the cop he was riding with. He had learned a lot, not so much about the engineering as the people and culture of this strange, flawed Solar System.

But as the journey wore on, and he adjusted to the sheer scale of it all, and was able to *think* again, he began to have doubts. This construction was enormous on a human scale, but, in a sense, not *overwhelming*. After all he and his crewmates, family and ancestors, had once crossed the stars . . .

He did try to talk over his feelings with the Lieutenant.

'Come on,' Planter said one morning. 'So you're stuck in a cabin on a speeding vessel. You grew up on a starship! A journey like this ought to be a walk in the park for you. If you know what a park is.'

'We had parks on our starship,' Brad retorted, bristling at another lazy put-down. 'The parks were nothing like *this*, this – rickety scaffolding. And at least on the ship we were going somewhere. Here, we're hurtling along in a great fixed framework, in a flimsy tube, at a huge speed . . . following tracks laid down by billions of others, probably . . . Doesn't it all seem futile to you? Everybody dashing around this huge web? I mean ... a track system more than a hundred astronomical units long –'

'More than a hundred and fifty.'

'I mean, why are so many people on the move, on such a scale. What's the point of it?'

Planter seemed to think it over. 'The point of it – is the thing itself. I guess. Look, this Solar System of ours is interlinked – in terms of resource provision, for instance. Water from Saturn's moons is used to feed the big population on Mars. Food from Venus, likewise. You're talking billions of people, all needing to be provisioned, continually.'

'OK. So there would be some human passengers to go along with all that. But not so many as are crammed into trains like this, scaled up across the whole Solar System. What's the economics in that?'

'Well, a lot of people with essential skill sets do get moved around, you know.'

'Like Rab Callis. He would have been moved to Mercury, right? But his mother ended up taking his place –'

Planter sighed. 'That episode follows me around. But that's a valid example. The Venus farms are hard work, but not so hard as the mines of Mercury. And so people might go from Mercury to Venus willingly enough, but not the other way around. But both Venus and Mercury have to be worked . . . And people grow old, or retire . . . There has to be a flow of people to keep all those work stations fulfilled.'

Brad thought that over. 'OK. But – the scale of this thing. And it seems to busy, day and night. Surely there doesn't have to be that much traffic, the freight, the people . . . A roadway connecting planets!'

Planter regarded him. 'OK. You have a point. You tell me. Why do you think we built this huge web of roads, why we encourage so much human traffic.'

Brad thought about that. 'Because it *is* huge. Because it

contains the whole Solar System. Because wherever you go, you can never forget – because you can *see* it – you never forget that you're just a tiny part of a huge machine, that you can never get out of it.'

Planter thought that over. 'That's a reasonable way of thinking about it. Although you make it sound punitive. Many people think it's – wonderful. Hmm. You look doubtful. Whatever. Anyhow I've spent most of my career in law enforcement, remember – and here I am back again, thanks to those two fugitives, I guess – and when I was on the tail of bandits or vandals or fugitives I didn't have time to indulge any phobias or prejudices. The job itself was always the top priority for me. *That* was what was trained into me.'

He paused, thinking further. 'I do know that there are some people who do nothing *but* ride the Frame. Never getting off save to change tracks. There are kids born, people die – I guess that's inevitable. There are people who spend their *entire life* on the Frame.'

Brad shook his head. 'That's – crazy.'

Planter shrugged. 'I wouldn't say so. Some call them the "dazzled". Live, work, die on the Frame. Have kids of their own. There's plenty of room! Maybe they're an extreme case, but I think there are a lot of people who are "dazzled" to some extent.'

'Dazzled, and easily controlled.'

'I'm an ex-cop. That's a good thing, for me. The Frame is just a means to an end. If it bewilders people, if it makes them feel controlled – well, good. To fret about such things is just weakness. You do the job, whatever. Oh, enough. Look. We have to work together, *now,* to resolve this transgression. The irresponsible abscondment of Rab and Muree – one of mine, one of yours. But this isn't your environment – even though you are subject to its laws and strictures, as am I, as is everybody on the

Frame. Well, we've got through ten days already, but five more to the interchange with the first radial track that will take us inwards.

'I suspect the chase won't end there. Our two refugees seem to be hiding themselves well so far. And interchanges are busy places . . .'

Planter kept talking, theorising, planning, mapping contingencies.

Brad tuned him out, and tried to sleep.

Time wore on, some hours rushing by, some crawling past.

Brad began to count the days more assiduously.

And he tried to keep up a routine. Two long walks per day, for instance, when the varying acceleration or deceleration allowed it. Also jogs when he found an empty stretch.

Not that there was ever anything new to see. Compartments, some closed, some open, some empty – maybe fifty per cent empty, in fact. People, generally scattered sparsely – there was *room* on this monstrous construction – people who sometimes looked out through their doors as he passed, some friendly, some suspicious, most indifferent. Some who didn't look out at all. Mostly the same people in the same compartment as the day before, he came to see, but not always. He wondered if people just moved for the fun of it, from one identical compartment to another, or if the authorities occasionally intervened, hauling miscreants off to some cell somewhere. Or even, maybe there were medical emergencies he hadn't been aware of.

There were limits to how far he could go, in either direction. Planter told him that passengers weren't allowed into freight cars, generally.

What freight? Materials of all kinds. And, Planter said, notably *water*. The lifeblood of terrestrial life, on new worlds now sustained by train-loads of the stuff. As if the Frame comprised the veins and arteries of some vast body.

And eventually, as yet again he followed his well-trodden linear route, Brad thought he glimpsed their first destination, up ahead. A cluster of lights in a kind of misty wall, orange, faint.

This was the fifteenth day.

He ran back to Planter, in their compartment.

But he slowed as he reached the door. Not wanting to seem naïve, the eager boy from the toy starship, in front of this sophisticated product of a sophisticated, integrated civilisation that dwarfed his own. He refused to give that impression, but probably failed.

Planter was sitting in what he called his 'reading' posture, legs crossed, one arm wrapped around his chest, the other holding his wrist bangle up to his ear – a bit of command-echelon tech he hadn't shared with Brad.

Brad himself just sat down and waited. He suspected most if not all Planter's messages were from his commanders at the Mask. If they concerned their quest in chase of Muree and Rab, Brad would no doubt hear what he needed to hear, eventually.

At last Planter spoke. 'I thought you were walking.' He closed his eyes, rubbed the bangle.

Brad knew he probably ought to be reticent, to make some kind of more sophisticated communication out of what he'd seen. But he was too eager. Simple as that.

'*Today I saw Saturn.*'

Planter looked at him, smiled a very superior smile. 'Good for you. I do keep forgetting you're a tourist.'

Brad felt patronised, and not for the first time. And not for the first time he struck back. 'In the Rossbee system we have two ringed planets, both ice giants—'

Planter held up a hand. 'Ah, then you win. Oh, come show me Saturn, then.'

Still more deeply patronising.

So they walked back the way Brad had come, along the length of the train segment, by the flickering, one-per-second beat of the lume lights, past compartments mostly occupied, it seemed, some open, some not . . .

Patronising. Brad had long had the feeling that Planter was patronising by default. With such power as he seemed to have over his fellow citizens, and an attitude that seemed to say that he also *knew* better what they needed than they knew themselves – poor Rab had been *better off* to be mutilated – a bit of loftiness was to be expected. But that didn't make it easier to take.

They passed through one more carriage, and came to one with an outer wall that was all window. Brad had run through this often, during his regular jogs, but it had always been deserted. Now there were a few people looking out at the view.

When they saw Planter's Lieutenant uniform, some drifted further away.

Planter looked around. 'You can see these cabins aren't so popular. Near the front end of the passenger carriages, near the viewing windows. People don't want tourists like you picnicking by their beds. Anyhow, so there it is: Saturn, just as you said.'

Brad turned to see, again.

In enhanced light, the disc of the planet was obvious, obscuring the deeper darkness beyond. He saw sparks purposefully crossing that huge face, their glow reflecting from turbulent clouds: spacecraft, surely. Beyond them, more sparks, more diffuse – as if there were craft working through the high clouds themselves.

Now Planter pointed out the moons, one after another. In the plane of the planet's equator, they were mere sparks of light. And in that plane Brad made out a fine line, broken in places, again apparently illuminated only by faint pinpoints.

The rings of Saturn, seen edge-on. So Planter said.

He gestured. 'All of this in shadow, of course, now that the Wrap has extinguished the Sun. What a sight it must have been before that. Now the illumination you see comes only from human activities, the sparking energies of our ships' drives. Everybody has heard about Saturn's rings . . .'

Brad hadn't. Planter showed him ancient images. To Brad the rings looked – impossible. Artificial, maybe. He wondered what else had been lost when the sunlight was lost.

'. . . And the moons – once this planet had more than two hundred *named* moons, and many smaller. This is one instance where the restoration of sunlight really would reveal great glory.'

'I have seen the old images. On the ship. I agree, it was a spectacular sight, if they did it justice.'

'But after the Neptune invasion – well, humanity had to protect all its treasures. If they came for Neptune, we thought, and then Uranus, then Saturn would be on the list, some day. But that didn't happen. Instead – look what Saturn has become instead.'

Brad felt oddly dismayed. 'What? What has it become?'

'Why, the pivot of the Solar System. The *human* system. The anchor of the Frame itself.'

They walked a little further, to another open area – without opaque cabin walls or roof, just windows, seats affixed to the floor. A viewing area, evidently.

Planter gestured for Brad to sit down.

'This is the Frame, Brad, and Saturn is its pivot. You know the scheme by now. We'll soon pass Saturn itself and go on a few more astronomical units to the spoke. An extension of the Frame, anchored to the ring we're following, a radial limb that reaches down towards the centre, the Sun. We'll drop down that spoke through seven or eight AU down to the Mars Frame-ring. And along there, a short ride of a couple of AU on the Mars ring to the planet itself—'

'Mars? Why not Jupiter? We're chasing Muree and Rab. Why wouldn't they go there? Or even stay here, at Saturn? The gas giants – big places to hide . . .'

Planter shrugged. 'Yes, but Saturn and Jupiter are basically industrial facilities – mines, if you like. Nobody goes there save to work, or to pass through to the inner System. And they have low populations, paradoxically enough. Try to hide there and you'll soon be discovered.'

'Whereas Mars—'

'Mars is essentially a city. A quarter of a billion. Plenty of places to hide. Plenty of secrets to dig up.' He looked at Brad. 'A city. I suppose you can't imagine that.'

Brad sat back. Settlements on Rossbee, under domes, held no more than tens of thousands of people each. Not that Brad, born on the starship, had seen any of those, even.

At length, he said, 'No, I can't. Probably.'

'Maybe you'll get to see Mars. Well, definitely, we need to go down there, unless we strike it lucky and find our refugees up *here*, hiding in the infrastructure. I've ordered screenings of the transit areas here, but most likely they'll have gone on further already.'

Rab thought that over. 'If the Saturn system is industrial, what is mined here?'

Planter considered. 'I'm not supposed to be over-briefing you, on this assignment. Fair question, though, not classified, and one that would be easy to research, so I'll tell you.'

So much for mutual trust, Brad thought.

'From Saturn itself we take essential gases – nitrogen, nature's essential buffer for habitat atmospheres. Helium isotopes for fusion fuel – the optimal fuel if you don't have the core of a star handy.' He waved a hand. 'Why, all of *this*, the Frame, is powered by helium-3 fusion, save for the lumes for their light. As to the rest – water. Simple as that. That's what they mine here, from the ice moons.' He studied Brad. 'I know that you are new to the Solar System. But you know already that there are trillions of human beings alive here today.'

'*Trillions*. You said so before. I . . . suppose I knew that. Hard to take in.'

'Well, it's true. It's thought to be multiple times the population of Earth at its peak, before supplies from space industries began to replace the extraction of resources from the planet itself.

'And such a population needs a lot of essentials.

'Just take water – I was once an overseer of the Venus water supply chain. Every human being alive needs something like two tonnes of water per day – that includes industrial purposes and so on, as well as drinking water. That number hasn't much changed since Earth was alone. Five *trillion* people need ten *trillion* tonnes of water per day, suitably distributed around the Solar System. And that's what we provide.'

'. . . Oh. And I'm guessing the Frame is used to ship all that water around the System.'

'Correct. The most basic need after air, and the first to be transported en masse. And most of it extracted from Saturn's moons.'

'But it can't last for ever.'

'That's true. Take Titan, for instance, the largest moon. If

Titan were all water, you'd have about ten billion times the daily human consumption, given the scale of the population now.'

'So it would last ten billion days—'

'Which is about thirty million years. And you can stretch that a lot with recycling, waste capture. The whole Solar System an integrated life support system.'

'And then what?'

He grinned. 'Then we'll think of something else.'

Brad looked around again, at the vast panorama of Saturn and its moons. 'You've united the Solar System, at least physically—'

'And logistically.'

Brad nodded. 'As if it were all one vast starship – a generation starship like the *Lightbird*. I can see that. I can see that everybody, every capable adult, can find a role in this vast system. I can even see the need for all this transport, all this travel—'

'Everybody gets trained up on a lot of professions. Mostly people cycle between the big centres, Mars, Earth, Venus. It makes for a – flexible culture. Wherever they are, everybody, every competent adult, can summon a flexible response in an emergency—'

'Nobody has a base.'

'Nobody but the duly appointed government,' Planter said.

'But I also grew up understanding that on such a ship you need tight political restraints on whoever is in charge. If a captain decided to turn off the oxygen, everybody would be dead in seconds. That's quite a power to hold. Here, you don't control the air, directly—'

Or did they? He knew he had a lot to learn.

'But the water supply is a pretty useful weapon to wield. All this control. And for what?'

'You know for what. In case the Neptune raiders return.'

'But there were no Neptune raiders.'

Planter touched his lips with his fingers. 'Perhaps not. But we did think so, once. Who knows, maybe we were right the first time?'

'You don't believe that—'

'And now – well, isn't this a better way? To keep everyone safe and calm and fed and happy, with a small lie . . .'

'A *small* lie?'

Planter frowned. 'I thought I made it clear. *Keep your voice down.* Anyhow, now do you see why we need to get hold of Muree and Rab? I'll put it in terms you'll understand. Just suppose they were running amok on a generation starship – *and they were the only ones who knew they were on a spacecraft* – wouldn't you shut them down?'

Brad had no answer.

But he saw that Planter's frown had deepened, even as he stared into the air, studying some virtual display only he could see.

Brad reached out instinctively. Pulled his hand back. 'Are you OK?'

Planter didn't turn his head, but he smiled. 'We got them.'

Brad stared. 'Muree and Rab?'

'Muree and Rab.' Now Planter did turn his head, and looked direct at Brad. 'We got them. I was right. They're heading to Mars.'

20

In the end, to get to Mars via the Frame, from the junction of the Saturn ring and the first radial strut, took them twelve days – eight descending the strut to the Mars orbital ring, and then four more days following that ring to its closest approach to the planet itself.

All that way, little to see.

Even from the closest approach of the Frame to the planet, and with much magnification, Brad first saw Mars as little more than a ghost, a landscape softly lit by sparse threads that might have been transport tracks. A shadow against the deeper, empty background of the masked sky. Even when he and Jeo Planter had boarded a small shuttle craft – the two of them and a score of other passengers – to fly them down from the Frame to the planet, at first there was still little to see save a spreading blot, a deeper darkness against the charcoal-grey of the sky.

At last, though, there was an elusive thread, which Brad saw as a finely textured loop, apparently circling the planet – and leaking light over a still dimly seen landscape below, and with more dangling threads beneath.

This structure was synchronous, Planter told him: a ring, complete and entire, closely orbiting the planet, but matching its very Earth-like twenty-four-hour period. Beanstalk towers connected sky to ring, set about half the planet's radius above the surface, to ground, combining the whole into a single vast structure circling its equator . . .

No, Brad thought, *vast* was too strong a word if you had witnessed the Frame itself, which spanned interplanetary distances, not just planetary. Impressive enough, though.

And, of course, a lack of sunlight.

Aside from sources on the synchronous ring, and a clutter of spacecraft around it, no light fell on the planet from above, and there was little enough glow from the landscape itself, only the lights of apparently scattered human habitations – some of which seemed very bright.

Brad had been born on a starship, he had never seen a planetary system before arriving at the Mask, and he realised that if he'd been born only a generation or two earlier he might have died on that starship before the completion of the *Lightbird*'s long journey.

But he knew enough to know, peering down at Mars, that this was all *wrong*.

He had grown up amid imagery and descriptions of the planetary system from which his thousand-year-gone ancestors had left. And he knew in the abstract what a planetary system was supposed to *be*: like Rossbee, with a star at the centre, the planets hanging in their orbits like pendants, each with one face illuminated by the light of the central star, one face turned away, waiting for that world's own revolution to take lands and seas, ice plains and lava flows – and humans, if any lived there – to take them all into the light of the sun-star. He recalled now those images of the prototype of all such systems, as far as humanity was concerned: Sol itself, not just *a* sun but *the* Sun; the planets, including old Earth. Planets so near and bright they could have been seen by naked human eyes – and named from antiquity. As, for example, Mars.

Nobody but himself, on this small shuttle, cautiously approaching, seemed to think there was anything strange about a planet defined only by a silhouette. Not even starlight.

Certainly not his sour companion Planter, who had walked on some of these worlds before – notably Venus, Brad knew, where he had performed his act of legalised mutilation.

But now, anyhow, came Brad's own first ever planetfall.

In the last hours on the Frame, Planter had been all business.

Before he allowed Brad to don his pressure suit for the transit to the surface, he took him back into the small cabin they shared, kicked closed the door.

And he produced an object like a small pistol.

'Give me your hand.'

'As you once said to Rab Callis . . . Sorry. Bad joke. Which arm?'

'Whichever isn't dominant.'

Left, then. He held out his arm.

Planter took the hand and held it tight – tight enough to hurt. *Serves me right,* Brad thought gloomily.

Now Planter took a swab and brushed his palm. It was some kind of oil, smooth, cold.

'Hold still.'

Now he held the gun-gadget against Brad's palm, pressed it – and there was a sharp snapping noise, and a sting in the palm that faded quickly.

Planter released him, and started to pack up his kit.

Brad dried off the palm, shook his hand. A slight itch quickly faded. 'What was that?'

'This is the seat of government for the whole of the human

Solar System. Everybody who lands here has to be tagged.' He held up his own hand. 'See? Had mine first done years ago, refreshed since. No scars. Don't go scraping it out in your sleep, or whatever. Even I couldn't talk you out of the holding cells they have down there.'

He tucked the kit into a pocket of his jacket.

Then, at last, to Brad's relief, they started talking about the destination.

They were to come down at Planter's chosen site, along with a cohort of other passengers, in a small private shuttlecraft – as opposed to a public vehicle – because Planter wanted them to be as anonymous as possible, all the better for catching Rab and Muree unawares. (*If* they were here at all, Brad thought.) And at Planter's insistence, both of them would wear pressure suits, without helmets, open at the neck, throughout the descent, so they could debark as soon as the shuttle landed.

A few more hours to wait.

A descent into a Mars without sunlight.

Still, there were lights in the darkness, at least. Brad, eager, leaned to see. As the shuttle continued its descent, at last he started to see some kind of texture in the darkened landscape below – a scattering of lights, apparently suspended in the thin Martian air, some of them bright enough and high enough to illuminate swathes of the ground. And on that ground now, he could make out long, straight-line shadows. Geometrical forms, circles, oblongs, lines that were obviously some kind of transport network. Maybe it was some kind of ground-version of the Frame technology. And at the obvious junctions of the network were more clusters of lights – that, and deep, dark scars in the ground.

Lieutenant Planter was watching Brad, not the scenery. 'With luck we won't spend much time down there . . . So what do you make of it?'

'I don't know what I'm seeing. Industry? Mining? I grew up in a spacecraft, remember. I don't know a great deal about what you do with a planetary surface. Still less *this* planet. I did look it up. I thought it was pretty much dormant – right? Smaller than Earth or Venus, lost all of its inner heat long ago. I'd have thought there'd be little that's useful to start with, and what there is would be mined out quickly.'

Planter pursed his lips. 'Not a bad appraisal considering you grew up inside of a tin can. Yes, compared to Earth with its core of liquid iron, Mars is pretty dormant, geologically – but not entirely. And the water isn't that plentiful – not compared to Earth, or even sources like Saturn – but it's not negligible, either. Enough for a start, although now Mars relies on imports.'

He glanced again, out at the complex landscape below.

'Only two significant settlements – aside from a scatter of smaller communities along the main roads. We're going to land at Hellas – you'll see. The political centre, the concentration of population. Right now we're passing over the other main settlement. A place called Cerberus Fossae, in an area known as Elysium Planitia.' He pointed. 'Just down there. The name means "heavenly plains" or something like that. And just here there's a mantle plume.'

'A . . . what?'

'Umm, a rocky planet's mantle is a layer of hot, liquid rock under the solid surface. Outside the deeper, even hotter core. If there are currents in the mantle you get fissures in the crust, earthquakes – lava flows that endure on million-year timescales. Here it's all a by-product of the great Olympus volcanoes. Most massive in the Solar System, and they perturb the geology across a swathe of the planet. Pushing up the crust and upper mantle, you see. Cerberus itself is a planet-scale feature.

'And so if you set up your colony just here you get heat, and fresh mantle rock to mine, and even water, forced out of the rock.'

'Water, on Mars?'

Planter eyed him. 'Water, the key to everything, everywhere humans go. Which is why so much of the capacity of the Frame is devoted to shipping it around the System. But if you have it on hand, you use that. Mars has some, not much compared to Titan – let alone Earth – but some. As I recall Mars has a human population of a quarter billion, and enough water to sustain that population for thirty thousand years. It makes economic sense to use it while it lasts. A lot cheaper than to ship it in from Saturn.'

Brad said, 'It's a proper planet, then. A functioning human world.'

Planter looked at him curiously. 'You grew up on a starship, and you never *saw* a functioning human world before.'

'True. But I can see why people would come here to work. A proper world, with gravity, and geology, and resources—'

Planter blinked. 'You see *why* they would come? You're still not getting it, kid. People don't *choose* to come here. Even the management and law enforcement layers are on assignment, not – voluntary. As for the workforce . . .' He studied Brad. 'Crime and punishment. What do you do about miscreants on a starship? You know, I never thought to ask that. Who does the dirty work?'

'There are volunteer police. You get trained up, assigned, rotated out – whether you like it or not, by the way.'

'And the miscreants?'

'Keep them isolated while they're re-educated. Show them

how wrong they were; give them some alternative responsibility. Train them up.'

'You'd always keep an eye on them, though?'

Brad shrugged. 'I don't know much about it. Never had to. There are supervision systems, hierarchies. Not my business, I never worked in that kind of department.'

Planter grinned. 'I bet you never did. Too young. And I suspect you are too naïve ever to be put in such a role.'

'So you say. There was a rota. If the mission had gone on longer, I would have had to take my turn, I guess. And if the *Lightbird* ever goes back to the stars, and if I go with it, I *would* take my turn. It's a duty. Like taking out the trash, as I've heard such things described here. So the workers here, at this – Cerberus Fossae. Are they indentured? Do they have – what, sentences?'

'Mars needs products of their labour. The water they mine, the minerals—'

Brad felt he was working all this out very slowly. 'But when they finish work – what then? At the end of the day. Do they – socialise? Under supervision or not?' He thought further. 'Can they have families? Are children *born* there?'

'You're getting the wrong idea here—'

'Do people live their whole lives in these – camps?'

Another hesitation. 'Some. It's unusual. It happens. You have to monitor things. People accrue power, in any situation. Any jail. Sometimes you have to move people around, take them out altogether. You don't want some kind of gang-boss dynasty to emerge. It's all about productivity . . .'

Planter ran down. Brad was just staring at him.

Brad said at length, 'I don't understand you, Lieutenant Jeo Planter.'

'Well, the feeling's mutual.'

'I know you are merciful. The evidence is the artificial hand on the arm of Muree's friend Rab. And you allowed his mother to proceed with some kind of life, didn't you? You could have seen her punished more severely, surely. Yet you spared her too. But you speak so harshly of people.'

Planter seemed reluctant to answer. 'I don't like talking about this stuff. Or rather, analysing this stuff. Look – you don't understand. Yet I think you ought to be able to.

'On your ship, out in the void, your generation starship, you were isolated in a fragile piece of machinery, with finite resources, with no possible chance of help if things went wrong. And so you couldn't *afford* to let things go wrong. Because if some system failed, even the slightest, there could be a cascade of faults which—'

'I know, I know. Obviously.'

Planter leaned forward, trying to make his case, trying to persuade Brad. Maybe easing his own conscience, Brad thought. Or trying to. And evidently the man had a conscience, or, for one thing, as he'd just said, he wouldn't have given Rab and his mother a chance at all.

'Systems, then,' Planter said now. 'You ought to be able to understand that. Think of the whole of this engineered Solar System as like – well, exactly like an engine. An engine that is keeping an awful lot of people alive, and has done so for an awfully long time.

'And it achieves that through systems and subsystems. Human-designed. Systems made *up* of humans. We can't rely on natural systems, as our ancestors did on Earth. Why, you've seen it – the whole of the Frame itself is an integrated transport system that carries people and water and whatever else we need, across the Solar System, to all the worlds. Water from Saturn's moons feeds the miners of Mercury. All intricately working together, and fast, and reliably. And all the energy is free—'

'The lumes?' Brad reacted to that. 'You get the energy you need from lumes. You can't call that *free*—'

'But they are, economically speaking. You know that.'

Brad tried to think that through. Was lume energy *free*? A lume was alive. Did lumes have rights? Were *they* like indentured labourers? Or maybe like the working animals humans had once used. Horses, dogs . . .

He glanced down at Mars once again. That patch of industry, over the Cerberus mantle plume, was free, was it? Perhaps the water and minerals and other products of the camp were free in the sense of coming from outside the assumed system. As if given freely by Mars. But the people labouring there, apparently for generation after generation, giving up their lives –

'What do you call it?' he asked now.

Planter seemed puzzled. 'Call what?'

'The . . . camp, the miners over the mantle plume.'

'It has an official title—'

'Tell me the unofficial title.'

'Most people call it the Gulag.'

Brad made a mental note to look up that word. *Gulag.*

The shuttle flew on, and soon began a descent trajectory. Heading towards a landing on Mars. Down to what Planter assured him was the other major settlement, indeed the most significant settlement on Mars.

Hellas.

21

As the final descent began, Planter called Brad to join him.

They settled in a lounge, cushioned in acceleration couches, in front of one of the lander's bigger viewscreens. Brad was surprised to find they were alone here. Everybody else was lining up for the airlocks.

When he remarked on that to Planter, the Lieutenant replied, 'So we'll jump the queue when it's time. You need to start figuring Mars out, if we're going to catch the two absconders. Sit down, shut up, and just *look*.'

Brad had no trouble with that. This was, after all, his first ever planetary landing.

The shuttle was still high above Mars, he saw, but low enough that the landscape filled much of the window, out to a horizon that flattened as they descended. At the view's periphery he made out slices of bare ground that looked a sullen red – illuminated thanks to what Planter told him were the low lights of occasional settlements.

At the centre of the image, Brad could see a *roof* – much the same brick-red colour as the landscape, but a smoother surface, clearly artificial as opposed to the grainier area around it. Human-built, then. A roughly circular form – a dome.

Its outer perimeter was ragged. A chain of eroded mountains, perhaps – hard to be sure, given he had never seen a mountain either, outside of a history record. All this was sprawling – rock walls, the dome – and reached over the horizon. Brad realised that the mountain chain was actually on the scale of the curvature of the planet itself. And so was the dome.

Planter was watching his reaction. 'So what do you make of it?'

Brad considered. 'That mountain chain . . . rim mountains? It looks like a crater with a lid on it. What is it?'

'A crater with a lid on it. Or rather, a roof. This is Hellas – named for the primordial crater itself. This is the only really large settlement on Mars, save for the Gulag. Two hundred and fifty million souls live here— You do know your jaw has dropped? I don't think I ever actually saw that before.'

'All of this is a *crater*?'

'Yeah. This is one tremendous crater, the best part of five thousand kilometres across. And one tremendous impact must have created it too, billions of years ago – when the planets were young, I guess. In fact its diameter is comparable to the planet's radius. You couldn't get a much bigger impact without splitting the planet itself.

'Meanwhile, the roof is three kilometres above the mean. People built *that*. After the Neptune incursion, after the Sun went out.' He grinned. 'Maybe *my* ancestors built that. Not yours. And that whole great structure is known as Hellas City – the political capital of the solar system. A single tremendous city, densely populated, hosting two hundred and fifty million souls . . . Plus two, if our quarry are here, as I expect them to be.'

'Why there?'

Planter shrugged. 'Where else would you go? What strategy would you adopt?'

Brad thought that over. 'Hide among people.'

'Right. And that's why we are approaching the largest crowd in the Solar System.'

And now, as the shuttle descended further, a slit began to open up in that domed surface – apparently to welcome the approaching craft – an aperture dilating to reveal a jumble of lights beneath, green, blue – and sheets of white that might be ice.

The revealed detail was complex – and yet oddly static, Brad thought, at first glance. But, looking more closely, he did see swarms of moving vehicles, mostly on the ground, some in the air, though nothing like the number he might have anticipated. But then that expectation had been set by shipboard studies, as he had tried to prepare himself psychologically. Images and records of the great, lost, *busy* cities of old Earth in times past. *This* was impressive enough, though – and totally outside his previous life experience.

The ship slowed. Brad stared out as the craft slid cautiously down through the complex cross-section of that parted dome.

Once through, they began a descent towards a broad, open area, more or less featureless, at the heart of a more crowded landscape – evidently a landing apron. Lumes hovered everywhere, casting a complex light.

Planter looked at him. 'First impressions?'

Brad thought it over. 'It seems – complicated. But not as – crowded – as the great cities on Earth, of the past, from the records I've seen . . .'

Planter grinned. 'You crammed knowledge of the old Solar System on your way?'

'Wouldn't you?'

Planter shrugged. 'OK. This city-state is just that. It's essentially a seat of government – not just of Mars, but the primary hub of our System-wide government, in fact. From Wrap to Mask, as they say, Hellas watches out for you.' He added, more cynically. 'Or at least, *watches*. Lightspeed delays always necessitate a lot of local control and decision-making. But for now this is the, the *hub*, the core of human governance. And the city itself is as big as can be sustainably supported.'

'You said, two hundred and fifty million people live in this place—'

'Quite so. Not many more on Mars as a whole. That's a big number, but given its size, that's about what the average population density of planet Earth was when your spacecraft left for the stars, Tenant. So this is – normal for humanity.

'And it's self-sufficient in some respects. Mars as a whole, I mean. As I told you earlier, it has enough water of its own for now. But very little food is produced here – manufactured or grown. Most of the food consumed here comes from—'

'Venus,' Brad said. 'The sky farms. Which you and Rab know all about.'

Planter acknowledged that with a nod.

The access port in the dome was already closing up above; the wide empty landing space expanded beneath them. Planter was silent, looking down frequently now, through the shuttle's windows, through various monitors.

When Brad ducked down to see, he made out much more detail than from elevation, much more intricacy. Human intricacy. He saw a tangle of roadways – some bearing vehicles, some speckled with what must be people walking, even running. Already he was low enough to see individual people, then. He noticed that the most major highways seemed to be radial, reaching from the crater rim to a centre he couldn't yet make out.

And between the roadways he saw buildings, sprouting everywhere. Some of these seemed modest – not that he was any judge – but others were like stretched pyramids, and some *soared*, remarkably, their tops now above the level of the shuttle: tall, slender buildings that seemed to be reaching to the dome itself, the artificial sky. *Low gravity*, he thought. *Of course you'd build tall.*

The imminent landing on Martian ground had exhilarated Planter. 'With luck, we might be minutes away from ending this. Or at least, the beginning of the end. Come on. Let's be ready to move.'

They were both suited already. Now they made their way out of the viewing lounge to the nearest airlock, crowded in, and began closing up their pressure suits, testing their integrity.

Brad manoeuvred himself next to the small port set in the outer door, peering through his faceplate to see outside.

More buildings. Buildings that seemed to scrape the sky. Or the dome, anyhow. And directly below, an empty area that loomed ever larger in his vision: evidently their ship's landing place.

It occurred to him to wonder if they would find Muree and Rab waiting patiently for the two of them to emerge. Maybe; Planter had sent out orders to apprehend the couple, if possible. There had been no reply, but Planter had seemed to think it worth a shot, and it would save a lot of searching . . . Now they were close to landing in this huge and complex place, that hoped-for prospect seemed too neat to Brad.

That moment of crisis wasn't here yet. Soon, though.

There was a jolt, a subtle quieting, a loss of vibration under Brad's feet.

Down.

Planter grinned. 'And now a bit more history for you to make. The first star traveller to walk on Mars. Or any solar planet. Well, here we go . . .'

A single glance between them, as they waited for the door to open.

*

As soon as it did, a short staircase folded out from the interior of the cylindrical shuttle, from the airlock door to the ground. Passengers were already crowding out of other airlocks and down the unfolding exit ramps.

Planter, flashing a Lieutenant's insignia, made sure they were among the first out, then hurried down the stair.

Once down, Brad immediately felt the subtly soft pull of Mars's one-third gravity. It wasn't uncomfortable. In fact it was like the partial gravity he had experienced in the *Lightbird*'s elevator shafts, en route from the Carousel to the ship's hub.

Planter had already marched away from the lander, towards clusters of buildings beyond the landing fields.

Brad had to jog to keep up. 'So why would anybody build such a thing? This domed city. On such a scale?'

'You might think of it as a backup. A backup for humanity, and at least some of Earth's biota.'

'A backup in case of what? Extinctions at human hands?'

Planter shrugged as he marched on. 'Human-caused but not necessarily deliberate. Planets are fragile things. Even on Earth, before humanity, there had always been extinctions. Solar flares and volcanoes and earthquakes and ice ages, continents crashing and disintegrating, waves of ice and heat. But humans didn't help, to say the least. In nature you have one extinction per decade; at its worst under humanity we were losing fifty *thousand* per decade . . .

'So, in a rare fit of unity – of biological generosity, I suppose, this was before the Neptune incursion – they built this compound, Hellas, here on Mars. They call it a "worldhouse" – a construction that would be able to contain enough of an atmosphere to emulate Earthlike conditions on an otherwise uninhabitable Mars. Under a roof kilometres high. As you will see.

They were determined to make Hellas habitable – and rebuild at least a chunk of Earth's ecosphere, here on Mars.

'They built those towers, two, three kilometres tall. Spread the first roof across the tops of them. And under that roof they gathered a thicker atmosphere than Mars could support itself. I believe it got up to about an eighth of Earth's atmospheric pressure.

'And it worked, to a degree. Meteorite strikes were a constant hazard, and the cycling of the air through the ecosystem they built, the lakes and the bacteria and eventually trees and grass and animals, had to be ten times more efficient than Earth's natural systems. But – it worked . . .'

Brad gazed at the buildings all around them as they walked, some wide, some slender, some functional blocks, others adorned with towers and spires. A monstrous urban landscape, all around the landed spacecraft. That extraordinary roof over it all, glowing by diffuse lume-light.

Planter talked on as he walked. 'That's all in the past now. All that was originally meant to be the base of an extensive human colonisation of Mars. But then, the invasion came. Neptune.'

And Brad, listening, was distracted by the sight of a lone figure who came walking out from the nearest building, towards the shuttle. With one gloved fist clenched.

Brad knew immediately who this was. He suppressed a laugh. He darted a glance at Planter, who hadn't noticed, and was still talking.

'After Neptune – well, then came the dark times, as the Sun was obscured. Large as it is, Hellas is nowhere near big enough to host a decent, sustainable ecosystem, even lit with lumes. But it served as a kind of seed bank. Preserving whole lineages of Earth life – until enough lumes had been spun into orbit around the home planet. Earth itself came out of the deep freeze. And life returned from Mars, from Hellas, A reseeding of Earth. Life that had been stored on Mars, now returned to Earth. And the old planet was resilient. Even after just a few centuries, there was a grand greening—'

He broke off, seeing at last who was approaching them.

Angela Plokhy grinned through her face mask.

Planter just stared.

'You,' he said to Plokhy, 'are under arrest.'

'Thought so.' Her grin widened. 'It's worth it for the look on your face.'

Brad had to hold Planter back. While hiding his own smile.

'Regards from Muree and Rab, Lieutenant!'

22

The ferry trip from the Frame down to Mars wasn't so bad for Muree. It was much as she had experienced before.

She was getting used to it.

But their destination was unexpected: a band in space suspended over the equator of Mars – and turning with Mars – a band that was untidy, a more or less continuous belt of structures and swarming ferry ships, some arriving from the deep-space Frame like their own craft, or ascending up from the planet's surface, or descending down to it. There were beanstalks too, fixed towers connecting the orbital belt to the ground, as well as independent craft flying up to the belt.

'Like bees flying up to a hive,' Rab said, watching. 'We'll take one of those ground-to-orbit ferries, rather than the beanstalks. Less chance of being noticed.'

So they waited for a ferry down to the ground – booked by Rab with his Plokhy-supplied ID. Much of this wait was in crowded, public spaces, populated by passengers alone or in groups, passing through as they were. Rab had never been to Mars before, but he knew the technologies and protocols they were passing through, and, they decided, he would do most of the talking.

And he was casually confident of being easily understood,

Muree had learned. The social unity imposed by the government had included a single basic official language, a common vocabulary and grammar. The Frame was monolingual by law. But the sheer size of the Solar System, of the dispersal of the homes of mankind, ensured that there was a constant battle, it sounded like, between the emergence of local dialects, vocabularies, and the standard imposed by the centre.

Muree herself could follow most conversations, she found, with the aid of translations through smart ear-buds. Still, they agreed it was best for her to keep silent as much as possible, in case of giveaway slips of vocabulary or traces of accent – always assuming anybody was paying enough attention to spot them.

Time passed. In a cramped waiting room, they dozed in turns, and if anybody disturbed them they made sure it was Rab who responded.

Until their hired local ferry finally showed up.

The compact little craft, smooth-hulled to withstand an atmospheric entry, was fully automated. For payment they had only to show their chipped palms on boarding, and Rab joked about how long it was going to take them to pay back Plokhy for all this.

They were two of a dozen paying customers on the ferry. Once they'd all paid and strapped in, the craft sealed itself up, briskly pulled away from its docking station.

At first it apparently descended fast – then tipped suddenly to the right. And Muree, disconcerted, shaken a little, pressed against a window, was granted a vision of the ground.

A ground at first glance pitch dark, under a starless, sunless sky. The only lights on Mars would be human-caused, of course, like all the worlds of the Solar System.

Now, peering out, Muree began to see such lights – wide

smudges that might be colonies, even cities, linear features that must be road or rail tracks. She enhanced the window's imagery, maximising what light there was, and was rewarded with a faint hint of rust-red over the black – the outlines of craters, canyons, eroded mountains – more roads, illuminated by human lighting technology – all of it softened by air that was really no more than a layer of mist.

And when she looked up to the horizon, even here, she thought she could see the straight-line gleam of the Frame – the fire of millions of lumes, giving up their lives, sufficient to light the Martian landscape, at least a little, across interplanetary distances.

But Rab was pointing, trying to get her to look straight down at the ground.

Where she saw a tremendous feature, a crater – so big it scaled against the curve of the planet itself, its rim standing against the black of space, its walls sprawling over the planet's own horizon. And the crater, huge as it was cradled a dome, she saw, a low, smooth construction reaching from the rim walls across the basin, enclosing the whole. Obviously human-made. An enormous engineering response to an enormous geological anomaly.

As they descended the great crater expanded in her vision, until most of its walls spread out of sight, over the horizon. In fact they would land outside the great dome, in the midst of a crater rim, itself eroded, that broke up into a chain of eroded hills and mountains, circling the great plain itself.

She looked at Rab. He grinned back.

'Hellas?'

'Hellas,' he said. 'De facto capital of the human Solar System, seat of government, and by far the largest concentrated human community anywhere – in this solar system anyhow. I can't speak for the interstellar colonies, of course. A city in a crater.'

She tried to focus. 'This is – overwhelming. I never saw an actual planet before coming through the Mask, remember, let alone made landfall. And we have to see it in the dark!'

Rab grinned. 'Unless they arrest us first.'

She grinned back. 'There is that—'

An automated voice spoke. *Prepare for landing. Please sit back in upright seats. Belts must be applied. Please secure pressure suits; we will open the hull immediately after engine stop . . .*

Muree heard a screech. The sound of hull metal hitting thin air. *Almost down.*

The ship landed beyond the south rim of the immense crater – so outside the crater itself, Muree realised. Outside the dome.

She stood, cautiously, testing the gravity – less than Earth standard, less than the carousel's spin gravity on board the *Lightbird* – but it felt heavy to her starship-bred frame, especially after so long in the zero-gravity of the Mask. Still, taking it easy, she was able to see out of the windows. That crater rim, close to, was essentially a much eroded range of hills, mountains, laden with red dust. There was no sense of curvature, just a wall of distorted rock, speckled with artificial light – and more lights illuminated what were evidently routes through the rim to the crate floor within.

Dark and bare it might be, but suddenly she was *in* a landscape, she realised. Created by nature, not humanity – if modified by humanity. For the first time in her life.

It took only minutes, after the lander's descent was complete, after the ship's engines shut down, for a flexible corridor to reach out and fix itself to the shuttle's hull, and for the doors in the passenger section to open wide.

Muree sensed the waking-up of the orthopaedic-support elements of her suit, and absently ran through a checklist.

She was aware of Rab watching her discreetly, but, checking over his own suit, he didn't intervene. She had found she liked that about him. No fuss.

When they were both done, they climbed down an easy staircase to the ground. She and Rab had nothing save their suits – and a few gadgets like Plokhy's identity implants.

Muree took her first few paces away from the opened-up ship, amid a small gaggle of folk chasing their smart luggage. The surface underfoot was dusty, reddish.

Once in the open, away from the shuttle, she looked around. The darkness was broken only by the vehicle's lights, and a few small lamps. The sky was black, of course, though she thought she could make out the trace of light that was a local arm of the Frame. And in a direction she thought must be the north, the shadow seemed a little deeper, darker. The crater rim mountains. Black shadow against black, starless sky.

Here and there sparkled some kind of frost.

She pointed at that. 'Water ice?'

'Carbon dioxide,' Rab said. 'That was what made up most of Mars's atmosphere before the humans came. All fell as dry-ice snow after the Solar Wrap was put in place, I guess, and cold Mars got even colder. A lot of the frozen air was mined for graphene and other products when they built Hellas City . . . You OK to walk?'

'Sure.'

'We don't have to go far anyhow.' He looked around, orienting himself. Eventually he ended up looking east, she figured. 'Come on.' He set off that way.

With care, Muree followed, one deliberate step after another. Soon the smart orthopaedics in her suit took over, and she could let it help – her suit following Rab's suit rather than the man himself. But even so she soon began to tire.

And she was aware that they had split off from the rest of the passengers.

Most of *them* were making their way north, towards that rampart of crater-wall mountains, and presumably Hellas City beyond. They were gathering at a cluster of lights at what must be the base of those mountains. Transport hubs, maybe, ways to get the passengers through the mountains and to their final destinations in the domed crater basin to the north.

North was Hellas, the city. East, the way Muree and Rab were going, was – nothing. Nothing but a slowly unfolding view of the rim mountains.

She called, 'You sure we're going the right way?'

'Sure as my suit can be.'

'What are you looking for?'

'Not "what". "Who . . ."'

And now she saw they were approaching a building, or complex of buildings, dimly lit.

She was distracted by flashes above them: another craft lifting into the sky, she saw.

'Busy place,' she said.

'I guess it always is,' Rab said. 'Incoming is mostly cargo, and *that's* mostly foodstuffs. You've got a city full of hungry people beyond that mountain range. Hungry and thirsty; a quarter of a billion of them . . .'

'Water? Food?'

'Well, they get the water from Mars itself. There are deep aquifers full of ice, and a lot of it in the caps at the poles. I'm told the masking of the Sun actually helped with the cultivation of Mars in that way. Without sunlight, in time, every drop of Mars's water froze hard, and could be harvested. On the surface no more than a thin frost – but there are aquifers, underground stores, that froze solid, waiting to be mined.'

'Food, though?'

'From off-planet. Mostly Venus. A nominal seven kilos per person per day.'

She was getting breathy. She concentrated on her walking in this sudden gravity field.

'The Martians import their food from Venus? From another *planet*?'

'The system works,' Rab said, shrugging. 'Globally, the supply chain. I should know. My mother worked on the administration of the Venus farms, until – well, you know the story. My family, my ancestors on Venus a few generations back, were farmers themselves, and much of our produce was destined for Mars – and a lot of that for this place. And at seven kilos per head per day, that's a lot of farming and shipping.'

She nodded and said carefully, 'You know something of your ancestors.' *Not from your mother . . . was that tactless?*

He glanced at her. 'I've been in a position to access the records about them. A few generations back. Nobody disapproved. It was good to learn about them. A kind of reconnection, after what happened to me as a kid.'

Stomping along in her exoskeletal hardware, she was getting tired and irritated. 'I don't get why we're walking off into the dark like this.'

He glanced back, she realised, saw she was lagging, and waited for her to catch up.

He said, 'Well, there's no easy transport *in* to where we're going. And still less *out*.'

She caught up with him, panting. She saw they were less than fifty paces from that forbidding wall. 'Then what—'

Suddenly light splashed over them, pouring from sources mounted on the top of the wall.

And a voice, loud in their helmets.

State your identity, state your business, or you will be confined.

Rab stopped dead, held out an arm to block Muree, but she'd stopped of her own accord.

State your identity, state your business, or you will be confined. State your identity, state your business, or—

'I hope this is a private channel,' Rab said. 'Should be. And I hope they fall for our bluff.'

'What bluff?'

She saw him grin through his faceplate. 'Stay here. And cross your fingers.'

He raised his arms, hands splayed, and walked carefully forward.

After a couple of paces he was bathed in more light, coming from still more sources embedded in the wall, it seemed. One beam hit him full in the face, making his faceplate opaque itself. He tapped the side of his helmet to override and clear the plate, and doggedly pressed forward, eyes open. He must be expecting retinal scans, Muree presumed.

And he held up his hand, palm out – the flesh hand inside its glove.

'My ID chip is here. My companion is similarly identified. We have come to speak to the prisoner identified in my ID chip—'

Display both hands.

He held up his left hand, his false hand, removed his suit glove. More lights bathed the metal of the prosthetic.

The lights dimmed.

There seemed to be a long lag before the next response. Muree wondered if the machines were referring this strange transaction to some human supervisor.

Then: *State your identity, your business, or you will be confined.*

Rab murmured, 'He means you this time. Show your chipped hand.'

Muree did so, nervously.

Once that was done, one more message: *Proceed to the decontamination area.*

Most of the lights cut out, save for a row illuminating a path running parallel to the wall.

Rab relaxed, and let out a sigh, crisply transmitted by the suits' comms systems. 'Come on. Let's get in there before he changes his mind.'

'He? I thought it was a she . . .'

He walked forward steadily, along the illuminated path; she had to hurry a couple of paces to catch up.

'You've never been to this place before,' she said, breathless. 'You said you'd never been to Mars.'

'Not this specific installation, no. Places like it, yes. On Venus. I hear they even have them on Earth. I didn't know for sure it would be here, this—'

'This prison.'

He glanced at her. 'You guessed it. This prison, yes. That's what it is. Every port, every landing point is going to have a prison, large or small, for holding arriving miscreants. Remember I've worked much of my adult life, such as it's been, with a law enforcement officer, or at least a former cop. Jeo Planter. So I did see police in action, a *lot*. Quite an education, over all those years. And useful, in certain situations. Like this. You get to know the procedures, the mindsets.'

She grunted. 'Well, now Planter is almost certainly following you, not the other way around. Who's the smart guy now?'

'Hmm. That's debatable. I'm not a Lieutenant of any grade. *But*.' He smiled through his faceplate, which she saw as a ghostly pale visage floating in the darkness as he walked. 'I was smart enough to take away some assets from my police experience. Such as an ability to pick up messages not available to the general public.' He tapped his helmet. 'Implants. Not entirely legal.'

She began to understand. 'You got a message. From – someone. To come here, to this prison.'

'Not specifically here, but I worked that out. They're going to be at this prison, almost certainly.'

'I'm barely following this.'

'You'll get it.' He grinned. 'Show time.'

They had reached a door in the dark flank of the compound. Still there was nothing to identify this place as a prison or anything else. Although, she thought, maybe that very anonymity gave away its function.

Rab waved a gloved hand – the false hand, Muree saw.

The door folded back, to reveal a brightly lit corridor. Muree thought she heard a hiss, as of air.

They hesitated, shared a glance. Then walked in side by side.

The door closed behind them. She heard another hiss.

A long, blank-walled corridor stretched out ahead of them, sparsely lit by lamps in the ceiling.

'Very institutional,' Rab said.

Muree wasn't sure what that meant.

Remove your face masks. Show your faces. Remove one glove to expose your ID chip. Remove your face masks. Show—

'We get it,' Muree said. She tapped the side of her helmet; her smart faceplate folded back and out of the way.

She found she was holding her breath; she always did when opening up a helmet. On some level her body, her reflexes, didn't seem to trust her judgement in such circumstances, and the suit had trained itself to reinforce that caution. 'Good thing too,' she muttered.

Rab had exposed his face, and was taking off his gloves. 'What's that?'

'Never mind.' She let out her suit air, took a deep breath. The air smelled of ozone, perhaps, and of some kind of disinfectant.

'Glove,' he reminded her.

When she had exposed her chipped hand again, a panel slid out of sight on the wall nearby to reveal a shallow alcove, with mock handprints within. An obvious instruction. She glanced at Rab.

He said, 'You first?'

She shrugged, and placed her left hand on the handprint. A green glow illuminated the little alcove immediately.

Welcome, said the robot voice.

She stepped back. Rab put both his hands, real and fake, on the handprint silhouettes.

Welcome.

They exchanged a glance.

Rab seemed relieved. He muttered, 'They might have queried the fake hand, identified it, if I didn't show it. If we ever get out of this I'll recommend an upgrade to security protocols like this—'

'Stop showing off.'

He grinned. 'Just nervous.'

'*You're* nervous—'

The inmate you requested to see is ready for you.

A door, some way down the corridor, swung open silently.

Rab led the way along the corridor to the door. That led into a small room beyond.

There was little in there, Muree saw immediately. Two chairs. An evidently transparent panel set in one wall. Low light on this side of the panel, darkness beyond.

A waiting room.

Another exchanged glance. Then they sat, side by side, still in their heavy exosuits, their helmets open, gloves still off.

'No drinking water,' Rab said. 'Nothing to read. Not very welcoming, is it? I think I'll complain—'

The panel lit up, or de-opaqued, revealing a room beyond. A matching layout: table, one chair.

And Angela Plokhy was sitting there, smiling.

Rab had clearly expected to see her.

Muree hadn't.

'Just so you know,' Plokhy told them, 'I'm assured that this conversation will not be recorded. You might ask why not.'

Muree, bewildered, just shrugged.

Rab said, 'Because the crimes of which you're suspected are low grade enough that your freedoms and right of expression need not be compromised. I'm quoting the law.'

'"At this stage", they told me,' Plokhy said. 'Suspected "at this stage". In an only vaguely threatening tone, but still. You two are still clean, by the way. I was specifically arrested for that illegal departure from the Mask, aboard my precious *Styx*. I covered your tracks; I claimed you were never aboard. As far as anybody knows, I *was* alone, and you got out of there some other way.

'Let's face it, they were going to get me for something. Every so often they take me in. Even though I have scramblers which will make it difficult to pin anything else on me. Actually it's the first time I've used my own identity for a long while.' She grinned. 'And now I'm in jail. Not for the first time, and not for long.'

Muree was deeply confused. 'But why are you in *this* jail?' She turned on Rab. 'And why are *we* here?'

Rab said, '*Because* she's here. Plokhy, here. She messaged me.

For one thing, I just wanted to be sure she's OK. After all, she wouldn't be in this mess if not for us.'

Plokhy shrugged. 'Hardly a mess. Not my original plan, I grant you. But I contacted Rab because I do have a – a message. A message to deliver. To *you*. In person, Rab. And so I chose to come here. I figured it was urgent enough . . . And I knew Rab's own chips would detect a message from me. All I could tell him was I was incarcerated and he'd come running.'

Muree thought back. 'OK. But, why *this* prison?'

'Saves time,' Rab said. 'Because this one is right by the spaceport. Generally used as a temporary detention centre for deportees.'

'Which happy band,' Plokhy said, 'I'll be joining soon.'

Muree faced Plokhy. 'Deportation?'

Plokhy smiled. 'Listen. I've trodden this route before. Yep, worst case I could be deported – and probably to Uranus, the lume mines. I've been there before too. A free ride from the government out to where I want to go anyhow, and once I'm out, my *Styx* will follow me. Or I could just pay a stonking fine. You see?' She smiled.

Muree tried to take all this in. 'You're serious, aren't you? You put yourself in this position for – us?'

'That's about the size of it. I wanted to be sure you've got the news I have heard since we last met. Whatever the authorities like to think, however they imagine they control us, news, fake and otherwise, seeps around this cage of a Solar System of ours. The Frame alone is a government-maintained conduit of information, some of it true, some of it false, as well as of lumes and water and the occasional plague vector—'

'What news?' Rab broke in. 'What information?'

She blinked. 'Well, about you two. Muree, for a start. About the *Lightbird*. About the newcomers from outside the Mask – the universe beyond. Just *that* truth is an unprecedented revelation, but the truth is spreading more widely. And because of your very presence, there is pressure on the web of lies that hides most of what those who rule us get up to, in normal times. This is a problem for the authorities the like of which they haven't encountered in – centuries, probably. In fact I don't know of a precedent.'

Rab and Muree exchanged a look.

'The truth is beginning to come out, then,' Muree prompted.

'Well – it's no longer contained, put it that way. And you two are already being chased, you know that. To the authorities you're the physical manifestation of this major leak, this breakdown – that's obvious, but the hunt is going to get more intense. Mars is a big place in human terms, so a good place to hide, but it's also the most heavily policed world in the Solar System, probably.'

'And here we are,' Muree said. 'Sitting on it.'

Plokhy glared. 'You need to take this seriously. You need to take *yourselves* seriously. And what you've done. You two aren't the only refugees with bits of knowledge about all this – and that knowledge is probably spreading fast. But you two are still the key, for now. Just because you were so visible at the beginning of all this, the encounter with the *Lightbird*. All those nursery-school kids! Shut you down and – well, the whole thing might still be shut down too. The openness, the shedding of the lies. We might go back to our bad old ways here in Fortress Sol.

'Which is why you need help.' And she looked at Rab gravely. 'And where I come in. Turns out there is somebody here who has pledged to help you. To understand, to break through all this. All the secrecy. *Here on Mars*. At Hellas. She got a message to me – don't ask how—'

Rab's jaw dropped. 'What message? . . . She?'

'It seems as if everyone knows I have a connection to you two. What am I, a postal service? Look – what she gave me is enigmatic, but it ought to confuse the authorities if they get wind of it, and it might make some sense to you, Rab. She said to look for her in *the most obvious place.*'

Muree was bewildered. 'She? Who? Who are you talking about?'

But Plokhy smiled. 'Didn't I say? It's her, Rab.

'It's your mother.'

23

The most obvious place.

It was a simple enough instruction, Muree supposed. But what could it mean, in terms of finding Rab's *mother*?

There was nothing they could do for now. Muree and Rab anticipated spending much of the rest of the Martian night thinking it all through.

They gravitated back to the main spaceport.

The area, not surprisingly, was crowded with short-stay accommodation. Most facilities were basic, just apartment blocks standing on the plain outside the uplands of the crater rim.

To Muree it all seemed strange too. Even the constant gravity was – odd. The spin gravity at the *Lightbird* Carousel, Earth normal, was three times higher than that exerted on Mars, but if you wanted a lighter gravity you could just climb away from the perimeter and in towards the axis, where the effective gravity dwindled to nothing. As used to house convalescing invalids maybe. Or extreme sports fans. People grew up amid these variations; getting from one place to another you could make use of the changing gravity in a three-dimensional way, instinctively using as little energy as possible.

Now it felt as if she was stuck halfway up an elevator shaft above a one-gravity floor.

But still, after so long away from the *Lightbird*, on the gravity-free Mask, aboard the *Styx* with its changing or zero acceleration – even after the light gravity of the Frame – after a few hours of walking around here, gravity had its revenge, as her muscles, joints, all ached in unfamiliar and unwelcome ways. Even her *feet*.

She walked in silence.

The accommodation block they chose for the night, randomly, was one of a nondescript row. It looked functional, not even interesting enough to be unpleasant. Sparse lanterns cast long shadows.

As they approached, nobody was around. Rab just marched ahead, as if, Muree thought, he owned the place, or at least was a pal of the owner.

Muree, by contrast, slowed up. To her, to be marched into yet another new confinement was bewildering, more displacement. She had grown up in a finite space where everybody knew everybody else. Now she was in an infinite space, it felt like, where she knew nobody, and everybody but her seemed to know the rules.

Rab was sensitive enough to notice her hesitancy. 'You OK? Nervous again?'

'Kind of. Maybe we should wait for another ferry-load to come pouring down from the sky, for cover. Just the two of us – we'll stand out. Especially if we're being watched. Tracked. A crowd might be cover.'

He shook his head. 'It doesn't work like that. You're not used to sigils. They're a common marker. Nobody sees you; they just "see" your sigil . . . Come on. Let's get it over.'

Glancing now at the dormitory block, she saw a small window set beside the door. Movement inside, somebody coming and going.

Muree stepped back into the shadows. 'There's someone in there. See? The window by the door. They must be screening everybody coming in.'

Rab looked over, and half-smiled. 'You're fretting about nothing. You'll get used to this stuff as we travel. This – protocol. It's the same everywhere, for good or bad. Across the worlds. It's not unusual to find attendants like that. I mean, human attendants. Anywhere you go. But not for security, not for ident. The systems take care of that.'

'Then for what?'

'Hell, I don't know. Illogical stuff. Maybe you don't like open places, because you live in the middle of some mound-city in Venus. Like I used to. It's not an illness or a condition; it's just a preference. Or you want to be in a certain room because your buddy is next door and you want to surprise them for their birthday. Totally illogical to a machine, understandable for another human.'

'OK. I buy that. But surely sometimes people will see things that a machine might ignore.'

'Like what?'

'How about an artificial hand? *Hey, like that guy on the run? With the hand, you know? Do you think it's him? . . .*'

Rab held up both his hands; he wore black gloves. 'When you travel, nobody *looks* at anybody else. Not beyond the surface. It's as if we were all disembodied chips, floating in the air.'

'Yes, but – fooling strangers is one thing. Lieutenant Planter has known you all your life, nearly. Surely he must be able to guess where you'd go, what decisions you'd make.'

Rab shrugged. 'Maybe. Maybe not. He knows me, but he hasn't lived *through* my life. He can't think like me – how it is to *be* me, how I make my decisions. And, listen – he did spare me Mercury all those years ago. Even cops are human. If I have to be hunted down, sooner by him. So you ready to brave the terrors of this totally ordinary overnight apartment block or not?'

She deliberately put aside her anxiety. 'I'll leave the talking to you.'

He grinned. 'And *I'll* leave it to my sigil. Come on. And then we have to start figuring out our next move.'

'Which is to work out where to meet your mother. *The most obvious place . . .*'

'After food and sleep.'

'It's a deal.'

The man behind the door barely glanced at them, as they outlined their needs for a one-night stay.

Muree couldn't help but stare at the guy as he did his job. Certainly no alarms went off. Plokhy's borrowed sigils were evidently still doing their job of hiding the refugees in plain sight.

At Rab's request they were given two connecting rooms, a short walk down the passageway, with a shared bathroom, food and drink dispensers.

After moving in and freshening up, they opened the communicating door, so they could talk while they were resting, each in their own room.

Rab seemed more reflective. 'You know, your questions are making me think. Seeing all this through your eyes.'

'Think about what?'

'Well, about my own assumptions about society. My society, I mean. Everybody tracked and controlled, as if the whole Solar System is like one big prison, with everybody tagged from birth – potentially at least.'

'You've just been telling me how inefficient it is.'

'Well, so it is. But it's the intent, you see, not how well that intent is carried out. The intent *is* to track every human being on every planet and moon and habitat – and for what? In case everything falls apart, like an out of control prison? It's not the effectiveness I'm seeing now. It's the *intention*.' He looked at her guiltily, then looked away. 'When I first met you, when I saw your ship – when I saw how *small* it was, if you'll forgive me for that – I thought it must be like living in a flying prison. Well, so it was to an extent. It *has* to be, in that case. Even your ratios of births and deaths have to be managed . . . Oh, I'm sorry.'

She shrugged. 'About my twin? Yes, the ship was a finite system – very obviously so. And we all grew up knowing that it had to be tightly controlled, by *us*, as individuals and as a community, over a time span of generations.'

He nodded. 'Sure. It had to be that way. But it's all a question of size. The Solar System is a finite system too, but so much bigger, at least on the scale of an individual human, that there ought to be room for *effective* freedom. Or at least the *illusion* of freedom.'

She thought that over. 'OK. But, for whatever reason, whatever the history, it's not that way. Evidently. The whole Solar System has been engineered into a prison – or that's how it feels to me. All of it encased in the Frame, that feels like a cage even when you look up into the sky, let alone when you ride it. And it's all sustained by lies – the Mask, which hides the Solar System from the stars, even from approaching human ships, and hides the stars from the inhabitants of the Solar System. That's not to mention the lumes that live and die all over this place. And all for what?'

He was grinning.

She smiled back. 'Sorry. I know I get obsessed about the lumes.'

He grunted. 'Somebody should. *I* never thought about them the way you do, not before the *Lightbird* showed up.'

Muree was starting to feel dopey. 'You know, for days now

I've had to make a conscious effort to remember when I last slept properly.'

He smiled. 'Me too, when I let myself think about it at all. And tomorrow's likely to be another busy one, whatever. Oh, by the way, I think I've figured out what Plokhy's "most obvious place" is going to be.' He hesitated.

'Save it for tomorrow,' she said. 'But for now—'

'For now we stop running for a while, and sleep.'

'Right. Good night. Or whatever it is—'

'The Architect Monument,' he blurted. 'You may as well know now. I've been thinking about that . . .'

'Never heard of it.'

'I'm sure I've mentioned it . . .'

'Oh. Yes. I do remember. Supposed to be at "a stable place", you said. Whatever *that* means . . .'

'Yeah. Whatever that means. I mean, maybe—'

'It'll keep. Good night, Rab.'

He shut up, thankfully.

But she'd heard what he'd said. And they *had* discussed this 'Architect' before. Or so she thought. And now the thoughts, the speculation ran round in her head, even as she stripped off her self-cleaning clothes.

Great. She was already over-tired – physically tired, thanks to Mars's constant gravity.

And now she was puzzling.

She knew what, in theory, an architect was. Architects had been involved in the inner layout of the *Lightbird*, in the design stages, long before she had been born. She'd been taught all that, growing up. So what? The generations of struggling colonists on the ship, indeed on Rossbee itself, had made for more captivating narratives.

Even here in the Solar System, what could any architect have achieved, what monument could have been left behind that could be so important? . . .

Damn it.

Her head was buzzing with speculation, her ever-present anxiety bubbling under the surface of her mind.

Deal with it tomorrow.

That was the advice her teachers had always given her when she had been small, and fretted about something; almost always it had turned out to be good advice.

But there wasn't always a tomorrow: her mother, dead years before the arrival at the Solar System, had not had the chance to see any of the extraordinary sights Muree had explored since leaving the *Lightbird* . . .

Nor had her lost twin.

Tomorrow . . .

Tomorrow, she would witness for *them*, she told herself.

When Rab knocked on the connecting door to wake her, after what felt like a very short sleep, he was already dressed, excited.

Eager to tell her. Waking early – in the Martian dawn – he had found out that *there was an Architect Monument on Mars.* And such a thing would surely be at the heart of the planet's greatest city . . .

Just a ride away from where they sat.

That was surely where they were being lured.

Suddenly they had a plan.

24

Leaving early suited both of them.

They'd slept enough, Muree felt. And it took only a couple of hours for them to eat, wash, check over their self-maintaining clothing and lightweight pressure suits.

When they made their way out, the same guy was working at the desk. He waved, with a half-smile.

Rab paused as they exited. 'Which way to the Monument transports?'

The guy raised his arm, his finger pointing back over his shoulder. 'Inward. You'll find it.' Then he waved them away, and turned back to whatever chores he had to do.

Chuckling.

Muree frowned. 'Asshole. It sounded like he thought you were asking a stupid question. And he didn't actually answer, did he?'

Rab shrugged. 'I have a feeling he did, on reflection. *Inward* . . .'

She thought it over. 'Oh. If this monument is at the centre of the crater—'

'Which is where you would put a monument. He sent us inward, into the heart of the crater. Which means if you head off at right angles to the rim, you'll follow a radius, wherever you start . . . It *was* a dumb question. Come on.'

*

He led Muree out through a door in the back of the office – it slid out of sight as they approached – and they emerged from a flat wall, with multiple doorways, all like the one they had come out of.

And found themselves facing a break in the ring of worn hills that was the crater wall – a break that led to a plain beyond – and a shallow dome, spanning the horizon, tinged a faint blue.

The dome of Hellas.

And here, what was evidently a transport node. Ways to get you from these rim mountains, and to the dome.

More trains, but not in the sky this time. Dead ahead of them, a single carriage was suspended from a slim monorail: a rail that arrowed straight to the central plain. A handful of people could be seen inside already, peering through picture windows; more were mounting, or hanging around along the line.

All this was dimly illuminated by scattered lumes above, like brilliant stars, evidently synchronised to deliver a kind of dawn – presumably across the whole of the Hellas complex. A cold, shifting light.

Muree wondered what this immense landscape would have been like under the light of the Sun.

Meanwhile Rab was walking forward, glaring around, evidently working the place out. Muree could see how multiple rail lines fanned out of this node in all directions, mostly snaking off into the crater interior, but others leading off to left and right, evidently tracking the curvature of the mountains. Away from the lines, more carriages sat backed up in a wider yard, on stubs of rail. They looked as if they could be transferred to a line quickly and easily.

A brisk, busy, complex transport node.

And now Rab forged on, to a rail dead straight ahead of them, running at right angles to the wall.

All this seemed dimly lit, to Muree. But when she looked up, she glimpsed a patch of blue sky, almost at the zenith. Blue, breaking through night darkness.

'That's a fake,' she said.

'What is?'

She pointed up. 'You need sunlight for Earthlike blue skies, on Earth or otherwise. There's been no sunlight falling on Mars, not for a long time – ever since your ancestors wrapped up the Sun . . .'

Rab grinned. 'Of course it's a fake. No Martian sky was ever like that, naturally. But this is Hellas. *The whole crater is under a dome,* five thousand kilometres across. And, yes, there's no sunlight, but—'

'Lumes. Lumes enough to turn the sky blue?'

'It took some engineering, I believe. The scattering of the light. And they make the dome transparent at night. Letting in the dark. You can *see* the Frame, on a good night, even from the busiest city areas. We should look for it tonight.'

Muree again felt overwhelmed. 'People did all this . . . I suppose if you do wrap up the Sun you have to compensate somehow.'

Rab frowned. 'The Mask is orders of magnitude more impressive an engineering feat than this.'

'Maybe. But *that's* monstrous. Nothing natural about it. This is on a human scale, at least. Or nearer to it. It's huge, but familiar. It's magnificent. Like they built a second Earth.' She didn't add, *It's also crazy.*

He considered that. 'OK. Anyhow, more travelling for us, I'm afraid. We don't want to miss that transport. You can gawp at the scenery out of the windows.'

He grabbed her hand – flesh on flesh, gently – and led her at a steady jog towards the coach ahead of them, suspended from its rail.

Muree kept up well enough, her main problem being the low gravity that still made it feel like she was going to float up in the air the whole time. She gritted her teeth and made sure she didn't fall.

They made the carriage easily, more would-be passengers following in their wake.

The coach was divided up into compartments, in an echo of the Frame trains they had taken. Many were already occupied, most by just one or two people. Some wore masks, for bio protection, she assumed.

They found an empty compartment.

They sat both facing forwards, the way the train was headed, Muree following Rab's lead.

Rab tapped a wall, and a tray folded down holding bottled water, what looked like snacks. He passed Muree a water.

It occurred to her she wouldn't have known how to work this simple tech, so well concealed was it. She remarked on that to Rab.

He just smiled. 'You want anything, just ask. It's all smart stuff. And free at the point of delivery. Your sigil, or other ident, will keep a record, to be charged back to your account.'

She grinned. 'You're saying, don't worry about it.'

'Don't worry about it. Remember, Plokhy gave us the sigils, and you can be sure she'll be paying for nothing.'

She had barely cracked open her water when the train started to move. Smoothly, silently – but she could feel a steady push at her back. And as the acceleration kept up, the couch seemed to grow a little softer, to accommodate the push.

Rab glanced at her. 'So, what do you want to ask first? I've ridden this rail a few times before. Always business. Inter-world police conferences. Note-taking for Planter . . . Though I guess *this* is business too.'

'We're heading for the centre, right? The centre of the great circular crater of Hellas. And that gentle push – I'll guess, what, there in ninety minutes?'

'Nearer to eighty, but that's a good guess. Good question, even.

'But then you were born a traveller. Sometimes I think there are people who don't know, truly, where they are, in space. Maybe not even in time . . . You get on the Frame at Saturn, you ride it to Mercury, you pass the time, you ignore what's outside the window, and maybe in your head those two places feel like they're next to each other . . . The person whose monument we're going to try to find would have turned in their grave if they heard that.' He thought that over. 'Or maybe they wouldn't have. Their whole ambition was to abolish distance, in a way. Or at least the dread of distance, within the Solar System anyhow. But maybe they did that too well.'

Muree shook her head. 'All this sounds like riddles. Better for me to see it for myself.'

'Sure . . .' He stared, absently, out of the window.

She gazed out too.

At a complex landscape increasingly crowded with buildings, huddles of cubes and domes, some looking factory-printed, some more customised, some standing alone. She guessed there must be a lot of industrial activity here, just inside the rim of the crater, where the space elevator cables were anchored and the shuttle craft landed. All of this under that blue-tinted roof more than five thousand kilometres across . . . This might not compare in scale of engineering achievement to the Mask, the Frame, the Solar Wrap, but she knew that roof alone would shame any structure, any city even, that her ancestors had built back on Rossbee.

Before the carriage picked up too much speed, she picked out people, walking, working, *outside* the inner buildings. No masks. Secure in the protection of the dome.

'It's a magnificent sight,' Rab said, watching her. 'If you think of it the right way. Before humans came here this world was a frozen desert. They say there had once been life, related to Earth life through some kind of early exchange across space – but while Earth flourished, Mars froze, leaving only traces of what had been in the planet's own deep aquifers, the ice caps at the poles. The planet was just too cold, too small.

'But then humans came and – well, look. Even after they took the Sun away, look what humans have made of this place. A dome over two thousand kilometres across and kilometres high. And a growing city. This will always be a city-world. But there are long-term plans to import more water from space – the ice moons – and nitrogen from Venus . . .'

Muree listened, fascinated. Disturbed. 'Now you sound as if you approve of it all. This – this regime that controls the whole Solar System. That engineers worlds.'

He shrugged. 'Maybe I've a little of the government thinking in me after all, thanks to my training. But I do know plenty of people have paid terrible prices to achieve all this.' He held up his own artificial hand. 'I guess you have to take what's been good about it . . .' He lowered his hand, stared out of the window.

Muree looked too, at the artificial sky, the watered Martian landscape.

And everywhere she looked in the faux-blue sky, she saw a sprinkling of light: dazzling pinpoints. Lumes, of course. There must be hundreds to light a landscape this size, with an illumination sufficient to support all the life she saw – hundreds of lumes living and dying every year or so, to be continually replaced by hundreds more.

She closed her eyes, tried to rest. But her vague, habitual sense of guilt churned.

That and the steady anxiety from which she had suffered since they had left the *Lightbird*. The endless strangeness. *What next?* . . .

Soon, the carriage tipped forward. They must be descending from the rim mountains, and heading for the crater floor.

She slowly fell into a troubled sleep.

25

A jolt woke her.

Startled, Muree found the train was stopping, and not too smoothly.

Rab was already out of his chair, looking through the big windows. Peering over his shoulder she saw an odd structure, a kind of bowl full of girders – that at least was her first impression – gliding past the slowing carriage. She stood to see better.

He glanced at her. 'You OK? You look a little groggy. You did sleep most of the way.'

She thought about that as she sipped water. 'I think I'll need to eat soon.' She stared out of the window, and was soon distracted.

They seemed to be somewhere near the great crater's centre, now. When she looked around, there was no sign of the crater-rim mountains – not in any direction. This was a crater so large that, from the centre, you couldn't see the walls.

She realised slowly that she had never been in such a large, open space, open in the sense of full of air and light, as opposed to vacuum. Her heart pounded.

Take it easy. It's just like the ship, she told herself. *That was big enough, wasn't it? A big enclosure. This is just the same, but bigger . . .*

But the bigness made a difference. The blue sky-dome looked

as if it was infinite – open, somehow, not enclosed at all. The lumes, on poles and hangers or drifting in the air under some kind of floats, were dazzling pinpoints that made her eyes hurt.

Rab was studying her. She had the impression she wasn't fooling him.

'Is it really just that you need to eat?'

She merely glared back.

He said, 'I did talk to some of your shipmates before we left the Mask. About how they were feeling, reacting, now they were off the ship at last. I know, it's a big ship – but there's actually only a few places in the Solar System like *this* – big in human terms, big and open and wide. Where you can walk around without a pressure suit. Earth being the ultimate, of course. They call it agoraphobia, a fear of big open spaces. Your ship is big but not that big. Whereas here—'

'Point taken.' That was snapped out. 'Oh, I'm sorry. You *have* got a point. No walls, yes, being able to see more than a kilometre or two in any direction, yes, it freaks me out a little. I think. But we've too much to do to fret about stuff like that.'

He grinned. 'Like liberating the human race? Well, we haven't liberated ourselves yet. Although we might be one step closer soon.' He seemed thoughtful; he was quiet for a while. Then, 'I'll tell you a secret. I've walked on planets before. I was born on a planet. This place, all this airy engineering, freaks me out too. As if the body knows it's all a fake. As if we all miss Earth, on some deep level. Sad, isn't it? Come on. We're slowing.'

Once the train had stopped, they half-stumbled out, together. Other passengers marched out without much hesitation.

Outside, Muree took her time over her first steps, though she shook off Rab's offering of a helpful (flesh and blood) hand. Standing still, stretching, she looked around.

There were clusters of buildings around the train stop – many advertising themselves as short-term hostels like the one they had stayed in at the crater wall. Also what looked like warehouses. Holding goods to be distributed across the crater floor, perhaps.

Further away she made out that odd structure she'd noticed from the train, like a tremendous bowl. An antenna of some kind? But the shape seemed too irregular for that, the interior too cluttered. Evidently it was a landmark, though. People were making their way towards whatever it was, some marching straight there from the train. As if it were the point of the trip.

She looked further, squinting in the bright lume-light. Beyond this stop she saw more carriages on diverging lines. Though some hefty buildings cluttered the near distance, she could see far across this flat landscape, scored by tracks, scarred by settlements, clusters of structures that might be warehouses, stores, engineering depots.

'Is that all freight traffic?' she said now. She pointed at a long train of sealed cars, heading across the landscape.

'Probably,' Rab said. 'And a lot of freight to traffic. Mars doesn't grow its own food, remember – or scarcely any. Most comes from Venus, more than a million tonnes a day, shipped across and fed into the distribution system down here. Feeding a quarter of a billion people, most of them here, in Hellas. Hence the number of freight trains.'

'You told me that last night. But still . . . even now I'm here, looking at it . . . I can't get around the fact that they *grow their food on another planet* . . .'

He grinned. 'Your mouth is open. You're the interstellar traveller, remember?'

She gave a wry grin back. 'All this is as remarkable as anything out there.' She turned to look in the other direction. One more distant settlement featured very tall, very spindly buildings: towers and blocks. Was *that* the true capital of Mars? She recalled images of cities on old Earth, featuring similarly grandiose monuments.

But the light seemed too brilliant for comfort, and she reflexively turned away.

Rab said, 'The light here is supposed to emulate what sunlight was like on Earth. Which makes it far more intense than on the original, unmodified Mars. You still OK?'

'Yes,' she said, knowing she spoke more from determination than from conviction.

She looked over again at the odd, bowl-shaped structure. People were gathered around it now, gawking, some holding bits of luggage, straight from the trains.

'And I have a feeling I know what *that* is. What we've come to see?'

He looked at what she was seeing. And he grinned. 'Let's get this done.'

Just as she had first observed, up close it was a hemispherical bowl, open upwards, containing some kind of framework.

And it was big, big enough for them both to climb inside – with a dozen others, she thought, if they tried – but that was evidently forbidden, given the imposing railings surrounding the monument. For surely that was what this was.

An enigmatic monument, if so. The structure within the bowl was complex, angular – a kind of compact geometry, with skeletal geometric shapes nested one inside the other. Shapes picked out in struts, each perhaps the length of her shin bone, struts assembled in triangles and squares and cubes and tetrahedra, one nested within the next.

'So this is the most obvious place on Mars to come find your mother, or whoever else it is? But what is it, scrap?'

He had to laugh, it seemed. But he looked around a little nervously, returning the glances of other visitors. 'Not that. I've been looking it up while you slept . . . You could call it the Architect's first vision, in response to the attack on Neptune, the start of the invasion.' He looked at her. 'The first conceptual sketch of what they came to call Fortress Sol.'

She looked at it with new eyes. 'Oh. The first representation of this great cosmic prison, then.'

'If you like. This – skeleton, this sketch of how it might have been – wasn't meant to be developed as it stood, but it's respectfully based on ancient ideas . . . And of course by now it's ancient itself. I've never been here before myself, but everyone – across the Solar System – every kid is taught about this structure, the Architect's first design . . .'

'Respectfully *ancient*?'

'Look, follow me around. It's better if you just see it. There's a stair that leads to a platform. For viewing.' He reached out. 'You want the fake hand or the human?'

She ignored him, folded her arms, and walked around the monument without help.

He followed.

She came to a steep stair, with a metal handrail. The small viewing platform at the top was unoccupied. She climbed briskly, still leading the way – and then found herself hanging on tightly to that handrail. Somehow the lighter gravity made the perch feel more perilous than it had looked. At least she would fall at only one-third Earth's acceleration . . .

Rab followed her up quickly. As he climbed, she heard the singing of his artificial hand as it scraped the metal of the handrail. When he joined her, she gave him a look to forestall his asking again if she was OK.

And they stood side by side, looking down into that bowl, the structures inside.

Nested structures, she saw.

A cube first, containing a pyramid-like figure, but a 'pyramid' with a base of only three sides, not four, not like the four-sided Egyptian monuments she'd seen in the *Lightbird*'s history gallery – a tetrahedron, that was the name. And more detail, deeper inside within the pyramid-like frame . . .

'It does have a certain elegance,' she said. 'Very complex to look at, but with a certain – symmetry. A logic.'

'So it does. And this was a first gut, mathematical, even artistic response to the threat of the destroyers, who were turning everything to dust and chaos. It's been called a frozen scream, or a desperate attempt at analysis, at comprehension, fitting the new horrors into old models . . . Anyhow, the sculpture worked, as a sculpture. With the Solar System supposedly threatened by chaotic invaders, it evoked a response that was based on something human, something much, much older . . .

'Of course this is a copy of the original, said to be on Earth itself.

'Look at it. Tell me what you see.'

When she looked again, as her mind slowly deconstructed the layered, nested structures, she was struck again by the elegance of it all . . . 'It's like – a mathematical puzzle. But there is a kind of rightness about it.'

He looked up at her. 'Yes. That's not a bad guess. It's more like a mathematical *engine*, though.'

'An engine?'

'Lesson time. Do you know much mathematics? Do you know what those nested shapes are?'

She looked at him. 'You wouldn't know this, but as a kid I *loved* math. I grew up on a starship that was in many ways restricted. There were a lot of things I learned about, but only through pictures, words. We didn't have much room to play, even. No room for *stuff*, and not much stuff either. *And* we were restricted in what we could make and do. You don't want your kids to start unscrewing hull panels. You want them doing something that's going to be useful, some day. *But—*'

'Math was different.'

'Yes. When I was old enough to get it – if I could get it at all. I was no genius. But, geometry. There's an infinite depth in there that you can explore through a screen. VR handling too.'

'OK,' he said. 'Well, that helps. So here's a physical manifestation of that same impulse, the impulse that motivated the Architect in their response to the invasion . . . I've heard people call it a sublimation. Taking the chaos and unease of the times and making something – well, orderly. Beautiful.'

'Safe?'

'If you like.' He grinned. '*You* studied these things because their images didn't take up any space. You could study them virtually. And the Architect turned to them because of their – abstract beauty.'

'The regular solids.'

'Right,' he said. 'I was never a mathematics buff myself. But I learned about all this, a lot of people do, because of this monument, and representations of it. What it meant to me, to us.

'So, as I can see you know – these solids, nested in the monument, are particular kinds of shapes in three-dimensional space. Frameworks with flat, regular faces, the product of a game with certain rules . . . The regular polyhedra.

'The cube is the obvious one. And that's the outermost here, of this – nest. Oh, but what were the rules of this game? You would only allow solids with certain properties. Think, Rab . . .

Yes. Every face of every solid has to be a regular polygon. So, for the cube, every face is a square. Another rule. The same number of faces have to meet at every edge – so, two squares meet on each edge of the cube. And the same number of faces have to meet at every vertex – so, the cube has three squares meeting at every corner.'

'OK . . .'

'OK. So there are only *five* such regular solids, mathematically. They're called the Platonic solids. The cube, plus the tetrahedron – like a pyramid but with only three sides, and a triangular base – then the octahedron, made up of eight triangles, the dodecahedron with twelve pentagons for faces – five sided panels – and the icosahedron with twenty faces, all identical triangles. And that's *all* there can be given the rules: the set of panels, the edges and the vertices. It's an expression of the three-dimensional space we live in. The ancient Greeks knew that . . . You heard of the Greeks?'

'No. And I don't know why we're looking at this – mathematical game. What does it have to do with the conquest of the Solar System?'

'Good question,' Rab said. 'I once asked that, and a smart teacher on Venus got me to study it, during a suspension. When I had problems with the hand and was finding it hard to sit still . . . For me, sitting and thinking wasn't punishment. A bit of abstraction took my mind off it . . .

'Look – this assembly is really all about between the Greeks, who thought the Sun orbited the Earth. *Somebody* had to be the first to figure out the structure of the Solar System. And they tried.'

'I know the math, some of it. But I just got off an interstellar spacecraft. Just imagine I never heard of these – *Greeks*.'

'Smart guys. Three, nearly four millennia back. They studied patterns in the sky, developed some smart mathematics.

'Look. The ancients knew of six planets: five visible plus the Earth. Also, you have the Sun and Moon – or we had them then. But why did the planets follow the paths they did? Why the different *times* they took to orbit the Earth – because that was what they thought was happening at first – why different *distances*? And why those particular distances? If the heavens are an expression of God's will, why isn't everything orderly? Nice and neat and mathematical?'

'And so—'

'And so there was a guy called Johannes Kepler, who lived just over sixteen hundred years ago . . . maybe two thousand years after the smartest of the Greeks. And he found some of the answers. Or thought he did.

'Kepler was a contemporary of Tycho Brahe, a great planetary observer, and Galileo Galilei, another – and a guy called Copernicus, a cleric, a kind of religious-minded mathematician-astronomer. And out of all this, all the new data, came new ideas. Following Copernicus, Kepler was able to *prove* that the planets, including the Earth, were orbiting the Sun. That was heresy for the dominant church of the time, and – well, it took some effort to make the case.

'But even when Kepler had proved to himself that the planets orbit the Sun, what kind of regularity is there in those orbits? In the end he was able to show that planetary orbits are ellipses with the Sun at one focus; that there is a regularity to the rate at which the planets sweep out areas around the Sun. The square of an orbit's period is proportional to the cube of the length—'

'Enough!'

He grinned. 'Sorry.'

'So what has this box of antique toys got to do with planetary astronomy?'

'Well, Kepler didn't just leap to the right answer. He knew from the data he had that there must be some regularity in the planets' orbits and their spacing – but before he got to the right formulation, he thought the regularity must derive from *the platonic solids*. He was clinging to that Greek elegance, you see.

'Those regular solids – the Platonic solids. This was the architecture of the heavens, he thought, and what better scaffolding than that? And he assembled all these ideas into what he called his *Mysterium Cosmographicum*. Cosmic mystery.'

She peered into that box again. 'OK. So I see all these nested shapes. Here's the cube on the outside. What planet's orbit does that specify?'

'Jupiter and Saturn,' he said briskly. 'The outermost planets known in Kepler's day. Now, look. Imagine you built the smallest sphere that could fit around that cube. Around the upright edges, the eight corners, OK? And then build the largest sphere possible *inside* the cube. One that just touches the centre of the six faces . . . you call those the circumscribed sphere, outside, and the inscribed sphere, inside.

'And Kepler proposed that *that* was how the dimensions of Jupiter's and Saturn's orbits were fixed. By the radii of the inscribed and circumscribed spheres, using all the platonic solids in a kind of nesting.'

'I . . . get it! I love it,' Muree said. 'If only it were true. And the rest of the planets?'

'Well, Kepler couldn't go further out. He didn't know about Uranus and Neptune – no observations yet. But, working *in* from Jupiter, the next in line is Mars, which is controlled by a tetrahedron – four sides, with Jupiter's orbit the outside sphere now, and Mars the inside.'

'It's like a – a ladder of geometry.'

'Right. Next in is Earth, surrounded by a dodecahedron,

Venus an icosahedron, and Mercury an octahedron.'

'Wow. But – how good is the fit?'

He grinned. 'Surprisingly good. It's only about twenty per cent out for the planets as far as Mars. Over thirty per cent for Jupiter and Saturn. In the end Kepler persuaded himself away from the model, and found the proper relationships – the orbits are actually ellipses – that eventually led to a full theory of gravity, which *actually* shapes the orbits—'

'OK, OK. You said that. I think I get it. But don't ask me to repeat it in half an hour. So what has this to do with the invasion, the Architect?'

'Well, because all this celestial geometry is – *cosy*. Safe. Orderly.

'There was a great wave of anxiety after the invasion. As you would have expected – as *you* know. Your ancestors were sent out to the stars. Mine hid away, from a hostile universe. But we seemed to need more. A cosy Solar System. And that was what Kepler had dreamed up in his *Mysterium Cosmographicum* – the cosmic mystery – that was what he called his nested figures and circles. Orderly, safe, logical. Well, we couldn't build the *Mysterium*—'

'The Frame.' Muree suddenly saw it. 'That's a sort of – flattened – version of this Kepler thing, isn't it? Squares and circles, into which the planets' orbits fit. And full of light, glowing, glowing light . . .'

Rab grinned. 'You get it. *That* was what the Architect finally dreamed up. It's based on the same principles, but it's simpler – and also pretty practical, of course.'

'So long as you have plenty of lumes to use up . . .'

'And,' came a new voice, 'of course, that dream gave us a fast transit system, which is a pretty good means of controlling a population scattered across the planets . . .'

*

The new voice was behind them, startling them both. They whirled around.

A woman stood there, evidently having approached too silently for them to notice. Tall, slender, dressed in dark green. Her face was pinched, her eyes deep, tired-looking.

Muree had no idea who this was.

Rab was standing open-mouthed.

The newcomer smiled thinly – nervously, Muree thought.

'I apologise for overhearing you. I'm glad my message got through to you via Angela Plokhy.'

'Plokhy,' Rab snapped. 'She knows everybody. Everything. Damn it. This is down to Plokhy, is it? Why are you *here*?'

The smile wavered. 'So I can talk to you. I've been following your – adventures.' She glanced at Muree. 'Since the starship docked. You've quite a high profile—'

That was when a surface vehicle rolled up, a bus with fat wheels. Muree was hardly surprised to see Angela Plokhy at the wheel.

Now Plokhy's familiar voice sounded in her suit's systems.

'Good. I hoped I'd find you together. Does save time.'

Rab was still glaring at the strange woman. He demanded, 'What do you *want*? Why show up *now*?'

'I want to go with you to Earth. Because that's where you'll find the truth. And I want to help you find it. I've been studying all this too.'

Plokhy gestured to Muree, beckoning. *All aboard . . .*

Rab stood frozen, staring, then shook his head. 'Why here, like this? Why now? Ah— *Mother*!'

And without another glance at the newcomer, he turned and left the platform.

Muree was astonished.

Mother?

26

Once the bus was rolling, all of them aboard – without any preamble, any introductions – Plokhy said she had been told, by Elinor Callis, to get them off-planet.

Elinor. Muree remembered Rab had said his mother's name was Elinor.

So Plokhy, in the driver's seat, informed them now that she would take them all back to the spaceport on the south side of the Hellas crater-complex, and pick up a shuttle from there. The most obvious route, the fastest way off the planet. Just like that.

And then, as the bus turned away from the monument site, Plokhy fished out a small gadget from within her tunic, pressed it against what looked to Muree to be a random bit of the bus's inner structure. Then she put away the gadget with a deft flourish.

Muree watched this with a smile. 'And so now nobody knows where this bus is going, and who it's carrying. Am I right?'

'The bus doesn't even know *my* name. Or our destination. And with any luck nobody's going to notice us trundling by, at this bus's normal speed, fake signature or not. We need to cover more than twenty-five hundred kilometres back to the spaceport. Take us about two Martian days. There are faster ways, such as the rail you used, but they are all—'

'All more visible,' Muree said.

'Correct. You're getting the idea, if not the paranoia. With any luck any pursuers will think you've gone on into the city.'

Rab grunted. 'Of course they will! Who'd be so dumb as to come all this way, all the way to Mars, to the monument, just to turn and go straight back?'

'Us?' Muree suggested.

His mother nodded. 'And then, on your ship, and off to Earth?'

Plokhy glanced around. 'Which is going to take us about fourteen days, by the way, at my standard five per cent of Earth gravity acceleration, and given where the planets are right now. I take it nobody wants to ride the Frame.'

Elinor shrugged. 'Your ship – you – are surely not perfectly secure. Nothing in this Solar System is; I've learned that often enough. But some things are more secure than others.'

Her voice was dry, almost cracking, Muree thought.

Elinor was tall, gaunt, her hair dark like Rab's, but streaked with white. She wore a nondescript surface suit, heavy, quilted – meant for Martian conditions rather than Venus or Mercury, Muree guessed. She seemed older than Muree might have expected. Withdrawn.

Still Rab wouldn't look at her.

And Muree saw how difficult this must be for him. Muree wondered how many encounters, how many conversations, in person or otherwise, they'd had since that first traumatic separation. If any?

On impulse, she reached over to him, and took his hand – choosing the prosthetic, deliberately. 'This is all of a rush. Or has been. And now the rush has stopped for a while, and once we get out of here we're all going to have plenty of time to – talk.'

'You've been aboard the *Styx*,' Plokhy said. 'Not you, Elinor. There's more room than in this rolling box. At least, more room for privacy if you want it, when we get there.'

Elinor said, 'I wanted to find you. I have contacts – I was alerted to the arrival of the *Lightbird* as it happened. Since then, Rab, your name has become prominent globally.' She seemed to allow herself a smile. 'I was – proud.'

Rab pulled his hand away from Muree's. 'I don't know what there is to say between us. We haven't spoken, face to face, since . . .'

Muree was struggling to keep up with these revelations. 'You have spoken since Venus, then. I thought you told me you hadn't—'

'No,' Rab said. 'Only – formalities. When I've passed life stages, particular ages, as I needed new idents and so on. *She* had to verify my existence, my identity. Ha! That's a joke.'

Plokhy frowned. 'What was done, was done. If not for your mother's intervention – well, the death rate on Mercury is pretty high, remember. You mightn't *be* here by now.'

Muree said to Elinor, 'Mercury. Which is where I guess *you* were sent after—'

'Not immediately,' Elinor said. 'The authorities are more subtle than that. They do, in fact, tolerate some independent thinking. The brute force stuff is left to the machines; humans need to exert judgement. But if your defiance is too overt, yes, the punishment has to be overt too. In my case there was some subtlety in the penalty, for my subtle crime. I had to be punished, but I was already being punished by the loss of my son . . .' Her voice seemed to catch. 'In the end, yes, it seems that a banishment to Mercury, for *me*, was sanction enough to satisfy.'

'Yet here you are, now,' Plokhy said. 'And you got in touch with me.'

'Yes. When I heard about the *Lightbird*, and Rab's involvement—' She sighed. 'You know, I learned a lot on Mercury. Achieved a lot. Made a lot of contacts.'

Rab snorted. 'You would. It's what people like you do. Whatever pit you are thrown into.'

Elinor seemed to ignore that. I did gain some freedom – including the freedom to get *off* Mercury, occasionally. Found my ideas developing. Opinions hardening about the regime we labour under.' She glanced at Rab. 'I always followed your career, you know. Even during the times when we were officially out of touch. And so I know about your absconding from the Mask, your travel across the Frame, your journey to Mars . . .'

Rab frowned. 'How *do* you know?'

Plokhy answered for her. 'We live in a very controlled society, but also a very old one. And the various mechanisms it has evolved to exert control over its citizens, while thorough, are also very old. And leaky. Which is how I make my own living. Exploiting the cracks.'

Elinor said, 'Sometimes I think the powers that control us *relish* the imperfection of the system. The rules, the monitoring, the oversight. If people think they can get away with breaking the rules, you might get more leaks. And a theoretically imperfect system is also a more flexible system.'

Rab held up his false hand. 'Like when I got this. Lieutenant Planter found a solution that bent the rules a bit – but which gave you what you wanted, Mother. Albeit at a price,' he said coldly.

Elinor turned away.

Muree exchanged a glance with Plokhy. *They so need to talk.*

'So anyhow,' Plokhy said now, 'the first major step for us is back to the spaceport. I will whisk you all as if by magic through the security clearances, load you aboard the *Styx*, and on we go to – wherever we go to next –'

'Earth,' Elinor said.

Plokhy seemed to think that over. Neither Rab nor Muree said anything. Muree wouldn't have known what to say, in this tangle of personal political, and *planets*.

It was Plokhy, predictably, who broke the silence. 'It will take fourteen days from here. And I intend to spend much of that time sleeping. Beginning now, if it doesn't offend . . .'

She pulled a curtain to isolate the driver's position from the rest of the bus, and was as good as her word.

That left Muree with Rab and Elinor.

'Earth,' Elinor said again.

Rab didn't reply.

There was a stiff silence between them. Mother and son. Muree could only imagine the conversations they would finally have, after they got through this unexpected reunion. If the events of this strange odyssey allowed it. But not yet.

Muree retreated to the back of the bus, pulled across a partition, and tried her best to emulate Plokhy and sleep, leaving the two of them to themselves.

But sleep was a long time coming for any of them save, it seemed, the phlegmatic pilot. If Rab and Elinor were able to talk, Muree wasn't aware of it.

When she did sleep, though, she dreamed of skies full of geometry.

27

Under Plokhy's guidance, their transit back through the south rim-mountains crater wall and to the spaceport beyond was as seamless and obstruction-free as the rest of the journey from the monument.

They didn't even have to change out of the bus they had ridden from the centre of Hellas.

As promised by Plokhy, the bus bypassed much of the spaceport infrastructure and its protocols, and docked smoothly with the flank of the *Styx* itself. So they were able to transfer from ground vehicle straight to space vehicle, avoiding another set of identity validations.

Muree was new to all this, but Rab and his mother were comparative veterans of travelling around the developed Solar System. Still, though they mostly stayed silent, they were both evidently impressed by Plokhy's expertise in concealment and subterfuge.

Once they were inside the *Styx,* as soon as the locks were sealed and tested for integrity – even before the passengers had discarded their emergency-protocol pressure suits – Plokhy had the craft disengage from the mechanisms of the Hellas spaceport and roll away on wheeled landing legs, already preparing itself for flight.

'Good,' said Plokhy decisively. 'That's that done. The sooner we are independent and can get out of here, the better – as always.'

As the craft quietly readied itself for take-off, she drew back the partition between the bridge area and the rest of the habitable hull, with its screens and tiny windows and deep acceleration couches.

As usual Plokhy took her own seat, the largest, facing banks of screens and touchpads. She slipped headphones on her ears, pulled a breathing mask over her face, and began pressing buttons, swiping touch screens, murmuring soft commands. Immediately Muree could hear soft noises, the low hiss of air circulation systems, subtle electronic chimes that told of engines and artificial minds waking up.

Rab was watching Plokhy as she worked. He murmured, 'You look so – comfortable.'

Plokhy turned. 'I'm back in a ship again. This is how I grew up. My environment. *My* ship. What's not to love?'

Elinor was sceptical. 'Really? But a ship like this can't protect you. You can't ever be secure – not in a System that's threaded through with global surveillance and controls on travel and transport. Despite your counter-measures, whatever they are – no offence.'

'None taken. Normally I would take it slower, be a lot more wary. But these aren't normal times.' She glanced back at Muree and Rab, and grinned. 'Not since that lot showed up. Anyhow, all I ever ask for is a fighting chance.'

Rab grinned back. 'You've certainly given us that, Plokhy.'

Muree felt a little bewildered. 'Somehow I never thought I would be back in this ship again . . . And certainly not going to *Earth*.'

'Get used to it,' Plokhy said, working her screens.

Watching her, Muree felt still more confused. 'And after Earth, then what?'

'Then we go wherever we need to be next. Or, more likely, get away from wherever it is we *don't* want to be.'

Elinor was curious. 'Why are *you* doing all this, Angela? What's in it for you?'

Plokhy sighed. 'I hate it when people ask that. Call it a character flaw if you like. I just don't fit. And – it's what I discussed before, with the youngsters. The political system we live under, while it keeps vast numbers of humans alive, is built on lies, and control. Huge lies. And I don't accept that. Call it a gut reaction. I guess I've felt like that since I was young, ever since I understood what a lie was – and that I was being lied to, by just about everybody around me.'

Elinor snorted. 'Have you ever studied history? Ancient history, I mean, pre-Neptune? Just about every political system humans ever devised was about control by a central few, generally with the use of monstrous lies. Look up religions – it took generations of geniuses like Kepler to start cutting through all *that* hierarchy of controlling untruth. The maturing of political science, and the development of a truly rational, truly fair form of democracy, didn't happen until it was born on the Moon – a lethal environment, where people *had* to cooperate and coexist just to stay alive day to day. But after the Neptune disaster, once they had brought in all this panoply of the Mask and the Frame, all that *control* – why, it's as if that ancient authoritarian method of government has come right back. In fact in this modern age it's finally reached its peak. All those long-dead warlords and emperors and popes would be proud.'

Rab seemed shocked by this little speech, Muree thought.

He said now, 'That sounds pretty cynical, Mother.'

'Cynical? That's from the boy whose hand was cut off to spare him a short life of dangerous drudgery on Mercury? Two choices, both existentially awful? Because *that was the law*? That from the boy, the *man*, who right now is on the run because he didn't want to be in on the birth of another huge lie? *That's* because of the law. And—'

'Well, OK. But I don't see why it's impossible to imagine a better system. For now, we're on the run—'

'Not me,' called Plokhy. '*You're* on the run. I'm just the pilot. Speaking of which, we're ready to go. Strap in. Literally, I mean. In five minutes we take off at twice Earth's gravity. Be seated or face the consequences.'

They hastily sat back and checked their couches.

In the last moment, Elinor leaned forward and held Muree's shoulder. She said softly, 'I'm glad you're in his life. You've shaken him, made him see other possibilities. You're good for him.'

Muree tried not to flinch at her touch, illogical as that impulse was. *Whatever happened on Venus, Elinor was a victim too . . .* She shrugged. 'And he for me. I'd never have dared take off on this adventure without him. If I'd just gone back to the *Lightbird* from the Mask, I'd have missed so much – all this – history!'

Elinor smiled, and would have leaned away.

But, impulsively, Muree grabbed her hand. 'And I wouldn't have met you,' she said.

'Me?'

Muree hesitated, hoping she wasn't speaking out of turn. 'I know how you saved your son. On Venus. You did your best.'

Elinor leaned back. 'Thank you.'

If Rab overheard this, as surely he must have in this very small cabin, he showed no sign.

The ship was starting to move. Muree leaned back in her

couch and let the strapping close tight around her. She shut her eyes, pretending she was back in the warm, noisy lume-creches of the *Lightbird*.

28

The trip felt like a long one. And it was, objectively.

'Well, this ain't the Frame,' Plokhy said sourly, when Rab complained about the slowness of it all – not for the first time.

With time, if they'd waited – or if they'd just been lucky – the planetary alignments *could* have delivered Earth and Mars in their different orbits closer to their minimum separation, and allowed a faster crossing. It wasn't to be. As Kepler's divine calculations would have it – and as Plokhy sarcastically put it – right now, travelling inwards from Mars's orbit to Earth's, they would have to cover a distance further than Earth's orbital radius. And so, at the ship's standard running acceleration of around five per cent of Earth's gravity, the journey would take about fourteen days.

Plokhy was blunt about it. 'Anybody who thinks that's too slow can walk.'

So they started to settle down, in their different ways.

Pilot and passengers kept themselves to themselves from the beginning. Particularly Elinor, Muree observed.

Plokhy stayed busy with ship's business, using the time to run through such maintenance as could be achieved away from a dry dock. That kept her in the small engine-access compartment, or else at her bridge station.

Muree, meanwhile, found a niche in the lounge, where, using the ship's extensive library, she skimmed through as much as she could of the history of Earth and its colonies – or its prehistory, before the 'invasion' from deep space, before Neptune, before the transforming aftermath. Why do that? Because she had a gathering, nagging feeling that her future was here, in the Solar System, rather than back on the *Lightbird*, even if and when it ever left for the stars. *Here* was where history had been made and the future would be born, for mankind . . . But right now that future was opaque, unmapped. And, maybe, just she might be able to contribute to that future.

That interval of calm study lasted most of the voyage.

On the last day Elinor asked to speak to her.

Muree hesitated before joining her, in a partitioned, soundproofed section of the lounge.

Through this long journey – ever since they had encountered Elinor – confined together as they all were, she hadn't wanted to get tangled up in any messy mother-and-son reunion, however well or badly it went.

But she could hardly refuse to *talk* to Elinor now. On what grounds?

When she reluctantly pulled herself through the partition, she found Elinor studying wall-screen images of what was evidently the Earth – images of the whole planet, or subsidiary screens containing magnified images of landscapes, seascapes, the intricate coastlines that separated them – or stylised maps, some of which showed terrain variations, plains and mountain ranges.

Green landscapes.

Smooth swathes that might have been grasslands or forests.

Bare stains that might be deserts . . .

Images of a globe lit up by the light of, apparently, a distant but bright Sun.

'Very old images,' Muree guessed. 'If that's sunlight. Before Neptune?'

Elinor looked back and smiled. 'What do you think of what you see?'

'It's – beautiful.'

'As you look at it now. I'm curious. Were you interested in Earth, before you got to the Solar System? Were any of you ship-born interested? In a planet that was still, what, light-months away from the *Lightbird* when you were born?'

Muree said, 'Well, we – my grandparents, the first crew of the *Lightbird* – had set off to the Solar System seven decades before I was born, specifically to see what had become of Earth and the other planets. And I grew up knowing that we were going to reach the Solar System and find out, *in my lifetime*. When I came to understand that, as I grew up, I felt – privileged – to have been born at the right time.' She thought that over. 'Of course I was interested in rather an abstract way. I had no idea what it would be *like*. But after all it's where we *all* came from.'

Elinor raised an eyebrow. 'In my experience, most people are mostly interested in the people around them – that's the beginning and the end. Granted, I'd already concluded that my son was lucky to have found you. That you had an awareness of your place in the long mission, as you say. But maybe you . . . self-selected. If you hadn't been *you*, if you hadn't had such interests, such a broad awareness, you wouldn't have come out here – and you wouldn't be able to help me now.'

Muree was getting lost. 'Help you do what?'

Elinor took a breath. 'Do what you're doing with Rab already. *Find the monument of the Architect*. He seems to have an instinct like mine. Maybe I even talked to him about it, when he was very small. Like a fairy tale . . . I can't remember.' Her face closed. 'There's a lot I don't remember of that time. Or that I've pushed away. And if we do find the monument, help me – understand it. I believe you have a unique perspective that – well, may be able to help us. You may see what we can't, from an outsider point of view.

'The true monument, I mean, not that medieval lash-up on Mars. *That* was just an exercise, in a way – I believe – a means for the Architect to work through their *own* thinking. Taking Kepler and those other ancient thinkers as a starting point. Certainly the records say that the final version of the monument was created on Earth, *before* the transfer of Earth's residual population to Mars. At the time it was part of a big operation; a lot of monuments were transferred . . . but not that one.'

Muree felt baffled, distracted by the background to all this. '*Why* would people leave Earth, for Mars?'

Elinor poured her tea, from a lidded jug onto a closed cup.

'Well, they had no choice. The central authority defined and implemented it all. I mean, the relocation of mankind. Part of a design, with a purpose for every planet of the Solar System. With Mars, specifically Hellas, taking over as the urban centre, the seat of government, other agencies. Earth itself was to be – repurposed. The cities abandoned as vast museums. Farmlands left to turn back to wilderness, the artificial sky farms of Venus cultivated in their place. All of this, and the outer planets, connected by the Frame – in fact the Frame made it all possible. And the energy of the Sun was drained in the process.

'We had cut ourselves out of the universe, Muree. Hidden by the Mask, left in the dark by the exhaustion of the Sun. That was an enormous trauma, for anybody who remotely grasped it – the human mind needed a new *image* of the Solar System.'

'And that's where the Architect comes in,' Muree said.

'And that's where they come in, yes . . . Inspired by their echoes of Kepler and his *Mysterium* – the Solar System a pocket universe, built on mathematical logic. A home where mankind could nestle in intellectual certainty, in symmetry, in order and safety. So—'

'A new *Mysterium*. A new mathematical structure, a new certainty – like Rab said at the monument.'

'Yes. A new logic after the terrible disruptive illogic of the invasion. It took me a long time to see it myself. Well, my excuse is I grew up *inside* the structure, I am shaped by it, as generations of others have been shaped. It fills space, it fills my head. We all depend on it . . .

'You need to have the right perspective. The Frame, and the processes behind it, *is* beautiful. A dream of mathematical logic, of design. With a beauty that echoes Kepler's dreams. And *we built it*. We humans . . . The Architect planned it to be a kind of solidified dream of order in the sky – the order we lost when the chaos of the Neptune invasion disrupted so much.

'And so the Frame, our own *Mysterium Cosmographicum*, was built. *But*, the Frame – the grand design . . .'

Muree prompted, 'Yes?'

'It was subverted,' Elinor said.

'Think about it. A transport network that covers the whole Solar System with geometric logic? It necessarily *controls* where and how you travel, what routes you can choose, the exchanges where you must make your presence felt – and records your actions every step of the way. You can subvert it in turn, of course – and your new friend Angela Plokhy is an expert at that – there will always be subversion. But any such acts are minor, easily tracked – usually casually discounted.

'And, more vital yet than the mere tracking of movements, *the*

Frame delivers water. Also power, light, heat – but, most crucially, water, from moons made of ice to worlds that were formed dry as bones. Even Mars, which has some residual water, will ultimately be entirely dependent on the Frame supply. And—'

'And lumes,' Muree said. 'The Frame brings these . . . subject worlds . . . heat and light, lumes, from the big Uranus pit.' She thought that over. 'Ah. And what an instrument of control *that* is.'

Elinor nodded. 'You see it now.'

'Yes. We all learned about that kind of coercion growing up on the *Lightbird*. A generation ship. It's an environment with an inevitable element of "benevolent coercion", the ship rules called it, when we studied them. Necessary for survival. But this was why we had check systems that didn't allow any one person to gain *total* access, total control. You see, we were told what might happen should things go wrong – it was gruesome . . . *If I cut off your food, you might last weeks. Without water, you are dead in days. But if I cut off your air, you are dead in seconds . . .*'

'Well, it's much the same here,' Elinor said. 'If I stop the flow of lumes to a world, if I cut off its light and heat – how long would the population last, days? Less? Or, the supply of Titan water to Mars? Can global thirst and hunger, darkness and cold, really be used as a threat? Such ideas are not voiced openly. But the capability is there. The threat implicit, unspoken. Everybody knows . . .'

Muree nodded. 'So what are you going to do about it?'

Elinor grinned. 'Tear it apart.'

'We're closing on Earth.' That was a shout from Plokhy at her bridge station. 'You might like to see it. Or not . . .'

They exchanged glances.

'Come,' Elinor said, leading the way out of her chair.

*

At the bridge station, Rab and Plokhy were peering into monitor screens.

At first, all Muree could see were flashes of dazzling blue-white, shifting, merging as she watched. All this was contained by a curving limb against the background darkness . . .

Earth.

Rab didn't turn around, even when his estranged mother came into the cabin. He, and Plokhy too, were evidently fascinated by the view, though she imagined they must have seen versions of this scene in the past.

Earth . . .

'Dawn on planet Earth,' Plokhy said. 'Delivered by a wave of lumes, continually being taken around the globe.'

Elinor stayed close by Muree. 'This is where we must go,' she murmured. 'This is where we must search. *Earth*. For the legacy of the Architect. The true legacy. The true model.'

Muree asked, 'And the one on Mars—'

'Is a mere representation of a medieval thought experiment. A starting point. But a starting point for what the Architect *did* envisage, and build.'

'And why is that so important? The actual Earth model, I mean. Why've we come all this way?'

Plokhy half-turned. 'Because of another legend.'

'It's a legend about that model itself. It supposedly represents features of our real-world *Mysterium*, the one that got made – the Frame, the Mask, the Solar Wrap, all the rest of it. But there are features that *differ* from the model. Somehow the Architect's plan has been hijacked, their intentions subverted. Those who control us have *weaponised* the *Mysterium*, the whole Solar System as we have rebuilt it. Or – you could say they have built it around a lie. And certainly have not delivered the dreams of the Architect.'

Elinor nodded. 'That's the conspiracy theory, all right. That our beloved governments have perverted the Architect's plans. And that those plans were either destroyed or so well hidden that no one has discovered them . . .

'The *Mysterium* model on Mars, the representation of Kepler's idealised geometry, is of course on display. There are other versions elsewhere, claimed to be copies of the Architect's model – but all tampered with, mutilated. Made to lie, like the one on Mars, if not replicating it, or else turned into other abstractions, like the Kepler original. Meaningless, some of them.

'But on Earth – it is said – the original model survives. The one the Architect built for themselves, or at least supervised its construction.'

Muree frowned. 'Why? Why should it survive at all? Why wouldn't the authorities just destroy it?'

Elinor said, 'Perhaps simply because they believed they could *afford* to leave it, because Earth's population is so low now. It's not likely to be stumbled upon. Maybe there's even a heavy conscience about destroying such a unique artefact. But that model holds the truth of what the Architect intended. *And if we can find it, so it will show us the lies, the betrayals*. It will be the proof . . .' She sighed. 'That's the hope, anyhow.'

Distracted by the images of Earth, Muree was only half-listening.

She tried to focus. She thought of what Brad Tenant, or her other friends from the cosy days of interstellar flight, would say about how she was handling this strange, obsessed woman.

They would say that Elinor was trying to fix the world, as a payback for damaging her own son.

They would say that Muree was no psychologist.

They would surely say that she should *do* something.

Help to find that damn model. And then –

Rab called, distracting her.

'Oh. Mother. Muree. You must come and see this.'

Mother. Muree saw that Elinor actually flinched at his use of that word. His first use since their reunion, as far as Muree remembered.

Elinor glanced over at Rab, then joined him at his screen. 'What is it?'

Plokhy said, 'Dawn on planet Earth.' She tapped a screen. 'As it is manifested these days.'

Muree leaned over. She saw a disc of darkness, and a kind of drizzle of light washing around the curve of the planet, thickening, brightening. Like a curtain being drawn back, slowly, slowly, to reveal a lighted stage.

She went to another screen, and swept a hand over the contained image as she had seen Plokhy do when she wished to enlarge a section. She managed to isolate a part of that horizon, between receding dark and advancing light. And as the light advanced further, so she increased the magnification, until the edge broke up into sparks, points of light. Ahead of the wave of dawn, a ruddy fringe – caused by the diffraction of the air, no doubt – and behind that soft edge a much more brightly illuminated landscape, vivid green.

'How many?'

Elinor frowned. 'How many what?'

'How many lumes must die to heat and light this sunless planet?'

Rab tapped a screen. 'It's quite a sophisticated process. You can emulate night and day, seasonal shifts, even—'

'How many?'

Plokhy looked up at her, her expression subdued, ashamed even. Then she tapped another query. 'Ten thousand, Muree. Ten thousand per year. Thirty, forty a day. More than one per hour.'

Elinor put a hand on her shoulder. 'This distresses you. The lives of the lumes give other beings life in turn . . . But perhaps we can stop this wastage altogether. Reduce it. At least rationalise it, justify it . . .'

Rab was peering intently into his screens. 'How?' he asked.

Muree turned back to the screens, the ports, as the green and blue of Earth unfolded before her, distracting her. Politics seemed irrelevant at that moment. Even, momentarily, the plight of those thousands of lumes.

She thought of the chain of ancestors in her own past, who had come from Earth and now she had returned to Earth. A loop was closing.

'I've come home,' she murmured.

29

Angela Plokhy decreed that they would stay in Earth orbit for two days and two nights. Universally used time periods with ancient definitions which, for obvious reasons, matched the reality – but only here. Even if the light was delivered, not by the planet's turning in the face of its Sun, but by a lume cloud, endlessly orbiting.

They all needed rest – needed to calm down a little. 'An exhausted pilot is a bad pilot,' Plokhy said, in a sepulchral tone. 'Not to mention would-be explorers.'

But first they had to figure out where to land.

After the two days, they discussed this with Plokhy in her command position, acceleration couches set out for the others.

Elinor spoke sagely. 'The only clue I ever heard about the Architect's monument is that it's in "the most stable place on Earth". Believe me, I've thought hard about that, researched it, when I've had a chance. But it's not much to go on.'

Muree and Rab exchanged glances. Rab looked disappointed, Muree thought, as if hoping for more insight from his mother.

Muree said, 'Well, I won't be much use. Before the *Lightbird* got to Sol system, all I really knew about the Earth was that it was the origin of mankind. I remember a lot of images . . . oceans, deserts, ice. Impossibly large crowds of people, at vast sport events, acclaiming some ruler or other. Going to war. Burning forests, flood barriers smashed. We saw all this in school; it meant nothing to us, my cadre.'

'Well, the population crashed after the invasion,' Elinor said. 'So the record says. During the rebuilding of the Solar System.

'The basic scheme was to evacuate Earth – not entirely, but to move huge swathes of the human population to other worlds, and to make those worlds independent of the Earth itself, if not of each other.' She glanced at Muree. 'They thought Earth could be the next logical target, you see – that if Earth were eliminated, if mankind were eliminated quickly, then the invaders' greater work of dismantling the gas giants, or whatever, could proceed without hindrance.

'So, at first, there was a mess of projects, more or less coordinated. The mass evacuations to the other worlds – especially Venus, now the main source of food for the whole System, and Mercury for its mines. Mars, Hellas, was to be the urban centre, with a relatively large population. Vast survival shelters for the survivors, as the Sun was exhausted of its energy, and finally covered by the Wrap, and the Earth briefly froze. This was before the lumes had been – harvested. Tamed. Our existing life-support systems were nowhere near adequate. There were mandatory birth-control regimes across the board. Still, the death toll was . . . more than it should have been, most historians agree, I think. But the overseers hoped to save most of the human race, if not all . . .

'Then the Frame came online. The human population was scattered and mixed further. All by design.' She glanced around, and swiped a screen to display a profile of the Frame. It was coloured, Muree saw, to show the current density of traffic. Heavy everywhere, brilliant spots of overcrowding at key junctions, where the wheel rims met the spokes.

'And the evacuations continued. Although, in a way, that refugee flow never ended,' Elinor said. 'There are probably hundreds of millions, billions, in transit at any one time. And as for Earth – at some point the flight from Earth became self-perpetuating. Unending. Eventually it was decided to abandon the planet altogether – well, mostly – as far as humans were concerned. Let it heal.'

Plokhy grunted. 'After millennia of human despoliation. At the very least – tens of millennia if you want to go back to the beginning of farming, and the forest clearings, the stone-tool users who inflicted the first mass extinctions—'

'It wasn't a bad reaction to an invasion,' Elinor said. 'I suppose. As far as Earth was concerned. To try to fix what we had done before, and preserve it . . . Even now there are always scattered populations on Earth, mostly visitors. Like us, I guess. Along with geologists, climatologists, naturalists, historians. Mostly it has been given back to the green, and the *science* of the green.

'And as for the Architect – they are supposed to have lived long before the final official abandonment. Even as the colonisation of the planets had been proceeding apace. A new interplanetary economy emerged. Raw materials from Mercury, food from Venus. Passenger ships criss-crossing the inner Solar System. But it was the Earthbound Architect who conceived the Frame. A new interplanetary unity.'

Plokhy grinned. 'We would all be wedged into the clockwork of a majestic, orderly, *visible* machine. The biggest comfort blanket anybody ever saw . . .'

Muree found herself intrigued by this. Or perhaps entranced. 'What a concept, though, whatever it was *for*. What a legacy . . .'

'True,' Elinor said. 'But there are also rumours of disputes with the governing bodies at the time. Almost from the beginning.'

'What about? Details of the engineering? Which planets got connected up first?'

Elinor grinned now. 'I wouldn't be surprised. The engineering was on a planetary scale. We developed the necessary, technologies. Planetary engineering. After my own bad start I've worked my way up to a reasonably high level in the management hierarchy on Mercury. There is one, you know; we aren't all punch-drunk miners down there. We're forever building or modifying transport systems to service newly uncovered lodes of some useful mineral or ore. And there's always somebody who wants new transit lines to reach *their* favourite patch, and preferably first, before everybody else . . . So, on Mercury, I've seen machines and processes and mining endeavours on the scale of a planet . . . Even compared to that, however, the Frame is magnificent. Overwhelming. But people are people, and will always be fractious.'

Muree watched Rab as Elinor described all this. Described the world his mother had been banished to – the world where he might have had to spend his own life. His prosthetic hand flexed and unflexed, apparently without conscious volition.

Elinor said, 'But I've studied the history, such as it was. I do know there was dissent during the building of it – of the Frame and all the ancillary components, like the Hellas spaceport on Mars, the space elevators. Disputes not just about the sequence of the build but about certain elements of the final design, as it slowly evolved. And, from what I've heard, some changes were imposed at quite a late stage – changes to which the Architect was adamantly opposed.'

Rab frowned. 'So this is the key. What changes?'

Plokhy said, 'All we have is rumour. As far as *I* know. But *that*, so the story goes, is why the Architect made their model of the completed system. As *they* had envisaged it. So, whatever was finally built, however compromised, at least they could deny the changes were ever in their design. A model they . . . sequestered, hid – somewhere on Earth, their own final home. *The most stable place they could find,* so it's said. A place untouched by time – as far as possible. As I say – so the story goes. And now all we have to do is find that place.'

Rab snorted. 'And then solve some kind of interplanetary riddle, centuries old.'

Muree frowned. 'Not for the first time I'm feeling a bit bewildered by all this . . . Our worldship was, *is,* a magnificent vessel, but pretty small compared to a *world.* You couldn't hide stuff or keep secrets very well. But here . . .' She looked around at them. 'So the plan is, we're going to have to search a *whole planet* for this . . . prototype, this model. *And* we have no clue as to where on Earth this thing could be. *And* Earth is empty of people—'

'Almost,' Elinor said. 'This is Earth. Home. There's always somebody who wants to be here, to visit, to study. To – reconnect. But on the other hand, they're not likely to welcome visitors like us who've come to loot the place of its greatest intellectual treasure. And to set off a bomb under the ruling regime.'

Muree frowned. 'Is that what *you* want to do?' She glanced at Rab. 'Would you?'

He grinned. 'Never thought about it. Maybe . . .'

Plokhy said, 'As for Earth, I've dropped a few people off here on occasion. Even stepped out of the *Styx* myself. Earth means nothing special to me. But, yes, those visitors always have their own agenda. Usually seeking some ancestral home, territory, nation . . . Even hunters of rare animals, plants. The security regime here allows for landings – it would be too disruptive to try to impose an impermeable cordon – but it's a tough ride trying to get away with your trophy. And such visitors, successful or not, generally want to keep themselves to themselves. Monomaniacs.'

Rab grinned. 'Monomaniacs who can pay *you*.'

'Nothing wrong with that. Anyhow *they* probably wouldn't be willing to help you even if they could.'

'So,' Muree said, 'we're going to have to figure it out for ourselves.'

Plokhy worked a console, and a virtual globe of the Earth and its atmosphere, maybe a metre across, hovered in the air. 'Care to make a start?'

And, entranced, Muree began to explore Earth.

Continents, brown-green. Blue-black oceans swathed in cloud, in whirls and streams. The white of ice at what must be the spin axis, the poles. And all of this only half-lit – lit by the lume swarms that emulated the day-night cycle of a lost Sun.

A virtual touch by her hand made the world turn, bringing new territories into her view, new rivers, seas, oceans. There was a surprising amount of detail everywhere, Muree thought, even in the cloud structures, for example. And – much further out – she saw that Earth had a *ring*, dim, wide. A ring of industry, almost as Saturn's ring of ice had been, as she knew from ancient images.

Rab saw her looking. 'Yeah. You star folk wouldn't have seen that before. More engineering. They built the Frame, most of the massive components anyhow, with material extracted from the Moon. Earth's Moon. I believe it took, what, a third of the Moon's mass?'

'More like half,' Plokhy put in. 'Leaving that trail. All that's left of a companion body formed from a primordial collision with Earth itself . . . Rocky debris and dust. It's not even *bright* . . .'

That felt viscerally wrong to Muree – ugly. But, as she knew from her occasional forays into the libraries of the *Lightbird*, Earth had been an old, much-used world long before the lume invasion . . .

Now her attention was drawn back to the brilliant, lume-lit landscapes of Earth itself. *This* world was a proper world, she thought, a complex, changing mechanism, even though she had seen no life yet . . . At first glance the detail seemed overwhelming.

But there was a search to be made, and she tried to focus. To think systematically.

'So, what do I know about Earth? Less than everybody else here . . .'

Elinor shrugged. '*Good question.* Maybe a fresh perspective will help. Help us make a start on our search for the Architect. What *do* you know?'

Muree frowned. 'You say that the Architect supposedly placed their model at the most stable place on the planet. Which surely means on the ground. Or under it, I guess . . . Not in the ocean—'

'Right,' Plokhy said. 'Or, a good guess. Ocean currents could take it invisibly far, sea-bed deposition could cover it quite quickly. Hardly stable. That knocks out seventy per cent of the planet's surface at a stroke.'

'And they *hid* it away, so it's not floating around in the air, in the clouds.' Muree glanced at Plokhy. 'Can you take away the clouds from the imaging, maybe remove the atmosphere altogether?'

Plokhy tapped a small screen; the clouds melted away, leaving an image that was sharper, much more clear – but oddly naked. Green, blue, white, the pale yellow of what must be deserts.

'If I turn it, tilt it?'

Plokhy nodded. 'Just imagine it's real, solid.'

Muree reached out as if to touch the globe with her two open hands. She was used to handling virtuals, though not in this much detail, this scale. She soon found it easy to swivel and tip the globe, revealing the land masses and ice caps, oceans and islands.

She pointed at the big land masses. 'Continents, right?'

'Correct,' Elinor said.

'At the poles, ice caps – but the northern cap is over a continent, and the southern is mostly frozen ocean.'

'Not quite – you have it the other way up. The continent of Antarctica is at the *south* pole. But the ice caps are more or less recovered from being almost destroyed at the peak of the human-induced heating pulse . . .'

Too many novel concepts were hitting Muree at once. *What human-induced heating pulse? Focus, Muree.*

Elinor went on, 'The lume radiation keeps the climate, and the biosphere, more or less stable, by emulating the day-night cycle the Sun provided before the Wrap.'

Muree, never having lived on a planet, needed a briefing on day-night cycles. Seasons too: more cycles in the climate forced on a world spinning on a tilted axis, orbiting a star. Now, she supposed, lume waves could be induced to emulate such patterns, once gifted by the Sun.

She asked, 'And the continents themselves move around, don't they? Over long enough timescales . . .'

Elinor nodded. 'Sort of. Earth has an *inner* core of solid iron and nickel, above that a liquid *outer* metallic core, then a mantle of molten silicate rock, and then a crust made up of plates that follow convection currents in that liquid upper mantle. The continents themselves ride on those plates—'

'And they crash into each other, distort, crack, coalesce. I know about *that*. Can you show me an example?'

The example was spectacular: a speeded-up view of the ongoing slow-motion crash of Africa into Asia, which threatened to close up the Mediterranean Sea, an arm of a greater body of water called the Atlantic Ocean. Throwing up mountain ranges in the process.

'So much for stability,' she said. 'When you're riding a raft in an ocean full of rafts.'

Elinor nodded. 'This is instability over millions of years, but – well, I imagine the Architect thought on such scales.'

Muree studied the images further. 'Still, I guess there are stable places even so. Temporarily. Relatively. If you are near the centre of one of those crust plates. And on a landmass that's far from other land masses. Are there any candidates?'

Elinor shrugged. 'Look for yourself.'

So Muree resumed her exploration. After a few more minutes she found ways to shrink the globe to a manageable size, or to expand it for a closer inspection.

For a while she considered Antarctica as a target, but all that ice, while semi-permanent, had a habit of accumulating at the centre of the continent and sliding off the edges. And the continent itself was forever scraped and shattered by the kilometres-thick ice layers above it . . .

Not there.

And then she found a blocky continent, apparently far from any others, surrounded by ocean, in the southern hemisphere.

Not the largest. Wider than it was deep from her angle of viewing. She saw what looked like a bare, arid interior, orange-yellow. To her right as she was seeing it, a crease that was a significant mountain range. And beyond *that*, a thin strip of green squashed in between the mountains and the coast of a grey-blue ocean.

'What's this one called? This small continent.'

The others had to check.

'Australia,' Plokhy said. 'That seems to be the name colonists gave it. The native peoples had many names . . .'

Elinor smiled, sceptical but encouraging.

'OK,' Muree said. 'Aus–Australia? Well, it seems a long way away from the other continents, so maybe more immune to crashes . . . We're looking for stability. It's a start, at least. Now what?'

'Now we hunt for the most stable place in Australia,' Elinor said. 'Can we take a closer look?'

Plokhy smiled in turn. 'I've just the thing for that. Let me programme a drone. If you need a break, now's the time.'

An hour later, the release of Plokhy's drone came with a jerky displacement of the *Styx*. Which made Muree feel somewhat uncomfortable.

Elinor noticed this, and touched her hand. 'You OK? You crossed the stars—'

'Well, my ancestors did most of the crossing.'

'I wouldn't have thought you would be nervous in a situation like this.'

'Hmm. But the *Lightbird* was a pretty hefty ship. She had been flying for decades without a serious hitch, by the time I was born. If not – well, I wouldn't have been born. Whereas this little ship—'

'Hasn't let *me* down yet,' Plokhy said, apparently slightly offended. 'I wouldn't stake good money on that drone, however. That was not my wisest purchase.' She glanced at the screens around her. 'Going OK so far, though.'

Muree turned to see screens full of a blur of cloud, flashing up and past the drone's point of view.

Elinor winced. 'Ouch. That *is* quite an authentic sense of falling. Did you know that a phobia of heights is endemic on Venus, where we live on top of cloud towers?'

'Sorry,' Plokhy said. 'But that's what you get for a fast entry. OK, until you tell me otherwise, I'm going to head for that strip of green to the right-hand edge of the continent. Umm, the eastern coast. Forests and plains, a river . . . I'll take us down as low as I dare—'

'Look,' Rab said, eager now. He pointed. 'There seems to be movement – *there*. On that green plain . . .'

Plokhy tapped a screen. 'So we're running parallel to that east coast, heading north . . .'

And suddenly the images came into focus, heavily magnified – an uneven shot, Muree imagined, stabilised by the advanced artificial intelligence and sophisticated aerodynamic capability that must have gone into the design of the drone. She saw what looked like another river, but this one full of smooth, flowing, light brown droplets –

Not a river at all.

'Animals,' Rab said. 'Those are animals. A great herd of them.'

Muree gaped.

'We're spooking them, clearly,' Plokhy said. 'I'm pulling the drone up and out . . . My systems are telling me those animals are called kangaroos . . .'

There had been few animals on the *Lightbird*. Small pets, dogs. Birds. Muree longed to see more, to go down, to see these great beasts thundering by. But she knew the drone must not pause, not descend for a closer look, if only for fear of harming the animals. Still—

'This is the point of the Earth,' she said.

Rab nodded. 'You mean, to host life.'

'At least this is the policy,' Elinor said. 'Ever since the recovery from the Neptune invasion. Most of the animal life on the planet had already been destroyed by human intervention anyhow, one way or another. Not to mention the other kingdoms – the plants, the insects, the fish . . . After the invasion, humans retreated, and left Earth largely to the surviving animals, plants and the rest. But there were interventions. Animals like rats and flightless birds were hastily genetic-adapted evolved to fill holes in the food chain, left by the human-induced extinctions. In some places the rodents predate on flightless birds; elsewhere the birds chase the rodents.'

'So it won't be as it used to be,' Muree said.

'It can't be. Of course not. But there is already a hell of a lot of grass, a lot of trees in the recovering forests. With or without human meddling, it will take more than the few centuries we've had so far to evolve, or co-evolve, a new wilderness. But it will come; life is adaptive – as is human life.'

'So long as alien invaders don't destroy *this* planet first. And the lume "sunlight" stays stable.'

Elinor said, 'Even that might not be the end. You know, there are genetic banks, stores, on Mars. Frozen life, in all its richness. I used to know the numbers. Once Earth had thirty million distinct species – that's aside from a hundred million microbe species. Thirty million insects, four thousand mammals . . . Relics of many of them, as well as genetic definitions, are stored offworld. On Mars, particularly. A prestige project for the new capital of the Solar System . . . And even on Venus there are museums where some surviving specimens of the old lineages can be found. Lions and tigers; oxen; wild sheep . . . Actual animals, I mean. Small populations kept healthy by careful breeding. A random selection of species, not an ecology. Not yet. Maybe someday . . . But, look, we're not here for animal-spotting. *People* lived in cities, towns, and that's where the Architect must have worked – and dreamed their dreams, and built their prototype.'

'I can take a hint.' Plokhy touched a screen.

The drone evidently sailed higher into the air. The grasslands, the forest clumps, the animal herds, receded, merging into a green-brown blur, broken by the bright blue of rivers. And now the landscape apparently fled under their view.

'We're heading north,' Plokhy said. 'To the remains of a coastal city they called *Bris-bane* . . . Relatively well preserved, as far as I can see.'

To Muree, what was left of the city looked, from the air, like a map. She saw an obvious layout of roads: straight lines, major routes through the city and a gridwork away from the centre lines.

Some of the roads terminated at the waterline, as if their extensions continued under the water. And out beyond that waterline there were hints of other, more substantial structures – piers, perhaps, harbours. What looked like the rectangular stubs of cut-down tall buildings.

Plokhy said, 'If you want me to go further down—'

'No,' Elinor said. 'I doubt there's much point.'

Muree saw she was consulting screens as she spoke.

Elinor went on, 'I think this is a typical coastal city – and typical now of how such cities were left after the worst of the climate-collapse flooding. When the ocean water rose *higher* than it does now. It receded somewhat with the cooling, the ice re-formation, remember, at the poles, in the mountains. And of course now the tides are much reduced, with the plundering of the Moon to build the Frame.

'In my online searching for the Architect I've studied these features, their history.

'Imagine it. The flood came from the rising seas, adding to run-off from the soaked landscapes inland. River water. Imagine a rise in water levels whole metres high, across the city. In some cases the drowning took only weeks, months, but was likely to linger for centuries, maybe.

'With time, if the city were abandoned, well, the taller buildings might survive up to the highest water line – at least they would be protected from the weather by that much – but debris and mud and silt would flood in and smash and bury anything it could reach. And later, when the water receded, you'd get this, layers of mud encasing everything . . . You'd have just what you see here, the stumps of once-tall buildings, amputated at the water line. And in that mud much would be preserved: brick, concrete, steel, aluminium. Building foundations, at least.'

'And bones,' Rab said.

'Oh, yes. Lots of bones. Human bones. In oxygen-deprived mud that will eventually harden to mudstone, leaving fossilised bodies to be retrieved by some future generation . . .'

'Then we are wasting our time here,' Rab said. 'If we're looking for the Architect's model. If it ever was here, it's surely lost in all that mud.'

'Good point,' Plokhy said.

Muree frowned. 'But the Architect would have foreseen that. Or, I hope they did. They'd choose a high-altitude city, then. Or a mountain. You wouldn't get buried in mud from the rivers and the seas up there.'

'No,' Elinor said, 'but up high you'd have other problems. *Without* all that protective mud, the wind and rain would erode any exposed structure. If the returned ice didn't get it first. Underground caches might survive, but there would be a lot *less* preserved than in the coastal mud. Depending on local conditions . . .'

'Then we're stuck,' Rab said. 'If the monument was at the coast, it will be either drowned or eroded away. If it's on high ground, it will *definitely* be eroded away.'

But Elinor shook her head. 'Maybe we're looking at this the wrong way. Maybe. Remember how we started this? We chose this continent—'

'Australia,' Plokhy prompted.

'Yes. Because we thought it was the most stable location on the planet – or we *guessed* it was, based on the shifting plates under the continents. We've gone for the coast, and the mountains, as candidates for where this monument might be. But maybe we should have kept to our original instincts. Seek stability. After all, stability and order would surely appeal to the Architect. Even if it means solitude. They were a loner, as far as anybody knows, a solitary genius . . .'

The insight excited Muree. 'Yes. You could be right. Why not?' She turned to Plokhy. 'Can you interrogate your systems again? I know it's a vague definition, but can you tell us *where the most stable location in Australia is*? Or was, when the Architect was drawing up their plans.'

But Plokhy just smiled. 'Ahead of you, as usual.' She tapped a screen; a map segment expanded, showing a parched landscape, thin rivers snaking through the image.

And a town, or the layout of one.

Plokhy studied her data. 'This place is the nearest settlement to the geographic centre of the continent. You probably won't get much more stable than that. The first inhabitants had their own name for it. Later colonists called it "Alice Springs".' She pronounced the name *A-lic-eh*, but her ship's systems corrected her. '*Ah-lees*, then. *Ah-lees Springs*.' She looked around. 'There's no sign of habitation now. You can barely see it at all. Just a grid pattern left by the latter-day colonists, their roads and buildings. Everything else worn away. But at least the floods would have been minimal here. Anything underground should have survived . . .'

They shared looks.

Muree thought the town itself looked like a huge map, with straight-line tracings of roads, buildings, perhaps a defunct monorail line, sketched in the dirt . . .

Elinor said, 'Can you drop the drone down there?'

'Can do, and more. I'll take *Styx* down. I take it you all approve.'

Three nods of confirmation.

Rab said. 'I guess we should be strapped in.'

'For sure,' Plokhy said. 'Also, brace for a full gravity when you step out into that desert. And watch the local heat: that's one thing the lumes have maintained, for better or worse.'

Rab grunted, as he started to strap himself into a couch. 'Just as well. If they'd let the climate drift, if that location was covered by jungle – well, even if there *is* something down there, we might never have found it.'

Plokhy secured herself in her seat at the command station. 'Oh, I'm confident enough that there's something to be found. And I even know precisely where to land.'

Muree squeezed in between Plokhy and Rab. She was puzzled by that remark. 'Where?'

Plokhy pointed. 'Next to the two people who are already down there. From that two-person lander I can see in my screens.'

That shocked Muree, and, evidently, Rab.

'Shit,' said Elinor.

Plokhy took her time bringing the *Styx* down into Earth's atmosphere.

Muree, looking over her shoulder, admired her skill as she led the ship with its suite of controlling AIs down through an ocean of air.

But in the final sequence – as the ground, here at the heart of the continent called Australia, flattened out, and antique dust billowed beneath the ship – Muree was distracted by those two figures, standing beside a small lander, near a worn-looking building. In fact the structure only had a single surviving storey; it looked as if it had been chopped in half by some vast axe, with pipes and cables draped across the open upper floor.

But, she saw now, a kind of sculpture, made of junk – metal bars and some kind of cable. All wired to make a tetrahedron, crude but unmistakable.

'A signature,' Elinor said. 'Crude but unmistakable.'

Meanwhile Plokhy sent out a drone to study that landed ship. Seen in increasing close-up through the drone's cameras, it had roughly the same characteristics as the *Styx*, Muree saw, evidently a standard design – optimised, after all these centuries? But with markings that she took to be official insignia. A blocky number painted on the hull.

Those two figures were anonymous in what appeared to be standard-issue pressure suits from the Mask – perhaps, she thought, standard issue throughout the complex state that ran the Solar System. Uniformity was evidently the watchword across this vast culture.

They wore helmets, but open, here in the air of Earth. Muree could understand the impulse to keep the helmets on.

Still the slow descent continued.

And, by the time the lander had touched down, helmets or not, she had no doubt as to who they were.

30

As soon as the *Styx* was down, as soon as the dust of landing settled, the two figures started to march straight over towards the grounded ship.

Plokhy climbed out of her command seat, and made for the cabin door. 'May as well face the music.'

Elinor groused as she clumsily clambered out of her own couch. 'Gravity again . . .'

Muree half-listened, but, as she waited her turn to crowd out of the cabin, she kept watching the two figures.

There's something missing, she thought. There was confidence in the two figures' stride. *Something these two know that we don't yet, that's – that's changing everything.*

It took only a few minutes for the four of them to clamber out of the side door, down fold-out steps, and to the ground. Following the others, with caution, Muree opened her faceplate. The air was hot, dry, dusty. It tasted dead.

Plokhy looked around. 'Don't breathe too much of this. The dust isn't healthy.' And she donned a fabric face mask herself.

The rest followed her lead, warily.

Rab stood with Muree. 'Welcome to Earth.' He bounced on his toes, heavily. 'Tough gravity. I was born on Venus; it's much the same there.'

Muree shrugged. 'Feels like the *Lightbird* Carousel to me. Although you could walk off that if you chose and go find lower gravity if you felt like it.' Such as the axial zero-gravity lume tank, that she missed all the time. 'Not here . . .'

Rab grinned. 'Your suit will help you walk, stand. If you do need it. Meanwhile . . .' He touched her arm and led the way, following his mother and Plokhy.

Who were heading for the two figures, now standing calmly, waiting.

So they gathered together, the six of them.

Those waiting were, of course, Lieutenant Planter from the Mask, and Brad Tenant from the *Lightbird*.

For a heartbeat they stood there, a tableau, Muree thought. Like six statues, another monument on this world of monuments.

It was Brad who broke the spell. From standing stiffly beside the Lieutenant – it was obvious who was in charge – he stepped forward and grabbed Muree in an enfolding hug.

She gave in to this for a few seconds. Then, evidently aware of the others, she pushed him back. She brushed the sweat from his forehead, cheek.

'You all right?'

'Yes,' he said. 'You know I didn't have any choice but to come with the Lieutenant – to come chasing you? Captain Tavar and Commander Revil both ordered—'

'It's OK. I get it. I'm sorry you got dragged all this way.'

'Well, at least I saw the sights,' he said ruefully.

'But you'd rather be in the lume tank on board the *Lightbird*.'

'Oh, yes . . .'

She was aware of Planter watching them. On his face a mix of triumph, and – something else, something deeper. He had been an officer of the law, she reminded herself. His reactions in the past to various situations had been pretty complex. She wondered what he was making of all this, this group gathered from scattered communities, their diverse goals.

This extraordinary place. The petty laws that they must be breaking when taking each breath. And Rab and Elinor reunited at last, all these years after Venus.

Rab, though, just sneered at him, and Muree felt vaguely disappointed by him.

'So, Lieutenant, you caught us up at last.' Rab held out his suited arms. 'You want to cuff me? Watch out for the prosthetic hand. Oh, you know about that already.'

Elinor touched his arm. 'Don't, Rab. Don't – provoke them. Or challenge them. Or insult them. We've all come too far for that. I mean – it's just us, here, in this extraordinary place . . .'

Planter smiled at her.

Almost regretfully, Muree thought.

He said, 'Hello, Elinor. We do keep meeting in awkward situations, don't we?'

Plokhy, meanwhile, just glared. 'You got here first. How did you manage that? In my slipstream?'

She sounded outraged, Muree thought, suppressing a grin. As if it was a race unfairly won.

'Not quite,' Planter said. 'We did follow the same reasoning, I suspect. We trailed you for much of the way, then figured it out for ourselves. The last part. Just before you got here. The logic of the most stable place. And Kepler – we set the smart scanners to look for Keplerian figures. That tetrahedron made it easy . . . We took a chance. And then you lot turn up. Saves chasing you.' He sighed. 'I still ought to arrest you all. Cuff you and bundle you into the hold of our ship, over there. But—'

'But what?' Rab snapped.

Planter actually smiled, through his faceplate. And relaxed, Muree thought.

'You came looking for something. We came looking for *you*. And we found something. What it means – well, I don't think we know yet. Come and see.'

He led the way towards that small, isolated building. He pointed at the tetrahedron on the roof and called over his shoulder, 'Not exactly subtle, is it? For now, we may as well work together. Arresting you all can come later. Well, come on . . .'

31

The main ground-floor structure, a concrete shell with an empty door frame, windowless, was mostly intact.

Planter seemed apologetic. 'You know, I think this might once have been a cistern. Or a waste disposal facility. Something humble. Yet it was built to last, evidently – after all, it has outlasted everything else around here . . .'

When they got to the door, he rubbed the wall, looking up at the exposed upper storey of this roofless building. 'This is very ancient, obviously. Yet it surely must have been no *older* than the other structures here. More or less.' He looked back, around. 'You can see there's a kind of grid pattern to the settlement layout. And this survivor has been built to fit into that grid. We'll have to take samples of the structures and materials to date all this. But for now it's enough that it's survived.' He returned his gaze to the four of them. 'And if it's survived until our times—'

'Then,' Elinor said, 'it must have been standing when the Architect came here. If they ever did.'

Planter, in command mode, ignored that and stepped forward. 'Well, let's go see. Come. Make sure you have your suit lights on . . .' But then he hesitated, turned to fix them with a hard stare. 'Before we go exploring – you know, my actual *mission* here, with Brad, is to arrest you, Muree, Rab Callis. Also Plokhy.'

'Thanks for the shout-out,' Plokhy said cheerfully.

Elinor snorted. 'On what charges?'

'Various, for them. You, I'm not sure about. I'll think of something.'

Plokhy coughed. 'Fine. You can cuff us all. Or you can help us find out the truth about the Solar System.'

He glared at her. 'You know, you really aren't as smart as you think you are, Pilot Plokhy.'

She grinned at him. 'Probably not. But I just need to be smarter than you, Lieutenant. And the institutions you work for.'

Rab seemed to lose patience. 'Ah, into the guts of Neptune with you old folk and your bickering. Let's get this done. As you said, you can arrest us all later, Lieutenant.'

And he turned away, and walked boldly into the structure. The first to enter.

Planter followed him.

Muree could see light from their suit lamps in the interior splashing through the empty window frames.

At first the rest hesitated. Brad hung back nervously, as if he thought he ought to watch over the prisoners. Muree grinned at him, and was pleased when he came over to her.

He said, 'Old Planter isn't so bad when you get to know him. When his sense of duty doesn't fill his head. Once he told me that when we caught up with you people he'd arrest all of you, then me, then probably himself by mistake.'

That raised a laugh.

At last Elinor shrugged. 'We've come this far.' She stepped forward.

Muree walked beside her. 'Yes. Far enough. Let's do this.'

*

For Muree, crossing the threshold into the derelict building felt strange, disconcerting.

Nothing to see but splashes of light from windows and suit lamps, on the walls and floor. Nothing here at first glance, except for heaps of anonymous dust and debris in the corners.

But at the far side, where Planter was standing, there was a hatch, set in the ground. Muree could see the dust there was disturbed.

Planter knelt down, explored this hatch with a gloved hand.

'I think this is wood. Very dry. If it hadn't been so desiccated, it probably would have rotted away long ago . . . There's no handle.' He pushed the surface, explored the edge with his fingertips.

Rab walked over, knelt beside him, held up his prosthetic hand, clenched into a fist. 'Let me try.'

Planter hesitated. Backed off, wordless.

Rab settled himself, leaned over on his real hand – and slammed the prosthetic into the hatch, near the edge, away from the corners. One blow, hard.

A loud crack, like the discharge of some weapon. The wood gave way in a sudden cloud of splinters and dust, leaving a hole wider than Rab's metal fist.

It occurred to Muree then that she had never before seen Rab *use* that prosthetic in that way, for a purpose that would have been impossible for a flesh and blood appendage.

Planter, unperturbed, nodded. 'Good work. Can you lift it?'

'Only one way to find out.' Now Rab knelt over the hatch, got his prosthetic in through the hole he'd made, grasped the broken surface, and hauled.

'Take it easy—'

But Planter's warning was drowned out by the noise of more cracking, splintering. The hatch began to break apart around that initial punch, and under Rab's heaving. Now Planter joined in, hauling back debris with his own gloved hands.

It didn't take long before the hatch had disintegrated completely, its fragments tumbling down into the cavity below.

And Muree could see a ladder, metallic, descending into that hole.

When she approached, Planter held up a gloved hand. 'I'll go first. It's easy enough . . . But maybe not if you grew up on a low-gravity starship.'

Muree said, 'I've climbed ladders before, you know.'

'Sure, sure. So follow me down. Use your suit lamps.'

Elinor caught Muree's eye. 'Once a hero cop, always a hero cop.'

Plokhy smiled. 'Quite right. Let him do his stuff.'

Planter gave them a reflexive glare. Then he leaned down, put one foot on the ladder's first rung, rested his gloved hands on the floor, and kicked, hard. 'Seems solid enough to take my weight. Rab, stay close. Grab me if –'

'Got it.'

Now Planter cautiously dropped his other foot. Gradually lowered himself further down, through the hole. Taking care, testing one rung at a time, avoiding the hatch edges.

Muree could see the ladder was awkward, but manageable.

When he was out of sight, he called back, 'I'm down. It's OK. Come down. Not you, Brad. Stay up there.'

Muree saw Brad was frustrated, but leaving somebody on ground level made obvious sense.

Then, after a silent conversation of shared looks, Muree herself was the first to move forward and follow Planter.

As she clambered down her first rungs, Earth's full gravity felt as difficult as she might have predicted, after so long on Mars and the Frame, but no worse. Brad hovered over the hatch above her, one gloved hand outstretched. She ignored the helping hand. Soon she was out of his reach anyhow.

Further down, the shadows of direct light made her nervous. But the descent remained manageable.

And soon enough she was at the foot.

She had to scoot out of the way, when Rab followed her down more quickly – more carelessly, she thought, his torch dazzling her. The other three were crowded around the hatchway, blocking any daylight, waiting their turns.

Planter was standing in the middle of the chamber they had discovered, screening whatever lay beyond him from view. His voice stern, he said, 'We'll wait until we're all down. Save you, Tenant; you keep watch. Then we'll see what we can make of this. I think I know . . .'

The small room felt crowded with all of them gathered, the splashes of light from their suit lamps overlapping, casting chaotic shadows. If there was anything in here, Muree couldn't yet see it for the Lieutenant's bulk.

At last Planter said, 'OK. Dip your suit lamps. Try not to dazzle each other. Here we go . . .'

He stood aside.

And the Architect's legacy was revealed.

It was like a sculpture hanging in the air, Muree thought. A circular mesh, standing with its plane vertical, apparently unsupported.

Six concentric circles, the spacing between them growing the further out they were.

And four radial spokes, reaching in towards the centre, cutting across the rings.

Outside the furthest of the rings, a semitranslucent bubble enclosing the whole structure.

And at the centre, something else. Something bright, reflecting the light – no, it was shining by its own light. A sphere? And meant to be seen.

'Like a spider at the heart of a web,' Muree murmured to Rab, pointing at the sphere. 'I wonder what the power source is.'

Elinor was walking around the model, looking at it closely – but with a kind of *sympathy* written in her face, Muree thought. A half-smile. A thin emotion, but more than she had shown her own son.

Elinor said now, 'Just as we guessed on Mars. This isn't another version of Kepler's dream. *This is the Frame.* A sketch of an engineered sky. And, standing here, *you can see it all,* see how the Architect took the essence of Kepler's design, that philosophical idea, and built again. Built *this.* A cleaner form, a form that fits our actual Solar System with its elliptical orbits, a unifying transport system, psychologically pleasing—'

Lieutenant Planter frowned. 'This was all about psychology?'

'Of course it was. In a mass sense . . . Think about the history. Think what the Solar System *was,* for humans, before the invaders came. We had long taken over the Earth: from about the twentieth century humanity had been in pretty much total control of its natural flows, of material, energy. Control that wasn't always for the best, I grant you – given how close we came to trashing the ecosystem, the weather system. Then came mankind's expansion into the other planets, taking over the entire Solar System.

'Our control was never perfect. There were always disruptions from a chaotic natural world – from earthquakes to solar flares – and disruptions from humanity's own dark impulses too. Accidents, wars, resource exhaustions, stupidity. But still we were in charge. We got an awful lot wrong, and kept on doing it when we knew it was wrong. But, *we were in charge.*

'And for all the damage we caused, the world we lived in, and managed, was at least comprehensible. Deliberate. Conscious. Controlled within the frame of natural law. It had been a very long time since humans feared the lightning.

'But then—'

'But then the invasion came,' Planter said.

Elinor nodded. 'And then the invasion came. We never even saw them, their mighty ships . . . All we saw was the results of their actions. Neptune. A whole planet disrupted. We weren't in control.

'And what was our reaction? We did what our ancestors might have done in the face of a storm they couldn't understand.

'We hid. We burrowed. And not just in caves like our forebears.

'We hid our worlds, even, from the universe – and we hid the universe from our own eyes. We took apart our Moon, just as the so-called invaders took apart Neptune. We exhausted the Sun in a spasm of building and rebuilding. And,' she gestured at the model Frame, 'we built *this*. A framework in the sky. As I said, an almost medieval conception of the Solar System – one *we* built. We shut out the universe.

'It was – a – a neurotic response, I suppose. We burrowed down into the little island of symmetry, of order, we had built. *This*. And, for better or worse, this was the Architect's legacy. Their gift to us.'

Muree was growing impatient. 'Yes,' she said. 'Yes, all that makes sense to me. So this is what humanity built after the invaders came. So we have been told, so your ancestors witnessed. The Mask, the Frame. This *is* the vision the Architect developed, and the interplanetary builders followed. But—'

She strode forward.

'But there's something wrong.'

*

She pointed boldly at the centre of the display.

Where, she knew, the Wrap, a black parcel containing an exhausted Sun, ought to be. She'd seen images; she knew it was like that.

Rather than a gleaming orb.

Rab leaned down to examine it more closely. 'I think this thing is actually *glowing*. Luminous. Just faintly . . .' He stood straight.

'Has to be radioactive,' Elinor said. 'The power source. If it's been here for centuries, a thousand years. Lumes could outshine this but could never match the endurance.'

Muree nodded. 'No. It's not lumes. But – that doesn't matter. What matters about the model is what this signifies, what it's trying to tell us.'

Elinor said, almost eagerly, 'Right. *That's no Wrap*. Far too small, too . . .'

'Bright?'

Rab shook his head, bewildered. 'What *have* we found? What does this mean?'

Nobody seemed to want to reply. Muree wondered if they, at least the natives of the Solar System, were undergoing some kind of conceptual shock. They had all come a long way to see this, and it was evidently not what they had expected.

Still Muree hesitated. Who was she, to speak first? But if not her—

At last Elinor spoke.

'All right,' she said briskly, breaking the silence.

'*What does this mean?* Go back to the basics. We've been told that the rebuilding of the Solar System was in response to the invasion. Correct? The Mask was built to hide the whole System. That entailed the start of the mining of Uranus. Large scale. The creation of the Frame that linked the planets – the plundering of the Moon. The rebuilding of the planets themselves – like Venus, those aerial cities we lived in, myself, Rab. And, alongside all this, maybe the crowning achievement – *the containment of the Sun*. To trap its energy – to reduce it to an exhausted black hole, in just a few centuries. OK. All that energy mined, we were told, used to construct the Frame, and the Mask, to light worlds like Venus and Mars . . .

'And *this* toy we've dug up is surely supposed to be a model of the modified Solar System, as it would be when the engineering was done. An integrated vision . . .'

She was speaking more and more slowly, Muree realised. As if she was hypnotised by this model, this buried, ancient artefact and its symmetries and enclosures.

But still something was wrong.

Elinor was hesitating.

'Elinor.' Muree grabbed the woman's arm, not tightly. '*Elinor*. You must be right – nearly. About the theory. The design. Right about some of it. But – look at it. Look!' She pointed at the heart of the diorama. 'What about the Sun? Look where the Solar Wrap should be. A Wrap that ought to be – how big?'

A hesitation. Then Planter spoke. 'About ten times the Sun's radius. A tenth the size of Mercury's orbit—'

'*A Wrap which isn't in this model*,' Elinor said. It was as if her eyes were suddenly opened.

Her jaw actually dropped, Muree saw.

And she reached into the heart of the monument, as if trying to confirm the reality of what she saw.

But there was no Wrap. Only that small, glassy, shining sphere.

The others stared too.

'Look at it,' Muree said. 'It's your solar system, not mine.

Where's the Wrap? It's supposed to take up the central tenth of the innermost Frame ring, the Mercury ring – correct? That's a pretty big feature. Well, where is it?' She pointed at the bright crystal at the heart of the diorama. 'And, what's this? What does it represent?'

In fact she thought she knew. She didn't want to be the one to say it.

'Come on,' she said, goading. 'Lieutenant Planter. Elinor . . . All this is to scale, you say. On this scale, *how large would the Sun be*?' And she pointed again to the central, glowing sphere. '*About this size* – right?'

'Shit,' Rab said. 'You're right for once, Muree. How could I not have seen that? . . . Because I wasn't supposed to see it, that's why . . .'

Elinor still stood, staring. Rab moved to her, held her hand in his own (flesh) fingers.

Lieutenant Planter just stared too.

'*That's* what's wrong here,' Muree said, as insistently as she could. 'The Architect left this monument, a kind of solid, sculpted description of what had to be done to the Solar System. What was *supposed* to have been done. A Solar System inspired by the cosmic engineering of the Kepler geometry, but heavily adapted. A Solar System united by the Frame – *but with the Sun shining, without any "Wrap", at its heart*. The Sun as it was – maybe unmodified altogether. That was the Architect's vision. That's what they are showing us here!

'And yet – *that was not what was built*. The Frame, yes, linking the planets. The Mask to hide the whole System from – well, imaginary invaders. But the Wrap at its heart – the Architect must have rebelled against . . . what was done there. As they saw their vision perverted.'

'Perverted,' Plokhy said. 'Yes, yes . . .'

Muree realised that the pilot had hardly spoken since the landing, the merging of the crews. But now she was grinning widely.

Muree said, 'Let's think it through. If this is so, if their vision was stolen and hijacked like this, the Architect must have become desperate. And so—'

'And so,' Elinor said, more softly, 'they must have found a way to hide this thing, this sculpture, this schematic, to prevent any chance of it suffering . . . umm . . . a *correction*. A modification to match what was *actually* built, as opposed to what they intended. They were betrayed. This is *their* betrayal in turn of those who controlled them. Perverted their design. They must have been watched, maybe everything they said and did was controlled . . .'

Plokhy grinned. 'A person after my own heart. They knew it was all wrong. They finally realised they'd been commissioned to turn the Solar System into a prison, not a refuge. Because that's the truth, isn't it? If you control the Sun, you control everything.

'But still the Architect got their message through, to us. To the future. *The truth*. Even if it's taken centuries and the arrival of a starship full of immigrants to shake everything up. *This* is how the rebuilt Solar System should look. And you figured it out. ' She looked around, at Muree, Rab. 'You kids. Well done.'

Muree felt uncomfortable. 'Come on. We couldn't have done it without you, Plokhy, Elinor—'

Plokhy snorted. '*You* did it, Muree. I've been flying around this cage of a Solar System and never once followed the clues you have picked up. Don't thank me. Thank *you*.

'So. What do we do now?'

Rab raised his artificial hand, clenched it in a fist, and grinned. 'We tear it all down. Or at least, whatever they *did* do to the Sun.'

Lieutenant Planter seemed to be thinking hard. He said, 'I have an awful feeling a lot of people are going to agree with you, Callis. My job has been to track you fugitives down. Well, I've done that. But . . . I'm not motivated to hand you all in. Not today, anyhow.

'There are bigger issues here, evidently. Somebody is going to have to handle all this, one way or another.'

Elinor nodded gravely.

Muree looked around at them all. 'So – what do we do next?'

They spent half a day studying the monument.

Capturing images, including uploading a detailed virtual replica to the memory banks of Plokhy's ship. Planter used various codes of his own to prove authenticity. Ensuring that even if the monument were destroyed right now, its message, its symbology, would survive.

They talked it over further.

They brought down food and drink from their respective vessels, and kept talking.

In the end they concluded their next step should be to go see for themselves what was going on at the Wrap, right now. Face the anomaly itself.

Even Lieutenant Planter agreed.

And to keep the secret of what they'd found, pending a wider revelation. When they could figure out what *had* been done to the Sun.

And that meant diving inward to the shadowed heart of the Solar System.

And so, twelve days later, the two craft sailed into the gravity well of Mercury. The last place where they could make a covert landing this side of the wrapped Sun itself.

32

Mercury.

From a preliminary high orbit, above Mercury, aboard the reliable *Styx*, Muree, peering out, was astonished by the view. Disturbed.

She had known that Mercury was both the innermost and the smallest of the major planets of the Solar System. But beyond those details she knew little of this new world, and what she saw startled her – *repelled* her – as she endured the approach orbit.

The others, Elinor, Rab, Jeo, Plokhy, took it in their stride. Planter too. But she, the interstellar voyager, was feeling queasy. Brad too maybe, that other interstellar veteran, but if so he was hiding it well – hiding it from Planter, his temporary boss, anyhow.

Maybe this was some kind of after-the-event shock, catching up with Muree.

She might be ship-born and -raised, but she thought her adventures since leaving the Mask with Rab had changed all her perceptions, had led her to believe she was growing accustomed to this strange environment of *worlds*. A world: a place where you were no longer stuck inside a box replete with life support. Where you stood on the outer hull of a much greater box, so to speak. Where there was no need to spin to generate artificial gravity, because a planet was massive enough to dimple space and create a gravity field on its own. On Earth especially, *you could open your pressure suit and not die screaming.*

Such an environment could hardly be more distanced from what she was used to. And yet on Earth she had never felt afraid, never uncomfortable – not in terms of the planet itself anyhow; its erstwhile inhabitants, and what they had done over their multiple millennia of civilisation, had been another matter. *This is home,* the planet had told her body, with its air and its bulk, its enfolding gravity field – even after her lineage had been a thousand years away.

But she had now come far from Earth, with its abandoned cities and recovering life, far from Mars with its giant crater-city. Mercury was yet another world, but one so strange, even at first glance, so different, so *bare*, so damaged, it was almost an abstraction. And oddly disturbing.

She tried to talk to Brad, her old shipmate. Get him away from the Lieutenant. But he was distant, withdrawn. Resentful. Had been, somewhat, since their reunion on Earth. So would she be, she supposed, if *he* had been the runaway, and *she* had been dragged out of her own life – out of the lume farm on the *Lightbird* – and detailed to cross the Solar System in pursuit, alongside a tough stranger like Lieutenant Planter.

All my fault.

She kept herself to herself, and tried to stay calm.

At last Plokhy, satisfied with her calculations and preparations, brought the *Styx* out of its approach orbit and headed down towards the planet. No helpful atmosphere here; the descent would be rocket-enabled all the way down.

As the ship made a preliminary low swoop over the landscape, Muree found herself skimming over a ground that, in places, was black as the inside of closed eyelids. Black save for where the lights of human settlements sparked in the dark.

But there were a *lot* of such settlements, she saw as the *Styx* flew on, many lights gathered in circles, or arcs of circles. And between these arcs were more lights, lights mobile in places, sparks crawling as lone specks or in longer trains. Human vehicles, evidently, snaking around unseen obstacles in the unremitting dark.

Around curving walls. Vast circular ramparts.

'Craters,' she said, to nobody in particular. 'The settlements, the transports. They're working around craters. They're built *into* craters.'

'Quite right,' Elinor said. 'And on Mercury there's not much to see other *than* craters. I spent enough time down there myself . . .'

She glanced at Rab. Rab, Muree remembered, the reason his mother had been banished to Mercury in the first place. She supposed it was too hard for him to acknowledge that, just yet. If ever.

And if Elinor was waiting for him to speak, it wasn't going to be any time soon.

She shrugged, and spoke anyhow.

'So. The landscape. Look at *it*.'

'Mercury. Innermost planet, hottest before the Sun was destroyed. Too small to have geological cycles like Earth or even Mars, nothing to shape it since its formation but impacts and cratering, and the heat and the tides of the Sun. Never had any significant weather, so nothing to wear down the crater walls save more impacts, and erosion from the cracking of the rocks by the sunlight, back when there *was* sunlight. The impacts – there are some *big* features dating back to the formation of the planets, the results of collisions that must nearly have cracked the planet in two.

'But on the other hand more recent craters, caused by relatively recent impacts – recent meaning millions rather than billions of years ago – these late impacts proved useful for us. They are like natural deep-mining excavations. And there *is* very useful stuff, deep down. There's a metallic core making up about eighty per cent of the mass of the planet. A rocky mantle and crust that are not unlike the Moon's upper layers – silicate rocks, metals like aluminium, some uranium.

'That's this planet: a lode of hugely useful resources deep in the heart of the System . . .'

Muree saw that Rab had lifted his arm, his artificial hand, and was flexing it, staring at it. '"Hugely useful resources,"' he said, 'The rocks. The mines. And people, all draining down into this great sink of industry. Endless flows of *people*.'

Jeo Planter faced him. 'I'm not going to apologise *again* for what might have happened if you *had* ended up as a miner down there. You wouldn't have been unique; as you say there are millions working down there. And some are there by choice, you know. There's even some archaeology being progressed down there. People came here, prospectors, miners, leaving traces long before the invasion and the creation of the Mask, the Frame, and—'

'And the Wrap around the Sun,' Plokhy murmured. 'We didn't come here to debate the ethics of mining on Mercury. We came for something else . . . Shall we go see?'

At that remark, with a tug at her controls, Plokhy coaxed the *Styx* into a steep climb.

Muree, like the rest, had been loosely, comfortably strapped in a couch, in the gravity-free environment of the *Styx*. But now, as Plokhy threw the ship around, Muree found herself forced back deeper, and her couch responded by pushing out belts to wind around her waist and across her chest.

Rab reached over and took her hand in his. He had got used to her reactions at such moments. She took hold gratefully, and by now it didn't seem to matter at all that he had offered her his prosthetic.

Elinor saw, Muree noticed. She smiled, but enigmatically.

Not for the first time Muree found it impossible to read Elinor. Even that smile seemed forced.

But now Elinor turned away, distracted by a view in a forward screen.

Muree looked that way – and saw, rising over the ragged rocks of Mercury, an abstraction. A looming disc of darkness, darker even than the general background of this strange, enclosed System. It looked like something missing in the universe. A flaw.

She asked, 'And what *is* that?'

Plokhy grinned, not unkindly. 'That, child, is the Sun. Or what we humans have made of it.

'That is the Wrap.'

The rest, even those who must be used to such sights, Muree thought, stared uneasily.

Having shown them this startling image, Plokhy glanced at her instruments and got on with the job. 'OK, we're starting our Mercury descent now.' She murmured commands, stroked screens.

Muree could feel the ship turn, bank, settling on a new trajectory.

She couldn't take her eyes off the wrapped Sun – though there was nothing new to be seen, as that black stain passed over their sky.

Planter glanced around at various monitors. 'Where are we heading, specifically? I'm no planetary explorer, but I remember that on Mercury we generally came down at spaceports at the poles.'

Plokhy grinned. '*You* probably did. That's where they built the first major port facilities. This was when Mercury was opened up for its first significant post-Neptune exploitation, when they planned the construction of the Solar Wrap. Lumes were being bred in seriously large numbers, and the miners were prospecting asteroids for carbon compounds to build what would become the Wrap.'

'Quite right,' Planter said. 'The authorities took a good hard look for suitable landing sites, and chose the poles *because there was water there*. Surprising, for Mercury, right? Relics of long-gone comet impacts, water that had settled in the permanent shadows of the craters up there, and frozen solid. A decent amount, given how close Mercury is to the Sun. I mean, when the Sun was allowed to shine on this place.'

Muree got it. 'Water's essential. You go to the water if it's there.'

'Exactly. And then, yes, of the two choices of water deposits, the north pole was settled on as the main drop-off for human travellers. The south was more dedicated to freight, in the early days—'

'But not today,' Planter said. 'So where are we heading, the equator? Something else you want us to see, is there, Angela?'

'You'll see.'

Muree, intrigued, looked around the cramped cabin's panels and screens, all busily showing fragments of the Mercury landscape, images that tilted and panned, magnified or shrank, as the ship approached. In a wider view she saw a horizon against a deep black background.

Now, suddenly, the craft swooped, disconcertingly, down towards the ground of Mercury.

*

Not for the first time, Muree noted, the conversation died down when there was something to see as they travelled, and people just watched and stared, through windows, into screens.

Now the ground loomed up, a ground battered and broken by the rims of craters, and, evidently, by the works of humans. Straight-line roads, some of which cut through huge circular crater walls. More cosmic geometry, Muree thought. Roads that connected equally huge rectangular excavation sites, from which much material had evidently been extracted. Deep pits, beside many of which sat neat little clusters of habitats, and the smooth surfaces of launching pads.

She shook her head. 'I can't get a sense of this – project. Why, *most of the planet* seems scarred. Did you really need to take so much?'

'Wait until you see what they built with it,' Elinor said.

Rab chose that moment to point to Plokhy's console, with one robotic finger. 'A hail light. Somebody calling, I think, pilot.'

Plokhy turned to see.

'About time. That's our invitation to land.'

Planter and Elinor shared a wary glance.

Planter asked, 'Who's "inviting" us? That hail's not the authorities, I'll bet. Since I *am* the authorities.'

Muree grinned. 'Well, that all depends on who is actually in charge down there right now, doesn't it?'

Elinor murmured, 'Don't push it too far,' but she grinned even so.

Plokhy looked around at the group. 'I'm taking us down into Caloris – Mercury's deepest, widest crater. I happen to know there's no active work going in there just now. And then we'll go deeper yet. Any objections?'

Muree shivered at that description. *Deepest. Widest. And, deeper yet. What now?*

Plokhy asked, 'Ready?'

Still no one objected.

'Just do it,' the Lieutenant snapped.

Plokhy shrugged, turned to her console, and tapped a screen.

33

Immediately, with a jolt, the ship began to move, down and over the broken surface of Mercury.

Soon they were skimming maybe a kilometre above the ground – so the screens told Muree. She found it hard to judge the scale of the features fleeing beneath their bow.

It wasn't until a range of jagged mountains hove into view, dead ahead, that she really got a sense of how low they had dropped, how fast they were travelling. The mountains were tall, eroded, a wall of uplifted rock – and they suddenly loomed out of the apparent distance, turning into a rocky barrier dead ahead.

All of this was only visible by the lights of the ship, and some splashes of illumination on the ground. A broken, jagged perspective.

And then the *Styx* dipped, banked, and was suddenly hurtling through a narrow-seeming gap between two sharp peaks.

Muree held on to a rail – the ride was smooth enough physically, if not psychologically – and managed to stay calm.

Until, in a flash, they were through.

And Muree, breathing hard, found herself facing a flat plain – flat for Mercury anyhow – a plain punctured everywhere with lesser craters, some eroded in their turn by later bombardments.

Rab drifted over to Muree, moving cautiously in the low-acceleration regime of the craft. He murmured, 'You OK?'

'Not the kind of space travel I'm used to. I never thought I'd miss that damn Frame.'

'You're doing fine . . .'

Now, ahead, Muree saw a dark ellipse on the ground – a crater, deep and neatly cut. She had yet to glimpse a floor. Very deep, then . . .

Planter glared into screens. He looked somewhat pale, but evidently he continued to function. 'Where are you taking us now, pilot?'

Plokhy smiled. 'See for yourself.'

The ship paused to a hover, stopping suddenly enough to make Muree gasp. Then screens in the lounge flooring lit up to reveal what was evidently, Muree realised, the view from beneath the ship.

She saw broken ground to the left, brightly lit, but, to the right, with a sharp dividing line between, pitch darkness – dark even where, she saw, the ship's lights splashed. Over a deep hole. *Into* the hole.

The craft drifted over it.

'Wow,' Brad said. 'That's not a crater. Or not just a crater. A shaft – a mine shaft? . . . But your light is shining straight down, without any reflection from the bottom, just a little roughness in the walls . . . How deep *is* that thing?'

'Also, how wide?' Rab asked.

Nobody answered.

Plokhy touched her controls. 'I'll take her down. You get a better sense of perspective outside the hull. Prepare to suit up . . .'

*

Once the craft was on the ground, they helped each other don their gear. As usual suiting up took as long as it took, whatever your enthusiasm or reluctance.

Elinor partnered Muree in the prep. They didn't exchange any words, and barely made eye contact save when the suit drill demanded it. Muree wondered if this was some kind of subtle gesture on the part of Elinor. A kind of tactile acceptance that Muree was part of her son's life now – even if Muree herself didn't know what part that would be.

She was starting to realise how complex human relationships could be when you were out of the orderly, reasonably enclosed environment of a starship in flight. Or, of course, a lume tank.

Anyhow, they got through the mutual prepping, and she did come out feeling they had made some kind of progress. Maybe so did Elinor, given the smiles they exchanged through their helmets.

And then they all followed Lieutenant Planter out onto the surface of Mercury.

34

Where Rab fell over immediately.

Planter was nearby, and went to haul him to his feet. 'You made a mess of your suit, man.' He contrived a few comedy brushing movements with his gloved hand before Rab touched a pad on his sleeve, and – Muree presumed – some electrostatic effect expelled the dust as a kind of sparkling shower.

A shower, Muree realised, lit up only by their suit lamps, and the landing lights of the *Styx*. When she glanced up at the sky, she saw nothing but darkness – featureless, save perhaps a faint scratch that might be a local arm of the Frame, and brighter, floating lights that might be the lanterns of robot tankers.

Plokhy, short, stocky, confident, came over to her with easy bounds in the low gravity. 'Couple of things to show you. *That*,' pointing up at the sky, 'comes second. But first—'

'The mine shaft?'

'The mine shaft.'

The company gathered close to the lip of the shaft.

'Not too close,' Plokhy said. 'Mercury's gravity is low – you can feel that – but not that low. If you fall in – I mean, you'd hit the bottom at about a kilometre per second. Your suit *should* save you, but I wouldn't bank *my* life on it.'

Muree was startled by all that, and she stepped back. 'So how deep is this shaft?' She tried to estimate it in her head, but the lighting was unfamiliar. 'A hundred metres?'

Plokhy smiled through her faceplate. 'More like five hundred, on average. On a *global* average.'

Everybody stepped further back, Muree was amused to see.

Brad murmured, 'Quite a signature humans are leaving on these worlds. '

Plokhy angled her head. 'But it's what humans have always done. At least now they're letting Earth itself recover . . .'

A little impatiently, Planter said, 'Enough of the angst. What are we doing here, pilot?'

'You'll see, Lieutenant. For one thing, refuelling. This is a dormant shaft. Now look, if you'll all back up from the shaft edge, there's something else I want to show you while we're out here . . .'

She led them perhaps a hundred paces away from the shaft, then gathered them in a rough circle.

And she looked up at the sky, directly overhead.

Muree, puzzled, obediently followed her example.

'You can see nothing, right?' Plokhy said. 'Nothing save the darkness inside the Mask, a structure that obstructs even the distant stars. But up there, right above us now, is the Sun. That's no coincidence; I had the ship calculate the position of the subsolar point right now. It *should* be shining down on us – and, right now, straight down into the shaft itself, given the angles . . .'

Muree looked up again, trying to see that black sphere. The Sun. The wrapped Sun, against the lesser black beyond . . . How large would it have looked here, on Mercury? Twice, three times its size seen from Earth?

She felt an odd stab of longing, illogical, unbearable. She had come from another star, to the home system, only to find the Sun itself hidden from her view. This – darkness.

But, so what? The Sun is exhausted. Reduced to a useless black hole.

Isn't it?

And she remembered the glass orb at the heart of the Architect's model Solar System. An orb that shouldn't have been there.

You haven't figured it all out yet, Muree.

She faced Plokhy. 'What do we do now?'

Plokhy grinned. 'The refuelling is done. Let's get back to the ship and I'll show you.'

As soon as they had clambered back aboard the *Styx*, Plokhy tapped at her controls, murmured verbal instructions to her systems.

And for her passengers, a louder warning.

'We're lifting out of here in one hour. A hard thrust out of Mercury's gravity well, and then we'll pretty much go straight up towards the Wrap, one Earth-standard gravity. At the destination in, umm, forty hours. You haven't been exposed to a full gravity for a while, so suit up now. In fact, anything you need to do out of an acceleration couch, do it now.'

Then she hesitated, uncharacteristically, Muree thought.

'In fact – anybody who doesn't want to come with me and *break the law* as we make for the Solar Wrap, debark now. This is all a rush . . . Well? Anybody want off? Lieutenant Planter?'

Nobody wanted off. Not even Planter.

Make for the Wrap. Those words echoed in Muree's head.

'OK, then. Make the most of your last hour in low gravity for a while.'

*

They scattered to bunks in the *Lightbird* lounge – all but Plokhy, who settled at her bridge position. They took turns to use the microscopic lavatory and shower, pulled on fresh skinsuits to wear under their pressure suits.

An hour.

Muree and Rab chose a temporary cabin together: together, much as they had been since the start of this long odyssey, all the way back to their unauthorised departure from the Mask aboard this very ship.

They weren't shy with each other after all these weeks, Muree had time to notice. Never had been, in fact. They'd always been in too much of a rush, she supposed. She liked Rab, and admired the way he had overcome a tough start in life – the loss of a mother, the loss of a *hand*. She'd grown to rely on him as they'd travelled across this extraordinary engineered Solar System. But then she felt she had supported him just as much.

Where was this relationship going, though?

Nowhere, she told herself, honestly enough, as she struggled back into her pressure suit. Not yet. Maybe never. Not unless there was some kind of resolution to be had of what might yet turn into a System-wide crisis, all emanating from the arrival of the *Lightbird* from out of deep space and deep time. A crisis of cognition, of trust, a challenge to a millennium-old authority . . .

And now Rab's mother was back in his life too. Damaged, difficult – but not going anywhere. That complicated things further.

Rab and Muree worked well together, and that was enough for now. If they all survived this moment, they could – reconsider.

First things first. A government to overthrow. Or not.

When their hour of grace was up, Plokhy slid into her command seat, with the others, seated, in their suits – Elinor, Planter, Brad.

Plokhy was murmuring into her comms system, too quietly for Muree to make out the words.

As they sat and strapped in, Brad leaned over to Muree and grinned, tentatively. 'I checked on the ship's lumes, by the way. On the *Lightbird*.'

Plokhy broke off from her messaging. 'I imagined your tank is full of sensors.'

Brad said, 'Never does any harm to go say hello.'

Plokhy's expression softened. 'I take your point. Anyhow, here we go. OK, crewmates?'

Muree grinned back. 'OK, Plokhy!'

'Right. Let's go!'

The drive cut in sharply.

The acceleration quickly mounted. Half a gravity. Muree felt herself being pressed down into her couch.

One day and sixteen hours of this to come. The locals, used to frequent changes, grumbled, but took it in their stride.

Immediately they were underway, in the background, Plokhy resumed her low-voiced messaging. Muree had no idea who she was calling, or why.

And Planter leaned over to Muree, spoke softly. 'By the way. Your attachment to the lumes – we've all observed it. And it's not so eccentric.'

She frowned. 'Who says it's eccentric?'

Rab grinned. 'I think this is a cop trying to be nice to you.'

'I mean it,' Planter said. 'Once, on Earth, you know, people relied on animals called horses to get around. The horses would pull wheeled carts and carriages . . . I saw a museum on Mars about it. Never any horses on Mars, or Venus. Plenty wild on Earth now, probably. But it was clear that people would care for their horses, even if they often wore them down with work

– and even used them in their wars. I know that the horses were pretty closely related biologically to humans, so empathy was possible – even likely. Both Earth-evolved mammals. But even so . . . I guess empathy for a lume, coming from an utterly different order of life . . . It's a stretch, but not outrageous.'

Muree said, 'I'm not surprised. Biologically we couldn't be further from those . . . knots of smart spacetime. But they are evidently alive, as we are. They live together, in . . . swarms – if not families. You can't get more basic a commonality than that. And they respond to what we do to them, for good or not.'

Elinor, looking over, nodded. 'I'm not going to argue with that . . . I've tried to study them myself, if only in the literature. Fascinating creatures, with a lifecycle we have barely glimpsed, still less understand. And, empathy with the lumes – it's not unknown, you know.'

Planter raised his eyebrows. 'As opposed to empathy with a cop?'

Rab grinned. 'Don't push it, Lieutenant.'

'OK—'

'I mean, at least lumes are *useful*, right?'

'OK! Leave it. Anyhow, I think our hero pilot has news.'

Plokhy had indeed finished her messages.

Muree was prodded by curiosity. 'Who were you calling?'

Planter grinned. 'I was wondering too. You're not much of a one for filing requests for flight clearance, are you?'

Plokhy glanced back. 'You can arrest me later, Lieutenant. Actually I did file a clearance request, just to get it on the system. But mostly I'm speaking to a few key . . . ah, colleagues. Mostly pilots, or those who employ pilots. Mercury is a busy planet, with a pretty high human population, and a mobile one. And most people own spaceworthy transport – as a utility if nothing else. You need a capable transport to get around the planet, just to get to work. So almost everybody has access to space. Or knows somebody who has. Perfectly legally.

'And, against that background, I'm spreading the word.'

Planter frowned. '*Spreading the word*? About us? Our own illegal flight to the Wrap? You do know we're already breaking the law by doing this?'

'So are you,' Elinor snapped.

'Yes,' said Planter heavily. 'I'm aware of that. But I'm also aware the arrival of the *Lightbird* precipitated a crisis in the governance of the Solar System. The old paradigm is stressed to breaking point. Something has to change. *But that change should be controlled*. Thought through. That's why I've come with you this far, in your quest for – well, what *is* it you're looking for?'

Rab shrugged. 'The truth?'

'But I'm not sanguine about your provoking some kind of popular uprising across Mercury in the process.'

Plokhy said easily, 'While *I* don't believe we've a hope in hell, on our own, of challenging the secrets that are wrapped around the Sun. We need a distraction. Something overwhelming, to divert the authorities' resources from blocking our path. Something that can't be stopped . . . *We need a fleet*, rising up to join us.'

Rab was checking various monitors. 'Ah. And I think you're getting one, pilot.'

They all huddled over screens.

Muree was still unfamiliar with the detail of the ship's tech, but she could easily recognise proximity warnings. A crowd of warnings.

There really was a fleet – if a ragged one: a flood of vessels lifting from the surface of Mercury, gathering in orbit, and then converging on the rough trajectory of the *Styx*.

All of them heading straight up towards the dark enigma of the Wrap.

All an obvious challenge to the authorities.

Planter was studying the monitors. 'Damn it. You're right. Your scheme is working, pilot.' He pointed. 'Look here. The police are setting up a cordon over the planet – over its Sun-facing hemisphere anyhow. More cordons are being set up further out, as the exodus continues. They're moving fast – *but it's not going to work*. It won't come to it, but there's no way they could shoot all those craft out of the sky, or disable them non-lethally. A few nuclear detonations, electromagnetic pulses, *could* stop many . . . But it won't come to that.'

'Maybe, maybe not,' Elinor said bleakly. 'But *we* started this. We're only one ship. If they were to take *us* down—'

'That's why I'm making sure we're in the middle of a crowd,' Plokhy said. 'Testing their consciences, the authorities, the police—'

Planter said, 'What you're testing is a regime a millennium old, pilot. I wouldn't be certain of anything. Of any reaction you might evoke.'

Rab said, 'It's not fair to press him on that, Plokhy. Not *him*.' He held up his mutilated arm. 'As you say, we already know this particular policeman has a conscience. The real question is how typical he is.'

'Just tell them what you're planning,' Planter said, apparently on impulse. 'I mean, the track record you people – well, *we* – have established must be pretty well known by now. Your odyssey around the Solar System, uncovering so many unwelcome truths.' He thought it over. 'But I think you should tell them *why* you are doing this, why you are challenging assumptions which have structured our society for a thousand years. Tell them about Australia. About the, the gap in the Frame. *Tell* them. I've already reported in what I could – you know that. Tell it now – tell it in your own words.'

Rab frowned. 'The officers in the pursuit convoy must already have guessed.'

'The officers will have been *told*. You should make sure the lower ranks are as informed as they are, at least. And then, when the crisis comes, they can make their own *informed* choices – to follow orders, or wave you through to – well, whatever there is to find. Police officers do think, you know. They do have judgement. They're used to having to make harrowing decisions out in the field, on their own, knowing there will always be an accounting to come.'

Elinor studied him. 'You really are on our side, aren't you? In the end, you couldn't help it. You've always been a complicated character. And conflicted. A policeman with a conscience.'

The Lieutenant shook his head. 'We're not as rare as you would think.'

Plokhy glanced around at the group. 'You all agree? Do we go in, yelling out our intentions? I remind you we've still got more than a day to fly before we approach the Wrap. Plenty of time to blast us out of the sky—'

'Or,' Elinor said, 'time for guilty officers and confused crews to think it over and put any such orders aside. Tell them. Tell them *all*. Citizens, police, the rest. Tell everybody what we intend to do. Keep telling them. And tell them what we might achieve, if we get that far.'

Planter said nothing more.

'If we live that long,' Plokhy murmured. 'OK. I'll set it up.'

35

One day and sixteen hours to the Wrap.

Muree tried to sleep, woke too early.

The others managed better, she knew. Even Plokhy had slept for a few hours, with Lieutenant Planter taking a watch at the bridge station. The unsleeping ship itself needed little monitoring, of course, but it was apparently an ancient tradition, even maintained on mankind's interstellar ships like the *Lightbird*, that some human presence should always be on the bridge, to watch over the smart systems that cradled all their crew's lives for the duration of the mission. Relics of too many smart-system disasters past, Muree supposed.

She knew she should try to sleep again. Failed again.

In the end, Muree went to where she probably felt most comfortable aboard the ship – its lume tank. This was about halfway through the forty-hour journey. Indeed, even as she made herself comfortable beside the tank, she could feel the brief, gentle tug of spin forces as the ship turned end over end, and began its long deceleration to the face of the Wrap.

The lume tank was a small facility compared to that of the *Lightbird* where she had spent so many hours – and with only two lumes. But lumes were lumes, and when Muree had first come through here she had been glad to see that these lumes seemed content, or at least not distressed. The lumes were the beating heart of the ship, now as always. Managing a flow of energy was what they were *for*, it seemed, in evolutionary terms. And here and now, as the energy they shed was fed steadily into the ship's main drive – and, as in other such ships, with feeds siphoned off for other systems such as lighting, life support – they seemed OK to Muree . . .

Perhaps.

Save for something odd in their movements, just now. Something about their placement around each other, perhaps. A certain restlessness in the way they jostled, gently, in their tank.

It puzzled her enough to run some basic scans.

After some absorbing (and time-consuming) work, in the end she found slight anomalies in the lumes' internal magnetic fields.

These fields could be powerful, a by-product of the huge energies contained within each lume – or accessed from some other branch of spacetime *through* each lume, depending on which theory of their nature you believed. And it was known that lumes used such fields to position themselves physically, especially in huddles and groups, or they could impel themselves through the magnetic fields of planets – as had been observed in the ruin of Neptune, in Uranus – and even, presumably, the magnetic fields of stars.

It was believed too that the lumes' fields acted as sense organs . . . There were even theories that the magnetic fields were one way for the lumes to communicate with each other, based on rumours that had never been confirmed scientifically.

It was believed . . . That was the way lume science had always been. To *Lightbird* officers and, she'd learned recently, officers on the Mask too, and presumably in the wider command hierarchies of the Solar System, lumes were useful tools, or a threat. That was all . . . When it came to lumes, Muree thought, even here, back in the Solar System, all humanity held of the lumes was beliefs, not solid theories.

Now, though, those magnetic anomalies.

She seemed to be finding traces of an alignment. The lumes were both seeking to 'face' in the same direction, their magnetic axes, north to south, lying in parallel. That chosen direction itself seemed random to her – until she belatedly thought to overlay the lumes' alignment on a diagram of the ship as a whole, and its orientation in space.

Suddenly it seemed clear. The lumes' magnetic axes pointed straight at the Wrap, lying ahead. Or whatever lay trapped within.

She was still with the lumes when Brad came to find her, as if he were intending to spell her on lume-watching duty. Just like their work practices in the long years of the flight of the *Lightbird*.

She told him what she'd found out, or guessed.

Brad shrugged. 'We always knew this was going to be a big day, didn't we? Even the lumes are agitated . . .'

'Not just agitated. Something's different.'

'Sure. But right now we need to go back to work.' He touched her shoulder. 'Come on.'

She clambered out of the small couch she had been occupying, and was surprised to find herself floating up in the absence of any apparent gravity. The ship's thrust was gone, the engines seemingly inert.

'Wow,' she said. 'We're *there*?'

He grinned. 'You didn't feel the shutdown? We're there. But there's not much of a view . . .' He squeezed her shoulder. 'I'll stay with the lumes. You – you go do what you do best.'

'What's that?'

He grinned. 'Stir everybody up. And have them do the right thing.'

When she got back to the bridge, everybody else had gathered – Muree was the last, save for Brad.

And she arrived to find the ports and screens blocked by darkness.

Plokhy and the rest were already in their couches, or looking out through simple transparent ports – looking out at the dark. Elinor and Rab were apparently running various tests. Muree imagined instruments probing the space ahead with electromagnetic pulses, with test particles from electrons up to heavy atoms.

Elinor and Rab, mother and son, working quietly together. As if nothing had ever come between them. A good omen, Muree thought.

Plokhy saw Muree looking, and winked. *Come on in.*

So Muree crowded forward, looking through the ports and into the monitors, trying to get an integrated view all around the ship.

To the stern, she could still see Mercury by the lights of its mines, the fine thread of the local Frame.

Ahead, though, still only darkness.

Rab touched her shoulder and pointed that way. 'This is it. Welcome to the Solar Wrap. A black wall.'

'It's just how we came upon the Mask.'

'This is a lot smaller,' Rab said. 'The Mask encased the orbits of the outer planets. This only needs to encase the Sun – whatever's become of it . . . Length scales of a million kilometres, as opposed to a *billion* . . . But still . . .'

A sun become a black hole, so their instruments had told them, as the *Lightbird* had approached solar space.

But all there was actually to be *seen* was the Wrap, another human megastructure, this one enclosing an entire star.

A movement caught her eye, off in the periphery. A spark of light, crawling past the vast flank of this wall, this tremendous artefact. Another ship? Her heart beat a little faster, and she strained to see more clearly.

Plokhy saw her and grinned. 'You saw that? Yes, *another ship*. Somebody else. We are far from alone. That's just the closest; there seem to be hundreds out there, according to my scans. There are even craft hanging back, behind the curve of the Wrap itself, to act as over-the-horizon comms relays. They're *organising*.'

Hundreds?

Planter grunted. 'They responded to your call, pilot, obviously.'

'They?' Muree queried.

Plokhy grinned. 'Whoever could make it here, I guess. We struck a chord.'

'Umm,' Planter said. 'But there are also plenty of police and military craft in the mix. Looks like everything the authorities had down on Mercury has been thrown up, for a start. Other would-be rebels, or grandstanders, will be incoming. The Frame will be full of traffic too – unless the authorities manage to shut it down, locally.

'For now they're just watching. Watching and listening.' He glanced over at Plokhy. 'Correct?'

'That's pretty much it for the little ships too. They seem to be waiting for somebody to take control. To *do* something. That's confirmed by fragments of decoded chatter I've been able to pick up. Just waiting for someone to make a move – on either side.'

Planter said, 'I suspect the cops won't make the first move, won't intervene until something happens – unless we, or one of the crowd here, do something obviously illegal, or dangerous. They're always happy if the crowds just disperse without any trouble.'

Plokhy said, 'As to the object itself – the Wrap – I've never been so close to it. Why would I? I'm trying to get a sense of any internal structure by having the dispersing ships take readings of any gravitational anomalies, irregularities, inside. Given a wide enough spread, we may be able to get some kind of three-dimensional map of the interior – unless the authorities manage to exclude us. Painstaking work. That kind of measurement is plausible given a structure on such a scale, even though gravitational waves are so feeble—'

Muree frowned. 'But we think we *know* what's in there, don't we? We of the *Lightbird* thought so . . . Let's go over it again. We knew, from far out, that the Sun our ancestors left behind wasn't sitting there in plain sight any more. And when we looked at the gravity waves, as much as we could pick up at the edge of the Solar System, we *thought* we saw a spun-down black hole, didn't we? A dead star, a collapsed back hole, all its useful rotational energy tapped out. Yes? So no kind of prize for any predatory industrial cultures that might come to tap such a star, to steal its mass and energy, regardless of any planets and planetary life and cultures that might depend on it.'

Plokhy shrugged. 'That's pretty much it. All a part of the grand plan for the post-Neptune Solar System. That's what should be there.'

'But,' Muree said, 'the Architect's model did *not* show a black curtain at the heart of the System. Or a spun-down black hole . . . It showed what looked like a star. The Sun. We're so close. Maybe we'll know soon—'

'I'm going up there,' Rab said.

*

That stopped the conversation.

Muree – like the rest – stared at him.

Rab seemed surprised himself, Muree thought, as if somebody else had spoken for him.

But now he repeated, 'I'm going up to the surface. Of the Wrap. Me and my pressure suit.'

Lieutenant Planter said sternly, 'I *am* still a law enforcement officer, you know. It's my duty to stop you doing any such thing, Callis. I would be sanctioned myself if I let this go forward . . . And what the hell would you do up there, anyhow?'

Rab shrugged. 'What do you think? See what it's made of. The Wrap. *See what's inside.*' He glanced around, more uncertainly. 'I hear what you say of having the little ships make some kind of integrated survey of the gravity field, Plokhy. But—'

Plokhy was grinning. 'But it never hurts to go see for yourself.'

'And I ought to find out, *test*, if it's physically possible to do that at least, I guess. To approach the thing. To land on it.'

Elinor shook her head at her son's latest crazy stunt. 'That's impossible. Absurd.'

'No. I did some figuring. I'm pretty sure I could make it up there with just a jet pack. *And* back.'

Plokhy was checking screens and readouts. 'Well, amazingly enough – given we know that the Sun is inside there, or at least some object with the same mass as the Sun – and given you'd be at ten solar radii out, there would be an effective gravity of, umm, no more than a quarter of Earth's gravity?'

Muree boggled. 'You're saying he could *walk around* on this thing? *On* the Wrap?'

'Well, it's similar to Mars's surface gravity, and you coped with that. Less, actually.'

Rab half-laughed. 'Sometimes I think the whole of the Solar System I was born into is just insane . . .'

Plokhy raised an eyebrow. 'My lifelong point entirely. As to other parameters – we know the surface is as cold as if it were in deep space. Your suit would protect you from that.' She laughed. 'What am I saying? You'd need to be protected from the *cold*, as you walked around on the Wrap of the Sun?' She nodded. 'But, yes. I figure you could walk around down there, work, get back OK without any more trouble than if you had landed on an airless Mars.'

Muree burst out, 'With luck. If there's nothing we've not foreseen. And what would you *do* down there? Or – up there . . .'

'Well . . . I hadn't thought that far.'

'I know what *I'd* do,' Muree said, thinking it through. 'Try to see what's what. Dig down into it. Into the shell around the Sun.' She looked around at them all. 'We would *know*, for better or worse.'

Now Elinor came forward, drifting in the air. She took Rab's prosthetic in her own flesh hand. 'And what then? Even if you survived – what do you imagine the authorities would do to you?' She gripped that metallic hand harder still. 'You would be taken back. You would be cast down into the deepest, darkest pit on Mercury – or worse. I saved you once—'

'Then let me go,' Muree said softly.

And once she had said it aloud, she found she had surprised herself by doing so.

They all stared.

'Let me go. To the Wrap. I'll go.'

Rab pulled his hand away from his mother's grasp, and drifted backward in the air. Now, clearly, it was his turn to be shocked. 'You? Why you?'

'Why not me? I'm just as capable as you of doing – well, whatever it is that's possible to do down there. I won't ask you to loan me your robot hand . . .'

Elinor watched this exchange, transfixed. Perhaps she was holding her breath. Muree could see how much she was longing for Rab to give this up.

Plokhy said now, slowly, sounding uncharacteristically hesitant, 'It actually makes sense. I mean, if Muree, a star traveller, goes down there, as opposed to one of us, the legal position would be complicated at least. It might offer some . . . protection for her – in that regard. Buy some time.'

Jeo Planter sighed. 'Unfortunately, you're right. This was all laid out for me when we were given the assignment to track you two in the first place, after you escaped from the Mask. Our mission of pursuit was a joint one, remember, sanctioned by both commanders. I could arrest you, Rab. I couldn't arrest Muree. She's under the jurisdiction of *her* commanders, not the hierarchy I report to. So the control I have over her is limited, in law. I could restrain her, send her back to her ship, confined. And I could always stop her if she laid about her with an axe—'

Muree glanced at Plokhy. 'Talking of axes. Have you *got* an axe?'

Plokhy grinned. 'You bet—'

'*Then*,' Planter went on doggedly, '*Then* I could restrain her from threatening or causing harm to citizens or their property or . . . But all I could do would be to hold on to her before passing her back to the *Lightbird* officers.'

Rab seemed furious. He held up his claw. 'You're going to let her go, aren't you? I have a missing hand. *You* have a blind eye.'

Planter shrugged. 'Always did, I guess.'

Muree was aware that Elinor was taking no part in this discussion. Very evidently she did *not* want to send her son on this mission.

Plokhy, as no-nonsense as ever, cut through it all. 'Well, we can't just sit here. Muree and an axe – that's the most useful idea I've heard all day. It's the *only* useful idea I've heard all day.

'Let's do this.'

And with that simple command, Muree saw Plokhy had taken control.

Her own mission was on.

'Muree, go check out your suit. I'll lay in a course. I presume it doesn't matter where you land – I'll just stand off, be ready to pick you up.

'And you, Rab, go find the axe in my store. Rear cargo bay. Who carries an axe on a spacecraft, you ask? Anybody who wants to keep alive. And add anything else you find that you think she might find useful. Put together a tool belt.'

'Like what?'

'How do I know? I've never cut through a solar wrap before. Use your imagination. If the axe doesn't work – knives, laser cutters. Laser might be best. We don't want to make too much of a mess of it all. Sharp-edged wounds, easily fixed . . .' She looked over at Muree. 'How are you feeling now, kid?'

'I . . .' *I wish I'd thought before opening my mouth.* 'Like I want to get on with it.'

Plokhy took her command seat, holding the ship steady.

Elinor drifted over to Muree. 'I'll help you check over your suit.' And she whispered, 'Thank you. For Rab.'

In the event, both Rab and Muree suited up – Rab in a strictly assistance role. They were supervised by Lieutenant Planter, who, if reluctantly, checked and double-checked their gear as they donned it.

As they prepared, much of Muree's adrenaline seemed to drain away, until she came to think this was the worst idea in the world. In all the worlds. But she was committed now – for pride, and to protect Rab, if no other reason. And his mother.

And to adjust the course of the whole future of mankind.

Not a thought you have every day, she reflected.

In the ship's cramped rear airlock, following Plokhy's instructions, they found a short ladder – rungs fixed to the wall – that led down a well, a few metres deep, to a small hatch directly below them.

When they were ready, they waited in the airlock while Plokhy cautiously manoeuvred the *Styx* down to within a few tens of metres of the solar sphere, and inverted the ship so that it felt as if it were landing on a flat surface beneath,

Waited in silence, as various screens showed a flat semi-infinite floor beneath them, dimly reflecting the light of the ship's lamps.

At last Plokhy warned them that contact with the Wrap was about to be made.

Muree held on to one rung reflexively. She could feel barely anything of the latest manoeuvres, so cautious must Plokhy be about damaging her ship in the process, let alone doing some kind of harm to the shell around the Sun.

But she could feel the gentle deceleration as the manoeuvre was completed.

And then the softest of jolts as the *Styx* finally made physical contact with the Wrap itself.

Muree and Rab exchanged a look.

'We're down,' she said.

'Yes.'

'Shit.'

'But down on what? Did we really just land on the Sun?'

And, as she shifted a little, she could feel that gravity – close to that of Mars as she remembered it, a steady pull, but light compared to Earth's, or even to the spin gravity of the *Lightbird*'s Carousel.

She was glad she was standing, and right way up too.

'Feels like it. We landed. Well, I guess we're going to find out.'

'All clear,' Plokhy reported. 'Now, listen. I'm told that there's no purchase on the surface of the sphere. There are people in the cloud, talking to me, who've sent probes down before, just to see . . . I need to stabilise the ship while you exit, but I'm wary of using any kind of grabbing claws on that unknown surface, even any kind of adhesive.'

Muree asked, 'So how will you keep her steady?'

'Thrusters,' Rab said.

'He's right,' called Plokhy. 'I'll keep the ship close up against the Wrap with the gentlest of thrusts from the attitude control nozzles. For as long as you need. You shouldn't notice a thing—'

'Except the gravity,' Planter called. 'Of the object itself. Watch out for your blood flow, any feeling of light-headedness – watch out you don't break your damn legs.'

Plokhy said, 'Oh, your smart suits will help. Don't fret it. Some people have the knack of reassurance. Some don't, Lieutenant.'

Rab glanced at Muree through his faceplate.

They both laughed.

Then Muree took a couple of deep breaths. 'So. Let's do this.'

'As we two crash through yet another massive conceptual barrier together?'

'It's getting to be a habit, isn't it? Help me.'

She held out her arm.

She didn't need the help, and he probably knew it, but he took her arm in his gloved hand readily enough. The fake hand, she noticed absently.

And, bracing against his support, she stood upright on the

ladder, above the open hatch. Rab fixed a safety cable to a hook on the waist of her suit.

Then he stepped back, nodded, let go her arm.

She stood alone.

'All right,' she said. 'I'm on the ladder—'

'We can *see* that,' Plokhy called.

A grin in her voice, Muree thought. Which calmed her.

'OK. I'm going down.'

One rung, two, three.

At the bottom of the ladder, above the closed hatch, she glanced up at Rab, who nodded through his faceplate.

'I'm down,' she called. 'At the hatch.'

'OK,' Plokhy called now. 'We see you. Just stand still for a few breaths, Muree. You're in gravity now, remember. We all are. Let your body get used to it. And your suit.'

And she could feel that adjustment as Plokhy spoke, a tightening of the suit around her legs, a slight sense of vertigo.

'You OK?'

'OK, Plokhy. Just a little clumsy. No whirling head.'

'Historic words,' Rab said, a little sourly.

She had to grin. 'Jealous, Rab?'

'Course I am. Wouldn't you be? You're already the glamorous star traveller. You're going to be even more famous, or notorious, or both, after this, however it turns out. And all people will say of me will be, "Who was that guy with Muree?" Well, let's get this done, and then we can write our biographies. Plokhy? Open the hatch, please.'

'Understood.'

The airlock door swung down at last, with the briefest hiss of escaping air. The ladder unfolded, reaching a little further from the base of the hatch.

Crouching a little, peering out by the lights of the ship and her suit, Muree looked down on a dark floor beneath the ship, infinite and flat as far as she could see – but with just a sparkle of what looked like ice.

'Hey, *Styx*. Did you get that? In the suit cameras?'

'A kind of frost,' Rab said. 'I think.'

'Could be,' Plokhy said. 'It's pretty cold out there. Any moisture in our escaping air will be frozen fast. Certainly any carbon dioxide. Frost on the box they put the Sun in. On any other day that would seem unusual.'

'Well, it's settled now,' Rab said. 'So—'

'The ladder,' Muree said.

She glanced back once more at Rab, who watched intently. She held on to the door frame with one gloved hand. She took one step down the ladder, two, three. Then back up, once.

'I can get back easily when I need to. The gravity is actually helpful.'

She stepped down once more. 'Bottom rung. So I'm going to step off the ladder now,' she called.

She stretched, and let her right boot settle on the surface below.

'Boot down,' she called now.

'There's poetry for you,' Brad called. 'Some story this will be when you get back to the *Lightbird*.'

'Yeah, yeah. Both feet down. Standing up. Letting go of the ladder. I'm standing *on* the Wrap. How about that? Walking away now . . .'

Cautiously she let go of the ladder, making sure she was still in grabbing range of it. She ducked her head beneath the hull of the ship, took one step, two. She had expected a slippery surface, given how sleek it looked, but it didn't feel that way.

'The walking is easy. Don't worry, I'll be cautious. The surface seems roughened somehow . . . It feels like there's a little give in the surface. *Oh.* I'm leaving footsteps.

'It's not like dirt, or snow, given I've only seen those things on Mars, and not close to. Not dust either. The Mask's outer layer is evidently a material that's compressing when I press down my footsteps. Feels like it's a material I could cut through with a hard thrust. Which is a promising observation. I get no sense of temperature under my feet, neither hot nor cold.'

'So your boots are working,' Rab said dryly. 'That'll go down in history. You want me to pass out the tools?'

'Please.'

She stepped back, and without difficulty took the bag of tools they'd selected: a shovel, a drill, a laser, other stuff. She lowered the bag carefully.

Then she walked further out, away from the cover of the ship's hull. She found herself under a darkened sky – the Masked sky. Perhaps she saw the lume-light of a Frame strut, a scratch across the dark.

To work, Muree.

She leaned down, took the shovel from the bag. The simplest tool of all. Set it on the Mask surface, pressed the blade with her boot sole, not hard.

She glanced back at Rab, who sat in the hatchway, one thumb up.

She said, 'Last chance to go back from this.'

'Let's make history,' he said.

She braced her boot on the shovel. 'Well, that's the plan—'

'Hold that thought,' Plokhy said sharply. 'Somebody on the line to speak to you.'

Muree lifted the shovel, staggered a step back from where she had been about to make the incision.

'On the line? Who—'

'Officer Muree? This is Mask Commander Edwina Revil. And I'm here to ask you to cease what you're doing.'

That threw her.

She stepped back again, back within reach of the ladder, holding the shovel.

'Commander Revil? But you—'

'Command the Mask, a great structure on the edge of the Solar System? So I do. Or have done. But I share joint responsibility for this, the Wrap, a great structure at the very heart of the System. There is a command team, a hierarchy . . . No matter. When news broke of the emergent crisis here at the Wrap—'

'Emergent crisis? What crisis?'

'The crisis you have caused – you and those who aided you – or are about to cause. When the issue escalated, I was seconded to handle the situation since . . . well, since you know me, I know you, and your crew . . .'

'How could you get here so quickly?'

'That's hardly relevant—'

'Not through the Frame,' Plokhy said. 'That will transport a lot of stuff, but it's not fast. You could get from the Mask to down here in days with a high-acceleration fusion drive ship . . . Another secret, Commander?'

Revil snapped now, 'How I got here is hardly relevant. The fact that I *am* here is what is relevant . . .'

Muree tuned out her words.

She still held the shovel in her hand. Tried not to think about Revil's ranting.

But still, could she, standing here, with this most rudimentary of tools, really achieve so much damage that a person the stature of Revil should be sent across the Solar System to close her down?

Her, and a shovel?

She suppressed a laugh.

'Am I really such a threat, Commander?'

Revil replied sternly, 'As an outsider to our System-wide culture, you have little or no understanding of the complex systems, technological, political, logistical and others, which maintain such high populations in harmony and safety. Yes, you are a threat.'

'A threat to safety? I haven't even got a spare shovel—'

'Yes, to safety. To safety from destabilisation, within and without. Safety from danger, psychological, political, and ultimately physical, technical. And that is why you *must* return now, to your ship, the *Styx* – and voluntarily. Given your physical location. You must be aware that the fragility of the Wrap is such that any attempt to apprehend you by force could end in disaster—'

'You would use force?'

'Of course not—'

'You just hinted at it. Why should I believe you would? Why should I believe you wouldn't?'

A pause.

'*Why should I believe anything you say,* Commander? Everything about your government is built on lies. You hid the whole of the Solar System in the Mask. And here is another Mask, your "Wrap" . . . You made it look to us, even, as we approached in the *Lightbird*, as if there was no Sun at the heart of the Solar System, just a burned-out black hole. Whatever I'm standing on here, I'm betting it's not that—'

'Who are you to question our ways – our methods, our *achievement*?' There was anger in Revil's voice now. 'In the face of an overwhelming existential threat, we have protected a stable community across a millennium—'

'I'm a citizen of a community of my own. The starship, remember? A mere century in our case. We were just as enclosed, confined, in our own technological bubble. We had rules to obey – even about the children we could have, or keep. But, you know, compared to this prison system of yours we were free—'

'*We were attacked*,' Revil said, forcefully. 'A thousand years ago. The Solar System. Humanity. *A planet was destroyed*. We found evidence of another, destroyed earlier. What were we, my predecessors, supposed to do? We did our best. We could not fight back – so we believed. So – we hid. We camouflaged a whole planetary system—'

'And you lied and lied to generations of your own people . . .' Muree glanced down at her feet, the rough surface of the Wrap. 'And what is there inside this final lie, this Wrap?'

She took a breath. And she wondered how many were listening to her words now – or would hear her voice in the future.

She said fiercely, 'Commander – admit it. *There's no evidence of a conscious attack on the Solar System*. Is there? All that you have is a lume nest in Neptune – and another, a planet exhausted, in the Kuiper belt. And you actually *seeded* Uranus with lumes for your own purposes, didn't you? But it's the threat to the Wrap that has forced you to break cover like this.

'So – *what's inside the Wrap*? And if there is no aggressor, what is the purpose, why the exhaustion of the black hole Sun . . .'

And yet she came to losing her nerve.

She looked back at Rab, touched her throat for private conversation. 'What am I doing? Everybody in the Solar System will be hearing this, soon if not right now. Even aboard the *Lightbird*, my Rossbee friends . . . *What shall I do*? Should I submit?'

Rab held up his arm, his prosthetic hand. 'It's people that matter. *This* can't be right. And for you, there was no room for your twin sister to be born, because her parents were aboard a ship that had fled from an imaginary foe. *That* can't be right. How many people, over the centuries, have suffered through such situations? What lie can justify such crimes?

'Enough. Yes, everybody's watching this, everybody's listening. And they'll watch it over and over, and listen to the words being spoken, for years to come. *Good*. So, for their sakes – follow your instinct.'

Follow your instinct –

She braced herself against the ladder, for purchase.

She held the shovel high.

Everybody's watching –

She slammed the shovel into the floor.

It was like stabbing plastic packaging – light, soft stuff. And after only a few centimetres, it seemed, any resistance gave and the shovel moved freely.

She had broken through already.

And light, dazzling, glistened through the slash she had made. Brilliant light.

She dropped the shovel, knelt, and dug her gloved hand into the crack. Grabbed a handful of a material that crushed easily in her fist. It was only centimetres thick, it seemed, even before her compression. She supposed that if you were going to make a bag big enough to enclose a star, using only the resources of a planet like Mercury, you would have to make it of thin, flimsy stuff like this . . .

She got her other hand in the crack. Yanked at the material. Hauled backwards. Felt a tearing through her clumsy gloves. A panel maybe two metres wide ripped open, causing her to fall back.

And that brilliant light splashed over her face.

She jammed her eyes shut, turned her head away sharply, until her helmet faceplate opaqued.

Maybe she hit her head.

She was falling back, falling in the light.

Later, it would be said that she had cast a shadow a million kilometres long.

36

Back, back. She was tumbling, backwards, away from the rent in the Wrap, away from that brilliant rectangle of light – back into the artificial shadow of this surface, a sphere that evidently did contain the Sun. A *star*. And not an inert relic, whatever lies had been told before. Lies upon lies.

What truth, though?

Falling back, helpless, twisting away from the light.

Falling back from that rough rectangle of impossible, mendacious brilliance.

Twisting helplessly, all sense of bearings lost—

Somebody shouting in her ear.

'Muree! Stop fighting your suit! It's trying to restore stability, orientation. Just let it do its job . . .'

Muree, disoriented, dazzled, didn't know who was talking to her. But she thought she was about to vomit with the tumbling. She tried to hold it back, a reflex born of a lifetime in a spacecraft. Endless drills. *You don't throw up in a pressure suit . . .*

'This is Brad. Let me try. . . Muree! Brad Tenant. Try to focus. Listen, Plokhy has a couple of lumes going crazy back here . . .'

'Lumes?' That she could visualise. She took a deep breath.

'Brad?'

'That's it. Yes – this is Brad. We've got you! Just relax. You're falling back from the Wrap, from the rip you made. All that light. But you're in no immediate danger. Just tumbling, that's all. And you still have your safety line . . .'

It was as if his words brought her slowly back to the world, to her anchor in reality.

'Tumbling?'

'Tumbling.'

She had been trained in how to handle a pressure suit since she was five years old: as soon as she had been old enough to wear her own suit, as opposed to riding in a papoose on the back of an adult. Starting with game-like drills at the spin-free axis of the *Lightbird*. Basically you let the smart suit do its job and stabilise itself, and you.

Now she murmured a command to tell the suit to do just that. And she starfished, head up, arms and legs spread wide.

Still the universe swivelled around her; the ship, the great wall that was the Solar Wrap, the hole she had dug in that pure black surface, the light that now poured out . . . But now she felt kicks, jolts, as the suit used built-in thrusters to right itself, to stop the tumbling.

Just follow the drill. Let the suit fix itself.

At last she stabilised.

Now she was hanging in space, her back to the Wrap, facing the *Styx*. Against the deeper darkness beyond, she thought she could see tracings of the illuminated Frame, the road between the worlds. That was lume-light.

The *Styx*, though, gleamed in the released sunlight, the light coming from behind her.

She murmured a command, and let the thrusters on her suit turn her around, so she was once more facing the Wrap.

It was an infinite wall, above and below her, to either side. So huge its curvature was impossible to discern. Just as it had been a few minutes ago. Like a black, limitless plain.

Save for that rent, directly ahead of her, a rough rectangle of brilliant light. The hole *she* had ripped.

Oh, and there went the bit of panelling she had detached, tumbling slowly away.

Without thinking, but in control once more, she had her suit push her towards the bit of debris.

'Handle with care,' came an immediate order from Commander Revil.

Sounding rueful?

'It's expensive stuff, and delicate. In fact don't handle it at all if you don't have to. It's already collapsed to a safety-fallback configuration, less thickness, more density. In places in the Wrap it would be about ten *metres* thick . . .'

'Copy that.'

When she reached the rip, she improvised a tether, pulling out a length of cord from a dispenser at her waist, then used a bit of emergency-kit vacuum-tolerant adhesive from a well on her sleeve to fix the cord to the fabric, near the tear.

'Got it. It looks less than ten *centimetres* thick.'

'. . . very delicate indeed. Once it's replaced – and that will be by our technicians, not by you – it should expand again, self-heal meld back into the overall surface. A wound that small should be self-healing, in fact, if it gets the chance. The Wrap as a whole is designed to recover from meteorite punctures and the like.'

Muree swivelled and looked back at the sphere, the darkness compared to the brilliance of the light that came pouring out of the wound she'd made. 'The Sun. It's inside there somewhere . . .' Something in her head connected. 'And so that is – sunlight.'

Rab laughed softly. 'Great deduction, oh bold explorer.'

*

'Great images,' Rab said. 'Just thought I'd mention it. The endless black wall . . . Remember, you're looking at a sphere of width ten times the radius of the Sun itself. And *that* is the Wrap. And now all anybody is looking at will be the light coming from that one tear, and you, in your suit, hanging in the light.' He laughed. 'In the future that's probably *all* anybody will remember of you. This one image.'

'The future? Out here in the present I'm taking it one step at a time, thanks. Anyhow I've never *seen* sunlight, if you think about it. Or even the light of another star, up close. But even so . . .'

'What?' Rab asked softly.

'There's something about it, this, the quality of the light coming out of the rip. It feels *right*. Even through my suit visor. Does that make sense?'

Plokhy said, 'Well, that's sunlight. The light under which humanity evolved. Maybe there's something deep inside you that's – responding.'

'So if the sunlight is *right*, does that make this thing *wrong*? This – shell?'

Revil said, 'I suggest you don't make any hasty judgements. Not until you understand what you are finding out, exploring, discovering . . .'

'Very well. So what's it *made* of?' A scrap of shell floated before her. 'Some kind of carbon structure? It's so light I couldn't feel it – like trying to grab smoke—'

'Even when you were punching a hole in it?'

'I guess it's highly reflective, to start with. To contain the sunlight, reflect it back? . . .'

'Reflective, basically, yes,' Revil said. 'It's actually a sandwich of dielectric layers. Thin sheets of the stuff. Dielectrics have complex internal electrical properties, and you can use them to control opacity and electrical conductivity in complex ways—'

'Basically the Wrap is a smart mirror,' Rab said bluntly. 'Is what the commander is trying to say. Smart enough, evidently, to reflect back the Sun's radiation. All but perfectly.'

'Correct,' Revil said. '*Very* efficiently, with reflection perfect to within one thousandth of one per cent. That's what the material is for, and it works just as my predecessors in the control hierarchy designed and built it to do. And it *has* worked for the best part of a thousand years. Even if it hasn't yet become fully effective as a Solar Wrap. Not yet.'

Muree still longed to understand what a 'solar wrap' *was*, what it *did*. What this monstrous structure was *for*.

But Rab continued to ask about how the fabric had been built, maintained – and since such monuments had shaped his whole life, Muree couldn't begrudge him using this chance to find out more.

'So,' Rab said now. 'You have a shell of material, ten metres thick, with a radius ten times that of the Sun. And all the material came from Mercury?'

'Correct again,' said Revil. 'The bulk components anyhow. Most of the structure consists of a silicate aerogel, very lightweight stuff . . . Much of the crust of Mercury is silicate material, in fact, usefully for this project. But even so the initial mining operation, and then assembly and maintenance, was hugely expensive in resources. Because the Wrap, though so thin, is extensive: a Wrap around the Sun – and at a distance. The mining on Mercury was brutal. They had to go as deep as five hundred metres as a *global* average, although in practice still deeper mines were dug into more useful lodes—'

Muree broke in, 'Been there, heard that. Can we get back to the point here?'

She was still drifting in space, still illuminated by the light pouring out of the rent she had made in the great sphere. *Sunlight*, where she should have been seeing the relics of a burned-out black hole.

'Indeed,' Plokhy called back. 'We didn't come here to marvel at a gargantuan, if insane, piece of planetary engineering. About which we know so far nothing except that from afar it *looks* like a black hole—'

'The hole Muree ripped in your Wrap, Commander Revil, revealed the sunlight she's been basking in ever since. When we should have been looking at – what? A Sun collapsed into a black hole, a black hole itself spun down to uselessness after a millennium of industrial exploitation. *None of that happened*, did it? All of it a clever fake embedded in the smart Wrap with which you have covered up the true Sun. And yet the Sun shines still. You even sent out fake gravitational waves to make it look like a black hole, by *that* measure.'

'Pilot—'

'Well, everybody knows by now. Or at least as much as has been revealed so far. I'm betting that the Frame is going to be crammed with travellers, right now, all of them heading as deep into the Solar System as they can . . .'

'Coming already, actually.' That was Lieutenant Planter. 'According to my own feeds. But she's right about the traffic on the Frame. All heading for the optimal route for Mercury. Links are being diverted, transits stopped – for now – though that can't last long, not if a sizeable population isn't to get trapped in bottleneck Frame links . . . And, ships, yes, like Plokhy's. Independents. More than I'd have expected, although the estimates of ship numbers are changing all the time . . .'

Rab said, 'But how can they have congregated so quickly? *We* only just got here . . .'

'Rumour,' Plokhy said. 'And not spread by me either, please

take note. People watch, you know. People *listen*. People interpret. You have connected mankind, Commander Revil, creating a mass mind of billions of brains. You have your Frame, commander, shuttling our bodies to and fro across the System in your neat arcs and straight lines. But there is another Frame, another network, even you can't close down. A network of words, of ideas, of bits of evidence, of pattern-matching.

'And now, today – well, here we are. People want to know the truth, Commander Revil. The truth *at last*. The arrival of the *Lightbird* was one crack in the façade, wasn't it? The colony ships were supposed to be just that – lost relics of a heroic gesture of the past, the age of the Neptune invasion. The starfarers weren't supposed to *come back* with a different version of history, were they? But you adapted, even so. You did your best to fit that new piece into the thousand-year mosaic of lies you've been constructing. But it just hasn't worked, has it? *People are coming down here because they want to know the truth,* Commander Revil.'

A furious mutter from Revil. 'I shouldn't have waited,' she said, as if speaking to herself. 'I should have come down here and put a stop to this sooner . . .'

Down here, Muree thought, drifting alone in space, idly listening. *Down here.*

Down at the bottom of the gravitational pit that was the Solar System. The pit containing the deepest, most ancient secret – most ancient *lie,* in a System riddled with lies.

It surprised her to hear that Revil was still talking.

'. . . Maybe if we'd acted as soon as the *Lightbird* swam into view . . . We couldn't turn her away. But if I'd had overall control over the incident, if I'd reacted more quickly –'

Muree was shocked. 'Did you even *consider* that, Commander? No matter what secrets you are hiding, or whatever – we couldn't be "turned away". We'd designed for a century-long mission, and that was what we achieved.' Her mind raced as she thought through this, for the first time. 'Oh, with the lumes we were never going to be short of power. But we were out of hydrogen for propellant; we'd already all but exhausted our inboard supply . . . If you'd turned us away, as you put it, it would have killed us all – maybe not for months, years even, but . . . Did you *discuss* that? Did you even *think* it?'

Revil hesitated. 'We were considering the survival of the species. We discussed all options. We – well, we were split. The governing councils. We took a vote—'

'A vote?' Rab asked. 'Are you serious?'

'*We had the gravest responsibility imaginable*. You must understand. That's what this has all been about, all the way back to the attack on Neptune, a thousand years ago. If you'd *seen* the destruction of that planet – the thousand-year-old relics are bad enough, but to witness it at first hand, as my predecessors did, indeed one of my own ancestors . . . Those who witnessed that, recorded it, analysed it, in response set up a new form of society – why, a whole new *architecture* of the Solar System, to try to enable humans to endure.'

'But those first witnesses were traumatised,' Plokhy said coldly. 'Shocked. Their judgement poor. Isn't that true, Commander? They couldn't see clearly what was in front of them. And they made poor decisions—'

'I think *I'm* starting to see,' Muree said, still drifting in space above the ripped-open Wrap. 'If you'd never seen lumes before – if you knew nothing about them—'

Revil said, '*The lumes, some of them, fell into the Sun*. That was what drove us to the strategy we had to adopt. Why we had to take on the lumes – and anything, anybody, that was controlling them. We thought might *lose* the Sun . . .'

And suddenly Muree saw it.

'Lumes into your star,' Muree said. 'That was what you feared. But what we saw – what I learned . . .

'Commander, you should have listened to us when we tried to describe conditions at my home star, Ross 128b. How we – umm – *live* with the lumes. As I learned, and you ought to talk to the Captain . . .

'Look, we get our lumes from a broken-open ice giant. Just like Neptune. And, ever since my ancestors arrived in the Ross system, *we've seen lumes, a drizzle of them, falling into the star*. It seems to be harmless. It's just – what lumes do.'

'But—'

'And,' she dared to speak over the Commander, 'and we've been watching this behaviour for a thousand years, remember. No harm has come to our star. And – *and*, before you shut me down – our star is a red dwarf, and it's much older than your Sun. Nealy *twice* as old, four billion years older, I think. Don't you think that if lumes were harming stars they'd have done it to 128b by now?'

Elinor broke into the feed. 'Ha! Of course . . . Good science, Muree. And if only there had been a full a frank exchange of data, rather than this paranoid effort to control, we'd have got to that answer a lot faster. And without a lot of pain.'

A short silence. 'This will have to be verified,' said the Commander.

Plokhy broke in. 'It will. And a lot of rethinking will have to be done. Your ancestor, and the governments she spoke with, *panicked*, Commander. A thousand years of panic.'

Muree said, 'Back on Rossbee we observed the same behaviour, of the lumes. It was history to me, but I read about it when I was assigned to the lume tanks on the *Lightbird*. Yes. But back then you couldn't know how they behave – how they live, what they *do*. But you know now.'

Revil waved a hand, away from the cloaked Sun, out towards the edge of the Solar System. 'That's the point. Even before they got in as far as Neptune, we, my predecessors, thought they were weapons. What were we meant to think? Any doubts were swept aside when the assault came—'

'But it wasn't an assault,' Muree said. 'You know that now. It was a migration. That's what lumes do, it seems. Migrate from star to star. We saw it at our own star! The lumes are, or anyhow *were*, not even aware of our – humanity's – existence.'

'They may have "fallen on" a planet earlier, further out in the Kuiper belt,' Revil pointed out. 'Don't forget that. We did find the debris of that event, and didn't understand its significance until Neptune—'

'Yes,' Elinor said. 'All right. *But this is just part of their life-cycle*. Evidently. They settle on worlds – big worlds, the giants of gas and ice – and they breed. They use their own energy to dismantle the planet, at least in part—'

'Turning it into one of their foul "nests",' Revil said.

'All right. But that's not the end of it. That's just a step on the way, to—'

'The Sun! Or the star of whatever system they infest. That's the ultimate goal of these – invasions. That's what we saw. We *saw* lumes invading the Sun! That's what we believed! We believed that just as Neptune was dismantled, so the Sun would follow—'

Now Elinor spoke. 'But it's not an *invasion*, is it? It would more appropriately be called a migration. All this is purely – biological, it seems to me. The lumes infest a planetary system, and ultimately its star. *Infest* – yes, that's a better word. Not *invade*. There's no sign of intention, is there? Any more than there is among the vectors of the plague the *Lightbird* brought . . .'

Revil growled, 'Then what's the point? What do they *want*?'

Muree was winging it – but she had studied lumes much of her adult life. 'Maybe what they *want* isn't something we can perceive. The lumes' migration is like a – cosmic process. And a process that doesn't play out on our timescales. They just head for stars because that's what they *do*.'

'Quite right,' Elinor said. 'Ah. But you *wanted* there to be signs of intention, didn't you, Commander Revil? You and your predecessors – indeed, your own ancestor at the first incursion. That was the story they concocted – the distant ancestor whose uniform you now fill, whose role you have taken—'

'Edwina. Her name was Edwina Revil. Show some respect.'

'Very well. Sorry. But you *wanted* to find the lumes harming the planets, the Sun. Intentionally if it could be proved—'

'*There was an invasion*,' Planter said now. 'That's what we were told – always. What I was told, and I've achieved a pretty high rank. The same story. There *must* have been an invasion by a species more or less like us, if not physically, necessarily. Technological. They came in mighty ships. They brought lumes, yes, but lumes were mere power plants. Or weapons. Bombs. We thought. Advanced, but nothing more than – tools. Engines. Or maybe even engineered organisms. It didn't matter. They, the Invaders, wrecked Neptune, as they had wrecked a planet further out – possibly before humans evolved. And if we hadn't camouflaged the Solar System – yes, using the lumes in turn, still breeding in Neptune – the Invaders might have come again. That's what we were told, Commander Revil. *That's what we were told*. And generations before us.'

Elinor said simply, 'Then everything *you* have been told is a lie.'

Revil had no reply.

The silence stretched.

Plokhy broke in.

'So,' she said cheerfully. 'To sum up. We're all going through quite the conceptual crisis here, aren't we? Not for the first time in this episode. Muree has a point. *It's all falling apart*, isn't it, Commander Revil? It doesn't matter what we know or say now. Because soon everybody's going to know about it. It's simple enough.

'The lumes came, yes. They had worked their way through some of the bodies in the Oort cloud or the Kuiper belt, always heading towards the Sun. They came to the planets of the Solar System.'

'And they took Neptune,' Revil said weakly.

'Yes, they took Neptune. They seem to need to breed in the heart of ice giants, before going on to their real target.'

'The Sun.'

'The Sun,' Elinor said. 'And evidently no more would have become of that. Not for billions of years, given the experience of Ross 128 . . . They wouldn't have infested any more planets. One per stellar system – maybe two? – is enough for a nest. Enough to launch them into their next phase. Yes, there are lumes now in Uranus, next planet in – but they're there because *we put them there*. Having seen how they transformed Neptune's resources, we wanted them to breed – for our purposes.

'Centuries passed. We studied the lumes – how to work them. How to use them. Why, we managed that very early, as the starships like *Lightbird* were designed around the lumes. And soon we were building the Frame and other monuments, like Hellas, similarly around their capabilities.

'Our esteemed Commander Revil – or your long-dead spiritual

ancestors – got it all wrong. Didn't you? You thought of the lumes as dangerous, but a dangerous *resource*. As earlier generations handled nuclear power, perhaps. They didn't *observe*, you see. They didn't try to grasp the picture. They didn't *think*, or *learn*. They thought only in terms of invasions to follow some day. They just panicked. Panicked on a scale of centuries . . . On an epic scale.'

For a moment Revil didn't reply. Then she sighed hugely. 'You could put it that way.'

There was a half-laugh, rueful. And suddenly Muree felt sorry for this extraordinary, extraordinarily powerful person.

'Look,' Revil said, 'we did what we could. What we thought we had to do. We – *hid*. Hid the planets in the dark behind the Mask.'

'And the Sun?' Muree said.

'The Sun, yes. We could trap the sunlight, but no mere blanket could hide the mass of the Sun. So – well, you know the second line of defence. We tried to make the Sun look – useless – to any invaders. As well as hiding the Sun visibly, the Wrap and Mask together were designed to give off fake gravity waves, which made it *look*, it was hoped, as if the Sun was a mined-out black hole, a stellar wreck.'

'But that wasn't enough,' Plokhy said. 'You were still afraid of the lumes. Or the invisible invaders you believe controlled them. And so you, your predecessors, *tried to make the Sun useless to them too*.'

Revil hesitated. 'Something like that. The theory was that the lumes might feed off the fusing energy of the Sun. So, in the longer term, we decided to shut it down.

'The Sun.'

Muree, hanging over a cloaked Sun, the rents in the Wrap, the leaking sunlight, listened carefully. Longing to understand. '*You shut down the Sun?* With the Wrap, then. It wasn't solely camouflage?'

'More than that.' Revil sighed. 'I myself worked on the Wrap, for some years. Part of my training for the outer Mask. Roles are exchanged across an integrated Solar System government . . .

'The Wrap design was originally *meant,* not as a camouflage mechanism, but as a means of extending the Sun's life. A dream of an earlier age, a more peaceful age . . . We hadn't given up on the present, but we were planning for the very far future . . .'

Muree hadn't expected that. 'You wanted to extend the Sun's life? How? It's a fusion engine a million kilometres across, isn't it? Tell me how.'

Revil said, sounding calm. 'The principle is simple enough. And the reason we dreamed up the technology of the Wrap in the first place. Because the Sun is a big heat engine, but a simple one, as engines go. If not, I suppose, perhaps this universe of ours would not be quite so full of stars . . .'

Revil spoke calmly enough, but Muree knew she must be hating this interrogation of and pressure from her juniors. *Get used to it,* Muree thought, maliciously.

'Look,' Revil said, 'a star is nothing, initially, but a clump of hydrogen – maybe already polluted with more complex elements, if your star forms from the debris of an earlier generation of stars. At the centre of the clump, gravity gets to work, the weight of all those outer layers compressing the core. And in that core, pressures and temperatures rise, until you reach a point where it's so hot and dense that the nuclei of hydrogen atoms, colliding, coalesce into the nuclei of helium, the next heaviest element. And energy is released by that process.

'Now, the trick is that four hydrogen nuclei combine to make one helium – but the four input hydrogens together masses a little *more* than the product, the helium. And that process, that tiny excess of mass turned to energy, is what powers the Sun, and all the stars. And that process will go on, by the way, until the hydrogen in the core is used up, the core is choked with helium. Elsewhere in the Sun, other fusion processes go on, as heavier elements are baked – oxygen, carbon. Meanwhile there is much more residual hydrogen in the outer layers, but no process to draw it down . . .'

'The Wrap, though,' Muree prompted.

'The Wrap. So, a star you have a ball of gas held together by gravity, and heated at the core by fusion processes. And in the beginning the star as a whole quickly finds a kind of equilibrium. Equilibrium, through a feedback between the energy output of the hot fusing core and the upper, cooler layers.

'If the core gets *too* hot, you see, the outer layers expand. But that *reduces* the pressure on the core. Which makes the core fusion rate go *down*, until you get back to the optimal temperature.

'Conversely if the core *cools*, the upper layers *collapse* a bit, which increases the pressure on the core, which makes it heat up again. It's essentially a stable heat engine with simple principles, but with huge energy flows—'

'Enough with the lecture,' Brad said. 'So what's this got to do with the Wrap?'

'I think I know,' Muree put in. 'Hope you haven't forgotten me. Bouncing around in the sunlight as I am.'

Plokhy called back, 'Not for a second. I think I get it. With the Wrap, you trap the Sun's heat, which would otherwise escape into space. All of it – correct? So, as you described it, with all that trapped heat, stuck inside the Wrap, the Sun gets hotter and hotter, including the core. So those feedback loops you talked about start to work, the expansion goes on and on . . . You end up with a much larger object, within the expanded Wrap, all at the same lower temperature. And a lower temperature requires a lower rate of fusion in the core, so the fusion fuel is used up more slowly. So how long does it take until equilibrium?'

Revil answered, but uneasily, Muree thought. She said, 'Perhaps a hundred thousand years.'

Muree thought she heard gasps at that.

Plokhy laughed. 'You think big, don't you?'

Muree asked, 'Then, when the Sun is quiescent – what?'

Revil sounded profoundly uncomfortable. '*Then* perhaps we will find a way to expel the lumes. Perhaps it will be safe to remove the Wrap. We will have the resources of the managed Sun at our disposal – a fusion-fuel lode to last not mere billions of years as promised by nature, perhaps *tens* of billions thanks to our management, the Wrap.'

'So you and your colleagues, your predecessors, plunged the whole Solar System, generations of your citizens, into the dark?'

'No – no – you have pushed me this far. Let me speak! And I speak for my ancestor, at the time of the Neptune invasion. Who left an account of her thinking, and her colleagues'.

'She, and I, follow an ancient philosophy sometimes called *long-termism*. We take a long view. In everything we do, the priority is to maximise the possible size of humanity in the very far future. For the generations to come, given room and time, will far outweigh us in numbers – even counting those in the past, to this point. The future will contain *more* people – and is therefore more valuable than the present, by any sensible measure – and so we must survive the present, doing as little harm as we can.

'The apparent invasion, the destruction of Neptune, seemed to threaten all that. Now we know better – and in fact we are using the legacy of our bold ancestors' response to that invasion to, to *ring-fence* the future for our descendants to come—'

'The Architect,' Rab said now. '*Their* work followed on from that, didn't it? You, your predecessors, had them turn the Solar System into one giant machine – powered by the lumes. An engineered sky.'

'So they did,' Elinor said. '*But you should have destroyed their model, their legacy, in Australia.* Because of the jewel at the centre. That should have been the Sun; *your* Sun is no jewel, but a black, choked stain. Did they *know* their model betrayed your lie? Were they speaking to the future through the model?'

Plokhy said, 'Well, if so, these brave people heard them. And now, Commander Revil – what now? Will you – and whoever follows you – really be able to keep up these falsehoods? . . . It's only been a single thousand years, and already the big lie is unravelling.'

And now Revil's voice was distorted, Muree thought, almost agonised by the weight of such responsibility. 'Then what are we to do? What am *I* to do?'

Plokhy said simply, 'I suppose you'll have to tell everybody the truth.'

'Never mind that,' Muree broke in. 'There's a bigger issue. After all we've seen – all we've discovered, discussed – how the lumes travel between solar systems, how they breed in ice giants, how they go plunging into the bodies of stars like the Sun – if they aren't weapons, not manufactured – *why*? They aren't just handy gadgets for us to use to power spacecraft and such. And they *don't* seem to be parasites on the Sun, the stars.

'What are lumes *for*?'

37

Murce had no answer to that question.

No answer, in the decades after the arrival of the *Lightbird* in the Solar System. Amid the political upheavals, the mass imprisonments, the rebellions, the crumbling of authority.

No answer before the departure of the *Lightbird* on her journey back to Ross 128b, after Muree had said her farewells to Rab, and his reconciled mother.

No answer as the human race diverged once again, still ignorant of the origin and fate of their universe.

Still ignorant of the true function of the lumes.

Until . . .

Epilogue

AD 3250

'I think I understand,' Elinor said.

Rab rolled on his back with a sigh. Distracted from his own reading, thinking.

He sat up, and searched for his loose, comfortable house shoes with his bare feet.

'Come and see me!'

'Mother, let me sort myself out . . .'

'I understand! I understand!'

He swore. And relished the quiet for just a little longer. But he heard his mother moving around her own room, here in their shared apartment on the roof of this Venusian berg stack, high in a temperate, colonised sky.

When she moved like that, he needed to go to her. Again.

As he walked past, he looked out of the big picture windows at the view.

This was a luxury apartment, as apartments went in this berg – an apartment with a window in the main berg outer wall, an apartment with a view.

Beyond the lights humans had draped across Venus, the lume-lights on these high-floating buildings, he could make out features of the true night sky beyond. The still-shining tracks of the Frame, set against the deepest black. And even from here, he could often make out scraps of a starry sky: evidence that the great dismantling of the Mask at the edge of the Solar System really was proceeding apace.

And when the Sun was high, you could see that too – or at least you could see what was visible through the neat rents that had been torn in the Wrap, in the decades since Muree had first thrust her crude spade into the flimsy fabric that had contained the sunlight for so long.

Muree . . .

Long gone from the Solar System, twenty years already into a new century-long mission for the *Lightbird*. A mission which Muree would not see out herself, of course – but her children might. Including the daughter they had shared, Rab and Muree.

A thought that gave him a kind of happy, sad ache.

But he had stayed home, daughter or not, to care for an increasingly frail mother. And back on Venus, where it had all started for him.

At least he was able to support his mother. And he could speak regularly, if through time-delayed channels, to his wife and daughter on the *Lightbird*.

Others had suffered far worse separations and dislocations in the great philosophical, political and social upheavals that had occurred during his lifetime. The collapse, after all, of a regime that had lasted a thousand years.

He told himself he was content. Sometimes he believed it.

In fact he had been thinking of Muree when his mother had called. He had been reading up on a partial analysis of the *Lightbird*'s current overpopulation problem – a five-year-old glitch in the latest reproduction rules . . .

'I . . . think I finally figured it out . . .'

His mother's voice cut through his rambling thoughts. He glanced at his reader screen, realised he had already lost his place in the study, let alone his chain of thought. But he managed not to cuss. 'Go back to point of loss of concentration minus five minutes, and hold.'

Then he dumped the reader, stood straight – and slammed his head against the ceiling of his small cabin. He managed not to cuss again. Well, not loudly.

He had learned to forgive his mother for her intrusive, interrupting presence in his life, as long as she *did* have something interesting to show him, to tell him about. Which wasn't always.

As it happened, this time, she did.

He made his way along the corridor, into his mother's room.

She was sitting up in bed, with three screens – no, four, two were overlapping – hung on wire-thin stands around her. Huge spectacles were held across her narrow nose by more wiry supports.

'You shouldn't swear,' she said as he came in.

'You shouldn't go shouting as you read.' Gently he took the nearest reader screen away, fixed her blankets again. Her wrists, where they protruded from her cushioned sleeves, looked more skeletal than ever. The bone loss was obvious, the related cancers not so.

Both common hazards of long-term deep-space flight. He'd grown to learn that, even after a millennium or more of travel in deep space, or residence there, the human body had not yet adapted to the conditions, particularly the loss of a stable, strong gravity field. And nor had medical advances risen to the challenge. Well, Elinor had been well cared for by her late-married husband – the former Lieutenant Jeo Planter – until he had lost his life in the line of duty, during the worst of the post-Wrap Mars revolution.

By then, his mother's condition had worsened and she needed to be brought back to Venus, the gravity field she had grown up in. And Rab had had to move down to Venus too, down into this deep planetary well, to be near her. Just as they had been together at the start of his life, now at the end of hers.

She was very perceptive, still, even looking out from behind those ridiculous spectacles, but a slave to her various intellectual obsessions.

'You don't have to stay so close, you know. I'm not a child. I'm pretty independent, always have been. Why, when you were getting those upgrades on that prosthetic hand of yours I did the work of two of us around here . . .'

'Yes, Mother.' He let her talk, as he fiddled around with her blankets, pillows, drink dispensers, screens.

'And if you'd stop your faffing I'll tell you what I'm so agitated about.'

But her wide grin – a few teeth gone – told him it wasn't agitation at all, but an impatience to share her latest bit of theorising.

'OK, OK.' He seized the opportunity to hunt for her latest food tray. It took him long seconds to find it, tucked under her cot – or more likely she had overridden the smart artefact's commands and told it to hide itself under there. He helped himself to a few of the little sandwiches he found there, nibbled one to make it last.

Then the tray pushed its way into its customary alcove for self-cleaning and reloading.

Elinor said now, 'If you'll just listen—'

'I can listen and eat at the same time. And I *know* you can talk and eat at the same time. You should have had some more of this.'

'Oh! And you should have been a cop like Planter if you're going to order me about!'

Behind the habitual quick temper his mother was easily distracted, a frequent occurrence these days. Thinking of Planter. Intertwined lives.

But at length she reached out, stroked his free hand – the flesh hand – and took a sandwich. Then she surprised him by biting it in two, chewing vigorously, and swallowing it down. And, even, taking a sip from one of the tiny cups. But when she was done she rubbed her chest, he noticed, and she suppressed a cough.

Good news, the sandwich eating; bad news, the cough.

He forced a smile. 'So tell me what's the big deal. What have you figured out now?'

'What have I *figured out*? I think I've *figured out* how the lumes are going to save the universe. *That's* what I've figured out.'

Well, that was unexpected.

He said, tentatively, 'Oh, is that all?'

'Sarcasm. That's just like Planter too.' But she winked at him, and snapped her fingers at one of the floating screens.

He was looking at a lume tank, a big one. All he could see was lumes, in fact, no edges to the tank.

Whatever drone had recorded this pulled back now, revealing more and more of the lumes, some glistening as if wet, others shining like – like stars, balls of light.

And still the viewpoint pulled back, until the individual lumes were hard to make out, and all he saw was the mass of them, speckled with brilliance. As if the lumes were behaving as a swarm, not as individual entities. But even now he thought he saw some details, some differentiation – some actually had bands of a greyish, silvery colour, on otherwise featureless surfaces.

The shining spheres swarmed over each other, looking like loose cells, he thought, like something biological. But then, he knew, the best theories of the lumes *did* treat them as living things, perhaps in a composite form – a mass of them working cooperatively like a multicelled creature, like a human, like Rab himself.

He remarked on all this to his mother.

'Well, that's obvious enough. The swarm behaviour has been known since before you were born—'

He held up his hands. 'I work on propellant tankage these days, remember, not on lumes.'

'All right, all right.' She stole a glance at him. 'You're *so* like Planter. Yes, lumes en masse do seem to have swarming, co-operative behaviour. But this has barely been studied. There are a few records of mass behaviour in the largest lume nests humans have visited—'

Rab knew about that. 'Planet Neptune.'

'Or what's left of it.'

'Uranus.'

'Not that. Humans have interfered with that one too much. You can't draw any sound conclusions.'

'The nest in the Ross 128 system—'

The home star of the *Lightbird*.

'Yes, but that doesn't compare in scale to the Neptune structure. Presumably from lack of opportunity; there are ice giants at Ross but nothing like as large as Uranus or Neptune. You know the story,' she snapped out.

One of her favourite shut-up phrases. *Shut up and listen to me . . .*

'So,' she went on. 'When the lumes first came to the Solar System, people thought they were some kind of weapon – maybe fired in from some unseen ship, or an invisible armada. Humans think in very narrow categories. They assumed that the rest of the universe was like *them,* with the lumes some kind of animated cannonball.'

Cannonball. He had to look up that term, discreetly, on a handy screen.

'And that froze human civilisation, here at least, into a paranoid huddle for a thousand years. But there was *no such ship,* no such fleet – no invaders of that kind. The lumes came alone, without any governing ship, or fleet. Just the lumes.

'And it was a migration, not an invasion. As we guessed in the end. Do you remember, when Muree vandalised the Solar Wrap? . . .'

Of course he remembered.

'That day, we started to guess the truth, finally. That – we believe – the lumes have been working their way out from the core of the Galaxy, along the spiral arms, until they reached us. And that, presumably, they will go on past us. Colonising stellar systems as they go.

'And when they crossed interstellar space, to the Solar System, they settled first on one suitable planet—'

'A body out in the Oort cloud. Then Neptune.'

'Then Neptune. Not to destroy it. Not wilfully. To use it. To, to *breed,* to transform its substance into lume-stuff, into their form of life.

'Just as we humans once took the products of Earth to make more of our own. Turning chunks of the biosphere into human flesh and bone. A lume cloud was a swarm, like a swarm of insects come to breed, not an invasion.

'I think I know why the lumes preferred the ice giants, by the way.'

'Oh, do you?'

'Because if you look across the cosmos, worlds like Neptune

and Uranus are *the most common type of exoplanet*. Did you know that? Most of them smaller than we have here, or had here, in the Solar System, but still.'

He nodded. 'Makes sense as an evolutionary target.'

She snorted. 'In hindsight, maybe. At the time, humans watching all this didn't understand anything. Strange to think that a few hundred years earlier we hadn't even known Neptune existed, the telescopes weren't good enough, and now we saw it destroyed . . .

'As it was, we thought of it in primitive terms. We thought Neptune had been attacked, or turned into some kind of planet-buster weapons factory, I suppose. Even as it was demolished itself. And we kept watching out for the armada to follow—'

'Which never came. The lumes just made more lumes. Hmm . . . lume stuff made out of ice and rock?'

'Remember, lumes work on principles that can transform matter itself into antimatter. A little transformative chemistry of that kind, ice to lume-stuff, is presumably trivial to them. But once the, umm, production line was established, humans took a more active interest.'

'Yeah,' Rab said, trying to keep sounding as if he was interested. Elinor would never compress a good preamble, though. He said, 'We learned how to handle lumes. Move them around. Prod them until they yielded up some of that matter-antimatter potential.' Rab had never thought too hard about this historical stuff, having been born generations later. 'Quite an achievement when you think about it.'

'So it was. Inducing a lume to destroy itself, to give up its potential energy. A slow matter-antimatter annihilation, controllable . . . It took some time, and a lot of human tragedy – and at the cost of a *lot* of lumes – before that control process was perfected. But the payoff was huge. A single lume could have produced the equivalent of an hour's insolation, back when the Sun still shone on Earth, an hour of planetary solar heating. *One* two-metre-wide lume.

'But by then there *was* no sunlight. Not after we created the Wrap. And no starlight once the Mask was completed. Because we *thought* we were under attack. Or under siege. The whole Solar System. A siege that might last millennia – longer. With the lumes as cannonballs . . .

'And that suspicion hardened when the first lumes started diving into the Sun . . .

'So we know what happened in response. Humans started scooping lumes out of Uranus – and began to *use* them on an industrial scale. And to build ships like the *Lightbird*, to scatter human colonies in case another *attack* came along. To transform the planets.'

'To build a huge rail track,' he said.

'The Frame. What an achievement *that* was. But I'm prepared to bet that by then, after the centuries it took to put all this together, people, or their leaders, were starting to think *there never would be* another attack. Maybe even then, discreetly, they no longer believed the first visitation had been an attack at all. But they had rebuilt the Solar System – had everybody working in wartime roles . . . Too much had been *invested*, in political capital, in specialised technology, for it all to be abandoned, just because of a foolish cognitive *error*.'

He said, 'In short, they wanted to hold on to power. They, the military chieftains.'

'Well, maybe. I'm prepared to be generous in my old age. I didn't have to make the decisions. They did their best to run mankind and its worlds, within the bounds of their shallow knowledge, their narrow thinking. I do agree, though, that their grip should have been lessened by the time the *Lightbird* showed up. And you and Muree might not have had to be chased across the System.'

But she was smiling.

Rab grinned. 'Come on. You wouldn't have missed that adventure for the world. All the worlds.'

She reached for his prosthetic hand. 'In a way it all started when I found you again. Do you remember, on Mars?'

He squeezed her hand back – gently, gently: he could feel the bones under her papery skin.

'And,' she said, 'everything followed from that, didn't it? The truth came out. And we started to tear down the Solar Wrap, the Mask beyond Uranus . . . We started the recovery. It's not finished yet. We had the fun part, though, I suppose . . . Future generations will envy us. We were there at the beginning. And now – oh, *that's* what I wanted to tell you. I'm so forgetful these days. What I've figured out, belatedly . . .'

'What's that, Mother?'

'What the lumes *are for* . . .

'Listen to me now. Show us the Sun,' she said.

A screen grew bright, casting the light of the Sun's image across the little room, bathing Elinor's gaunt face.

'The Sun. What about it?'

'What about it?' She sounded indignant. 'Do you just take it for granted? The Sun won't last for ever, you know. None of the stars will. You understand that a star like the Sun is mostly hydrogen. It shines by fusion, in its core, of hydrogen into helium – with other elements created later.'

'Yes, I—'

'But the Sun won't last for ever.'

'You said that—'

'It's maybe five billion years old now. It's already more than halfway through its useful lifespan. Soon enough the hydrogen in its core – which is where all the fusion happens – will start to become depleted. Just the core, mind. That failing core will implode, dumping heat into the outer layers, which will expand in response—'

'A red giant.'

'Yes. Without protection, life on Earth wouldn't be viable after three, four billion years from now. The other planets, similarly affected. And after *eight* billion years, the maximum red giant stage, the planet itself might be destroyed. Earth, consumed by its own dying star. *But*—'

He had to laugh. 'That has to be a big "but", coming after that lot.'

'Yes, yes. I told you that the hydrogen *in the Sun's core* will be depleted. Not elsewhere in the Sun. And even the fusion process itself is inefficient . . .'

'Hmm. Four hydrogen nuclei bond to make one helium nucleus—'

'But only a fraction of the mass-energy of the four hydrogens is released, as free energy, you see. And the rest of it, all that potential mass-energy, is stuck as helium, for ever. Which slowly clogs up the core, by the way.

'And as the Sun goes through its evolution, even by the time the core is choked and shut down, *most* of the Sun's hydrogen is left unburned. Not to mention the fusion products, starting with helium.

'The numbers are dismal if you look at it from an efficiency point of view. Over its lifetime, fusion processes will release only about *six per cent* of the total potential mass-energy of the Sun. Leaving ninety-four per cent inert, useless, slowly cooling. All that lovely unfused hydrogen, just sitting there, getting cooler and cooler. All that possibly useful energy – wasted, locked up for ever. The same argument applies to every star in the Galaxy. Whereas a lume, you see, unlike a star—'

'Ah. But a lume burns the hydrogen it stores to near a hundred per cent of its mass-energy.'

She looked at him closely, the way she had when he was a very small child, trying to make him think. 'Yes? And so?'

'And so, on the one hand, hungry lumes. On the other, all that waste hydrogen,' he said. '*Ah*. And if the lumes get a chance to breed in the hearts of stars – even inert, dead stars—'

'Yes. Yes! The lumes are like little matter-antimatter engines that can turn *all* that waste post-solar hydrogen into energy, with *maximum efficiency*. All of it. All that hydrogen in dead and dying stars . . .'

He nodded. 'I do know a little cosmology.'

'Hmph. So you say.'

'The stars won't last for ever. The universe is already less bright than at its peak. It will take a long time. But . . .'

'But in ten billion years,' she said, 'the Sun will be dying. In a *hundred thousand billion* years the last stars of all will be dying off, and no more star-stuff to make more. After that there will be darkness, nothing but cooling embers – red dwarfs – alleviated by the odd collision, perhaps . . .'

He saw it. '*But not if the stars are seeded with lumes*. Each star could be made to burn ten, a hundred, a thousand times as long as it might have before.'

'You've got the idea. Oh, those are round numbers, there's a lot of technical modelling to be done before we can be sure—'

'But I get it,' he said. 'A new phase in cosmic evolution. Wow!'

'And *that's* what the lumes are *for*,' she said. 'So I believe. Survivors of the Big Bang at the dawn of the universe, coming into their own at the end of the universe – ultimately extending the potential of the universe for supporting life and mind by orders of magnitude.

'Maybe – and this is *very* fanciful – maybe the lumes are the product of some wider kind of *evolution*, a pan-cosmic process. Maybe they evolved through a chain of cosmic creations, one universe budding others, and the ones with the lumes lasted more, and spawned more lume-habitat infants of their own . . . I need the time to write this up, of course. Maybe present it to the academies on Mars . . . even at Hellas . . .'

She was running down, he saw, as she always did, after one of her bursts of energy.

But she said now, 'There's no point in being a mad old person if you haven't the licence to come up with mad ideas.'

'Not so mad.' He smiled. 'As a kid, you know – and even after I found you, on Mars – I didn't know you were ever such a – scholar.'

She shrugged. 'Without you, I needed a distraction. What better than to figure out the salvation of the universe?'

'So now we know we've got all the time anybody could need,' he said. He grinned at her. 'Thanks to you.'

But she reached out and held his hand. Her touch was clammy, weak. Weaker than before? And she was closing her eyes now.

She whispered, 'Starlight, life and mind, for so much longer. Thanks to the lumes . . .'

He said, 'We'll tell Muree. She always wondered about the true nature of the lumes. She would love to know all this.'

'Who would?'

'Muree – she—'

She stroked his face with cold fingers. 'Tell her what, love?'

And his heart broke a little more. 'It doesn't matter.' And he clasped her hand more firmly. 'Come on. I'll make you some tea.

And let's watch some of it again. When they took off the Wrap.'

He waved his free hand in the air.

And above them a new image of the Sun had coalesced – a darkened sphere, still mostly covered by its Wrap. But, in an accelerated display, he could see the little ships coming from all over the Solar System – probably including the indefatigable Angela Plokhy aboard the *Styx* – diving down again and again at the flimsy structure of the Wrap, creating huge rents, the whole leaking light like shining blood from multiple wounds.

'I'm glad I was born at a time when I could see that,' he murmured now.

But Elinor didn't reply.

'Mum? Mum?' He put down his tea and held her close, gently raised her chin with his prosthetic hand. 'Mum? . . .'

The freed sunlight was bright in her closing eyes.

Afterword

The lumes are my own irresponsible invention, based on musings about how the useful life of the universe and its contents could be extended. If they don't exist, perhaps they should be invented. I leave that as an exercise for the reader.

Early speculations on exploiting black holes for useful energy – the 'Penrose process' – were published by R. Penrose and R. M. Floyd, 'Extraction of Rotational Energy from a Black Hole', *Nature Physical Science* vol. 229, p. 177 (1971).

I discussed the social challenges of a 'worldship', a ship containing its crew for generations, in C. Cockell, ed., *The Institutions of Extraterrestrial Liberty*, Oxford University Press (2022).

Useful and informed speculation about archaeological remains of humanity on Earth in the far future was given by Jan Zalasiewicz in *The Earth After Us*, Oxford University Press (2008).

The idea of covering Venus with an artificial buoyant 'cloudscape' was inspired by 'Cloud Continents: Terraforming Venus Efficiently by Means of a Floating Artificial Surface', by Alex R. Howe, *Journal of the British Interplanetary Society* vol. 75, pp. 68–75 (2022).

The idea of enclosing much of Mars under a roof has been studied by Richard Taylor (*Journal of the British Interplanetary Society* vol. 45, pp. 341–52 (1992)).

A recent review of what is known of the 'ice giant' outer planets is 'Uranus and Neptune: Origin, Evolution and Internal Structure', by R. Helled et al., *Space Science Review* 216:38 (2020). Though many such planets have now been discovered orbiting other stars, the ice giants are not well understood, with only one space probe having visited them – *Voyager 2*, which made flybys in 1986 and 1989 – but at time of writing more ambitious international probes are being planned.

The 'solar wrap' idea for extending the useful lifetime of the Sun was developed by astronomer Martin Beech, in *Rejuvenating the Sun and Avoiding Other Global Catastrophes*, Springer (2008). I had previously sketched the idea of cloaked stars in my story 'Lakes of Light' (2002; collected in *Resplendent*, Gollancz (2006)).

The star Ross 128, eleven light-years away, actually exists, as does its planet Ross 128b.

The speculative designs for antimatter-rocket spacecraft described here are mostly based on the relevant discussion in *Frontiers of Propulsion Science*, ed. M. Millis and G. Davis, American Institute of Aeronautics and Astronautics, Inc., Reston, USA (2009) (pp. 73ff); and see *Indistinguishable from Magic* by Robert L. Forward, Baen Books (1995).

On the astronomer Johannes Kepler, David K. Love's *Kepler and the Universe*, Prometheus (2015) is a fine recent biography.

All errors and misapprehensions are of course my sole responsibility.

Stephen Baxter
Northumberland
September 2024

CREDITS

Stephen Baxter and Gollancz would like to thank everyone at Orion who worked on the publication of *Fortress Sol*.

Agent
Christopher Schelling

Editorial
Marcus Gipps
Zakirah Alam

Copy-editor
Elizabeth Dobson

Proofreader
Bruno Vincent

Editorial Management
Jane Hughes
Charlie Panayiotou
Lucy Bilton

Audio
Paul Stark
Louise Richardson
Georgina Cutler

Contracts
Dan Herron
Ellie Bowker
Oliver Chacón

Design
Nick Shah
Rachel Lancaster
Deborah Francois
Helen Ewing

Finance
Nick Gibson
Jasdip Nandra
Sue Baker
Tom Costello

Inventory
Jo Jacobs
Dan Stevens

Marketing
Javerya Iqbal

Operations
Group Sales Operations team

Production
Paul Hussey
Katie Horrocks

Publicity
Jenna Petts

Sales
Catherine Worsley
Victoria Laws
Esther Waters
Tolu Ayo-Ajala
Karin Burnik
Anne-Katrine Buch
Frances Doyle
Group Sales teams across Digital, Field, International and Non-Trade

Rights
Rebecca Folland
Tara Hiatt
Ben Fowler
Alice Cottrell
Ruth Blakemore
Marie Henckel